Dedication
For my sister Cheryl and my daughter Ellen and in loving memory of my dear Mother Patricia, my mentor and my friend.

Acknowledgements
I would like to thank Jane Gardam for taking the time to read my first novel, Catalyst, and for giving me encouragement to proceed with my writing. Thanks also to Annika Sneller for being a sounding board and a true friend.

My special thanks go to my daughter Ellen and my sister Cheryl for their support and invaluable input and advice without which I may have lost my way.

Finally, I extend my thanks to my publisher and designer Michael Pennamacoor for his tolerance of my fidgeting and nagging and for a job well done.

Val seen here with her two dogs in Sandwich, Kent

Val was born in Gloucestershire and spent many family holidays in Devon, which is the location for her novel 'Catalyst'. The vast, beautiful and sometimes treacherous moorland of Dartmoor has always held a fascination for her and whenever possible she re-visits it.

Coming from a family of artists and artisans she was drawn to craftwork from an early age and on leaving school after her 'A' level exams she spent four years at Art College training to be a three-dimensional designer specialising in silversmithing.

For six months after graduating she sojourned on the island of Mauritius where her artist sister Cheryl worked for the International Voluntary Service.

On their return to England they spent many years renovating run down properties from London to Kent. During this time Val learned how to brick-lay, pitch and tile a roof, construct a staircase and various other building techniques as well as executing architectural plans for the jobs in hand. In the fullness of time this gave them the wherewithal to purchase their own commercial outlet in Sandwich, Kent, from where they were able to successfully market their produce.

Whilst running the business Val also held a contractual lecturing position at Kent Institute of Art and Design where she taught for approximately ten years.

Val was recently forced to give up silversmithing due to cervical spine surgery resulting in a fusion of three vertebrae. She continues to run her gallery and picture framing business in Sandwich but, missing the creativity of designing, she began writing 'Catalyst'. The bug took hold of her and she has now written this sequel – 'Legacy' – and is already well into her third novel.

Val has one daughter who graduated from RADA in 2015 as a theatre prop maker, and two dogs.

LEGACY
BY VAL P GOULD

AbgrundBooks

Legacy

Published by AbgrundBooks, Sandwich, Kent, UK (michael@abgrundrisse.net)

Cover painting 'Mauritian sea' by the pastel artist Cheryl Culver PPSA RBA
(www.cherylculverpaintings.co.uk
Cherylculver@btinternet.com)

Layout and design by michael pennamacoor of Abgrundrisse
(michael@abgrundrisse.net)

Printed by Lulu (www.lulu.com)

ISBN: 978-0-9555869-4-1

CHAPTER 1

A WEAK MORNING SUN cast elongated shadows of the grave stones; some square topped, some rounded and from other older ones, huge angels reached unnaturally long limbs out across the cemetery. Miss Hazlett, her walking stick echoing a third footstep on the paving slabs, walked slowly to the graves and took from her bag two bunches of flowers from her garden. In foresight, as the tap was at the far end of the cemetery, she had brought a Tizer bottle filled with water with which, after removing the dead flowers and emptying out the now stale and brackish water from the vases, she replenished them both and resting uncomfortably on arthritic knees she arranged the posies to her satisfaction.

Miss Hazlett suddenly experienced a tingling up her spine as though someone or something was behind her, she started and turned but the graveyard appeared empty. She shrugged herself back to normality and giving a final touch to her arrangement she made to rise. This necessitated putting one hand on the grave stone and, with the help of her stick, forcing herself to a standing position. Again, she felt that prickly sensation of nerve endings rising and with her back to the graves she gazed in earnest around the cemetery. The sun was a little higher now and the shadows shorter, she imagined that she could vaguely make out the shape of a person but it remained static and with the sun in her eyes she assumed it to be one of the angel monuments some people favoured for their family plots. Telling herself to stop imagining things she turned back to Paul and Sally's stones to say goodbye.

As she sadly read their inscriptions for the umpteenth time, a peacock butterfly settled itself in the sun spot just above Paul's engraved name where it slowly fanned its wings and then was still. She gazed at the beauty of the wings as the insect seemed to lay claim to the name and sadness and anger merged and came surging to the surface. *Why, oh, why did this have to happen?* Turning abruptly from the graves she strode to the gate, banging her stick on the path in time to her thoughts *why, why, why?*

When Sally's body had finally been released for burial Miss Hazlett had attended the funeral along with neighbours and other parents who had known Paul and his mother from the school. An added grief had overshadowed the service as the news had spread that Paul was also dead, hence the release of her body. None of the friends and neighbours could believe him guilty of murder, especially that of his mother whom he adored. Miss Hazlett had visited her grave regularly, knowing there were no relations to tend it she had taken it upon herself to do so. When, a few months after Sally's burial, the plot alongside was taken she had paid it little attention until the stone was erected. Whilst tending the flowers on Sally's grave, Miss Hazlett had glanced at the neighbouring stone out of curiosity to see if it was anyone she knew. She had to read it twice before her brain acknowledged the name. Dear Paul had been found and laid beside his mother. Thenceforth she had tended both graves and grieved for their untimely and unnecessary deaths.

"I am terrified of going home." Sandy's voice caught in her throat. "I haven't even spoken to Mum for weeks now, how am I going to make it better?" Sandy had remained at the farm after the funeral and no contact had been made either way. Life continued as normal but there was a vacuum in their lives. Alice and George ran the farm as if on auto-pilot and laughter seemed a thing of the past. Six months ago, Paul had been a stranger but they were mourning him as a family member.

"It all seems so pointless, Mum's estranged herself from us all and Paul didn't even know the result of the hearing." Oliver turned her to face him and as she looked sadly up at him he replied firmly

"No not pointless. Yes, he died in ignorance but don't forget that he was happy with us and in particular – with you. I honestly think he had put everything else out of his mind. He felt secure and his trust in us gave him peace of mind." Oliver and Sandy walked in silence for a while, Lilly trotting alongside. "And," he added "there was nothing pointless in clearing his name and at the same time exposing those dreadful people at the Asylum. If nothing else, we might save other unfortunate inmates being abused and misused." As they reached the top field with its views across the moor, Oliver beckoned Sandy to sit beside him on the sunny verge. With a sigh, she slumped down on the dry grass and together they surveyed the vast expanse of moorland with its hues of purple and white heather interspersed with bright sun-shot gorse flowers.

"On a day like this it's hard to imagine how treacherous it can be out there isn't it?" Sandy relaxed a little and lay back against the slope. For weeks now she had been questioning everything regarding Paul and 'did they do right?' Or 'maybe if...' and although Oliver was by nature an impatient and quick tempered man his affection for Sandy and his empathy with her personal situation inclined him to kindness and tolerance – but he was not sure how many more times he could re-assure her without losing his patience. Oliver could well understand her unhappiness over the breakdown of her family unit and in particular her ruined relationship with her mother but there was only so much anyone could do or say to alleviate the sadness. Thus, he was relieved when she seemed to soak up the beauty of the day and cease talking about Paul. But barely five minutes had passed when she said

"I just can't get the image of him that last night out of my mind. I keep asking myself if there was anything that could have been done to save him. Would he have stood a better chance in hospital or would that have merely made him fret and still die in the end?"

"Stop it!" Oliver wrapped his arm around her shoulders, "Mike knew it was the end, he would not have hesitated to get him admitted if there had been any chance at all and sod the fact that he 'didn't exist'."

"All those lies, even at his funeral. And none of his old friends there to say goodbye, do you think we should have done it like that?" It had been a quiet affair at the huge cemetery twelve miles away from his home as the small local burial ground was full. They were able to secure a plot next to his recently buried mother and keep the whole affair out of the public eye.

Strangely for Sandy, whose emotions were volatile, she had not cried at the service and in fact she had not cried at all since but suddenly she felt her eyes prick and she got up from the grassy bank where they had sat to talk and vigorously brushed the bits of hay from her jeans. With her back to Oliver she reined in her desire to weep and turning dry eyed to him grabbed his hand and he heaved himself to his feet. They walked along the footpath leading to the meadow where the sheep grazed, their woolly coats giving them the appearance of animals twice their size. Yellow heads of dandelions and celandines sparkled in the sun and the golden buttercups nodded as if in agreement with each other. Along the verges wild scabious rose tall and blue from the springy tufts of grass. The field beyond the sheep was always left untouched and over the years an army of teasels with their strange purple ring of blossom had made it their home. Amongst the young plants, that stood tall and purposefully, their parent plants, now brown, brittle and bent backed, with heads bowed succumbed to their fate. Plucking a scabia from the verge and handing it to Sandy, Oliver replied

"I know what you mean, but imagine the explanations and possible repercussions if we had made it public."

"Do you think we could still be in trouble legally if the whole story came out? After all, we all lied through our teeth and harboured a murder suspect."

"Yes, I think we could. Let's not go down that route. In time the past will knit over just like Baggins' front door. Come on it's lunch time and I'm bloody starving!"

Tim joined them at the farm later that afternoon and he and Sandy took a stroll across the fields with Lilly.

"Have you seen Mum? Is she alright?"

"Yes, I have seen her, she was very cold with me, with good reason I suppose. We talked briefly on the doorstep, she said she didn't need anything and virtually sent me packing."

"I have been on the point of ringing her loads of times but I just didn't know what I'd say. Oh Dad, I just want to run away and forget any of this happened." Tim stopped by the stile adjoining the teasel field and leaned his arms on the top rung. Sandy did likewise and they quietly watched the little chalk blue butterflies flitting amongst the thistles and the red admirals seeking the last of the sun, their wings spread wide to expose a pair of staring eyes. A small flock of goldfinches dipped and soared, harvesting the remains of last year's fallen seeds. The young teasel plants were as tall as Sandy and the evening sun slanting through the alder trees threw the prickly stems into shadow whilst illuminating the purple flower bands. Tiny pearls of dew, dyed orange by the setting sun, hung like miniature rose hips from the jagged leaves. In the centre of the field a large clump of brambles spread their thorny shoots wide, claiming territory at an alarming rate. A little white scud of a rabbit caught Lilly's eye as it darted under the protective briars and others followed swiftly as Lilly scrabbled through the stile and gave chase.

"She'll never catch them, thank goodness." Sandy said with a smile. "You'd think I'd be inured to the thought of killing a rabbit by now wouldn't you after all the ones I killed and gutted?" Calling Lilly back she added "But that was in a different life."

Lilly appeared to be obeying orders but, in reality she returned to the stile because she had lost the chase. She sat panting, showing her white teeth and pink lolling tongue as though she were laughing.

Tim turned to Sandy, a cheeky look on his face.

"What?" She asked pulling back from him to better assess his expression.

"I've got a surprise for you" he chuckled.

"What sort of surprise?" Sandy looked worried. Had he arranged a meeting for her with Mum? Or done something on those lines? God, she hoped not, it was too soon.

Back at the farm Alice appeared to be in a sweat

"The blasted Aga's gone out! George!" she hollered "I asked you to bank it up, the food's ruined!" George ambled into the kitchen an apologetic smile on his face.

"Sorry love, I forgot. Oli, be a sport and protect me from your mother."

"Oh, go on with you, you great long streak, what are we going to do for dinner?"

"Funny you should ask, I've booked us a farewell meal for Sandy at The King's Arms."

"Dad?"

"All will be revealed." Tim winked at George. "Come on get yourself cleaned up and brush your hair Sandy it looks like a porcupine." Sandy looked at the grinning faces around her, including Alice's.

"What's going on you lot? Alice, you haven't got any food in the

Aga have you?" Sandy reached past Alice and placed her hand on the stove, "Ouch it's hot!" For a moment, Sandy looked near to tears, "You're all in on it except me, what do you mean by 'farewell', are you kicking me out?"

"Don't be daft lass, come on let's go before Bert gives our table to someone else. Has Ali arrived yet love?"

"You bet, I wouldn't want to miss a slap-up dinner!" Alistair sauntered into the kitchen, "Let's go."

Sandy hated being kept in the dark and all the way to the pub she probed Tim and Oliver as to what all this 'farewell' business was about. None of them would answer her questions and they irritated her by giving each other knowing winks.

"I feel like a child!" She exclaimed.

"Well stop acting like one!" Tim laughed back at her. "You'll find out soon enough."

Bert greeted them in his usual friendly manner and showed them to the big table in the dining room where they had all last sat together was on Paul's birthday.

"Right, let's order food and drinks and then we can put Sandy out of her misery." George ruffled her hair affectionately.

"Get off George I've just combed it!" Sandy ran her fingers through her hair and the spikes sprang up again much to George's amusement.

"Do that again Sandy, it's as though you've been plugged into the mains!" Sandy pressed her hands hard on her hair to flatten it and then with a flourish she whipped them away and up came the spikes again. After they had all had a good laugh at this they placed their orders and George called for their attention in a mock judge's voice. When all were quiet he gave the floor to Tim.

"Well, there's not much to be said, except that I have a surprise for my incorrigible daughter."

"What is it?" Sandy asked impatiently, "Stop keeping me in suspense." She suddenly thought *what if I don't like the surprise?*

After all this build up it would be dreadful if she were disappointed – she wouldn't be able to hide it, she was still a child at heart in so many ways.

Tim reached into his pocket and brought out an envelope with a ribbon tied round it and handed it to Sandy. She had absolutely no inkling of what could possibly be inside; maybe it was keys to a car, Tim had mentioned he might get her a little banger to replace the burnt out one.

"Well aren't you going to open it?" Oliver gave her a nudge, "You haven't got x-ray eyes!" Sandy lifted the flap and drew out two plane tickets. For a second she just stared at them then turning to Tim she threw her arms around him knocking his full pint of beer into his lap.

"Shit Sandy!" He cried as he backed away from the table grabbing his napkin to staunch the flow. "Sorry, excuse my language!" he said to the bar in general as his expletive had managed to come out in a lull in the conversations around the room. A few old farmers at the bar guffawed and one wisecracked 'the gents is over there, mate!' More laughter followed and Bert rushed over with a cloth to mop up.

"Sandy you're hopeless!" He chuckled as he beckoned his barman to bring a dry chair for Tim and a refill 'on the house'.

"Dad that's fantastic, I'll write to Josie, I think she's still got six months left on her contract. She can show us around!"

Tim put the plane tickets to Mauritius back in his wallet a grin splitting his face in two.

"You'll have someone your own age to have fun with rather than a geriatric fat old Dad." He laughed.

"Too right! She's made loads of friends out there, sorry Dad, not that you're very fat and only just a bit senile!"

"Thanks, for those kind words. And," he added sponging his trousers with the last of his napkins "making me look as though I've wet myself!"

Sandy turned to Oliver and his family, her eyes sparkling with excitement

"It's not farewell though, I'll be back sooner than you may like!"

Sandy cleaned out her brushes and put them in the ceramic pot she had made at college which had been deemed 'a schoolgirl's effort' by the tutor. A judgement she couldn't help but agree with. What a waste of time that was! All she had wanted to do was paint but the course required them to experience other mediums before the final choice in the second year. She couldn't believe she had actually packed it along with her paints, just because it was the pot she always used! She had been in such an excited state that her packing had left out necessities and included idiotic items such as this pot and her old threadbare Teddy named unimaginatively Ted-Ted. He was one of the few possessions she had not packed for removal into June's new house before the final breakdown between them when Sandy had chosen to remain with Paul during his last days. The surprise holiday which Tim had booked secretly for them both was better than she ever imagined. The Mauritian sun blazed down on her shoulders and she slipped on a cotton shirt. Tim was sitting in the shade reading a book and sipping a glass of local beer. He glanced up at her as she approached, her make-shift easel, constructed of bits of plank from an old pirogue, slung over her shoulder.

"Beer, or a swim?" He asked.

"Swim, I'm melting." The coral reef strung along the horizon, its surf a meringue white, the Indian Ocean lay beyond like a dark blue ribbon. At night, the sound of the ocean breaking on the reef in the distance and the soft wavelets rippling inside the lagoon was as soothing as a lullaby. In the darkness, the phosphorescence glittered, the cicadas chirruped and it surely was paradise. Mornings were a pleasure to wake to and began with a pre-breakfast dip or snorkel in the clear turquoise waters. Just hanging there, face in the water, watching the amazing assortment of brightly coloured fish swimming beneath them never failed to give them unfathomable pleasure. Donning their snorkel masks, father and daughter slid into the warm, salty, unpolluted water where the sunlight filtered down to the sea bed. Inside the reef the depth seldom reached more than twenty feet. When Sandy's first snorkelling swim had taken her over a sudden drop in the sea bed she suffered a sensation akin to vertigo. It was as though she had floated gently off the top of a cliff causing her a moment of panic. During their first week, they spent most of the time relaxing and swimming broken only by one big shopping trip to Port Louis for provisions. Tim had hired a beaten up old Hillman Minx and it coughed and spluttered its way there and back. The local taxi drivers turned their engines off on the downward approach to the town and free-wheeled, barely in control of their vehicles, hoping their brakes worked at the bottom. Tim refused to emulate them in spite of Sandy's pestering. So far he had not been too enamoured with the reliability of the Hillman and the last thing he wanted was to find that the brakes were as faulty as the headlights, indicators and clutch.

They had ventured out as far as the reef on one occasion and after braving the crashing waves and the coral scratches had snorkelled beyond it. Gazing into the deep Indian Ocean's clear depths which graduated from turquoise to deep navy blue down to the depths beneath put Sandy's small panic of vertigo within the reef into perspective. The ocean was remarkably warm in spite of its depth and expanse, though not as warm as the lagoon where at times it was like slipping into bath water. Fish life was all around them, some a good deal larger than those within the reef. They didn't venture too far out for fear of strong currents sweeping them away, in fact they were horrified to find when they managed to re-enter the lagoon that in a very short time they had been taken quite a long way from their starting point. Tacitly they agreed to stay landward of the reef in future. *Mum would have a fit if she were here*, Sandy's thought seemed to echo Tim's as they reached the shore and pulling off his mask he grinned conspiratorially at her

"Lucky June didn't see that!"

At the weekends, Josie was free and spent much of her time basking alongside Sandy by their sugar cane thatched cabin, catching up on all that had happened that year. Some weekends there were parties on the beach, scuba diving lessons and water skiing. Tim excused himself from most of these as being a boring old fart who was happy to sit, Panama hat over his eyes a book in one hand and a local beer in the other.

Being physically so far away from England it was quite easy to mentally disengage herself from the unbelievable few months Sandy had experienced. All she wanted and needed was to recuperate and to go home refreshed: ready to continue her life, wherever that may lead. Therefore, when Josie asked about the road accident which had prevented her from catching her flight, Sandy was at a bit of a loss to explain why she hadn't tried to catch a later flight. After stumbling a bit on her off-the-cuff story about dislocating her shoulder during the accident, Sandy decided to tell her about the whole episode.

Josie was amazed when Sandy recounted the horrific time they had spent in the moorland prison. She sat open mouthed throughout most of the tale.

"Hang on a minute, I must get a beer and a note book, this would make a brilliant film!" Josie interrupted as they reached the bit about Jimmy dying in the bog.

"Bring the sun tan oil I need to do my back!" Sandy called after her. Telling the story to someone who hadn't been involved was cathartic to Sandy and she found some of the sadness lift. But when it came to her parents' breakup she cried freely in Josie's arms.

"Somehow I have to face Mum again and try and put it all to rest and I'm dreading it."

"I love your Mum, she's a worry guts I know, but what mother isn't? Just have fun now you're here and things won't be so bad when you finally get home, I'll bet."

The photograph album lay open across June's knees. One small wet mark had soaked into the black paper on which the pictures were affixed with little white paper corners. She dabbed her eyes with her handkerchief, fearful of spoiling the photographs with her tears. Sandy's little face gazed up at her, Tim smiled lovingly into the camera. Then the roles were reversed and June looked at her own happy face; who was that woman? She tried to think herself back into the old June's mind but failed and closed the album with a snap. She started as the post fell on the mat; the silence of her home now she was on her own made every small noise sound like a thunderclap. She placed the album carefully on the coffee table and supposed she had better see what rubbish had been delivered.

June picked up the postcard from inside the front door. The message was brief; 'It's beautiful here Mum. Love Sandy xxx'. She was torn between hugging it to her and throwing it in the bin. Would Sandy ever live at home with her again or had their relationship truly been torn to pieces? Three months had passed since Tim had purchased the house for her and again that Paul had managed, even in death, to stand in her way of getting her precious daughter back. Sandy had never seen the house let alone moved in. Slipping the postcard into her pocket she wandered out into the cottage-style garden which the previous owners had maintained meticulously; she hated it. In fact, there was nothing in her life which gave her any pleasure. The Squires had made overtures of friendship, well, Sylvia had 'phoned to invite herself to see June's new home. June had pretended to be going away and Sylvia had not 'phoned since. June wandered sadly into the garden where she sat heavily on the seat under the laburnum tree, and watched the sun flicker through its long golden tresses. In the opposite border a buddleia's deep purple flowers beckoned the butterflies and bees. A bushy laurel hedge provided privacy from the neighbouring garden and coincidentally, a nesting place for birds and in front of this, an herbaceous border was stocked with delphiniums, lupins, anemones, tall spikes of astilbe, yellow coreopsis and many more, all arranged to give a gradual colour change from white through reds and oranges and finally to blues and deep purples. Soft fronds of decorative grasses waved in the light breeze. A smaller border held annuals such as stocks and sweet-willams, snap-dragons, wallflowers and aquilegia, jostling for space with californian poppies. The little orange flowers reminded her of her mother's garden and how, as a toddler, Sandy loved to pull off their little pointed bonnets to expose the flower within.

"Look Mummy, the flowers have pixie hats."

A honeysuckle trailing over an arbour, its perfume filling the air, completed the cottage garden scene. June wept with sheer loneliness, made more poignant by the fact that the garden really was lovely but having no one with whom to share it made her hate it for its beauty. Never having worked and being married to a practical and clever man, June had concentrated her whole life on being a wife and mother: all she had ever wanted to be. She had no hobbies, belonged to no clubs, had very little interest in reading and, so it would now appear, had no friends. After leaving her, Tim had taken semi-retirement, working from home in that scruffy little cottage; gone were the invitations to and from colleagues' homes for drinks or dinner; she felt as though she no longer existed. *They even left the dog with the Tregowans to look after when she could have come to me! I may as well be dead.*

As June sat weeping in her garden she heard the doorbell ring. Whoever was that? She had not had a visitor other than Tim who had called briefly to check everything was alright before he took Sandy on holiday. He had been pleasant enough but neither of them had wished to prolong the visit. June had not invited him inside and he had made no move to enter, merely enquired if she needed anything. Declining his offer she primly thanked him as he awkwardly pecked her on the cheek whilst saying goodbye. She had closed the door before he had even turned to walk down the drive and had gone directly into the kitchen at the back of the house as she didn't want to see him not look back. *Oh Tim, if only I could put the clock back.* Whoever it was at the door could jolly well go away, it was probably a salesman. She remained seated but dried her tears and attempted to think positively. She would never get back together with Tim, she knew that, but she must salvage her relationship with Sandy. *Does she hate me after all the love I have given her?* June's life without Sandy's love, even if she never actually lived with her again, was something she could not contemplate. *I will make it better.* She took Sandy's postcard from her pocket and kissed the name.

The wretched doorbell rang again, more insistently, as though the caller had all their weight behind one finger. This was followed by a loud rapping on the knocker. *Drat*, thought June, she supposed she had better see who it was. She opened the door to her flushed faced elder sister, Gillie.

"I was beginning to worry!" Gillie pushed her way indoors. "Why don't you answer the bloody 'phone?" Then, seeing June's pink rimmed eyes she threw her arms around her and hugged her. "Pack a bag, you're coming to stay with us for a while, you look as though you haven't eaten for a week!" Then, picking up the 'phone receiver "I'm just going to ring Stewart to tell him."

"No don't, well you can ring him to say I'm alright, but I would rather stay here in my own home."

"Would you like me to stay a few days with you, I haven't got anything on and we could get out, go somewhere, even just sit and eat fish and chips in the park, anything you want?" June slumped down on the kitchen chair and ran her hands through her hair.

"Oh Gillie, I'm so miserable" she cried. "Whatever has happened to my life?" Just a year ago, she and Tim had stood, arms around each other waving Sandy off on her holiday. "We were so happy; I can't believe that it's all gone. They were my life, they are still my life, both of them. I can't go on without them." June's face was an anaemic white and her eyes seemed sunk in their sockets, Gillie looked down on her and found it hard to believe that June was the younger of the two, she looked ten years older than Gillie, rather than two years her junior. She seemed to have shrunk, not only in weight but in height also. Gillie was at a loss as to what to do. It was no good feeding June placebos or saying 'it'll be alright in the end' or some such placatory remark as so far there was no indication that this would be true. Tim had certainly turned against her and there seemed no going back on this score, but surely Sandy, who had always been so close to her mother, wouldn't turn her back on June for ever! On this point, Gillie felt that she could venture a comforting word.

"June, please don't despair completely, Sandy's due home at the end of the month and she's had time to think and also time to realise that she misses you. Now all that business with Paul is over she will get back to normal even if it takes a bit of time. She loves you June, you are her mother and the bond you have is still there, I promise you she will come back."

In her spare time, before Sandy had arrived, Josie, who had attended college with Sandy, had accumulated a vibrant selection of paintings done in a style reminiscent of Gaugin.

"It was the heat!" Josie laughed when Sandy remarked on her

deviation from her normal work. They included mostly studies of locals, fishermen, women in the sugar cane fields and villagers outside their corrugated tin roofed huts. She was very vocal about the treatment of the local Creoles by the sugar cane barons and the 'houses' they were expected to live in as maids, servants and cleaners to the huge colonial style homes of the rich land owners and the High Commission employees on government postings. This did not, however, stop her from attending flashy functions when her most recent boyfriend, David, invited her. David was doing some sort of study about the Russian presence in the Indian Ocean. Josie explained to Sandy that Mauritius was strategically placed and for the time being, although independence from Britain had been granted, the British government still kept a retainer High Commission in the country as it needed a foothold in the Indian Ocean to counteract the Russians who were looking for a similar foothold. Also, the necessity to establish an electoral system and boundary demarcations which were fair to all the ethnic groups, had fallen to the British government before they were able to finally cede complete independence to the island.

"It's all a bit hush hush. David wasn't supposed to tell anyone what he was doing so don't let on that I told you."

"So, he's not exactly prime James Bond material, is he?"

"No but he's really dishy, just wait 'til you meet him. Hey, do you want to come to a cocktail party with David and me at the Governor General's on Saturday." *Josie was mixing with the upper echelons!* Sandy shied away from the idea.

"God no!"

"Oh, come on there's loads of free booze and free men!"

"I'll think about it. Dad as well?"

"I'll be sneaking you in as it is, David is only allowed one guest and that's me, so sorry, no. Anyway, I doubt he'd want to." Tim agreed later when Sandy told him of the invitation that he wouldn't want to go but encouraged her to attend if only for the experience of mixing with the 'gin crowd' as he put it.

"What do you mean 'gin crowd'?"

"Well, their weekends go like this: breakfast at 11am, first drinks (gin) at 11.30am, lunch at 1pm with wine followed by more gin, afternoon nap followed by a bone shaking manic spin around the bay in the motor boat, a quick swim followed by sun downers (gin) then evening meal with wine followed by liqueurs and probably more gin. Thanks, but no thanks, they're not my kind of people."

"Oh, I forgot to tell you in my letter that you may need something dressy, did you pack anything like that?" Josie was priming Sandy for the coming event.

"Nope, I wasn't exactly planning to go to a ball!"

"What have you got then?"

"Shorts, t-shirts, bikini, jeans. So, it looks like I won't be able to come."

"No problem, I'll lend you something of mine. I've found a dressmaker who makes fantastic silk saris."

"I'm not wearing a sari, I'm not Indian, I'd look ridiculous!"

"No, no, I was about to say she makes all sorts of dresses in fantastic Indian silk. I've got one which would look great on you."

"Okay, but if I don't like it I'm not going to wear it, no matter how much you nag me." Sandy had forgotten how forceful Josie was and how used to getting her own way. It was the main thing about her that had got under her skin at college.

The evening was incredibly sultry and almost as soon as Sandy had donned the dress she felt sweat patches under her arms. The shoes Josie had lent her already pinched and she felt as though she was walking like an old woman with corns.

"Don't worry about the sweat, everyone will be much the same, at least you don't have B O!" Josie had sprayed them both liberally with deodorant followed by an ample helping of perfume. The ensuing mixture of smells began to turn Sandy's stomach and excusing herself she went into the bathroom to wash the perfume from her neck and wrists. At least the smell of soap was a clean one and not one smell masking another.

Finally, they were ready. The cocktail party began at six pm and would finish at about eight. After this David was taking them to the casino and a meal then probably a party back at his place. Sandy was already planning her escape; a headache, stomach ache, anything to get her out of the party.

David parked his Mercedes in the space allotted him and whilst he locked it and gave the keys to the attendant Sandy took in the affluence of the place, the crowds of people looked rich and self-assured. Mauritius had an eclectic mix of cultures: Chinese, Hindu, Muslim, Franco-Mauritian, French, British and American. Some of these were resident Mauritians and others, visiting dignitaries or government representatives. David took Josie and Sandy's arms and escorted them in. He had a smug grin on his face as he introduced them to other High Commission men and their over-tanned middle aged wives. Sandy recalled her father's description and thought, *no gin for me!*

The party was not as bad as Sandy had feared, the main reason was the interest taken in her and Josie as artists. Requests were made for them to paint various portraits, mansions, yachts etcetera, all for decent fees. Sandy's bag or rather Josie's loaned bag bristled with visiting cards by the time the party was over.

By this time, Sandy had genuinely had enough, her feet hurt and her head ached and swam from the noise and having drunk more than she should have. All she wanted was a large glass of iced water and bed.

"David, thank you for the evening but I've got a really bad headache. Do you think you could drive me home please?"

"Oh, what a shame, I was enjoying having two beautiful young ladies all to myself. Tell you what, I'll drop Josie off at the casino, it's on the way and I've booked a table for dinner so she can take her time deciding on the meal. Is that alright Josie?"

Josie looked a bit put out and she pouted in a spoilt child manner.

"I suppose so though I don't mind the drive especially with the top off the car. It's so hot I could do with some wind in my hair." David ignored Josie's request to accompany them to Sandy's and pulled up at the casino.

"That's enough wind in your hair. Be a good girl and get the champagne on ice." Josie gave David a pointed look.

"Try not to be too long I don't want to be waiting half the night." She blatantly gave him a long and embarrassingly for Sandy, loud wet kiss and waved Sandy goodbye in a casually dismissive way. David beckoned Sandy to sit in the front seat which Josie had vacated and Sandy, although quite happy to remain in the back, obliged. He gave her a charming smile and they roared off into the night.

As they reached the beach road not far from Sandy's cabin David manoeuvred the car to face the sea and turned off the engine. The silence after the noise of wind in her ears seemed thick as though she had suddenly become deaf. The full moon reflected its lemon light back off the water and she could see David quite clearly in the borrowed beam. The gentle hiss of the sea on the coral and the chirruping of night creatures gradually ousted the feeling of deafness and closing her eyes she let the peace of the place soothe her headache. Through her lashes, she studied David's profile as he too had closed his eyes, with his head leant back against the seat he almost looked asleep. His dark hair, dark beard and tanned skin made him look Spanish or certainly of southern European origin though when he spoke his accent was perfectly English. An image of ginger freckled Oliver came to her mind and she smiled at it, remembering his green eyes and those ginger curls corkscrewing over his ears. The sight of them silhouetted against the sky when he came back to rescue them from Baggins Hall and his long legs also covered with fine ginger curls when he stripped off his jeans to dry them over the fire reminded her of how much she owed him and how dear a friend he was. Tom, her ex-fiancée, had been dark haired with almost black eyes which flashed when he was angry or excited but through which one could never see his soul. She remembered how blank his eyes had appeared when she had refused to go along with his idea of how to live her life; as though he had pulled gauze over them to shut her out. No, she wasn't particularly fond of dark men. That evil murderous Jimmy who had imprisoned them in the bunker had black stubble and the black of his shaven head where the hair had begun to grow through had repulsed her. Every time she saw a man with a dark five o'clock shadow she thought of him with both fear and disgust. Oliver is a gentleman not like this phoney twat sitting beside her.

"My word, what an expressive face you've got." Sandy jumped

"What? I mean sorry I was miles away."

"I've been watching you; your thoughts may as well have been written on your face. You were smiling; a gentle smile, were you wondering what I kissed like?"

"Heavens no! I wasn't even thinking. I was just enjoying the sound of the sea." How dare he presume that about me! Sandy began to feel exceedingly uncomfortable in David's company and remembering Josie's look and her last comment she had an overwhelming desire to get back to the cabin.

"Oh, come on, you and I are very alike you know, we're both assessing the other to guess the mileage." He reached his hand over on to her knee and squeezed it "You are a bit of a conundrum; I would like to get to know you better."

"I'm just me, nothing more and I think it's time you got back to Josie, she'll be really sulking by now." Opening the door, she said "I can walk from here, it's no distance."

"Do I not get a kiss goodnight?"

"No sorry, I don't think that's a good idea. Thanks for the evening and give Josie a message for me, would you? Just tell her 'think again'".

As Sandy hurried along the shore she heard David drive away his tyres spinning angrily on the sandy ground.

"Creep" she muttered and away from any eyes she thrust her fingers in her mouth to simulate gagging. "Shitty little creepy bastard."

She ran the rest of the way, Josie's shoes in her hand and with each step she described her impression of David with an increasingly vulgar cuss word at an increasingly louder volume until she ran out of vocabulary and breath and collapsed on the veranda steps in stitches of laughter.

"I am me! Foul mouthed, common, and happy to be so!" she shouted to the sea.

"Sandy?" Tim's worried voice preceded him as he emerged sleepy eyed, "Are you alright?"

"Never better Dad!"

CHAPTER 2

LACKING A CAR, Miss Hazlett had, as usual, taken the bus which wound its way around the countryside picking up passengers from the outlying villages and hamlets. Sitting near the door at the front for easy disembarking she had a panoramic view of the landscape. The first harvests were well on the way to being completed, hayricks with their air spaces between the bales stood like the battlements of a castle and the remaining yellow grey stubble in the shorn field was already showing little shoots of fresh green growth. Further along the journey they passed the huge sheep farm from which one could buy fresh lamb directly from the farmer. The flock grazed the steep sloping field and from a distance looked like random dots of grey wool dropped on a green carpet. The ewes who browsed nearer the road looked up at the passing bus with blank incurious eyes. Miss Hazlett noticed that they bore the coloured dyes on their haunches indicating that in the spring they would bear lambs which, if they were unfortunate enough to be male would spend a happy few months bouncing on their woolly legs before being slaughtered.

Miss Hazlett made the journey once a week specifically to visit the graves and the driver had become accustomed to seeing her over the previous months. He noted the chrysanthemums in her bag and the white fronds of Goat's Beard which she had picked from beside her ornamental pond.

"Beautiful 'Mums' love." He nodded at her bag as she rose to alight. "Home grown?"

"Yes, they are thank you." She smiled "Would you like me to bring you some, I have plenty?"

"Tell you what," he replied with a grin "how about I bring you some of my Victoria plums, they are ripe and ready to be picked and we can do a swop?"

"Splendid, I'll see you next week then."

The storm broke as she stepped off the bus and Miss Hazlett quickly put up her umbrella. The heavy rain drops turned to hail and battered it like gravel. The icy pellets splashed in the rain puddles and soaked her shoes. She dashed to the shelter of some overhanging trees and waited for the storm to abate. The sky was dark purple black and a cold wind attempted to snatch the umbrella from her hand. She gripped it as tightly as she could, her finger joints screaming in protest, but the wind fought back and she was forced to grab the umbrella with both hands. Her stick slipped from her hand and clattered to the floor. Bending awkwardly to retrieve it she was too late to catch the flowers as they tipped from her bag into the puddles. Already the chrysanthemums had begun to resemble old dish mops and the Goat's Beard sported two broken stems, now they were scattered in disarray across the pavement. It was pointless to take them to the cemetery and subject them to a final disintegration, so, with a sigh of resignation she stepped out into the storm and crossed the road to hail the next bus home. Another person was standing at the return bus stop in a hooded raincoat but as Miss Hazlett approached the stop the figure turned and walked away. Strange, the bus was due and in this weather who would choose to walk?

On her return home, she sat drinking tea in her kitchen. She had a strange feeling about the figure at the bus stop: all the way home she had experienced an anxiety for which she could find no reason. Thinking back to the sensation she had of being watched in the cemetery she tried to tell herself it was her imagination but still the feeling persisted. Why would anyone be watching or following her? This was ridiculous she had to pull herself together.

That evening after the ten o'clock news had finished she did not turn the television off as normal but decided to watch the film which followed to take her mind off the nagging thoughts that somehow, she was in danger or, as her imagination went wild that she had seen a ghost. Unfortunately, the film was about the supernatural and she turned it off in disgust. As far as she knew, Paul was buried in the cemetery, a Christian burial; Professor Small had pleaded and won a posthumously innocent verdict. But what if Paul was not dead, what if it had been him watching her, and if so who was buried in the plot and furthermore why didn't Paul approach her if it really was him...? *You stupid old woman* she told herself, *you are going senile.* She decided that she had to speak to Professor Small, though quite why, she was not sure.

The following day Miss Hazlett took the bus into town to visit the small library where she requested to see the back dated copies of the local newspapers. She imagined that any news of Paul's exhumation, were it an official retrieval of his body, would have been reported sometime between November when Paul's mother, Sally, had been buried, and May the following year when his stone was erected. She felt sure her memory served her well with these dates and settled herself at a table distant from the other people in the room where she diligently scrutinised the papers from front to back including obituaries. By lunch time she had not even reached half way through the pile and her old eyes were beginning to sting and water from trying to read the small type in a rather poor light. This was something which surprised her as a library was for reading in and a forty-watt bulb was hardly adequate! She reminded herself to say something about it to the librarian on her way out. Enough was enough for one day, she thought, tomorrow she would complete her search. At least then she would have some information of her own to present to the professor. An idea entered and then was quickly banished from her mind; an enquiry at the police station would definitely give her the answer she required, but somehow, something was telling her not to pursue that course. She couldn't quite put her finger on why she was loath to involve the police other than that Paul had been accused of matricide, albeit that he had been cleared of the charge. Maybe, she supposed, they might be unfriendly or say something unkind about him so she decided that she would see what the professor had to say first. The next day saw the completion of her search and she had found absolutely no mention of Paul after the report that he had been presumed dead. No mention was made of his posthumously proven innocence. Typical, she thought angrily, people only want to read about bad news, no wonder the world is such an unhappy place. That poor boy is still thought of as a murderer who got his just deserts.

"Sandy love, have you thought what you're going to do when you get home?" Tim took a break from the barbecue to pour a beer. He stood hesitantly in the doorway of the hut as Sandy rubbed her hair with a towel. They had been in and out of the water nearly all day, the temptation to soak up as much of their paradise as possible before returning home was too great to resist. Sandy sat in the canvas chair opposite him, her grey blue eyes filled with pain.

"Oh Dad, I really don't know. I miss Mum like crazy but how can I reconcile myself to what she did and worse, why she did it? I still can't understand why she was so horrible about Paul. He hadn't done anything to merit it." Tim lit the green mosquito coil on the veranda as the first mosquitos of the evening began whining around them. Sandy slapped at her cheek as an errant insect landed on it. "Got it! Look it's full of blood – ugh!" She wiped her hand on her shorts and continued "I can't understand why she couldn't feel the same sort of compassion we all felt, after all, he was the victim, his life had been ruined and all Mum could do was try to ruin it further. I don't know if I can ever forgive her." She turned to face Tim, puzzlement and sadness showing on her face, "Dad have you any idea why she turned into someone we didn't know any more? She seemed to have a complete character change, I just don't understand." Tim sighed, a deep heartfelt exhalation

"I really don't know why she became so bitter. I understand that the relief of knowing you were safe led naturally to the expectation that you would come home again." He paused, searching in his mind for something, any small thing which might have set June on her vindictive and destructive course but he had not understood her then and he did not understand her now. "I simply can't believe it was just the delay of that happening which made her so angry, after all, she knew that it was not going to go on for ever. Also, I don't think it had anything to do with breaking the law by sheltering Paul, although I did have some misgivings about that myself at the time. It is hard to credit it but your mother seemed to positively hate Paul, I've never known her to feel and to blatantly show such antipathy towards anyone in all our lives together, it just wasn't in her nature. At least I didn't think it was."

"It's dreadful Dad, I don't know if I even love her anymore. It's not just her attitude to Paul but I keep thinking about how she was with me! She rang off on me and she didn't make contact, she accused me of leading him on as if I was some sort of tart! She even looked at me as though she hated me."

"No darling, that would never happen. She loves you with an intensity which I have always thought a touch unhealthy, you know why that is of course; you were like a miracle after losing her first two babies. We are going in circles and keep coming back to her love being the reason for her behaviour, but I believe it's something more than that, but for the life of me I don't know what it is." Tim and Sandy sat quietly side by side each deep in their own thoughts and pain. The meat on the barbecue spat and sizzled as it cooked taking Sandy back to those dark days when the three of them cooked whatever they could find or kill and her stomach turned at the thought of eating.

"Dad, I'm not hungry, I'll just have some bread and cheese later." She stood up and leaned on the veranda facing out across the lagoon where the phosphorescence sparkled under the stars.

"I feel so guilty. I've wrecked our whole family. It's all my fault, isn't it? Don't deny it Dad!"

"Darling, tell me straight, would you rather have seen Paul locked up for something he didn't do? Would that have made us a happy family?"

"Of course not! I know we did the right thing but why couldn't Mum see that? Oh, Christ Dad, what the hell am I going to do? I feel so alone, I know I've got you and Oli, Alice and George, but Oli's got his own life to pick up on and I can't hang out on the farm any longer." Adding in a near inaudible voice "I want my Mum, the way she used to be." Tim caught her in his arms and ruffling her hair like he would Lilly's ears he hugged her to him and as she buried her face in his neck, he felt her tears on his skin. She felt so small in his embrace, so vulnerable and in the warmth of the night she was shivering.

He held her until she, with an effort, gulped a deep breath and wiped her hand across her eyes then taking her hand he led her back to her chair where they sat in silence. Tim sniffed the air, an unpleasant smell of burnt meat told him that he would be having bread and cheese as well. He removed the food from the hot coals and threw it in the rubbish.

"Another beer?" he asked, Sandy nodded

"Yeah why not." The sounds of the night as it fell, grew louder; filled with the pinging of moths' fat bodies hitting the glass of the

Tilly lamp as they flung themselves in their pointless quest for light, the trilling of cicadas and the gentle hiss of the lagoon as it gently washed against the shore. They each drank the last of their beers and turned their chairs to face the water and the vast expanse of night sky where, unpolluted by man's illuminations the moon shone upside down and the stars glittered like chips of broken glass. Tim reached out and took Sandy's hand in his.

"Darling, I wonder if when we get home you should visit Mum and try to find something of your old love for each other."

"To be honest Dad, I'm scared to see her, scared that she hates me and that she blames me for everything. Can't we stay here a bit longer, please Dad? I'll write to her and see how she responds and if it sounds hopeful then I'll visit. Do you think we could do that?"

"Sandy, my love, we have to leave at the end of the month, the place is booked out to someone else. Maybe you could invite Mum to go on another holiday with you, away from England, away from me, away from everything which reminds you and her of Paul. Maybe in a different environment where there's no-one to take you away from her you could heal a few of the wounds?"

Tim was met with silence. Sandy gently pulled her hand away from his and through her tears she answered

"I can't Dad. I can't forget the horrible things she said about Paul's Down syndrome. It was unbelievable; as though it were his fault he was like he was."

"Yes, I know, she called him a 'mongol' to me and spoke about him as though he were some sort of monster, it was such a shock to hear her speak like that." Tim's cheerful open face closed with pain as he recalled how this had been the beginning of their breakdown. The woman who had up until then been loving and caring suddenly became a cruel vindictive person whom he didn't recognise. "Darling, I can't explain or excuse her, I wish I could, but no matter what, she is your mother and one thing for sure is that she loves you. Try to remember that."

Their departure time was drawing nearer and Sandy was becoming more withdrawn. Tim watched her little figure wandering over the sand or sitting pensively on a rock with an ache in his chest. Even Josie failed to cheer her up with tales of her latest conquest. David was history now and it amused Josie that he hadn't liked the fact that she had finished it and not him.

"I knew he was a two timer but for a while I thought he really cared about me. Then he abandoned me on a trip to Flat Island and finally reappeared at the end of the day with that drip Cynthia, you know, the one from the Foreign Office. I honestly thought about throwing myself off the boat on the way back but I didn't have the nerve."

"He's manipulative, I didn't trust him from the moment I met him."

"You're right. I just wish I hadn't told him so much about me, my mistakes and things I'm a bit ashamed of. I hope he goes home soon. I feel sort of exposed, it's as though he's got a dossier on me and is just waiting for the best time to use it."

"Bloody hell!" Sandy almost shouted, "anyone would think he's squeaky clean!"

"Yes, but he's a man isn't he and men who are promiscuous are just sowing their wild oats but a woman is a tart, the village bicycle, a temptress – you name it!"

"I'm just glad he doesn't know anything about me." Sandy blew out her breath, what a meal he could make of that!"

During the last weekend of Sandy and Tim's holiday Sandy and Josie held a lunch time exhibition on the beach of all their paintings. The invitations were issued to not only those people who had commissioned work but to Josie's friends in the VSO and the Peace Corps. Tim employed some local women to provide cold food and had a crate of beers delivered by taxi. After the lunch and the sale of much of their art work everyone swam and sat around chatting. Sandy was just handing over her last sale to a big blond woman who should have been wearing a horned helmet when Josie rushed up to her

"Sandy, why don't you renew your visa and stay on for a bit? You could share my flat!"

"Oh wow, that would be fantastic, how long for? But what about living money? I've earned a few rupees today but that won't last long."

"Don't you see? If you could sell even just one painting a week it would pay for food. Living's bloody cheap here."

CHAPTER 3

PROFESSOR SMALL ANSWERED THE 'PHONE in his study. A small elderly voice quivered in his ear

"Professor, this is Miss Hazlett, do you remember coming to visit me?"

"Why hello Miss Hazlett, of course I remember you, what can I do for you?" There was a longish pause before she answered.

"I'm worried and confused; may I come and talk to you?"

"My dear Miss Hazlett, I can come to you if you like, I'm free this week and I can drive over on Friday, would that be alright?" He replaced the 'phone and jotted the appointment in his diary. Leaning back in his chair he stroked his chin thoughtfully.

That Friday, Miss Hazlett answered the door to Professor Small who grasped her bird-like hand in his large paw and shook it warmly. He ducked his head below the lintel, an obviously habitual reaction to having cracked it many times before on various doorways owing to his height and she showed him into her sitting room where she had laid out a tea tray with some cakes and biscuits. His towering form lost some of its slightly intimidating appearance when he gently eased himself on to the proffered chair thereby reducing his height to that of the still standing Miss Hazlett.

"I'll just make the tea, or would you like coffee?"

"Tea is splendid, as strong as you like!" She scurried off into the kitchen and Professor Small let his gaze wander the room. He noticed that there were quite a number of school photographs on the shelves. They showed a young Miss Hazlett with neat dark hair dressed back in a bun, a high-necked blouse and a sweet smile, Miss Hazlett with greying hair and a sweet smile, Miss Hazlett, smaller, with white hair and that same sweet smile. And the children, all with some disability, lined up either side of her all sporting huge grins. Some were laughing and some were looking shyly under their lashes at the camera, heads turned slightly away and cocked over one shoulder; her rotation of 'families' through the years. He rose to take the tray from her as she entered but she told him bossily to sit down as he made the room seem very small when he stood up. He immediately resumed his seat.

Wincing slightly as she bent to pour the tea into the fine bone china cups she skipped the obligatory 'did you have a good journey?' type of conversation and went straight for the kill.

"Have you told me the truth about Paul?" The cup in the professor's hand looked like one from a dolls' house set which might shatter with the slightest tightening of his grip. He took a sip of tea and carefully placed it back in the saucer. "Is Paul buried in the cemetery or is he not?" The professor was taken aback, why ever did she think he might not be?

"Yes, of course he is, why do you ask?" The professor shifted uncomfortably in his seat and took another sip of his tea.

"I don't know, but I have a strange feeling that he is watching me. I know that sounds stupid and I know I'm an old woman but I'm not senile and..." she trailed off.

"I can assure you that Paul was certified dead from pneumonia and properly interred..." He caught his breath, damn it, would she notice the slip? They had told her that he had been exhumed from the mire, it had been easier that way rather than explain everything that happened on the moor and afterwards. Apart from the need to protect Sandy and all the others he had had to protect himself, the truth of their sheltering a suspected murderer held unfathomable consequences should it get into the wrong hands.

"What?!" Miss Hazlett prompted him sharply. He gave a small start at her tone which indicated that she had noticed his slip.

"Paul is buried in the cemetery." He repeated.

"No! And you know very well that wasn't what I meant. I am not a fool Professor and I don't like to be made one. You just said he died from pneumonia yet before you told me he had died in a mire."

The professor sighed, it was no good procrastinating; he had opened his big mouth and now he had to explain.

"I repeat, he is buried alongside his mother but, please forgive the lie I told you, he didn't die on the moor, he died in a warm bed surrounded by people who cared deeply about him."

"So, he wasn't exhumed. Why did you tell me he had died such a dreadful death? Didn't it occur to you how upsetting that was for me? And who are these people who 'cared' so much about him" she emphasized the words with sarcasm, "but not enough to let him see me and to let me know he was safe?" Miss Hazlett's face and neck were flushed scarlet as her anger rose. "You have lied to me and put me through anguish. How could you?" She fetched his coat from the hall and thrusting it into his hands as he rose to attempt to calm her she said curtly "I think you should leave now."

"I will go if you wish, my dear," the professor rose from his chair, "but I beg some more of your time if only to justify my actions and to ease your pain." Miss Hazlett didn't reply but merely glared at him with tears of anger and grief in her eyes, then, snatching his coat back she rammed it on the hook creating a pokey in the back by ignoring the hanger and resumed her seat.

"Well?" She fixed him with a cold look. "Continue."

Small took a deep breath

"I will not presume to have your blessing with what we did but

I sincerely hope you will understand why we kept the truth from you." He reached for his teacup which was now empty and placing it back in the saucer he smiled rather coyly at Miss Hazlett, "May I have another cup before I begin?" Miss Hazlett's sigh didn't escape his notice as she picked up the pot to refresh it. Whilst the kettle came to the boil in the kitchen he gave himself a minute to decide where to start. He had realised that once he had made his slip this woman was not going to be satisfied with some half-cocked tale and so, teacup replenished, the professor began the story of Sandy's meeting with Paul. She started with shock when she heard that Sandy had run him over, questions already hovering on her lips. Small gently but firmly bade her hear all he had to say and he would answer her questions then. As he recounted all that Sandy and Oliver had told him about the traumas Paul had suffered both at the Asylum and at the hands of Jimmy, tears spilled down her cheeks, but she remained silent and attentive. The affirmation that Paul was indeed buried beside his mother and had died in a warm bed surrounded by friends drew an audible sob from her. The account of the kindness and gentleness shown to Paul by Sandy and Oliver and Oliver's family, at risk to themselves in the eyes of the law, the support and medical care given to him by Doctor Mike Squires also at risk of losing his license should the facts come out made her smile with gratitude through her tears. Breaking her agreement to save her questions until the end Miss Hazlett butted in with

"My goodness, you were breaking the law – and in your position!"

"Well, yes we were, although at first I wasn't aware that I would end up doing so."

"I don't understand, surely Professor, a man in your profession would know whether or not he was breaking the law!" It was becoming more complicated, he realised that he had missed out the initial subterfuge when he was first persuaded to take on the case. It seemed so long ago when Alistair had come to him with his request to clear a man's name who was presumed dead.

"I'm sorry my dear, I have jumped ahead of myself. Alistair, Oliver's brother asked me if I could act for the presumed dead Paul, spinning a tale which was to a large extent credible; that he had a Down syndrome cousin who was being bullied after the news of Paul's arrest. It wasn't until I was well and truly involved that I had my suspicions that this wasn't just some extracurricular project for Alistair. I was intrigued and I contrived a meeting with the fictitious cousin at the farm. It turned out to be Paul who was being sheltered by the Tregowans. I should have withdrawn from the whole thing or indeed reported them all to the police but Paul's nature, which you and many others gave testimony to and which I experienced first-hand left me in no doubt that this young man needed my help. Once I was *au fait* with the facts and had met them all it became a mission for me." He was greeted by a lengthy silence as she took in the complicated sequence of events and their implications. Small fidgeted a little in his rather too small chair as the thought occurred to him that he had perhaps made a mistake in telling her of the illegality of what he had done. This appeared to be confirmed when she suddenly sat forward in her chair.

"But your oath, don't you swear an oath to become a barrister?" Miss Hazlett looked shocked.

"Yes, we do. We swear to uphold the law and the breaking of the oath is termed as perjury."

"Do you mean to say you broke your professional oath to save Paul?" Miss Hazlett clasped her hands to her mouth; her bright blue eyes were shining with a mixture of tears and gratitude. She took a moment to control her emotions, "Oh Professor, here I was thinking such bad thoughts about you and accusing you of treating me like a fool when you have taken such a risk, how can I ever thank you." She beamed at him.

"I broke the rules yes, but if upholding the law means that justice is denied an innocent person then I'll be buggered if I care if I break it!" He reached for her small hand and grasped it in both of his.

"If there is one person in this who deserves thanks it's young Sandy, her behaviour extended far beyond what could be called duty." His face fell as he said "It resulted in a complete breakdown of her family unit." Miss Hazlett's smile vanished immediately,

"What on earth happened? I thought the families were united in the whole thing? Surely it cannot be connected?"

"I shouldn't have said anything, but now I have, I'd better explain briefly."

"Before you do, I'm going to fetch us both a drop of whisky, or would you prefer brandy?" Miss Hazlett didn't wait for an answer and to the professor's delight produced a bottle of fine malt whisky from the sideboard. They settled themselves comfortably in front of the open fire in her tiled hearth and Professor Small attempted, but failed, to argue both sides of the story. However, Miss Hazlett, on hearing how June had behaved so irrationally was not as surprised as the professor had assumed she would be.

"I have no children Professor, I lost my fiancée in the First World War and I never married. I loved the children at the school but they were not mine. Sally and Paul became my family; neither of us had any other relations. We were drawn together through loneliness. Had I had a daughter, especially if I'd lost babies before, I imagine I would have mown down everyone in my path to have her back, as it were, from the dead." She met his surprised look with one of resolve. "What a dreadful dilemma for Sandy. Was the marriage shaky anyway? Surely her husband understood what she was going through?"

"I can't tell you the intimate details, for a start I don't know enough to pass comment, all I know is that she apparently turned into a harpy, though God knows why she let it get so out of hand. She was the biggest loser in the end."

"How incredibly sad, the poor woman."

After seeing the professor off Miss Hazlett quietly cleared the tea tray away and pensively washed the cups. Although the situation was now clear in her mind and she was grateful for having been told the truth, she felt a nagging in the back of her mind; one of those feelings which are difficult to rationalise. Paul's case was already old news and most people would have forgotten about it as soon as the next day's papers had landed on the mat. However, as the professor had said, it only took one person to start a rumour before things became ripped open like a badly healed wound.

The main reason for inviting Small had been to discuss with him her anxiety that she was being watched, but after the exposure of his lie the subject had been forgotten. Now that she was alone she went over her experiences both at the grave and at the bus stop and bearing in mind what she had just been told she felt sure that her instincts had been right – she was being watched. But by whom and to what end? She paced the kitchen, leaving the cups to drain rather than drying them and methodically putting them back in the cupboard as was usually her wont, and returned to the sitting room where she sat heavily in her chair. Leaning back against the antimacassar she closed her eyes and silently wept.

The professor was exhausted and drove home slowly musing over how humanity never ceased to surprise him.

The 'phone rang at the farm. George answered in his soft Devonshire burr, "Professor, good to hear from you, how's business?"

"George, we need to talk, can you get in touch with the others and arrange a meeting, preferably at the farm?" George felt a shiver of anxiety run up his spine.

"Is there a problem?" He hesitated, "Is it about Paul?"

"Yes, a small problem, we need to meet and I will explain. I will be bringing someone with me, Miss Hazlett who was Paul's teacher. Can you get everyone together for next Thursday?"

"I can get Ali and Mike but Sandy and Tim are away. Oli's here of course and Alice."

"Damn, I really wanted Sandy there but never mind we can introduce them at a later date." Hearing Alice's questioning voice in the background he added "Don't worry it's just some ends we have to tie up."

Oliver tried not to show his disappointment when Sandy's letter arrived. However, he had no right to feel let down; he was meeting Susie later that week with a hope deep in his heart that things would work out and it would be uncharitable for him to wish Sandy back if she didn't want to face reality just yet. He strode over the fields with Lilly running ahead, worrying about what he would say to Susie, his lack of communication had put him at a disadvantage with her and she had been cold and initially reluctant to see him. It had taken a lot of persuasion to get her to come and he was both excited and trepidatious; was Susie thoroughly fed up with his lack of contact and was meeting him just to tell him it was over? Or would they pick up where they had left off? They had been seeing each other every weekend before he had been stranded on the moor and even talked about engagement. However, Oliver's experiences over the ensuing months had confused him as to who or what he was. He had never formed such a close friendship with anyone as he had with Sandy and Paul, especially Sandy. But, did that preclude his love for Susie? What did he really want from Sandy? Was it merely brotherly love and friendship or was it more? Furthermore, what did Sandy want from him? Surely, they would have progressed further were they in love with each other? They seemed to know each other in a way that only siblings did, each was comfortable in the other's company without even thinking about it, they behaved like mates, irrespective of gender. Also, he mused, Sandy *is* a bit of a lad! *Ergo – she's a mate, a bloody good mate.* Dragging his mind back to the task in hand he grabbed an ear of wheat, rubbed the chaff away with his thumb and tested the corn between his teeth, it would soon be ready for harvesting weather permitting.

The drought and heat wave which had begun in June had finally come to an end on the 26th August. Having battled to maintain their harvests with water pumped from the rapidly diminishing dykes and ponds the Tregowans were now faced with torrential rain just at the point of harvest.

"The bloody wheat is sodden and so is the mowing grass." George stomped angrily into the kitchen shaking his waterproof like a man fighting off a wild animal. "I can't harvest it in this weather – it'll just rot."

"We've got a bit of time yet Dad, all we need is a few days of sun and we can crack on, work half the night if needs be." Oliver followed George into the kitchen whose floor was now puddled and muddy.

"Can't you ever learn to shake your waterproofs in the porch before you come in and damn it all George, you've still got your gumboots on!" Alice thrust a mop in Oliver's hands. "Swab it up please!"

And it poured, day after day as if the rainfall which should have fallen over the last three months had been stored in a huge vat which was now being overturned. The only good thing for the Tregowans was the cattle pasture began to green up again albeit too late in the year to benefit grazing. However, the ground quickly became a quagmire and the livestock, especially the sheep and goats, had to be housed in the byres and fed on pellets.

"This is costing us too much money." George signed the last cheque to the fodder suppliers. "Thank goodness we cut the winter wheat when we did but if the second crops fail we're going to have to sell some of the animals. It'll be winter soon and then three months or more before they can be put out. The upper field isn't too bad at the moment but the top soil is beginning to wash down and that'll bugger up the spring growth." He rested his head in his hands and sighed "Who would want to be a farmer? I can see '76 doing for us; I've never known such contrary weather."

Thursday evening came and Professor Small collected Miss Hazlett in his car and they set off to the farm. The roads were awash with water from the persistent rain and thunder crashed almost continuously. Professor Small drove with his nose virtually pressed to the windscreen, the wipers were on full speed and still the rain cascaded down the screen as if from a hose pipe. Trying not to distract him from his concentration, she took the opportunity to finally tell him about her experiences at the cemetery, the reason she had asked to meet him in the first place. "Hmm," he murmured, "this has happened twice you say?"

"Well, not exactly, I just felt something the first time and then the person at the bus stop made me feel very vulnerable, I'm sure they were watching me."

"We need to discuss this further my dear." There was a massive crash of thunder and the sky lit up as a huge streak of forked lightning flashed across it. Miss Hazlett gave a little shriek and covered her face with her hands.

"Chin up! We're nearly there." Small grunted. As they approached an avenue of tall dangerously swaying trees he thrust his foot down on the accelerator, ignoring the bow wave of water he was creating as he ploughed through the flood.

"I'm sorry," he cast a hurried glance at Miss Hazlett, "but I don't want to be crushed by a falling tree." Finally, the lights of the farm could be seen in the distance, distorted and dancing through the wet windscreen.

"At last!" he bellowed, "Thank God for that."

Mike Squires had already arrived and been taken into the kitchen where he stood by the Aga, a towel in his hands.

"I got soaked just coming from the car." He laughed as he held out his hand in greeting. The Tregowans had not heard his arrival and apologised for not opening the door as quickly as he would have liked. They had spared Miss Hazlett from a similar soaking by rushing out to the car with umbrellas and oilskins as soon as the professor had parked.

Introductions were made and Alice beckoned them all to sit at the table which was laid for supper.

"I thought a hot-pot would be a good idea tonight bearing in mind the weather." Alice placed the casserole on the table mat. "I hope you like lamb Miss Hazlett?" A brief image of woolly bundles of happiness bouncing in the fields made Miss Hazlett pause before assuring Alice that she loved lamb casserole and how she often bought lamb from her local farmer.

"This is one of our own." George added "Alice will give you some from our deep freeze to take home, do you have a freezer?" Alice shot him a quick look to remind him that their supplies were rather precious given their conversation earlier but it was too late as Miss Hazlett thanked him saying that she did indeed own a freezer, whilst silently wondering who she could give the meat to when she got home. The casserole was, as usual for Alice, very good and overcoming her aversion to eating lamb Miss Hazlett managed to swallow the meat well-disguised with potatoes and vegetables. After an apple-crumble had been consumed with a tankard each of scrumpy for the men and wine for Alice and Miss Hazlett it was time to get down to business.

"Let's go into the sitting room and relax over a glass or two." George suggested. "Brandy for you Professor?"

They made themselves comfortable in the easy chairs and Chesterfield sofas and George deposited a tray of glasses and bottles of various sorts on the low table. He had brought sherry for Miss Hazlett and beer, wine and spirits for the rest of them.

"Actually, George, I would prefer a whisky if you don't mind." A little voice rose from somewhere deep in the soft cushions.

"Righto!" George beamed at her and poured a good measure into a glass. Alice had already poured her own glass of wine and Oliver helped himself, Alistair and Mike to a beer each.

"Professor, say when."

"When. Thank you George. And don't you think we have known each other long enough to drop the title, just call me Jeremy."

"Oh," Alice interrupted "on your notepaper it says your name is John." Small grimaced and then let forth one of his huge roars of laughter.

"Can you imagine what my parents were thinking when they christened me John? Apart from the fact that my father was called John which caused no end of confusion, put it with Small and you have a ready-made nickname." He chuckled at the memory. "It started when I was in infant school when my teacher made a joke about me being bigger than my name and in front of the whole class called me Little John." He took a large swallow of his drink and sighed in appreciation. "Good stuff George. Anyway, Jeremy is my middle name and as soon as I moved from the prep school I gave my name as Jeremy and cajoled and bribed the teachers to refer to me by that." He leaned back in the chair and Oliver held his breath waiting for the crack of breaking furniture. "There are only so many times you can laugh off being challenged to a fight with wooden staves and being asked where my Sherwood Greens were."

"Was there a Maid Marion?" Alistair asked giving George a wink.

"Ah, now you've put me on the spot Alistair, yes, there was one little girl I took a fancy to but she was called Gertrude!" He sighed, "What a dreadful name to give to a pretty little thing. It all came to nothing though; she never noticed me which is odd considering my huge presence." George offered him a refill of brandy and Oliver took the opportunity to top up his own beer. Small continued "One day I retaliated to the ragging and ended up sitting on a boy who was half my size breaking his arm. I was dreadfully upset, it wasn't intentional. I'm not physically confrontational by nature. I was sent to the classroom as punishment and spent the playtime crying in the corner facing the wall." He looked around at the grinning faces and added "You may well laugh young Alistair but at six years old being sent to the corner was a really severe punishment."

"It's better than getting the cane though!" Alistair remarked and wriggled in his seat as though he had just received it.

"True, but humiliation is sometimes worse than a slap. Anyway, by the time I was seven years old I was already as tall as many boys in the upper school and my bulk made me seem even bigger. As time went on I soon learned to go along with the jokes and laugh, tongue in cheek, along with the little sods." He nodded in the direction of the ladies "Apologies for my language ladies."

"I've heard worse!" laughed Miss Hazlett.

"Try working on a farm and you'll hear a lot worse." Alice added.

"You should hear the language of some of the criminals I have to represent!" Small replied. He paused and becoming more serious he addressed the family and Mike and began to explain why he had asked for this meeting, "I have already taken Miss Hazlett into my confidence," he added with a smile in her direction, "this dear lady has more reason than all of us to mourn Paul and his mother and yet we mislead and bemused her about the facts. We know, and now so does she, the reasons for this and

I ask her now if she understands and forgives us?"

"I do understand, er, Jeremy, and I suppose I am of a forgiving nature should circumstances merit it. From what I have been told, they certainly do." She pushed herself forward from the deep cushions to the front of her seat and perching like a bird on the very edge she continued "You have no idea how distressed I was firstly by Sally's death and then the accusations against Paul." Her voice faltered for a second but she straightened her back and took a sip of her whisky, "I have known them for years and Sally and I had become firm friends. And then the news of Paul's death in the mire broke my heart. I dreamed of him struggling to get out, I imagined his terror, I heard his voice calling for help..." She took a deep breath and with a small cough continued, "then his stone was erected next to Sally and I assumed he had been recovered, and I thought at least the poor boy had not been left there un-mourned, like a common criminal of the eighteenth century with no Christian burial and I was thankful for that at least." The Tregowans could identify with these dreams as Oliver could testify having been plagued with similar ones when Alistair had nearly perished in the same way. Alistair sat rigidly in his and looked at the floor, no one spoke for a while until Mike in his kindly way reached his hand out and clasped Miss Hazlett's in a warm comforting way saying

"Jeremy mentioned over dinner that you had a disturbing experience at the cemetery, but he has not had time to update us, do you think you could tell us what happened?" Miss Hazlett looked embarrassed, what a fool she must seem, imagining that Paul was watching her – wishful thinking she supposed. However, her feelings of being watched may sound fanciful but she was now fully convinced that they were accurate and that it had something to do with Paul's death. She explained how she had felt she was being watched and described the shadowy figure in the cemetery whom she thought had been Paul, blushing a little as she heard how silly it sounded. But the person's behaviour at the bus stop had been strange, of this she was sure.

"Maybe they just changed their mind and went home." Oliver suggested in a slightly bored voice.

At this point Jeremy Small took over.

"Who knows? However, now you can see that I needed to tell Miss Hazlett the truth, well, to be honest I made an error and let it slip that Paul had died from pneumonia, hoisted on my own petard!" He smiled wryly "The problem now is who is following her and why?"

"If she actually *is* being followed." Oliver continued dismissively.

"Could it be June?" Alice asked "She has a vindictive streak."

"Jeremy told me about Sandy's mother on Friday but I still don't understand why her marriage broke up or why she and Sandy became estranged – surely Paul can't have been the only reason? And even so why should she want to follow me? From what you tell me she knows everything that happened and where he is buried. I can't see that it would be her, can you?"

"I'm afraid it seems that Paul was the reason for the breakdown, but I agree I can't see your watcher being June, she's far too involved in her own misery, poor woman. Tim and June were a very happy couple before all this happened, I have known them for years and never for the life of me did I imagine them ever breaking up." Mike looked vacantly into his glass before taking a small sip and placing it on the table. "It's very sad but I don't think they'll ever get back together again."

"Well, she blamed Paul for everything, she was unbelievably vitriolic. I don't understand her at all!" Alice got up and stomped across the room to draw the curtains with an angry swish nearly knocking a vase from the corner table and then stomped back again. "She hated Paul, she had the stupid idea that he was taking Sandy away from her."

"In fairness to June, my love," George interrupted "she had just had three months of not knowing whether Sandy was alive or dead and in the end, she had to accept that she was probably dead. And then Sandy turns up and she thinks everything is going back to normal and then it doesn't. And, why doesn't it? Paul! Don't damn her to hell completely. I think she behaved like she did because of her love for Sandy and not necessarily because she hated Paul."

"Well I think she was dreadful and spoilt and selfish in the extreme!" Alice was getting more heated and Oliver spoke over her

"Mum, you're sounding just like her, for God's sake calm down." Alice flashed him an angry look but resumed her seat in an embarrassed silence. George reached over to her and gently took her hand. Oliver continued, "I'd like to be able to say that I understood why June was so aggressive to Paul and forgive the way she hurt Sandy but I can't, that poor kid was torn to bits. It'll take her a long time to get over it." He took a long drink of his beer, topped it up from the bottle, "Mike, you've known June and Tim for years, has she always been difficult?"

Mike sighed deeply, "Poor June, and I say poor June, because whereas all of us are feeling so righteous she is desolate and alone." Alice began to interrupt but George squeezed her hand saying quietly,

"Go on Mike."

"It must be embarrassing for her to know that you are all aware of her miscarriages and her need for medication on and off for years. Even after Sandy was born she sometimes slipped into depression. Sadly, I found I was unable to cope with her during those months after you returned with Paul. I should have made more effort and, I hesitate to say it but I feel it was wrong and hasty of Tim to give up on her and leave. He was her support and she relied totally on him."

"But what about Sandy?" Oliver exclaimed to Mike "Tim was put in a horrible position, it was a choice between June, and her refusal to budge and support us all, and Sandy who refused to give up on Paul." Murmurs of assent came from Alice and Alistair. Oliver opened another bottle of beer and drank it down greedily. "She made life hell for Sandy."

"Oli, that's your third beer in a row!" Alice remarked "Go easy my lad. Sorry Mike, please go on."

"I agree the choice eventually had to be made, but only as a last resort. I'm sure that in time Tim could have coaxed her round and maybe got to the bottom of why she found Paul so deeply abhorrent. I understand that she may not have taken to him and been a little repulsed by him but I can't understand her full blown hatred. It's almost as if she feared him. Ask yourselves, if Paul had been a normal young man, intelligent and wholesome, would she have supported him then?"

"I suspect that she would have Mike, I know she was terrified of Paul's obvious love for Sandy and the thought of her daughter loving a Down's man and maybe even marrying him was enough to send her bonkers!" George released Alice's hand and indicated Oliver, tall and strong, "She liked Oli and welcomed him into her home. Had they announced that they were a couple she would have been thrilled no doubt. Even though it would boil down to the same thing – someone would be taking Sandy away from the nest."

"So," Mike picked up the thread "was it pure prejudice? She must have known in her heart that Sandy's affection for Paul was platonic and that there would come a time, when his case was all over, when she would have Sandy back again."

"Loads of people have a thing about what they call 'mongols' or anyone who's a bit odd." Alistair muttered "You've only got to watch how people stare when that school for, and I quote, 'spastics' in Exeter has an outing. It's as though it's contagious!"

"Unfortunately, the public in general are very prejudiced, be it mental problems or the colour of skin, people can be very unkind." Mike agreed. "Going back to your question Oliver, has June always been difficult? My answer is no. She has always been vulnerable and a little over emotional but a more loving mother and wife you couldn't find. June could be great fun, flirtatious, humorous and honest. Perhaps it's her honesty which couldn't make her pretend to care about Paul when in fact she didn't. The only person she cared about was Sandy."

"And herself!" Alice couldn't help interjecting.

For the next half hour or so they exchanged views and ideas on what could have motivated June's behaviour and with no absolute knowledge the conversation wove aimlessly and tediously until Oliver, on his fourth beer, suddenly slammed his bottle loudly on the granite hearthstone, surprising them all with an aggressive outburst.

"Frankly, I don't think we're getting anywhere with all this talk about June. I thought that the main reason we've met is to discuss how the professor here has thrown shit in the fan and to pacify Miss Hazlett. Quite frankly I've got better things to do!" Oliver got up "Anyone for more drinks?" Without waiting for a reply, he made for the kitchen and in the absence of ensuing conversation could be heard clinking beer bottles and cussing quietly when the bottle opener wasn't immediately to hand.

When Oliver finally returned to the sitting room clutching a fresh bottle of beer Professor Small pointedly waited for him to sit down before continuing.

"I was wondering whether we should call on June. Miss Hazlett in particular, you should be there to perhaps supply some background to Paul – his mother, his nature and his neighbour's persecution of him. Her maternal instincts can't help but be moved by their closeness and the horror of finding his mother dead and so on."

"Please call me Hilda, everyone else is on first name terms and though I am senior by many years to you all I would like to drop the 'Miss Hazlett'." She pondered a little over the request but, shaking her head slowly she replied "I don't know if I would do any good, she would sense my animosity, I wouldn't be able to hide it if she was unpleasant about Paul."

"Well think about it, she may refuse altogether to see us but if she agrees it's a step in the right direction. Otherwise we'll just have to wait for Sandy and Tim to return and seek their opinions on what to do."

"We could have decided that in the first place and not wasted an evening with pointless chatter!" Oliver's voice boomed across the room, he was a bit slurred and pink in the face. "You're a sweet old biddy Miss Hazlett but p'raps if you didn't spend so much time in a cemetery you wouldn't imagine ghosts or have you been reading too many crime novels; imaginary stalkers, hooded figures, murder in the library with a poker, who did it? The butler."

"Oli, keep your toys in the pram! Is there *any* beer left?" Alistair tried to joke away Oliver's blatant rudeness.

"If there is it'll be a miracle. Enough's enough Oli, you're drunk!" George stared him down as in his inebriation he looked to become confrontational. Oliver slumped into his chair and flung his feet out across the fender dislodging a burning log which rolled onto the hearthrug.

"For God sake man have a care!" George rushed to grab the log with the tongs and return it to the fire whilst stamping on the scorching the rug which was giving off a smell of burning animal hair. Oliver shrugged uncaringly

"Sorry."

"I'm not sure this conversation is getting us very far." Hilda ventured. "Perhaps we should meet again at a more convenient time."

"Yeah, what a waste of an evening, nice meeting you Hilda. Goodbye."

"I think we should definitely call it a day." George declared "Oliver is in a belligerent mood and obviously drunk. I apologise everyone for my son's manner." He rose to his feet and with flick of his head he ordered Oliver to accompany him to the kitchen. Oliver slowly pulled himself to his feet and staggering a little followed his father from the room.

"I don't believe what I'm hearing Oliver, Hilda has known the family for years and she has none of her own, they were like family to her. When your mother or I die will you just forget about us and never visit our graves? Come on, out with it, what's your problem? Why have you embarrassed us all with your drunkenness and outright rudeness to Hilda?"

"If you must know, I had better things to do with my time than sit through that load of claptrap tonight. Didn't you think to ask me if I had any plans before you agreed the date with everyone else?"

"Just what is more important than protecting everyone, especially Jeremy and Mike?"

"Susie. That's who. I arranged to meet her tonight. She finally agreed after basically telling me to sod off because I haven't been in touch for ages and then I had to cancel."

"Well I'm truly sorry if I've ruined your date, but firstly, this situation is more important and far reaching than a broken date." Taking a deep breath, George attempted unsuccessfully to keep his temper. "And it does not justify your behaviour tonight." His voice by this time was all but a shout, "I thought you were a man not a simpering pansy, get a grip and get in there and apologise!"

Oliver sprang to his feet, his face scarlet with rage

"No I will not go grovelling like a naughty schoolboy. I will join you all in my own time." He flung open the door and stormed off into the rain.

George stood for a while in shock at Oliver's behaviour, he knew Oliver could be petulant but since his meeting with Sandy something had changed in him, he had matured and this side of his character had lain dormant. He must really care for this girl; the relationship had been pretty serious before Oliver went trekking but when he returned home and seemed so close with Sandy George had assumed that Susie and he were finished. However, his behaviour this evening had been unforgivable and George was shaking with anger and embarrassment. Pulling himself together he tried to assume a nonchalant air as he returned to the sitting room but from the awkward silence in the room it was apparent that most of the exchange had been heard.

Thus, the meeting ended with no solution. As far as June was concerned, they would discuss her with Tim and Sandy on their return. It had, if the truth be told, indeed been a waste of time.

The atmosphere was very tense as they finished their drinks and Alice's offer of beds for everyone was politely declined. George and Alice waved them all off and returned to the sitting room where they found Oliver who had returned through the back door. He was soaked and red eyed.

"Mum, Dad, I am so sorry." After a moment's hesitation, George strode up to him. Oliver looked sadly up at his father. The anger in Georges' eyes faded to be replaced by kindness; he ruffled Oliver's curls saying,

"Go and ring your lass, invite her out again and don't take no for an answer."

Susie refused to speak to him when he rang, her mother told Oliver coldly that she was out with friends, the sort who didn't let her down! But finally, after badgering her all the week she reluctantly agreed to meet Oliver at the Kings Arms. They sat in a slightly hostile silence in the seats favoured by Sandy when she and Oliver used to pop in for a break from the family and all the anxiety over Paul, which made Oliver uncomfortable.

"Shall we sit outside?" he asked as he brought the drinks to the table, "It's a lovely evening, shame to waste it." The rain had finally abated and the evening was calm and crisp.

Susie nodded her agreement and they moved to a sunny sheltered table in the beer garden. Sitting back in his chair, Oliver stretched his long legs out in front of him and breathed deeply the fresh autumnal air. Susie sipped her cider whilst Oliver took a long draught of his bitter. He smiled inwardly as he thought *I'd be getting a refill for Sandy by now.*

"I think you owe me an explanation." Susie said abruptly. She was unsmiling and a small frown creased her smooth forehead. Her usually sparkling brown eyes had a dull flat look in them and instead of her soft hazel hair gently framing her face she had pinned it back in a pleat which Oliver thought was not very flattering and which emphasised her severe expression. Oliver knew that he would have to give an account of himself but still had not formulated exactly what he was going to tell her. His dilemma being that he should tell her the truth as they could not start their lives together with such a huge lie between them. But, and here he dithered, it wasn't just he who had been involved, the culpability spread beyond him and his immediate family, did he have the right to reveal all? At last he spoke and reaching across the table, he took her hand which he was sorry to find was unresponsive.

"It's a long story." Susie removed her hand from his and fixed him with a sad but direct look.

"If you can't or won't explain why you have not been in touch with me for a year, then I don't see why I'm sitting here."

"I'm sorry Susie, I got involved with someone else's problems and I had to see it through. It's all over now; please don't ask for too many details, I don't want to betray a trust."

"It was a girl, wasn't it?"

"Yes, a girl was involved but not in the way you think. Sandy and I became very close during this time, but as mates, I've been loyal to you even though I didn't get in touch. Maybe in the future when it's all history I'll feel able to tell you everything. But, please trust me, I can't tell you now." Oliver could feel anxious sweat breaking out in his armpits and between his shoulder blades. For a while Susie didn't answer. She had finished her half of cider and Oliver, in an attempt to relieve the tension he was feeling, suggested a refill. Susie accepted with a shrug.

"Just a half please and then I think I ought to get off home." Oliver put the empty glasses back on the table and leaning over the back of her chair he stroked her cheek and then gently kissed the back of her neck.

"If that's what you want okay, but I was hoping you might stay for dinner, I've booked a table for us, we need time. Please Susie give me a chance."

Susie cautiously agreed to dinner later, much to Oliver's relief. Bert showed them to the table Oliver had booked, a quiet and private spot at the back of the bar overlooking the garden and the countryside beyond. Susie looked vacantly around the bar and seemed reluctant to meet Oliver's eye. He began to fidget with the cutlery, re-arranging it and polishing it with his napkin. The silence between them stretched on and Oliver was relieved when Bert brought them their drinks, at least it gave him something to do with his hands. The sun was beginning to slip down behind the trees throwing them into silhouette; a shimmering orange outline trembled around the branches as if they were on fire. Bert lit the candle on their table giving Oliver a badly disguised wink as he handed him the menus. Over dinner Oliver began to try to explain to Susie why he was unable to tell her everything that had happened since they last met. Susie was aware that every now and then Oliver took himself off to spend some time in solitude and she had always encouraged him in this knowing it was an integral part of who he was. She listened for a while then butting in to his floundering excuses and disjointed sentences she said

"Oli, please stop, leave it. When you are over this Sandy give me a call, if I'm still around maybe we can meet again." They finished their meal in silence neither eating much, Oliver paid and they left. Susie drove away without looking back. Oliver dejectedly began to walk home, he preferred walking to driving the five or so miles. Glancing at the sky he thought it looked stormy but there was no storm, the swirling black mass darkening the sky was accompanied by a thousand different birdsongs, he gazed at the murmuration of starlings mesmerised by the patterns as they swooped and soared, twisting and spiralling until finally they broke apart and the evening sky was clear. "Look Susie!" He said to the empty space beside him.

CHAPTER 4

TIM WAS SYMPATHETIC to Sandy's wish to stay on in Mauritius for a while; it would give her a bit more freedom to enjoy herself and to maybe make new friends.

"But you can't keep running away for ever my love."

"I'm not running away Dad, I just want to get the most out of this holiday." There was a big element of truth however in what her father had said; she had no idea what she was going to do when she got home.

What was her career? Teaching? What else could she do with a diploma in fine art? She might just have well stayed with Tom and married him. At least she would have been spared that last year of her life, June and Tim would still be together and Paul would have been someone she might or might not have read about in the newspaper. Maybe he would have been better off in the institution – he might even still be alive. No. She pulled herself up, he would have been murdered by that bastard Jimmy there was no doubt about that. It was no good thinking of what might have been, things are what they are. At least Paul died in a warm bed and not on a cold and lonely moor. Sandy knew in her heart that life with Tom would not have worked out, she would have been bored and frustrated and her resentment would have been directed at Tom. She doubted if their relationship, sexually charged though it was, could have survived Tom's controlling character and her own black moods.

But her life was far from perfect now. She had been instrumental in breaking up her parents' marriage and in turn was now a floating body dependent on others' charity. Her conversation with her father about her mother sat like an undigested meal in her gullet. June was her mother and Sandy loved her deeply. But did June still love her after all the hurt and accusations? Sandy missed her mother; or rather she missed the mother she used to have. Had June really changed completely into the spiteful woman they had witnessed over those months or had she always been a selfish spoilt bitch under the veneer of a doting wife and mother? Sandy couldn't bear to think of her mother like this; she resolved she would write to her that afternoon, she may be able to repair some of the damage from a distance before meeting face to face.

Sandy moved her luggage into Josie's flat and made up her mind that she would damn well enjoy herself and put everything else out of her mind. Josie had been allocated a little motor scooter to get her to and from work in Port Louis and on days when Sandy didn't fancy painting the two of them would ride to a different beach each time where Josie offloaded Sandy and her snorkelling gear, water, lunch and something to read. Endless sunshine and empty white sandy beaches were hers for the day. Other than the occasional fisherman Sandy experienced a rejuvenating solitude. Snorkelling interspersed with reading, dozing and sunbathing re-enforced her initial impression of this island being pure paradise. After work Josie chugged up on the scooter and flinging her sweaty work clothes on the beach she'd throw herself into the water. The family planning department for whom she worked was established by the British government in an attempt to introduce contraception to an increasingly over populated island. Josie spent most of her days painting billboards or designing posters to persuade the inhabitants to take the pill or to use condoms as small families were happier and wealthier. One poster aimed at the male population showed a pregnant man with the slogan loosely interpreted as 'If YOU were pregnant you would cry for Family Planning!'

"Guess what?" Josie called out as she came in from work. Sandy was busy painting and scarcely glanced up "Hang on a minute I'm at a tricky bit." Out of the corner of her eye she could see Josie impatiently hopping about. "Alright, you've wrecked my concentration, what is it?"

"There's a Russian battleship parked outside the bay!"

"Anchored, not parked! Do you mean Grande Baie?"

Yes, Grande Baie. Everyone at work is talking about it."

"Gosh! I wonder what's happening." Sandy's interest was taken. "That's what David's involved with isn't it? All the powers wanting control over the Indian Ocean or something." Sandy wasn't particularly knowledgeable when it came to world politics.

"Yes, and did you also know that the British Navy have ships dotted around the place?"

"Can't say I did. Are they always there?"

"Yes, but they move about and are quite far out generally."

"Christ I hope there's not going to be any fighting!"

"Nah, they're just keeping an eye on each other. Still, exciting, isn't it? Have you ever met a Russian?" Sandy shook her head. "Me neither. They're not allowed out much are they? Certainly not without complicated visas and things in case they defect."

"It must be horrible to be confined and not be able to see the world, look how free we are to travel just about wherever we want. It doesn't say much for communism if they have to imprison their members does it." Sandy shuddered, the thought of anyone or any regime restricting her movements made her feel cold inside.

"As it happens, we've been invited to a barbecue this weekend at a *campement* at Grande Baie and we can have a good old snoop."

"Not anything to do with David I hope." Sandy was suspicious.

"No, no, I haven't seen him for weeks. It belongs to one of the bosses at work, his daughter's getting married and he's full of bonhomie." Sandy's curiosity was piqued, the invitation was innocent enough and she'd never seen a battleship up close.

"Okay, let's go."

Sunday morning, they packed their swimming gear as no barbecue on the beach was complete without half the time being in the water, and chugged their way on Josie's scooter to the large privately owned beach. Josie shouted over her shoulder to Sandy as they slowed down to approach the house.

"How can he afford this place on his income?" They parked the scooter and Josie enlarged

"Judging by the salaries we all get he must be creaming some off for himself."

"Hush, someone will hear you. Anyway, you don't know, he may have independent means and is working for the good of humanity."

"Yeah and I'm the Queen of England!" Josie laughed back. "Anyway, let's have some fun."

From the beach they could see the ship quite clearly out to sea beyond the reef.

"I wonder why they are here and not berthed in Port Louis." Sandy commented.

"No idea."

The weather was typically very hot and sunshades were erected over sun loungers for the faint hearted which didn't include the girls. They basked in the sun and ate the food and drank the beer and chatted to the other guests whom Josie introduced to Sandy. As the afternoon wore on people became sleepy and many dozed off in their chairs or on towels under the palms. Sandy and Josie sat at the edge of the water allowing the warm wavelets to swirl around them and then with an almost imperceptible hiss drain through the white sand back to the ocean.

"Hey look!" Sandy pointed towards the ship, "It looks like they're coming ashore! But how will they get over the reef?"

"I think it's a bit lower, or there's a gap in it. The trip to Flat Island left from here so smallish boats can get in and out okay." Josie explained. As they watched, a number of men in swimming trunks steered a motor dingy towards the beach but then veered off and headed to a spot farther up from where the party were now all gathered to watch. The boat didn't come into the bay but disappeared around the small headland towards Pointe Eglise. Everyone lost interest once it was out of sight and went back to their drinks or siestas.

"Well that was a bit of excitement – not!" Josie laughed as she and Sandy returned to the party. "Anyone would think they were aliens or something, I'm sure they look pretty much like us."

"Yes but it would be interesting to talk to them wouldn't it? I assume they speak English – most people do, it makes us lazy about learning other languages."

The party were called to drink the health of the young couple whose engagement party this had turned out to be and there were cheers all round as they shyly held hands in front of everyone. The party was drawing to a close and the fresh pineapple desserts were rapidly disappearing from the spread. The girls quickly grabbed a slice each and wandered away from the others.

"Shall we have a little walk?" whispered Josie to Sandy. Sandy grinned and noting that the other guests were paying them no attention she grabbed her towel and slipped on her flip flops.

"Let's go." They walked along the water's edge in the direction the sailors had gone until they were out of sight of the house and not very far from the little boat pulled up onto the beach.

The sailors were swimming and laughing, oblivious to being

watched. One man appeared to be racing another in the sea heading away from the shore. The laughter ceased abruptly and was replaced by cries of alarm. Another man launched himself into the sea and he was followed by more sailors all swimming to the man who was in front.

"That bloke's in difficulties! Look!" Sandy pointed to the man who was now being carried by the current farther towards them. He kept disappearing under the water and then they saw a good deal of thrashing water around him. "My God I think he's drowning! Where are the others?" As they watched he sank under once more and this time he didn't re-surface.

"I'm going to help him!" Josie set off at a run.

"Don't be stupid, you could drown as well." Sandy panted as she caught up. "Look the other blokes are there now."

"I'm going to get help then." Josie ran off without waiting for a reply.

One after the other the sailors dived and surfaced, dived and surfaced until finally one of they came up again pulling a limp form as he swam backwards towards the shore. They laid him on the sand and began to pummel his chest but he remained still. They tried mouth to mouth resuscitation but to no avail. The man was dead.

Very soon, alerted by Josie, a crowd of people from the party came running up the beach.

"I'm a doctor let me through!" one man shouted. But as he approached the sailors formed a ring around the dead man and refused to let him pass.

"Dead." one said bluntly. The doctor attempted to talk to him but he seemed to have very little English and that plus his reluctance to let anyone near his shipmate made it a pointless exercise.

The sailors were in shock and some had begun to shiver although it was still very warm.

"Come." Josie's boss beckoned them "Come we have hot drinks. We have brandy." He made gestures to explain. Josie ran up panting.

"I've rung the police and they're coming and so is someone from the High Commission." She explained to Sandy quietly that she thought they ought to know because of the politics.

"Het." The Russian who had pronounced the man dead shook his head "No" he repeated in English "we go." He indicated the ship and ordered some of the sailors to carry the body back to the motor launch. They turned their backs on the party guests and with the dead sailor slung over the shoulder of the biggest man, they left.

When the police and the representative from the High Commission turned up they had already reached the ship and boarded it.

What happened after that, they never found out. They assumed that the sailor would be buried at sea and the incident logged as an accident. They wondered if the sailors had been breaking the rules by leaving the ship but it was all surmise.

"Weren't they odd." Sandy and Josie were talking it over later that evening. "If they'd been American or English or *any* other nationality they would have welcomed some comfort and refreshment."

"Not the Japanese. They'd have closed us off too. They're full of dignity and honour and not showing emotion and all that rubbish." Josie had no qualms about making generalised sweeping statements based on no knowledge whatsoever.

"Odd behaviour though. I'm off to bed. Night." Sandy yawned.

"Me too, night."

Sandy was swimming and diving for shells one afternoon when, glancing towards the beach she caught sight of a figure sitting beside her towel. It was, as far as she could tell with the sun glinting on the surface of the water, a man. Treading water, she slipped her mask to the top of her head to get a better look. Yes it was a man and he was changing into swimming gear. What the hell! The beach is a million miles long – why has he plonked himself literally on top of her space? Well he can bloody well bugger off! As she began swimming back to the shore he entered the lagoon and began swimming directly towards her. Tucking her head down and flipping her bottom up she dived down and swam underwater away from him and headed farther down the beach. Approaching the shallows she pulled herself along with her hands on the coral until she lay in just a foot of water at the edge of the beach. Wearing flippers whilst swimming in the shallow coral reefs was more of a hindrance than a help so she had taken to wearing an old pair of plimsolls to protect her feet from coral scratches which could quickly turn septic. Thus she was able to exit the water and run quickly back to her possessions before he realised she had gone ashore.

On reaching her bag and towel she took the time to inspect the clothing lying nearby as the swimmer was still a way out. Somehow, she knew it would be his. David, having caught sight of her on the beach waved and began to swim a strong crawl towards the beach.

Sandy had no option but to sit on her towel and wait for him. If she left the beach there was nowhere to go and the walk home was too far especially in the heat of a hundred degrees. Anyway, why would she run away, he isn't dangerous – just a creep.

Sandy wrapped her towel around her waist and assuming a nonchalant posture she picked up her book and began to read, totally ignoring the tanned figure striding up the beach, mask and flippers dangling from one hand.

"What a coincidence!" he smiled, "Had I known you were here I'd have brought a bottle of champagne."

"Are you in the habit of intruding on a person's space?" Sandy replied without looking up. "Or do you just plonk yourself down by just anyone?" When he answered Sandy could hear the grin in his voice and she felt angry and vulnerable.

"You've caught me out Sandy, I'm afraid I just had to see you again, I must have given you a very bad impression of myself when we last met."

"Yep. You did. But I don't think it was just an impression." She rummaged in her bag to find her watch. It was three pm thank goodness; Josie packed up at three and would be arriving soon to give her lift home.

"I know, Josie will be here soon and I shall disappear before then." He rubbed the towel over his hair and left it standing in tufts making him look slightly boyish. "Truly, Sandy, I'm very attracted to you. Josie and I were already beginning to tire of each other, or rather, tire is the wrong word; we disagreed on so many things that we rowed more than we made love."

"She was fed up with you two-timing her. Or was it three-timing? I think she lost count."

"Well that's all over now. I was unhappy with Josie that's why I behaved so badly. I'm not naturally like that."

"Well that's nice for your next girlfriend David. Sorry it won't be me." Sandy heard in the distance Josie's scooter hiccupping its way down the track, David quickly gathered his things saying as he turned to go

"I won't give up."

Later that evening Sandy told Josie about her encounter on the beach. Josie laughed, then looked sad.

"Bloody man, I was passionate about him and he knew it. That's why he knew I'd forgive him every time. I don't know what it is about him but he's sort of Svengali like. It took a lot of willpower to break free."

"Has he got some hold over you? You remember telling me you

regretted how much you'd told him about yourself?" Josie grimaced,

"I was involved with a married man when I first came here. Then I met David and poured it all out to him. He's a good listener and made me feel better." She sighed, "Then when we started to argue he used it against me and threatened all sorts of exposures both of me and the married man. He stores things up; he's got gossip about nearly everyone on the island including 'high ups'. In fact it was a relief in a way when he started showing an interest in you 'cos it sort of let me off the hook. I hoped he'd forget all about what I'd told him."

"Christ! What a bastard!" Sandy exploded.

Sandy began to feel very uncomfortable on the deserted beaches and for the next few days she stayed home with the door locked and painted furiously. David did call on a couple of occasions but she didn't answer his knock and actually hid in the bathroom in case he should peer through the window and see her. His predatory nature was spoiling her holiday and making her wish she was back in England. This in turn made her angry; how dare he ruin things for her! She decided that the next time he called she would have it out with him. After building herself up to a confrontation she was almost disappointed when he didn't call again and she was left with an unspent anger but this was tempered with relief; he must have finally got the message.

CHAPTER 5

"CHRIST I'M HOT! Do you think this was such a bright idea?" Sandy sank down in the shade of the rock and took a long drink from her flask. "This water's damn near hot enough to make tea with!" Mauritius lay just north of the Tropic of Capricorn and the sun cast very small shadows, even in the shade of the rock the temperature must have been at least ninety degrees. The volcanic rock of the mountain had absorbed the heat and Sandy could feel it radiating onto her back. "How much further to the top? Then we have to come back down again!"

"Stop complaining. This is something I've been wanting to do since I got here but I didn't think it was very safe to go on my own." Josie sat beside Sandy and drank deeply. "Must make sure we don't drink all the water, how much have you got left?"

"I haven't touched my other bottle so we should be okay but I could easily drink the whole lot now." Sandy tucked her flask back inside her backpack and together they began the steepest and most treacherous bit of the climb. Pieter Both, the jagged mountain with the ball of rock on the very pinnacle had already claimed the lives of a couple who were climbing it in a thunderstorm. They had been struck by lightning and fallen to their deaths into the sheer chasm over which Sandy and Josie were now making their careful crossing. The ridge of rock was only a few feet wide with drops either side and Sandy was tempted to crawl on her hands and knees, she didn't dare look down and when she looked up the sky seemed to swirl in front of her eyes. Finally they reached the top and there above them was the massive round ball which topped the climb. Someone had hammered iron rungs into the side and those who were brave or foolish enough could climb up and stand on the second highest point of the island. 2,700 feet is not high in comparison to Everest or other huge mountains ranges but Pieter Both's incline was sharp and jagged and the rock coarse and rough. They agreed that tempting though it was to reach the very top they had no idea how safe the rungs were and decided that they had gone far enough.

As they made their way carefully back down the mountain Sandy mused that she had done some pretty hairy things in her life so far but this must top them all – literally. She smiled to herself as she visualised her mother's face if she told her what she had done.

After a walk on the flat for about half a mile they arrived at the corrugated roofed hut where a family lived along with a few scraggly chickens and a goat. They had left Josie's motor scooter with them for safe keeping and Josie offered them five rupees for their kindness. However, instead of accepting the money the father waved them inside saying

"Ou pral mangje avek nou, vini vini!?

The wife then thrust bottles of Pepsi Cola into their hands and beckoned them to drink. Inside the hut, it was clean and homely, plastered on the walls were pictures of Queen Elizabeth and the Duke of Edinburgh, Union Jacks and a photograph of the Mauritian Prime Minister cut from a newspaper. When Josie and Sandy had been seated at the rustic table a bowl of fish curry was placed in front of each of them. Sandy was a bit horrified to find that she had been given the head in hers and, she hazarded, most of the bones! As they ate Josie chatted a little in her basic Creole to the family and discovered that the man was a fisherman, hence the fish curry and the wife and children worked in the sugar cane fields for a pittance. Josie thanked them warmly as they left and forbore to re-offer them the money for fear it would be taken as an insult to their generosity.

The bug had bitten and the following weekends they climbed Trois Mamelles, a gentle but long slope to the top of one of the three summits and Le Pouse, the third highest on the Island. For such a small country, which measured approximately 45 miles by 30 miles it contained a disproportionate number of mountains in relation to its land area, all thrown up by volcanic activity.

Sandy's extended visa was due to run out and she half wanted to extend it again and half wanted to go back home to England. She and Josie were discussing it one evening over cold beers on the terrace behind the flats when they heard the unmistakable purr of David's Mercedes followed by skidding gravel as he slung it round to park.

"Oh, damn it's David, do you want to see him or shall we pretend we're out?" Josie noticed Sandy's face flush with anger.

"No I don't *want* to see him but we may as well find out what he wants; he may be coming to say goodbye for all we know – ha ha." Sandy was aware that much as she tried to disguise it, Josie still had feelings for David though God knows why after his treatment of her. They heard the doorbell ring followed by knocking and Josie went through to open the door. When she got there David had vanished. She returned to the terrace to find him nonchalantly sprawled in her vacated chair having climbed the back wall. Sandy was looking daggers at him and Josie arrived at their chairs to hear her saying

"You've got a bloody cheek to just come in uninvited."

"Hi David," Josie smiled at him "can I get you a beer?" David nodded barely glancing at her and Sandy felt for her friend whose face showed the hurt he had purposely inflicted.

"A please or thank you would be nice. You may drive a flashy car and turn on the charm easily enough but you're hardly a gentleman are you?" she snapped at him. David smiled his smooth urbane smile and turning to Josie he drawled in an exaggerated tone of apology

"I do beg your pardon. Yes, please I would like a beer." When Josie had left the terrace to get his beer he said to Sandy "Your visa runs out in a week does it not? Are you thinking of renewing it?" Noticing Sandy's look of annoyance, he added, "I work at the High Commission remember, it's my business to know who is outstaying their visa."

"And it's my business whether I decide to stay or go." She reposted.

"I only asked because I can pull some strings if you want, the powers are not happy about people staying on for a second renewal." Josie returned, with beer for David, and some olives and cheese in a dish. She stood awkwardly by the table as if waiting for David to offer to get another chair but he remained seated and ignored her.

"Here, sit in mine, I need the loo." Sandy was on her feet and striding indoors before Josie had a chance to answer. For a while she and David sat in silence neither looking at the other, then Josie, pulling her chair around so that David had to look at her, said

"Sandy isn't interested David, I think she's got a boyfriend back home."

"It's none of your damned business!" he snapped back at her. "If she's anything like you, that shouldn't stop her having a good time with me. You'd sleep with half the husbands on the island if you could get away with it." He added with a sneer "I'm having dinner with your ex and his wife tonight at the High Commissioner's, it would be a shame if his wife caused a scene over the dessert, and he's due a promotion as well..."

"Can't you let it go David?" Josie pleaded, "I told you in

confidence, it was a mistake on both our sides and I don't want to break up his marriage!"

"I suggest then that you persuade your little mate to cooperate and then I may keep schtum about that and other things you've told me."

"I can't make her do something she doesn't want to, you don't know Sandy; she won't budge."

"Well say goodbye to your job at Family Planning and any references you hoped to have." He drank down the remainder of his beer and with a scathing look at Josie's tearful face he pushed his chair back and went in search of Sandy. Josie heard the door to the flat slam as David left and Sandy appeared from behind the potted palms on the far side of the terrace where she had been secreted and had heard the whole conversation.

"I'm going home when my visa runs out." she said bluntly. "If I were you I'd get the hell out of here as well; you don't need his bloody references, you're an artist, you paint, you're not some ineffectual secretary at the mercy of jumped up bloody men."

"Oh Sandy, I love it here, it's as though I belong. I don't want to go home to dreary rainy England." Josie was crying properly now and Sandy put her arm around her shoulders

"He's probably just bluffing. Don't worry, just forget you ever met him."

"Maybe David's posting will finish soon and he'll be sent to Outer Mongolia or somewhere dreadful and then I can relax. I want to stay here as long as I can." Josie smiled through her tears.

"Okay if that's what you feel but I'm leaving, I have a longing for the wet dreary days back on the farm."

Josie went with Sandy by taxi to the airport. They travelled without speaking, the holiday had ended on a low and they were both too unhappy to converse. The charter plane stood on the

tarmac shimmering like a mirage in the heat. Josie hugged Sandy and waved her goodbye as she crossed to the steps. As the plane sat with its engine idling waiting for permission to take off Josie saw David hurrying through the departure lounge doors. She ducked down behind a dhal puri stall to avoid meeting him, however, if he saw her he ignored her and made for the runway, but he was too late; the plane had begun to taxi prior to take off. Josie watched as it turned and began to accelerate and as it rose and banked away on its long journey back to England she felt very alone. When she had told Sandy that she had been relieved that David had taken an interest in her she had really been pretending. David had got to her in a way that no one else had ever done. She couldn't help it but she was very much under his spell. Sandy had advised her to get away from him and in her heart, she knew she was right, but she couldn't help herself. Sadly, Josie watched David exit the departure lounge, he appeared not to have seen her and she was undecided whether to call out to him. It was impossible to read his face as he passed within feet of her with his eyes on the ground in front of him so she held back a little until the doors had swung closed behind him. Then she too left the airport to make her way to the waiting taxi. As she approached the taxi rank her spirits rose as she saw David waiting – he must have seen her after all.

"It's okay I'll give you a lift." He handed the driver a note and dismissed him.

"Thanks David." Josie smiled at him as he led her to his own car and opened the door for her. *Maybe*, she thought, *just maybe he'll forget about Sandy now she's gone.* She settled herself comfortably in the passenger seat and watched David's profile as he pulled away in his usual manner leaving a cloud of dust behind him. He didn't speak to her or even acknowledge her presence in the car until he pulled up outside her flat.

"Are you coming in for a coffee?" Josie put her hand on his

which was resting on the gear lever. Pulling his hand away he turned to her with such a look of dislike that she gasped.

"You are some little bitch!" he spat at her. "I warned you didn't I?"

"But David, I told you I had no influence over Sandy, you have to believe me." Josie pleaded "I did try, honestly."

"Not hard enough. I warned you that you'd be sorry if Sandy went home." He leaned over her and unfastened her door "Get out!" Josie scrambled out of the car tears pouring down her face.

"You had better start packing," he called after her as she stumbled up the path to her front door, "it's not only me who has a score to settle with you." Josie stopped in horror

"What do you mean?" she cried.

"To put it in a nutshell, your ex's wife did rather spoil the dessert – and now she knows where you live." So that was the reason for the lift – one more gloat and yet another threat. Josie felt the bottom fall out of her world, Sandy was gone and she had absolutely no-one to turn to. She went indoors and collapsed in tears on her bed.

CHAPTER 6

JUNE READ AND RE-READ Sandy's long airmail letter. How she longed to see her again. The tone was gentle, there were no accusations or blame, just a long and excited tale of her holiday and the people she had met and right at the end she had written 'I love you Mum. XXX'

The plane landed at Heathrow. Sandy tanned and healthy looking disembarked. Oliver and Tim were waiting for her in the arrivals lounge and the sight of Oliver's ginger curls above the heads of other waiting friends and relations and her dad's beaming chubby face sent a warm glow through her. Dear old Oli, always there for her. The glow faded when the realisation that she was back to reality hit her. She still had not decided what the hell she was going to do, not just with her mother but with her own life.

It was a long drive back to Devon and Sandy said she could have caught the train. Oliver shushed her saying he enjoyed driving and had been looking forward to her return. He added that he hoped their journey across the moor would be uneventful! Neither of them could decide whether to laugh or cry.

Alice and George suggested that Sandy stay at the farm until she had made up her mind about her future as Tim only had one bedroom. Again, Sandy felt a surge of annoyance with her father for buying such an impractical house. It put her in the position of having to sponge off the Tregowans, yet again, or move in with

June. More than a year had passed since she had graduated from college and other than earning a few pounds by selling her paintings in St Ives and Mauritius she had done nothing to further her career. Perhaps she should re-apply for a teaching qualification; at least it would, as her father had said, 'give her more irons in the fire'. She dithered over this and finally decided against it. Being a student for four years was quite enough and the teacher training would involve academic studying and dealing with children when all she wanted was to paint. Also, playing on her mind was her mother, she still hadn't had a reply to her letter sent from Mauritius, had her mother received it? She decided to write to her again; she couldn't even think about her future whilst they remained estranged.

After his upsetting meeting with Susie Oliver had devoted his time to the farm and had taken much of the load off his father. Although he retained the desire to write, he found the farm work therapeutic whilst giving him time to himself. Walking the fields and supervising the planting and drainage, he decided that this was in fact the life for him. If only he had Susie to share it with. However, he found it hard to imagine Susie helping with the lambing or sitting up half the night feeding an orphaned calf.

This particular afternoon, Sandy had gone shopping with Tim to restock his cupboards and her painting materials. The gallery in St Ives having requested some more paintings for the last months of the tourist season had thrown her into a manic state. At least six local paintings were needed for the show but her portfolio contained mostly Mauritian coastal scenes which could in no way be mistaken for the grey and often angry English sea.

She was taking her painting seriously and was enthused by the reception they had had in Mauritius. However, there was still no indication as to what she was going to do with her life, whether she was going to move in with June or stay with Tim or, and Oliver rather wished she would, stay on at the farm. Underneath her show of independence, she was still the sad little girl who had poured out her heart to him on their trip to St Ives. He had tried to get her to make a decision, but she seemed to be in denial and refused to talk about it other than asking him heatedly on one occasion if he was trying to get rid of her and if that was what he wanted then she would bugger off tomorrow! Oliver and the rest of his family would be happy for Sandy to stay indefinitely but in what capacity? A lodger, a friend or a daughter in law? Oliver tried to imagine Sandy and him running the farm and living together 'til death did them part, but it was no good, love Sandy as he did he knew it was a brotherly love and that sooner or later they would go separate ways. Maybe he should get out more and meet someone new.

Oliver recalled a conversation he had had with Sandy shortly after her return and noted the mention of a number of men's names in her account of her holiday. He half hoped she had kept in touch with one or more of them and maybe she would settle down and be happy.

"Dad," Sandy put her arms round Tim's neck and gave him a kiss on the cheek, "I love you Dad." Tim pulled back from Sandy and looked suspiciously at his daughter.

"What do you want?" he asked smilingly. "You always start by telling me you love me before you ask for the moon."

"Fooled you this time then. I've had a letter from Mum. I'm going to see her this weekend."

"That's great, are you thinking of staying over?"

"I don't know, maybe, it depends on how things go. I'm nervous in case she starts on about Paul and you and the Squires and everyone who abandoned her, but I do so much want to make it up with her."

Tim drove Sandy to the station Saturday morning and watched her on to the train, her small back pack sitting high on her shoulders indicating that she had packed very few things. Tim drove slowly back to the cottage wondering what reception Sandy would receive from June. He had high hopes for reconciliation between them but also anticipated that it would be an emotional strain for them both. They had to thrash it out and hope to get it out of their systems or to pass over the whole episode and bury it. Tim hoped they would talk about it maturely and that Sandy would be able to make June understand why she had seemed to abandon her. Hopefully June would realise that if she wanted Sandy back she had to forgive her and in turn Sandy would have to forgive June. Tim didn't envy Sandy the weekend, he knew that were it him and June they wouldn't last a morning before recriminations started flying.

From the bedroom window June saw the small form with its spikey hair and scruffy jeans walking hesitantly down the front path and her stomach clenched. She felt her heart flutter and noticed she was trembling uncontrollably. Drawing a steadying breath, she rushed down the stairs to open the door just as Sandy reached it. For a long moment neither spoke or moved, then June spread her arms wide and Sandy fell into them.

"Darling little girl," June sobbed, "my darling girl, I've missed you so much."

"Oh, Mum I've missed you too." June took Sandy's back pack from her shoulders and remarked sadly to herself how it didn't appear to hold more than some nightclothes and a change of underwear. When Sandy used to hitch-hike home on an impromptu visit from college taking illicit time off from a subject she wasn't enjoying and stretching a weekend to four days, she would arrive with her pack half filled with LPs and enough books for a month. One early summer night she had arrived well past twelve o'clock and finding the house locked and bolted had climbed the drain-pipe to her window which was partially open and clambered in. The following morning when Tim had gone to work and June was busy vacuuming the landing, humming along to a tune in her head, under the impression that she was alone, Sandy had opened her bedroom door and tapped her mother on the shoulder

"Mornin' Mum." June had nearly passed out with shock.

"I'll put the kettle on and we can have a cup of tea in the garden, it's looking lovely." June found herself chattering on as if making up for all the lost words over the last months.

"Great Mum, then you can show me where my room is." June burst into tears.

"Will you stay a while darling? Please?"

"Yes Mum, we have a lot to talk about. Oh it's so good to see you!" Again they hugged closely both crying freely.

Sandy stayed with June for the week but her commitment to the gallery necessitated her early return to the farm to complete the work for the exhibition. During her stay they had caught up and made up but it was all on a superficial level. Neither addressed the biggest issue between them. Every time Sandy thought to approach the topic something made her hang back. She supposed she was afraid to destroy the fragile peace they had between them; it was too precious.

The week was up and it was time for Sandy to get on with her painting. As she was packing her few items of clothing into her bag June entered her room and perched on her bed. Her face fell with every item Sandy packed.

"Sandy darling I want to tell you something before you leave."

"Okay, tell on." Sandy answered stuffing the once carefully ironed shirt into the top of her bag.

"I folded that Sandy, now look at it, it'll be creased!"

"Sorry Mum, I shouldn't bother next time." She grinned mischievously at her mother. "What do you want to tell me?"

"Sit down Sandy I want to explain about my feelings regarding that man Paul. I think you'll understand when you hear what I have to say."

"Oh Christ Mum, you do choose your moments don't you? I've been here for a week and now when my train leaves in twenty minutes you want to talk about it!"

"But you should hear me out, I'm not to blame for my reaction to him, it was because of something that happened to me years ago." Sandy's hackles rose when instead of showing any remorse her mother had immediately started by excusing herself. Sandy pulled back; a black cloud had descended on her mood. Zipping up her bag she flung it over her shoulder and walking out of the room before she could show her anger she said over her shoulder

"Not now Mum, I've got the exhibition to do and we need longer than we've got."

"But you need to know Sandy, you'll understand then and we can put it all behind us."

"Next time Mum, we have to talk but not now, I don't want to start something I can't finish." And so Sandy left June's house and an uncomfortable atmosphere behind her as she strode to the station, already sensing the smell of grass and hay in her nostrils. Her feeling of pleasure at returning to the farm was overshadowed by guilt as she turned to wave at the lone figure at the gate. Her relief of leaving June and her neediness nagged at her conscience, striding purposefully towards the station she attempted unsuccessfully to erase the sight of her mother's sad face from her mind.

The next few weeks were taken up with painting and delivering and then the exhibition itself. Winding down after painting like a mad woman, Sandy spent long relaxing days wandering the farm, or helping out with the animals, collecting eggs and milking the goats. She remembered Paul's love for them, Daisy in particular, and the way he had fetched them blankets worrying about them being cold. And when she helped Alice bread making there was Paul's grinning floury face across the table as clear as if he were standing there. The memories made her smile but saddened her also. Paul had been such a kind man and so vulnerable, why had life been so cruel to him? Sandy kept bringing to mind the last thing that her mother had said to her; whatever was she on about? What could have happened to her in her past which had anything to do with her horrible attitude to Paul? And furthermore, she still didn't seem to have any remorse over it or indeed over Paul's death. She would ask her father what June had been referring to, he has known her nearly all her life as they met when they were at school; if anyone knew, he would. At least then when she returned to June's she would be prepared and maybe more inclined to understand and not to lose her cool. In the meantime she would throw herself into helping run the farm, it was the least she could do as she wasn't paying towards her keep.

After a long day driving alongside Oliver in the tractor as he ploughed one of their largest fields, bouncing uncomfortably all day as they trundled up and down the long furrows she turned up at her father's cottage, windswept, dirty, and even with bits of straw in her hair and clothing.

"I thought you were ploughing, how did you manage to get straw in your hair?" Tim brushed her down outside before letting her in.

"Yes, well you can blame Oli for that. He knocked into the bales when he was putting the tractor away – I was lucky I wasn't brained! Then we had to pile them up again which took ages. After a dozen or so bales they start to get damned heavy." Sandy threw herself into the armchair and stretched out her limbs. "Phew, I'm knackered. I need a break."

The nights were getting longer and a damp cold air permeated the ill-fitting wooden framed windows of the little cottage. Tim had lit a fire in the tiny sitting room, the kettle was whistling on the stove and whilst Tim made tea Sandy spiked crumpets on a fork and watched them brown. Melted butter dribbling down her chin and her face red from the fire made Sandy look five years old again, Tim wanted to sit her on his knee and read her a story, the one that always made her giggle about Pooh Bear and the Heffalump. The image broke as she expleted.

"Shit Dad, I forgot. I told Mum I'd come back for a while after the exhibition was over, can you give me a lift to the station tomorrow?"

"I shall have to think of getting you a little run around, it'll be cheaper than the train fares."

"Before I go Dad can you remember anything that happened to Mum in the past which would explain why she hated Paul so much?" Tim looked up questioningly,

"Such as what?"

"Oh, I don't know, she just said that something happened to her in the past and that I would understand when I heard about it." Tim sat wracking his brains for a memory but nothing came to mind.

"Frankly I have no idea what she's talking about."

"Oh well, never mind then Dad, I'll have to wait until I get there."

"When you do find out what it is let me know will you? I can't think what it could be, I thought I knew everything about her but there you go... It won't be the first time she's proved me wrong!"

Sandy took a larger pack with her to June's this time as she was intending to stay for a few weeks. They had got on well on her previous stay with no recriminations, it was as though the past year had not happened, with the exception of course that Tim was no longer living with them. It was quite soon into this latest visit that June hugged Sandy tightly and begged her to come back home permanently.

Sandy hugged her mother back and, to gain a little thinking space, said

"Yes Mum, but not quite yet. I need a bit more time to sort myself out." The truth was that much as she loved her mother Sandy was extremely happy on the farm, it was such a natural way of life. It was a hard full-time job, all day and every day there were animals to look after and fields to plant or mow or harvest and sometimes during lambing time the farmers were up all night. But Sandy felt at home there and at peace. The thought of living in a row of suburban houses after the wilds of the country-side didn't appeal any more. However, she couldn't say this to her mother. June looked disappointed saying

"What is there to sort out? Surely you're not thinking of staying with *them* for much longer? And you can't live in that little hovel with your father."

Hmm, you're sounding a bit more like normal, Sandy thought. She was a little upset to hear June refer to Oliver's family in the old derogatory tone, having hoped her attitude to them had changed over the months. However, at least she knew she was talking to the real June and not a 'how a mother should be' persona. "Let's get some fish and chips tonight then you won't have to cook and we can have some time to talk." They wandered to the chip shop arm in arm, stopping to throw some stale bread to the ducks on the pond and laughing together as the birds squabbled over the scraps only for them to be stolen by a swooping seagull.

"It's nice here by the park, your father did well when he found the house for me. You'd like it living here darling, there are nice walks for you and Lilly and the train station isn't far away."

"Yes, it is nice Mum." Sandy didn't want to discuss her moving back, not yet – if ever. Changing the subject she asked after Gillie and whether she saw much of her.

"Yes quite a bit, but we live our own lives and Gillie is always busy with something or other."

"You should join something, a bridge club or the WI" Sandy

could see June's loneliness through her pretence that she was happy in her new home and wished she could honestly say that she would live with her again. If only June could make some new friends or even find a male friend, the pressure on Sandy would be lessened. They hurried back home from the chippie before the meal cooled and whilst June removed mugs from the cupboard for tea Sandy laid the cutlery on the table.

As she plated up the fish and chips Sandy asked hesitantly

"Mum, why did you hate Paul so much?" There, she had said it and hopefully they could talk it through and put it to rest.

For a while June didn't answer, she busied herself putting the kettle on for tea and asking Sandy if she still took sugar.

"What do you mean 'do I still take sugar?!' I haven't taken sugar for years!"

"I'm sorry darling, I wasn't thinking."

"Mum, leave the kettle alone – we need to talk things out." June continued making the tea and only when she had placed mugs before them both did she give her full attention to Sandy.

"Yes darling, but where on earth do we start?" June was being evasive and impatiently Sandy blurted out

"Mum, I don't understand what came over you and why you were so horrid to Paul."

"I did try to explain when you were here last Sandy, but you refused to listen!" June replied tartly.

"Mum, I was just about to leave! You knew I had the exhibition to do and that time was short. I stayed longer than I intended as it was."

"Well why do we have to talk about it now? It's over and done with isn't it?"

"No Mum it isn't!" Sandy's frustration was growing and her voice becoming more and more strident. June put her hands over her ears

"You don't have to shriek at me, I'm not deaf and neither do I wish to be bullied by my own daughter!" Sandy took a deep breath and forced herself to be calm.

"I'm sorry Mum but you keep avoiding the issue, sit down and eat these damned fish and chips before they get cold." After a few mouthfuls June put down her knife and fork saying

"I didn't hate Paul."

"Well you behaved as if you did. I saw the way you looked at him when you came to the farm and we were sitting on the settee together. It was horrible. I ignored it at the time because I was so pleased to see you."

"I did not look at him in any particular way, I was confused as to who he was and what he was doing there that's all."

"Oh, come on Mum, you greeted Oliver with grand overtures of gratitude but you totally ignored Paul when he tried to speak to you." June was becoming flustered and pink, she tried to deny the accusation but knew it was true. After a while of procrastinating she said again

"I didn't hate him it's just that all I wanted was to have you back and everything was in such turmoil."

"You had me back Mother, why was it so difficult to be nice to Paul, he didn't stop you having me back?"

"But he did!" exclaimed her mother, "He took you away from me, all you cared about was him!" Sandy sat open mouthed at what June had said, how could she possibly have thought that?

"Do you think I am so shallow that I can only care for one person at once? All I wanted was to help him, it was my fault he was there at all."

"But you turned against me Sandy, you accused me of all sorts of things..."

"And so did you accuse me of all sorts of things – like leading him on, and you made lewd comments about him sexually!"

"That was in the heat of the argument I didn't mean it. I just wanted you back and he was preventing it what with that court case then him being ill..." June pushed her plate of food away from her wrinkling her nose at the smell of the now rapidly cooling fish.

"And dying!?" Sandy shouted at her mother, "No doubt that pleased you as he couldn't get in the way anymore then could he." Sandy leapt to her feet and June followed suit. They glared at each other.

"How dare you say that? I didn't wish for his death and anyway by that time I had lost you and your father, how can I forgive him for that?"

"Paul didn't do anything to make you and Dad split up Mum! That was between you two!" The conversation was getting out of hand; Sandy didn't want to row, just to understand. The way they were going they would be back where they had started: estranged. She took a breath and tried to calm herself.

"I'm sorry, that was unkind but just a bit true wasn't it Mum?" Seeing June looking near to tears she added in a softer tone "But you haven't lost me Mum, have you? Look I'm here and I love you." June slumped into her chair and tears began rolling down her face.

"Yes darling, you are." she sobbed. "Don't ever go completely away from me will you?"

"No Mum, I never stopped loving you and I never will." Sandy stroked her mother's hair as she cuddled her and waited until June's sobs subsided. Her mother gazed lovingly up at Sandy, wiped her eyes and with a huge exhalation she leaned back in her chair, emotionally exhausted. Sandy poured them both a glass of wine and led her mother into the sitting room where they remained quietly absorbing the love they had so nearly lost. But the issue was still unresolved. Sandy couldn't face opening the subject again, her mother was too fraught and so was she. Turning on the television and hoping for some light entertainment she curled up by her mother on the settee just like old times. When the programme which neither of them had really watched finished June turned to Sandy and hugged her tightly saying

"Oh Sandy, I love you so much it hurts." Sandy began to return the sentiment

"And I love you too Mum..." but was confused by what her mother said next.

"Thank God you're normal."

"Of course I'm normal, what makes you think I may not be?" June put her head in her hands and wept bitterly. Sandy, bemused, put her arm around her sobbing mother and shushing her as one would a child begged her to stop crying and tell her what she meant. Finally June dried her eyes and pulled Sandy close to her.

"I have wanted to tell you my darling but I didn't know how to start. I'll try to explain for all the good it will do for our family, but it might help you understand."

Haltingly, June recounted her experience of Sandy's birth.

"I was so happy, we both were, your father and I. I don't think I'd have tried again if you hadn't survived the full term. Everything had gone well, I had taken Mike Squires' advice and had plenty of bed rest and then the time came for you to be born." She leaned across the table and squeezed Sandy's hand in hers. "I'd gone into hospital just in case there were any complications but everything went smoothly with the birth and you were delivered alive."

"Obviously!" Sandy laughed. *What's this got to do with Paul?*

"In fact the birth was quite short and out you popped. I was a bit dopey from the gas and air but when I heard your first cry my heart nearly burst with happiness and I wanted to leap out of bed and hold you close." Seeing her mother's face glowing with the memory of her birth Sandy smiled lovingly at her.

"Go on Mum, was my hair as spiky then as it is today? Or was I bald and bright red and wrinkly?"

"I didn't see you immediately. I expected them to put you to my breast straight away as you were obviously hungry but the nurse took you and put you in a cot. You were bawling loud enough to wake the dead and my poor breasts were aching and pulsing." June paused and gripped Sandy's hand harder, tears welling in her eyes. "I heard Tim knock at the door and ask to be allowed in but the nurse said the doctor had to examine you first. I so wanted him with me I cried out 'what's the matter? Is she all right?' I was terrified that there was something wrong with you and that was why they wouldn't let me see you. Tim was peering through the glass in the door trying to see between the curtains, I waved at him to come in but he didn't see me and then the nurse left me alone to fetch the doctor."

"But surely that happens at every birth doesn't it Mum? They have to check everything before shoving the baby into your arms, and they have to weigh them and everything." Sandy knew very little about childbirth but surely that was how things went?

"Yes I know that but the nurse said there was something funny about your head and my imagination went wild – did you have water on the brain? Would you die before you ever walked? Oh Sandy just you wait until you give birth, it's a marvellous thing but terrifying as well."

"Mum, I don't know why you're torturing yourself about it now, I was okay wasn't I?"

"Yes darling you were. But it took the doctor ages to examine you and all the time I was fretting and hoping upon hope that you were normal. I'd read up on how to prevent miscarriages and also what symptoms to look for in a new-born to tell if it was... well..."

"Yes Mum, if it was what?" Sandy asked sharply.

"A mongol!" June spat the word as though it were phlegm. "But thankfully you were 'passed' healthy by the doctor and given to me to feed. I was frightened to look at you in case you were deformed or something. After all that time waiting for a baby, everyone knowing I was pregnant and all the good wishes from the family and neighbours – to then give birth to a mental defective – how could I have borne the shame if you had been one of them?"

Sandy was very quiet, then she felt a prickle of sheer anger. So this story *was* about Paul!

"What would you have done had I been 'one of those'?" She tried to keep her voice calm, "Would you have loved me or got rid of me?"

"Oh how can you say such things, of course I would have loved you," she paused to wipe her eyes, "but the shame! I don't know if I could have borne the shame."

"I just don't get you Mother. Where's your compassion? Where's your humanity?!" She shrugged her mother's hand off as June reached for her arm, "No! Don't! Just don't!" Sandy turned away from her mother's tearful face and without looking back she left the room closing the door quietly behind her.

Back in her room Sandy sat on her bed and stared blankly out of the window overlooking the garden, her thoughts in upheaval. Try though she did to see things from June's point of view and to imagine herself giving birth to a Down syndrome child, she couldn't shake off the feeling that had she been one herself her mother would have put her away somewhere. Somewhere where the neighbours wouldn't see her, somewhere where no one would ever know... because of the 'shame'.

The fish and chip supper slowly coagulated into an unpleasant smelling greasy mass as Sandy and June held their own lonely vigils; Sandy in her room and June, her head pounding due to her sobbing, remaining slumped on the settee.

Sandy's reaction was surely out of proportion, after all it hadn't happened, she had been born perfect... *why, oh, why did I tell her?* Looking back over the past year she should have realised that her daughter held a more altruistic view of life than she did.

It was not like that when June had been Sandy's age; people didn't understand or care about mental or physical impairments then. They were not talked about, they were sent to institutions or in some cases even quietly smothered at birth. June asked herself if she could have done that. Honestly, she probed her conscience; no she could never have murdered a child. But would she, *could* she love one who was defective? She found herself unable to answer her question.

As the night drew in and the last of the birdsong faded June heard Sandy's tread on the stairs. The door to the sitting room opened quietly and Sandy, pale and expressionless entered. June caught a fleeting look of disgust on her daughter's face when she saw June's tear stained face and puffy eyes which sent a shiver of despair through her causing her eyes to water once again. This provoked a small impatient sigh from Sandy. Quickly June brushed her hand across her face and rose from the settee with an attempt at a smile and opened her arms to her daughter. Sandy didn't know how to respond; how could her mother indulge in self-pity when she had no compassion for others? Who was this person? This person whom she had loved all her life, was it all a sham? She retained her distance from June's still outstretched arms and attempting to be calm and rational which she certainly didn't feel, she said

"Mother, I wish you hadn't told me about my birth. I do understand how you must have felt after waiting for so long for a baby, but I can't help imagining where I might be now if your fears had come true." June began to speak but Sandy, raising her voice over her mother's continued. "Who knows, I might have met Paul in an institution and been bullied like he was. But at least *he* would have loved me." She was breathing quickly and shallowly holding back her tears and anger. Taking a deep breath, she steadied herself and looking at her mother as though she were a perfect stranger she added "What I can't get is why you were such a bitch to Paul! Just because you had had some stupid unfounded scare twenty-five years ago you hated someone who had done absolutely nothing to deserve it other than being unfortunate enough to be born with Down syndrome. His own mother had loved him so much that she kicked his father out because his attitude was like yours. She would have gone through fire for him but she died. He was put through hell with no one to speak out for him. He was accused of killing the only person who could see the beauty in him and when he did find some people who cared enough to help him YOU tried to destroy that as well! Honestly Mother do you ever think of anyone but yourself?"

June stood rooted and aghast at Sandy's outburst. No sound came from her open mouth. She was ashen and looked about to faint.

"Don't go all frail and pitiful on me. I'm sorry Mum but that's how I feel. I'm going to bed now and so should you. I'm not going to rush off back to farm in the morning so don't panic. Tomorrow maybe we can talk about everything in a slightly less fraught way. Goodnight." She gave her mother a perfunctory kiss on the cheek and avoiding her attempt to hold her close she left the room.

June watched her beloved daughter leave the room with such pain in her heart she thought she would die. She almost wished she could. As if in a trance, she wandered into the kitchen, picked up the plates of food and scraped them into the bin, then running the tap until it was scalding, she washed and dried them. She then walked around the house turning off lights and checking doors as if behaving with normality would restore normality to her life. When all this was done June slowly climbed the stairs to go to bed. One look inside her room sent another dart to her chest; one set of pillows on the bed, no men's slippers under it, the only evidence of Tim having been part of her life was the beautiful oak bedside tables he had made. Returning to the kitchen she unlocked the back door and walked out into the night. As she wandered sadly across the park to a lone seat under a spreading chestnut tree she heard the last train pull away from the station and wished she were under its wheels. Instead of the close mother and daughter evening she had anticipated Sandy and she had pulled even further apart.

It seemed to June that the hole she had dug for herself was getting deeper and she could see no way of getting out. She had no answer to Sandy's accusations as they were all so horribly true. She hadn't really considered Paul as a human being with a mother who loved him, just as the obstacle in her way. Her only excuse was her overwhelming love for her daughter and that, it seemed, in Sandy's eyes wasn't enough.

CHAPTER 7

TIM AND MIKE SQUIRES had met for lunch as they did periodically and were sitting back in their chairs replete and enjoying a small brandy each. This was their time to be old friends together away from everything else in life and they treasured it. Mike took a sip of his drink and remarked on the never-failing standard of food at their favourite restaurant. It was conveniently situated near Mike's home so he and Sylvia could put Tim up for the night to save him a longish drive home with half a bottle of wine and a couple of brandies inside him.

"I saw June the other day, she looked quite perky."

"Yes, Sandy has been spending quite a bit of time with her and, fingers crossed, they seem to be making it up." Tim tensed when Mike added

"And what about you and June, do you think you'll ever get back together?"

"Don't ask me that Mike. I have absolutely no idea, but at the moment the answer is no." He looked up sadly but defiantly adding "I just don't know her anymore." When they were together Mike and Tim often sat for long moments not conversing, they were relaxed like only old friends can be in each other's company. Stretching his legs out in front of him Tim eased his belt around his slightly corpulent tummy and the two of them sighed with pleasure as they drank their brandies.

"Tim, what do you make of this Miss Hazlett or rather, Hilda, and the cemetery business?" Mike asked. Tim had not been in

England when they had all met the school teacher and had been updated both by Mike on his return and by George who skimmed over Oliver's drunken rudeness as quickly as possible.

"I don't know what to think, it certainly wouldn't be June. I know she was spiteful about Paul but I can't see her stalking an elderly woman at a grave?" Tim grinned foolishly at the thought.

"What're you smirking about?" Mike grinned along with him.

"Oh, just the image of June in a brown raincoat skulking behind tombstones and jumping out saying 'Boo!' A bit like a Spike Milligan or Monty Python sketch."

"Spike Milligan was 'The Phantom Raspberry Blower of Old London Town' if I remember correctly." Mike burst out laughing "Can you imagine June blowing raspberries at Hilda in a grave yard and then running off laughing maniacally?" Tim choked on his drink.

"Don't make me laugh when I'm drinking brandy!" he spluttered, "it really burns when you breathe it in!" They began to make so much noise that other diners began to cast them irritated glances only to be surprised that the rowdy blokes were middle-aged professional looking men and not a couple of teenage bikers. Wiping tears of laughter from his eyes Tim returned to the subject

"No. Maybe Oliver is right and she was imagining it. Who knows or, in fact, actually cares?"

"The prof took her seriously enough, he has a soft spot for dear little Hilda. I think it's because she is quite dominant and doesn't bow to his superior position as a barrister." Mike chuckled, "She's like a little bird but one with a sharp beak."

"What does he think then, the professor?" Tim was intrigued, he had dismissed it as nothing to worry about when he had been told but if Small was taking it seriously then maybe they all should think again.

"He doesn't think anything. But he's sure Hilda is telling the truth."

"Well he knows her better than we do, maybe there is something in it, but what and who and why?" Tim mused.

"Whoever it is must show their hand sooner or later, that is if there's more to it than some weird sort of coincidence." Mike added "Of course it could be completely unconnected with Paul, maybe her routine has been noticed by a local villain who intends to burgle her house."

"I don't know, that seems a bit far-fetched to me, after all she's been visiting the graves for ages, why hasn't she been burgled before now?"

"Hmm you're probably right. But I must say I do feel sorry for her, it was bad enough losing her friend but to now be intimidated and anxious about visiting their graves is shocking." Mike looked saddened. "What a maelstrom of events over these last couple of years! It's hard to believe it all started with Sandy's holiday plans."

"Yes, it's as though a whirlwind has whipped through all our lives." The tone of their lunch was becoming maudlin, unlike their usual cheerful bantering and Tim held up his hand.

"Enough of this miserable talk, did you hear the one about the three nuns?"

June was hardly aware of the drizzle that had begun to fall and mist her hair and lashes as she slowly made her way back home. She knew she hadn't the courage to throw herself under a train or to drown in a river and she put those foolish thoughts away. Thinking back to her reaction when she saw Sandy with Paul at the farm she remembered the way her stomach had clenched at the sight of him, bringing back all her fears. The consequence of this instinctive reaction was hatred. So blinkered had June been that all reason had deserted her. The result of which was the loss of Tim's love and although it had begun to seem that Sandy was prepared to forgive her, now even that had all fallen apart. All those years she had lived with the memory of her anxiety at Sandy's birth and it was only now, after blurting out the whole story she realised how unimportant and irrelevant it was to re-live a groundless fear over and over. She had let it get so deep inside her that it had coloured every aspect of her reaction to Paul. For the first time since Sandy's return from the moor with Paul June felt ashamed and deeply sorry. Thus, when Sandy emerged the following morning June handed her a mug of tea and asked if it would be alright to talk now. Sandy nodded without looking June in the eye. For a while June said nothing. She feared saying the wrong thing and losing Sandy for ever. This was her last chance it seemed.

"Sandy darling," she reached out to tilt her daughter's chin up forcing her to meet her gaze. "Darling, I am ashamed. Never have I felt so utterly bad about myself, last night after you had gone to bed I tried to put myself in your place and to imagine having a mother like me. It wasn't nice. You were right, I behaved dreadfully over Paul, all the time thinking it was all about you and me. But it wasn't, was it? I was so relieved when you were safe I just ignored anyone else's problems, I wasn't interested, I didn't care. All I wanted was to be back to normal. But where did that get me? Not only were things never going to be the same as no-one can live in the past but I destroyed all the happiness I once had." Sandy's eyes grew large with astonishment, she never thought to hear her mother speak like this. June had been so adamantly against Paul and what she had said last night had underlined her behaviour and even justified it. Had June really repented or was this a last-ditch attempt to throw a blanket over everything and hope never to mention it again? She studied June carefully and June met her look steadily, the sadness in her eyes was no longer that of self- pity but genuine remorse. "I know it's too late to undo all that's happened and probably too late to have you love me like you used to but maybe one day you will forgive me." June turned away sharply to hide her emotion, again this was something she never normally did as her tears were usually contrived to evoke pity, kindness, concern, anything which was centred around her feelings. Sandy felt her own emotions well up and hastily supressed them, sure though she was that her mother was being wholly truthful there was a lot of shit to be cleared away before anything could be normal between them again. She rose and gently rested her arm around June's shoulders feeling her mother's barely controlled quivering in her attempt not to cry.

"Mum, you don't know what that means to me. I never thought you'd see that you were wrong. I do love you Mum, even if you hadn't just said all that I would still have loved you but Paul's existence would always have been between us ready to come boiling up at any time." They remained quietly holding each other fighting back the tears, the only sound being the ticking of the mantle clock and as it struck the hour Sandy pulled away gently and as June looked up at her she leaned down and kissed her mother's forehead, noticing sadly how much more grey her hair had become. "Let's go out for a long walk and just – be."

Sandy returned to the farm after prolonging her stay with June for a further week; the dross of the last eighteen months or so had to be cleared away before either could effect a closure. June's parting words were something Sandy never expected – a request to the Tregowans for June to visit in order to try to right some of the wrongs she had done.

As usual, Oliver was waiting at the station for her and was relieved to see her smiling as she threw her backpack at him to stow in the boot.

"Good visit then?"

"Yep. You'll never credit what has happened! I'll tell you all about it when we get home." Oliver relished the reference to the farm as 'home' and hugged her happily and ruffled her spikey hair.

"Brill!"

"What about you Oli, how's the romance going? Engaged yet?" Oliver grimaced

"I have absolutely no idea where if anywhere Susie and I are going. To be honest I think it's over." Sandy was a little ashamed of the fleeting feeling she had of relief. Somehow Susie just didn't fit any more, she sounded just a bit too girly for a farmer's wife. But at the same time she felt for Oliver, he too had lost something precious to him due to their chance meeting on the moor – so much had changed in all their lives. Paul had been the catalyst which turned their paths left instead of right and had thrown their emotions in turmoil. Would they have wanted it any different? Who could tell? Fate had grabbed them all and played out its game then abandoned them to the new lives they now had.

As they reached the top of the long slow incline, the farm, surrounded by acres of pasture with hazel woven hedgerows, came into view. The foul weather had died off making it possible for the cows to be out to pasture for a few more weeks before winter drove them back inside. George was a small figure in the distance distributing extra feed to them in the meadow as the grass had still not replenished itself enough and the sound of their lowing floated across the fields accompanied by the unmistakable aroma of cow pat.

"I never thought I'd love the smell of cow shit!" Sandy laughed, "But, and Josie would die if she heard this, it's sort of homely and comforting."

During dinner that evening when Tim had joined them all Sandy told at great length what had happened with June. Alice sat with her mouth open until Oliver threw a pea at her.

"Shut your mouth Mum you look gormless!"

June having carried her anxiety of that episode after Sandy's birth deep inside her, never once alluding to it during the ensuing twenty-five years wrenched at Tim's heart. Had he known about it he probably would have behaved differently, maybe he could have helped her cope with it and maybe they would still be together. What an absolute mess he had made of everything. He sat unspeaking slowly swirling the last of his wine in the glass and a deep empty hollow feeling in his chest.

CHAPTER 8

MISS HAZLETT WAS BOTH ALARMED and furious to find that she was being watched yet again on her next visit to the graves. From the moment she got off the bus, she was aware of someone walking a small distance behind her. This, in itself, did not alarm her but when she heard the gravel crunching on the path behind her as she approached the graves, she turned to see who it was. It was a middle-aged woman and judging by the hooded coat she was wearing it was apparent that it was the person from the bus stop. As she came nearer Miss Hazlett felt sure she recognised her but couldn't place who she was. She turned away and busied herself clearing away the dead flowers hoping the woman would walk on past to attend to another grave.

"Not many people would bother to put flowers on *his* grave, after what he did." Miss Hazlett started and turned to face the woman.

"Why are you following me?" Miss Hazlett asked sharply, "And what business is it of yours if I choose to remember a dear boy?"

"I didn't hear anything on the news about any recovery of those bodies from the bog. I'm sure they didn't bother, they were criminals after all and who cares if they stay there to rot!" She added with an insincere smile "What a waste of money to put a stone on an empty plot." Miss Hazlet was sure now that she knew who this person was.

"Why, I know you don't I? You're Sally's neighbour." Miss Hazlett shook her stick at the woman angrily, "You caused his death with your accusations!"

"I saw him do it and I'm not letting it rest. I've seen your solicitor friend coming and going to your house plotting and scheming and covering up the facts. The truth will out I can assure you!"

Miss Hazlett, visibly shaken and speechless turned away and stumbling on the uneven path she hurriedly made her way to the bus stop and was relieved to see the bus making its way up the hill. She clambered as swiftly as she could up the step and sank breathlessly into her seat. As the bus began to pull away she caught sight of the neighbour hurrying to wave the driver down but she was too late and was left standing on the curb. Miss Hazlett breathed a sigh of relief and allowed herself a small smile of satisfaction.

Sandy relaxed into life again and spent longer with June each time she visited. It was during her stay in the latter part of September, the third anniversary of her aborted holiday that as she scanned the local paper she came upon a report of a body being found on the moor. The cadets from the barracks at Eastleigh in North Devon out on manoeuvres had discovered a body, perfectly preserved, which had risen to the surface of a bog. According to the experts, the drought followed by the prolonged rain had been responsible. The extreme dry weather having shrunk the peaty morass had allowed the sunken body to become loosened from its hold. The ensuing rain had floated it to the shallower part of the bog where it had remained until found.

At the farm, George crashed into the kitchen clutching the newspaper

"Alice look!" He thrust the open paper into her floury hands. "Surely it can't be the same place, can it? There are hundreds of bogs on the moor!" George rang Tim and Tim rang Mike.

"Jesus Christ!" Tim swore, "Is this going to haunt us for ever?" Mike Squires, now well into his retirement choked on his tea at the breakfast table and Jeremy Small cursed volubly into his nightcap of a large scotch whilst watching the ten o'clock news.

"Turn on the news Mum." Sandy, visibly shaking sat close to the television as the report came through. The photograph of the preserved body flashed on to the screen during the interview with the officer in command of the cadets. It was browned and mummified but identifiable as Jimmy.

"Oh, my God!" Sandy exclaimed, "It's him Mum. It's the same bog – I can't believe it!"

"Shush a moment, let's listen to what they're saying." June increased the volume. The police had done their research and Sandy's recognition of Jimmy was confirmed by the pathologist.

That evening Sandy rang Oliver.

"Oh Oliver I can't bear it – they're going to realise that Paul isn't there aren't they?"

"I don't see why they should. After all they have no real idea how deep it is and he could have sunk further. All it proves is that they did drown there, I doubt they'll bother to dredge the bog."

"Yes but don't you see? Paul was proved innocent and they may want to find him to give him a proper burial now that Jimmy's been exhumed; it would be sort of humane and Christian."

"I must admit I hadn't thought of that," Oliver fell silent for so long that Sandy thought she had lost the connection.

"Oliver!"

"Yes I'm here. I'm thinking. You may be right but frankly I doubt they will waste public money on it. He has no kin to push for exhumation so more than likely they will let it go. Don't worry, even if they do find he's not there, there's no reason to connect us to his disappearance."

"What!? How can you think that? The police saw him as Peter at the farm and we discovered the coats – there's loads to link us, it would hardly be difficult for even a basic plod to work out."

"We didn't discover the coats – remember? But you're right

there are too many connections. All we can do is hope. Come down to the farm this weekend and we'll talk then. It might have all died down by then anyway."

The secretary tapped and entered Professor Small's office.

"There's a lady to see you Jeremy, she's very agitated shall I show her in?" Small knew at once that it was Miss Hazlett and rose from his chair to usher her in himself.

"Thank you Mary, Hilda would you like tea or coffee?"

"Oh Jeremy, I'd love a cup of tea, preferably with a shot in it!" She attempted a joke but her trembling hands gave a lie to it. Hilda, her voice shaky with anxiety, recounted her confrontation with the woman at the cemetery.

"Tell me exactly what she said – this neighbour. I've met her don't forget and I'm afraid I disliked her on the spot. It wasn't just her adamant condemnation which I found hard to contend with but the weird vicarious pleasure she seemed to get from it all."

"Quite, but I'm really concerned that she knows more than we think she does and she's like a dog with a bone; she won't let it rest." Hilda recited the conversation in detail to Jeremy who noted it on the pad in front of him. The tone of the exchange added to the feeling that she had been watched each time she had visited the graves sent shivers up Hilda's spine. The professor's face flamed up with anger.

"Bloody woman! What's the matter with her? Hasn't she got a life of her own?" He scribbled a doodle on the pad, the pencil nearly shredding the page. "Has she got any family, a husband or children do you know?"

"I believe she is on her own but I've no idea if she has any children. Why do you ask?"

"I don't know really, just trying to get a picture of her and trying to understand her motivation I suppose." He replied gloomily.

"Just supposing they do decide to dredge the mire and don't find another body..." Hilda faltered

"My thought exactly. That being the case we are in for a very stressful time. In fact, I'm very surprised that the authorities haven't come knocking before."

Miss Hazlett looked puzzled

"Why's that Jeremy?"

"I was very concerned at the blatancy of his burial and named stone but Sandy and Oliver were insistent that he be laid alongside his mother and buried under his proper name. They just relied on it all being old news and the fact that one more grave in that huge cemetery wouldn't draw the crowds or if it did attract any attention it would be assumed it was just another person of the same name."

"I see, of course anyone who knew them would start to wonder why there was a grave for him if he died on the moor, just like that neighbour did. She, that woman, implied that she thought it was an empty grave. But there was something about the way she said it that makes me suspicious; as if she was goading me into saying something about it. But I was too shocked and angry to reply or I might have said something I regretted."

"But this discovery is going to stir up interest again and Paul's name will be used in the reports – someone will say to themselves 'hey that's the same name as the bloke buried next to our gran' or some such remark." Jeremy began to look extremely worried. "Damn and blast it all!" he exclaimed. "Just let's pray that they leave well alone or that it rains like buggery and they deem it too dangerous to mess about in the bog." He scribbled another doodle furiously on his pad then his face lit up.

"Hang on a minute..."

"Yes?" Hilda leaned over the desk to look at what he had written, but it was purely and simply a doodle. "What?" she prompted him.

"Just a small hope to hang onto, even if they do exhume the mire and find no other body, it doesn't mean that Paul didn't die on the moor, he could have died anywhere and with foxes and buzzards and the like there wouldn't be much left of him by now."

"Oh what a terrible thought!" Hilda exclaimed.

The news was avidly watched by all and as time progressed little more was reported about Jimmy's reclaimed body other than after an autopsy which confirmed the cause of death it had been buried. His only apparent living relative was his octogenarian mother who, in the advanced stages of Alzheimer's had forgotten that she had a son. It was a very bleak and lonely funeral attended by one police officer, the pall bearers and the vicar. At the service the vicar in an attempt at smoothing Jimmy's passage, be it up or down, claimed that it had been Jimmy's experiences in the war which had disturbed his mind and that he had been haunted by demons, thus explaining his irrational and murderous behaviour which had condemned him to life in the institution. However, the police officer in attendance knew better; having been a contemporary of Jimmy before the war but out of respect for the vicar's benevolence he held his peace.

Winter was upon them and true to George's predictions the livestock had been housed sooner than usual in the byres. November saw the first snow flurry followed by freezing winds and very little sunshine. Luckily, they had managed to harvest the bulk of the wheat and hay in the lull between the rain storms; a strong wind helping dry the crops well enough to be cut, but a third of the harvest remained to rot and had to be ploughed back in. Money would be pretty tight and George was loathe to sell his breeding stock, unless absolutely necessary. From a domestic food point of view, they would be fine as the chicken laid eggs and the goats and cows produced milk for butter and cheese. Alice tended the vegetable garden and boasted that as always she had enough coming on to feed an army. Hopefully they would get a good price for the smaller harvest as owing to the inclement weather many farmers had suffered bigger losses and this would increase the going rate for the wheat. The hay was needed for their own stock.

"If we can pay our way over the winter we'll be alright as long as we don't have any major vet's bills." George finished totting up the accounts and poured himself a large scotch, added another log to the fire, settled into the armchair and lit his pipe.

"It's a shame that your Digger Honeydew doesn't taste as nice as it smells Dad." Oliver remarked as he walked in. He had attempted smoking George's pipe when he was in his teens and on his own in the farmhouse. Alice had come in from the garden to find Oliver being violently sick on the floor of the sitting room.

"Serves you darned right young man. Hopefully that'll put you off for good, filthy habit – I wish your father would pack it in."

CHAPTER 9

SANDY HAD A DILEMMA – where to spend Christmas? How she wished that her family was whole again and that they could enjoy it all together. Tim thought she should spend it with June and fought with the feeling that he would like to be there also. Oliver would have liked her to stay with them but understood Sandy's choice to be with her mother as the thought of leaving June on her own was too cruel. Alice astounded them all by suggesting that June came to them for the holiday 'to try and heal the wounds'.

"No, no, no!" Although grateful for Alice's thoughts Sandy was terrified of the antipathy coming to the surface again and putting them back to square one. "I'll bring her for a visit just for the day after the new year then if things get a bit hot I can whisk her off again." Tim breathed a sigh of relief, no it was not a good idea to throw June in their midst, she might feel like a fox tossed to the hounds. Although Tim knew that the Tregowans would make her welcome and show her kindness she would be outnumbered and consequently could be defensive. He determined that he would meet her alone prior to any visit to the farm; they needed to talk.

"No Sandy my love, let's take it one step at a time. I don't think it's a good idea for June to come here at all during festive seasons. It would underline too much what she has lost."

"But I do think it's time all of us got together and became friends. Sorry Tim but there's no reason why you can't get along with June; no one's going to force you to get back together if you don't want to. No doubt she feels the same but let's lay the ghost don't you think?" George had always been more kindly disposed to June than the others. He seemed to possess the ability to see beyond the immediate impression and had shown pity and understanding where the others had not, with perhaps the exception of Mike Squires, although in Mike's case this had been in retrospect.

"That's not what I mean George, I agree with you totally but it is about June and me and nobody else. I'm sorry if that sounded rude and ungrateful," Tim searched for the words to explain what he was feeling, "you see, I loved my wife deeply before all this happened and our breakup was torture but I felt I didn't know her anymore; I hated who she had become. I sort of need to know her again." George nodded and reached for Tim's hand which he shook firmly.

"You're a fine and decent bloke Tim; you must lead the way in this. I promise we won't interfere but we'll be here for all of you if you need us."

That evening Oliver invited Sandy to go to the King's Arms for a beer as it had been a long time since they last went anywhere away from the farm alone.

"Do you fancy a winter break back at the cottage in St Ives?" He handed her a pint in a jug. "I know it may bring back memories but that's not always such a bad thing."

"I'd love a break Oli but maybe not there. I want to be happy not sad although it was nice there with the views and the open fire."

"I think it'll be good for both of us. We can remember how we laughed at Paul when he was bundled up against the cold and we can cry too if you like." He opened a packet of crisps with a bang which made Sandy start then burst out laughing as they scattered all over the table.

"Idiot school boy!"

"Say yes Sandy." He gave her a comically pleading look reminding her of Lilly when she wanted the leftovers from dinner.

"What's this then, a proposal?" Bert interrupted their laughter with a rather dirty chortle as he brought the menu to the table.

"Go on Sandy say yes; he's a presentable lad!"

"Bert, stop eavesdropping. I might have been asking Sandy to rob a bank for all you know. And yes, it is a proposal but not of marriage."

"Going to live in sin are you!?" Bert guffawed and ambled back behind the bar. When Sandy grinned up at Oliver expecting him to make another humorous comment she was surprised to see his face suffused with embarrassment.

"Oli, he was only having us on. What's wrong?" Oliver sidestepped the question and excused himself to go to the gents. On his return his colour had returned to normal and grabbing the menu he asked Sandy what she'd like to eat. When they left the pub at closing time they were very slightly tipsy and sauntered along the lane in a not very straight path. The waxing moon in the clear frosty air and the millions of bright sparks of dying planets gave a festive atmosphere to the night like a child's painting of the nativity with glitter scattered on to glued black paper and a stable drawn underneath the brightest star. A silent barn owl drifted over the hedgerow and a squeak owl called in the distance. Hoar frost was already beginning to coat the twigs which shimmered in the night light as the temperature dropped and they pulled their scarves tighter around their necks.

On reaching the farm Sandy caught Oliver's arm and led him to the little pond in the garden where often they had sat to talk out of earshot. The night was completely quiet and still, everywhere you looked frost glimmered in the moonlight, wafer ice had begun to form at the shallow edges of the pond and the grass of the lawn crackled beneath their tread. Their condensing breath merging as one, they made their way to the seat on the far side of the pond.

Pulling him down to sit beside her she asked him again in her typical forthright manner

"What's up Oli? Why did you react like that with Bert?" Oliver shuffled and made to get up

"It was nothing – indigestion I expect."

"Come on you, I know it wasn't. Was it because you thought I wanted you to ask me to marry you? Don't worry" she added quickly "I wasn't expecting that and anyway I'd have said 'on your bike' in the nicest possible way of course." Oliver grunted a laugh

"Thanks, lucky I didn't ask then! But don't ask me what was wrong, it's not important honestly."

"Then why can't you tell me?" Sandy persisted.

"My God they say people resemble their dogs; you're as bad as Lilly when she wants food. Look I don't want to tell you – you'll laugh at me or think I'm odd or something. Please let it go Sandy." Sandy huffed and got up from the seat.

"Alright if you feel like that but I thought we were special friends, after all, you know all about me, the good and the bad and I thought if there was anyone you could talk to it was me!"

"Sandy sit down. Okay I will tell you and then you'll be happy. But please don't repeat it to anyone." Oliver took a while to get started but finally he said "I'm glad it's dark as you won't see my embarrassment and I won't see your disbelief and amusement. Well here goes. You know that Susie and I were very seriously involved before I met you, we had talked of marriage. She was my first really serious girlfriend and I respected the fact that she didn't want to have sex with me before we were married and though it was difficult I kept to my promise. Some blokes would have gone off and got it on the side but I didn't because I cared too much about her. Need I say more? You must have caught on by now – I'm still a virgin. Twenty nine years old and never been fucked!" For the first time since Oliver had met Sandy she had nothing to say. No doubt she was sitting with her mouth open in surprise or disbelief, Oliver didn't want to look to find out. "Now you know and you must think I'm a wimp or abnormal or something."

"Oh Oli, I don't think that at all. I can't think why you're embarrassed about being a decent bloke. She's a bloody fool to let you go." Sandy flung her arms around his neck and hugged him to her. Sandy's art college life had been quite free and easy and before she had left she had slept with a number of her fellow students. Most of her friends had been boys and sometimes the moment was there and they had sex in a sort of platonic way. Looking back she felt a little ashamed at the memory, especially whilst she sat beside this wholesome respectful guy. "Maybe she'll come back but you need to meet other girls. You're stuck out here on the farm and you never go to dances or parties, do you?"

"I don't dance and I don't really like parties except with close friends." Oliver lifted her chin so that she looked up at him, "You're the closest friend I've ever had." Very gently he caressed her forehead and sighing softly his lips found hers.

Next morning when Sandy awoke the sun was already up – she had overslept by hours. Jack Frost's swirls of ice on the small cottage style window panes were slowly melting away and tiny driblets of water ran slowly down to the cill. *Bob's going to win – no John is...* Sandy replayed her childhood memories of guessing which raindrop would reach the bottom first. One memorable holiday the family had rented a caravan at Dawlish when she had been about four years old. It had rained steadily for five days out of the seven. Trapped inside those four walls her mother had tried every game possible to entertain her increasingly fractious daughter. Strangely enough this had captured her attention more than Ludo or Tiddlywinks and when Tim had returned from the shop looking like an oilskin clad fisherman he was thrilled to be greeted by infectious laughter. Sandy's reveries were halted by a tap on her door and Alice entered with breakfast on a tray.

"Hey I'm not sick Alice, just lazy!" Sandy protested.

"We did wonder if you had caught a chill sitting out by that pond in the frost last night!"

"Oh. Well it was a bit chilly yes…" Sandy felt her face flush as she remembered Oliver's kiss and realised that it must have been witnessed by George and Alice.

"George was just about to pop Lilly out for a last pee," Alice explained with a big smile "but he took her out the front door instead, not wanting to intrude."

"Oh God, how embarrassing, it was nothing, we were just talking and…" Sandy wasn't at all sure what she felt and was more than a bit annoyed that something private was now common knowledge. If they hadn't been seen they could have both pretended it hadn't happened and carried on as before. Now it was bloody complicated. When Alice had left the room she quickly dressed and calling Lilly she went out to hunt down Oliver. They needed to talk away from prying eyes, well-meaning though they may be, they were not wanted. Oliver was ploughing the remainder of the wheat fields in readiness for the winder sowing. Sandy decided to take Lilly for a long walk and to time her return with his lunch break. It was good to be alone to think and with her parka hood up against the cold wind and strong walking boots on her feet she strode off into the woodland on the edge of the farm. The naked skeletal deciduous trees traced linear patterns against the sky like long bony arms and fingers. She thought how apt it was that a branch was called a limb and the main body was a trunk and that the trees had the equivalent of a human circulatory system; they even bleed. Browned leaves lay thickly in the dells and Lilly rushed through them, her short legs sinking in the crackling fall, squirrels darted up the trees as though being pulled up on elastic thread. Out of the corner of her eye Sandy caught the rapid movement of a tree creeper, so camouflaged that it was barely discernible from the trunk. A pheasant squawked in alarm as Lilly flushed it from the undergrowth. Further on she came to the tall firs under which footfalls were silent and the ground was soft with its covering of needles and the essence of pine was strong in the air. It was here that she rested, her back against a tree, closed her eyes and let the peace flow over her. Lilly woke her with a sniff in her ear and a huge lick in her eye. Gosh, the time had flown by and she had probably missed Oliver's lunch break. He'd be back at the farm now and they were all probably wondering where she was.

This was in fact the case as when they had all started lunch there was and still no sign of Sandy or Lilly Alice began to wonder if her tactless comments had upset her and confessed to Oliver what she had said. He was both embarrassed and annoyed; he too presumed that his kiss had been a private affair and that it meant nothing, well almost nothing. As he left his chair, scraping it back noisily across the flags he shot his mother a withering look and leaving his food untouched grabbed the dog whistle off the hook and left without saying a word. Scanning the fields, he saw no sign of Sandy or the dog so he gave a long whistle and waited. No black and white form came running from behind a hedge so Oliver's natural assumption was that she was quite a distance away. The farm covered forty acres and in the main was either cultivated or pasture land with the exception of the woodland which was maintained merely as a place for game. He strode off in that direction. His main concern wasn't that anything had happened to her but more that he wanted to clear things with her before his Mum booked the damned church! Nearing the trees, he whistled once again and this time Lilly charged out from the eaves of the wood and galloped up to him tail wagging. She was followed by Sandy brushing the pine needles from her hair and coat.

"Hi there." Oliver waved and Sandy waved back and jogged up to where he was waiting. "Are you okay?" Oliver detached Lilly from jumping up his legs as if she hadn't seen him for a year.

"Yea I'm fine just lost track of the time. I came out to find you but you were ploughing so I went for a walk." She found it difficult to look Oliver in the eye; she was embarrassed by what had happened last night and no doubt so was he. They fell into step and began walking back home, both wanting to say something but neither sure how to begin; not knowing what the other's reaction or thoughts might be. Finally, Oliver began

"Sandy, I'm sorry about last night, I really am. I just felt sad and somehow it seemed right at the time."

"Yes, it did, didn't it?" Sandy replied, swiftly following with "but that was last night and it was all about Susie really wasn't it. Let's forget it eh?"

"Yes let's." In spite of 'clearing the air' they both remained pensive as though there was more to say but not sure what it was. Lilly ran on ahead of them to chase one of the farm cats into the barn and they followed her out of the cold wind that had blown up with a promise of snow. Calling Lilly away from the cornered hissing cat they sat on a hay bale and through the open door saw the first powdery flakes begin to fall.

"Damn, I've still got to finish the ploughing and it'll be dark in an hour or so. I hate doing it by headlights."

"I doubt this will come to much," Sandy reassured him, "it said on the forecast that it would turn to rain. You can finish it tomorrow."

"Thanks." Oliver laughed, "It's your fault I haven't finished today."

"Oh no, it's yours. If you hadn't sexually assaulted me last night in full view of your parents, we wouldn't be sitting here now when you should be working!"

"I'd hardly call that a sexual assault. More like a friendly peck!"

They both relaxed having broken the tension and laughed about it. "We'd better get back before Mum rings the vicar." Oliver stood up and looked down on Sandy's upturned face, her nose pink from the cold and the remains of the forest still in her hair. She looked a mess. Leaning down to her he lifted her bodily off the bale and whilst she was still captive in his arms he kissed her again. Sandy reluctantly found herself responding until she gave in to her feelings and returned the kiss.

"Well that wasn't about Susie!" Sandy said rather breathlessly. "Oli are you serious or just mucking about?"

"Deadly serious Sandy. I realise now that mates don't have to be just mates. Do you mind? Do you feel anything for me?" He hesitated before asking nervously "It's not that you pity me is it, you know, after what I told you last night? Are you humouring me just to make me feel better?"

"I may care about you as a mate but I kissed you back as a girl. Honestly Oli I never imagined us actually being a couple even though we've been living in the same house, done so much together and been through so much together. I thought I loved you like a brother, I never dreamed I'd care for you in any other way. And as far as making you feel better – well it's made me feel better too so we're quits!"

Alice spied them as they approached the house walking close together and laughing. Breathing a sigh of relief that she hadn't done any damage she hurriedly returned to the kitchen to continue her bread making.

Life continued as normal and Sandy and Oliver, although obviously close did no more than hold hands occasionally or give each other a kiss goodnight. Neither was ready to commit to a sexual relationship; their friendship still felt too much like siblings. Maybe it would come and maybe not; they had plenty of time.

CHAPTER 10

SANDY BORROWED TIM'S CAR and drove to June's where she would spend Christmas week and return to the farm for New Year. Although both felt happy at being together for the 'festive season' the absence of Tim cast a shadow over the week and they pulled their crackers half-heartedly, paper hats placed on the table rather than their heads. In truth, they were both glad when things returned to normal without the artificially imposed necessity of Christmas cheer.

After Boxing Day, the shops re-opened and the milkman delivered again as did the baker and the postman; his deliveries were mostly belated Christmas cards which the senders had posted at the last minute in response to having received one from someone they had forgotten. However, the card Sandy picked up from the mat felt different from the usual cheap flimsy cards people sent. It was in a strong white envelope with a franked postmark from London. Taking it into the sitting room she placed it on the table.

"What's this darling, why haven't you opened it?" June picked it up and inspected it. "It looks important, have you applied for a job in London?" She added with an attempt to hide her disappointment should Sandy move so far away. But now that she knew Sandy still loved her she had vowed to herself that she would no longer be a clingy mother no matter what.

"No Mum, I haven't applied for any jobs."

"Well aren't you going to open it?"

"Okay, here goes." Sandy tore the flap open and withdrew the card. It wasn't a Christmas card but a Mauritian hand-made card.

"Oh, it must be from Josie." She read the message inside and swore. 'Dear Sandy, I haven't forgotten you. I am back in England and want to see you. Love David.' Beneath the message was an address and 'phone number. Well he can think again she thought and stopped herself short as she was about to throw it on the fire. The only thing to do was to confront him and put a stop to his persistence. "It's just a card from someone I met in Mauritius, nothing special." She screwed it up and shoved it into her jeans' back pocket. *Shit and shit again, what's the matter with that man?* Sandy fumed inwardly at the audacity of David to track down her mother's address. How the devil did he get it? Wheels within wheels she supposed. He must have access to all sorts of private information, but, she thought again, he probably just looked her up on the electoral role, it wouldn't be difficult as Sandy had been automatically placed at her mother's address when she moved. Putting him out of her mind she opened her portfolio and set about drawing up her latest picture from the sketches she had made. However, she found it difficult to concentrate with David's card burning in her pocket. Putting away her materials she wandered into the kitchen to make a cup of tea for herself and her mother. Helping herself to a large slice of Christmas cake she turned on the radio and sat at the table where her mother joined her.

"How long are you staying darling?"

"I promised Oli I'd be back for New Year, are you going to Gillie's?" She nearly asked June to come back with her to the farm for the celebrations but remembering Tim's advice she bit her tongue just in time.

"Yes love, don't worry about me, I'm fine. You have a good time with Oliver, he's a nice lad."

The 'phone rang in the hall and June answered it.

"Talk of the devil!" Sandy heard her say. This was followed by some laughter as Oliver replied and June handed the receiver to Sandy. June withdrew to the sitting room with her tea and closed the door behind her. No more interfering or eavesdropping, she was content and secure again with their relationship now on a completely different level. Sandy chatted for some long time to Oliver and when she came in to join her mother she was flushed and smiling.

"Oli said they're missing me. He said it was too quiet without me throwing my paints across the room when things didn't go right!"

"He's certainly got to know you well!" June laughed. "So, when do you want to leave?"

"Not yet Mum, I've got a lot to think about before I go back." She relayed her conversation with Oliver in her mind, he was missing her and begged her to hurry back.

"I need to talk to you Sandy." he'd said. "When you're not here it's as though nothing happened between us and I keep thinking I imagined it all."

"I know Oli, I feel a bit the same but I can't leave Mum just yet. You do understand, don't you?"

"Yes of course I do but that doesn't stop me wanting you here. I need reassurance that you still feel the same."

"I do, honestly. I'll be back for the New Year and we can talk about where we're going then. Okay?" She glowed as she recalled his endearments just before they said goodbye. She was pretty certain how she felt but after years of regarding him like a brother this new relationship still felt just a little odd. June was looking at her expectantly and Sandy felt suffocated. She needed some time alone to think hard about Oliver and her.

"Lilly needs a walk, Mum, do you want anything from the shops?"

"No thanks darling, you will be back for lunch at one?" Sandy called Lilly, clipped on her lead and headed for the park. One or two dog walkers were out and some young families trying out new bicycles and roller skates. Avoiding the majority of them, Sandy made her way to the far side which was away from the tarmac path and let Lilly off. It was pleasant and Sandy was thankful that she was alone but it was nothing like as therapeutic as the open fields and the aromatic woods around Oliver's home which overlooked the stunning scenery of the moorland and its many moods. She had promised her mother to stay for the week but she yearned to be at the Tregowans' farm. Should she take her mother back with her in spite of what Tim had said? On second thoughts, no, Gillie and Stewart had invited June for New Year as they hadn't intruded over Christmas, Sandy would give Gillie a surreptitious call later tonight and confirm it. Also, Sandy suspected that June's intuition was telling her that Oliver and she were more than just friends, judging by her expression when Sandy had finished her 'phone conversation. Should she confide in her mother or wait until she and Oliver were certain? Yes, she decided, that would be best just in case it had been a huge mistake and everyone would feel awkward if nothing came of it. Sandy shivered as the weak winter sun disappeared behind some yellowish clouds which looked very much as if they held snow and calling Lilly to heel she headed back for lunch.

"Brr it's chilly out there, Mum, have you kept the fire going?" She called as she slammed the front door shut.

The Christmas period was drawing to a close, and New Year was on the horizon. Just one more day with her mother and then back to Oliver. Sandy began to feel ridiculously nervous. The day was bright and frosty when Sandy took Lilly for her morning run across the park and half-heartedly attempted to stop her chasing the ducks or belly-flopping into the pond after them. Although it upset the parents whose children were feeding the fowl Sandy couldn't help laughing at her hooligan of a dog sending the moorhens clucking furiously to the other side of the pond.

"I say miss, call your dog back!" one man shouted at her when his children ran crying to him that the horrid dog had chased away the pretty ducks. Sandy relented and put Lilly on the lead.

"Come on Lil' home time and... nosh!"

As Sandy closed the door behind her, Lilly began barking and June, looking a bit flustered, met them in the hall.

"Hush Lil'." Sandy began to shrug off her coat. "Whose coat is that Mum?" Sandy noticed a lush sheepskin jacket hanging on the peg. Has Stewart come already?" June shook her head.

"No, it's not Stewart, I don't know who he is except that he said he knew you." Sandy looked puzzled, whoever could it be? "He said his name is David." Sandy stopped dead in the act of taking her coat off

"What?! What's that creep doing here?"

"He said you met him in Mauritius." June simpered a little, "He's very good looking!"

"Why the hell did you let him in Mum?" Sandy was furious. How dare he come uninvited and wheedle his way in to her home? June jumped in alarm at Sandy's reaction.

"I'm sorry darling but he said he was a friend. What was I to do?"

"Oh, never mind!" Sandy snapped at her mother, "You weren't to know." Seeing her mother was upset by her manner she added "I'm sorry, I just don't like him and I certainly am not pleased to see him!"

"Hush darling." June gestured to the partially open door. But Sandy just chucked her coat on the floor and crashing the sitting room door back against the wall she shouted at the handsome tanned man who was sitting nonchalantly on the settee with his elegant suited legs crossed.

"What the fuck are you doing here?"

"Why hello Sandy. What a greeting to give a man who has travelled hundreds of miles to see you."

"I don't care how many miles you've travelled you can just turn around and travel them all back the opposite way. I told you in Mauritius that I wasn't interested and now I'm even less interested as I've got a boyfriend here."

"Do you Sandy?" June interjected with a big smile on her face.

"Yes, Mum I do!"

"You never told me, is it...?"

"Mum!" Sandy cut in. "I'll tell you later, okay!"

"Alright darling, I'm sorry, now, David, would you like some more coffee?"

"Mum he doesn't need any more coffee. He's leaving now!"

"Mrs. Williams, do you mind if I have a private chat with Sandy?" David requested as he got to his feet to return the coffee cup to June, by doing so indicating rudely that she should leave the room. Poor June didn't know how to handle this suave man and was acutely embarrassed by Sandy's language; whatever had happened in Mauritius to make her so aggressive? Casting a worried glance in Sandy's direction she nodded and placed David's cup and saucer on the tray which she returned to the kitchen.

"Sandy, I'm sorry you feel like this and I'm sorry for springing my visit on you but I had to be sure I'd find you in. I know that you'd have disappeared had you known I was coming."

"Yes, I would have. Look David, I know what sort of man you are and I don't want to get involved with you, you're fickle and promiscuous I don't like people like you and I don't like you." Sandy breathed heavily with anger, her cheeks had reddened and he could see her trembling from where he stood. "What do you want from me David? I thought I'd made my feelings clear; are you so thick skinned that you didn't understand or is it conceit? You can't believe you have failed to make yet another conquest, one more notch on the bedpost. You're a male tart, have you had yourself checked for diseases lately?!" David flushed up with anger at being insulted so crudely. For the first time since she had met him David lost his cool demeanour. His dark eyes flashed and he visibly stiffened, he thrust his hands in his pocket and Sandy heard him jangling his keys, an irritating habit she had noticed before when he was a little agitated or impatient. He came very close to her and through his teeth he replied.

"I resent those comments. I have tried to show you how much I am attracted to you and all I get are insults in return. I think you should listen to what I have to say, before booting me out. I could make trouble for you and your boyfriend – Oliver, isn't it?"

"How the hell do you know his name?" she cried but David merely grinned smugly at her discomfort.

"And what do you mean – make trouble for us?" Sandy felt panic rising up, which she strove not to show. Now he was back in control David smirked and nonchalantly resumed his seat. Leaning back in the chair he linked his hands behind his head and said

"Josie told me all about him and," he paused, a cruel smile spreading over his face, "Paul, that was his name wasn't it?" Sandy's stomach lurched at the shock of this revelation. She stood for a moment speechless. Josie and her bloody loose tongue and her obsession with David, she must have repeated the whole story to him. And the damned girl hadn't the decency to warn Sandy that she had done so!

She drew the image of Oliver with his honourable and gentle loving character into her mind and managed to control the panic welling up inside her. Resolutely determined not to take his bait and let on he was right about Paul Sandy drew herself up and said "I have no intention of going out with you David, and yes Oliver is the man I want to be with. Why don't you just leave me alone!"

"I'll give you some time to think it over Sandy, how about a week, will that be long enough for you to realise that I don't make idle threats. The last thing I want is to see you with a criminal record but there's no need for that is there?" He smiled at her and she wanted to smack him in the face. He continued "All I want is for you to give me a bit of yourself and who knows, you may even grow to like it." Reaching into his inner pocket he withdrew a silver card holder, took from it a heavily embossed visiting card which he placed on the coffee table as Sandy refused to take it from him, then gathered up his sheepskin coat in readiness to leave. "Say goodbye to your mother for me and thank her for the coffee." He moved closer to Sandy and grabbed her by the shoulders forcing her to look up at hiim

"I'll be waiting. *À bientôt.*" With that he let himself out of the front door and with one wave and a blown kiss he turned the corner and out of her sight.

Sandy flopped into a chair exhausted by the exchange and very worried. Damn and blast that trip to Mauritius; it had been jinxed from the start. *Why did I have to open my big mouth to Josie?* Oliver would be horrified at her stupidity, why couldn't things just go smoothly for once in her life?

The thought of sleeping with David was abhorrent, not because he was unattractive; he was extremely attractive, but because he was a thorough shit. No way was she going to succumb to his blackmail. But what should she do? Sandy was loath to admit her mistake to the rest of them, they'd think she was a fool and no doubt they'd be angry with her. *Bloody Josie! And bloody stupid me!* June came quietly into the room to see Sandy with her head in her hands.

"Darling, what's the matter?"

"Oh Mum, I don't know what to do. He wants to go out with me and he won't leave me alone."

"He's a very presentable young man and polite, why don't you like him?"

"Because he's a creep and he sleeps around and anyway I think I love Oliver." Sandy still couldn't bring herself to admit what she had done by telling her story to Josie. They had all just relaxed again after nothing more had happened after Jimmy's body had been found. Oliver had been right; no exhumation had taken place and as far as anyone else knew Paul still lay deep in the mire. Anyone else that is, except David. Whatever was she going to do?

For the remainder of the week with June Sandy remained agitated and withdrawn. June tried to ask her about David and why it was so difficult for her to just tell him no.

"You don't understand Mum." was all the answer she received.

"I've never known you not to be forthright with people Sandy, sometimes I thought your tongue would hang you!" June was exasperated, Sandy was behaving completely out of character.

"Just ring the darned man and tell him you're going to marry Oliver, that'll put him off surely!" Sandy agreed to do this just so that her mother would leave her to think things through in peace. Finally, she made up her mind. June had gone to the shops and Sandy rang David to reason with him.

"David, it's Sandy."

"Hello Sandy, when are you coming to see me?"

"David, please let it drop, I have a boyfriend here and I love him. I can't cheat on him surely you can understand that?" She tried to be reasonable and not to lose her temper or emphasise her dislike for him, which would only make him more stubborn, she hoped to draw on his better nature which must be in him somewhere.

"I do understand Sandy but he needn't know need he? I fancy you like mad and I'm sure you don't hate me as much as you pretend to. Just come and see me, we can talk it over, I don't want to hurt you or get you into trouble, I'm sure we can sort it out." Sandy felt a glimmer of hope that they could, he sounded more amenable than he had on his visit; maybe he had just lost his temper because she had been so rude to him. She ended the call with a promise to ring him after the New Year to talk again.

Sandy felt a little more cheerful after the conversation, he was just trying it on, by the time she spoke to him after the New Year he would probably have a new girlfriend and have forgotten all about her.

⌢ ᵕ ⌢

New Year came and Sandy was back at the farm. They saw 1977 in with champagne and laughter. When everyone had retired to bed Sandy sat with Oliver on the large settee, her head resting comfortingly on his arm, Oliver drew her to him and kissed her.

"Happy New Year my love." he murmured in her ear.

"Happy New Year to you too." She returned his kiss. "It's been a lovely evening, hasn't it?"

"Sandy?"

"Yes?" Oliver slipped off the settee and going down on one knee he clasped her hands in both of his large freckled ones.

"Sandy my love, will you marry me?"

It was too soon! Sandy sat up in alarm and Oliver looked worriedly at her.

"Will you?" he asked quietly "You do love me, don't you?"

"Yes, of course I love you Oli, it's just a bit sudden that's all. We were mates a couple of weeks ago, with no thought of being in love. It's all happened so quickly I haven't caught up with it yet." She laughed and tried to lighten what seemed like a refusal. "I *do* want to marry you Oli, but not yet, it's too soon, I have to sort myself out a bit, career wise and everything."

Oliver deflated a little. He had planned this proposal, on his knee in front of the open fire at the start of the New Year and had thought that Sandy was ready. He had hoped that he would celebrate by losing his virginity with her after she had accepted his proposal. But now he felt her subtly pull away, just a little, but enough for him to release her hands and sit back on his heels.

"That's okay, there's no rush to marry. If I know you want to be my wife I can wait," adding "but please don't keep me waiting too long." They climbed the stairs to their bedrooms and at the door to Sandy's room Oliver hovered hopefully and expectantly and Sandy kissed him lovingly but did not invite him in.

In her room, Sandy was near to screaming. She had wanted to make love to Oliver, she would have loved to marry him next week but she had to get rid of David and his threats before she could plan her life with Oliver and she would rather not complicate things by telling him about it until it was sorted. Then she would admit to her stupidity and tell everyone what an ass she'd been.

Sandy decided not to ring David as she harboured the hope that he would have moved on and become intrigued with some other girl. If she rang him it could just give him that little push to re-sume his pursuit. Staying on at the farm for a few weeks before visiting June again, she tried to put all thoughts of him from her mind. Oliver seemed happy even though his proposal had not exactly gone as romantically as he had wished and he and Sandy often worked together at the various chores. Now was perhaps the time to admit to her mistake. As the family and Sandy, who was becoming more and more accepted as family, gathered around the dinner table one evening Sandy waited for a lull in the conver-sation. But this was forestalled by the 'phone ringing. George called Sandy from the hall where he had gone to answer it.

"Sandy, it's your mum."

"Hi Mum, how are you?" A pause, "Me too, we've been very busy but I'm hoping to come up at the weekend. Is that okay?" There was a rather long silence from Sandy as she listened to her mother then she said "Oh, I see. I'll deal with it when I come home." She was aware that she could be heard from the kitchen and kept her voice calm and succeeded in allaying any questioning looks from the family.

"Mum okay?" George asked, "Missing having you around no doubt."

"Yes thanks, she's fine. I'll go and stay for a while if you can spare me?"

"We can't ever spare you love, but you go on and give her some of your time, we've hogged you for long enough." The conversations continued over pudding and somehow there didn't seem a right time to tell them what she had done. She let it pass. Once she had spoken to David who, her mother said had rung asking, apparently quite politely, if Sandy could ring him at her convenience, she'd have sorted it all out with him and then there would be nothing to worry about.

On her return, she waited until June was out and then she rang David. Attempting to be friendly and unfazed she asked him how he was and what he was doing, she chatted about her time on the farm and how she had enjoyed helping there.

"It's so nice to be in the countryside, I don't know how you put up with being in London." In the end, she ran out of pleasantries and David cut in.

"When are you coming to see me?"

"I don't really want to come to London David. Can't we sort it out over the 'phone? All I want is to get on with my life, don't you want to do the same?"

"Yes, and that's where you come in Sandy."

"Please David, let's just be friends, you don't need to keep doing this. Let it drop and maybe we can go for a drink some time or you could come and meet Oliver and we could all be friends." She crossed her fingers hoping for a laugh and an 'okay, let's do that' from David but no, he merely replied

"Come to my flat, I don't want to talk about it over the 'phone. I'll make us dinner and we can thrash it out. How about this

Friday. I finish work at four. I'll pick you up at Paddington say five o'clock?"

There seemed to be no other way, she had tried to avoid having to see him but perhaps if she dealt with him face to face she might make better headway. Sandy agreed to be there, she'd buy a return ticket and hopefully be back on the last train.

"Alright, but can we eat early I don't want to miss the last train?"

The 'phone conversation had not achieved anything and Sandy was angry. She had really tried and had forced herself to be friendly. *Damn him!* Sandy slammed the 'phone down so hard that she cracked the receiver.

During the week, Sandy mentioned to her mother that she was going to meet a friend in London Friday evening and quickly changed the subject before June asked who it was. For the rest of the week she went over in her mind all the arguments she could muster to get David to leave her alone. She could tell him to do his worst and storm out or she could plead with him to forget what Josie had told him saying that by doing so he would prove that he was really a nice guy... on and on she turned it over in her head until Friday came, all too soon. Sandy waved good bye to her mother saying

"I'll be back late Mum, don't wait up." She trudged off to the station, bought her return ticket and waited for the train to arrive.

David met Sandy at Paddington Station. He leaned forward to greet her with a kiss on the cheek but she recoiled violently causing a few strange looks from other passengers. He escorted her to his car, his diplomatic number plates allowing him to park in a restricted zone. Sandy snorted with disgust at his smug use of the immunity when they could quite easily have gone by tube or walked.

David's flat was the whole top floor of a beautiful Georgian property in Pimlico. The opulence took Sandy's breath away.

Original paintings and antiques adorned the walls and surfaces and the furnishings had obviously come from Harrods. Either he held a far superior job with the government than he let on, or his family had wealth in its own right. Whatever the reason the memory of him sitting on June's slightly shabby settee made her feel awkward and inferior.

"Sit down and I'll get us some coffee, do you prefer high roast or mild?" Regaining some of her dignity Sandy replied that she didn't give a shit if it was out of a tin. David grinned, he really did like her feistiness and my goodness didn't he fancy her. He wished she had been just a little more willing but the chase was exciting especially as he was sure she could not refuse in the end. She sat primly in a chair, avoiding the large settee so that he couldn't sit beside her. When he had ground the coffee, and put it to percolate in the kitchen David offered to show her the bedroom where she could hang her clothes for the duration of the stay.

"I'm not staying! You said come for dinner, I told you I wanted to catch the last train home."

"Well, just in case you change your mind." David said with a smirk. Sandy didn't answer, she was determined to keep it civil, but what she really wanted to do was smack him in the face.

"Now, for dinner, it will be ready quite soon, I prepared it earlier to give us time to talk." He left the room and returned with two glasses of red wine. "I hope you like red, it's a very good one." Sandy thought, *it would be!*

David served the meal, he was a good cook and it was a pleasant meal, Sandy ate quickly as she wanted to get the visit over as quickly as possible.

"That was very nice, thank you." She drank the remainder of her wine and put her napkin beside her plate. "David, have you considered at all the pointlessness of what you threatened to do? It's all in the past now and no one was hurt. On the contrary, a vulnerable man was saved from a dreadful life." David listened attentively.

"Go on, tell me why breaking the law is okay just because it's in the past?"

"What would you have done? No, it's stupid to ask that as unless you were there and experienced the whole thing you couldn't understand; Paul was the sweetest man alive, he was wrongly accused and by sheer chance I met him under the weirdest conditions. We went through hell on that moor and he took his share in keeping our spirits up. He tried to help where he could even though he was still a child in a man's body. He was terrified and totally confused. All we did was try to help him." She stopped talking, the memories of that time would never go away and after all they had been through dear Paul had died before he knew he was proven innocent.

"That's all very moving and commendable but you should have let the law do its job. It's not up to you to decide whether a man is innocent or not, the courts do that. And as for that solicitor, he should be struck off." He poured more wine for them both and continued "So you see it's not just that I want you to be my lover, it's more to do with whether, as a law-abiding citizen and a member of Her Majesty's Diplomatic Corps, I can keep quiet about it. You see, I am now implicated by proxy."

"No, you're not, it's only hearsay as far as you're concerned."

"Oh, but I am. Now, tell me why I shouldn't report you all this minute?"

"You have a cruel streak David. Can't you leave it alone? None of us has ever done anything to hurt you or damage your career, why ruin all those decent people who only acted out of human kindness?"

"I might consider forgetting I have any knowledge if you really want me to, but I'd be putting myself in a vulnerable position should it all come out and it's found that I was complicit."

"Oh, would you, please David, we are all just recovering from the trauma of it all and my Mum and Dad's breakup was awful, Mum and I were estranged for months afterwards. We've finally made it up and we're happy again." She nearly mentioned Oliver but thought better of it.

"I'll think about it. Come on let's have another drink, the evening's still young and you've hardly touched a drop." Sandy glanced at her glass, it was empty; when had she drunk it? She must have been sipping it automatically without even noticing she was doing so. David filled it up again and went to fetch another bottle. He took it to the sitting room and Sandy joined him, she sat in the arm chair and left the space in the settee beside him empty. He smiled as he took note of this.

"I'm not going to hurt you Sandy. But sit there if you wish, now let's discuss this a little further."

"You said you would forget all about it. I'm so grateful David, You have got a decent side to you after all." she joked feebly.

"Yes I have, but it takes the right person to bring it out." He smiled at her adding "But I did say 'might'." Sandy' heart sank, she thought they were getting somewhere and that her reasoning had swayed him, she had even for a moment thought he *did* have a better side.

"Don't play with me David, either you will or you won't, just tell me which it is."

"Look at it this way, all I want from you is for you to like me enough to go to bed with me just once and then we can all go our separate ways."

"I can't do that, I've agreed to marry Oliver, I won't do that to him even if I wanted to, which I don't."

"Well you can't blame me for trying. Have a liqueur with me before you go to catch your train, I'll run you to the station afterwards." Sandy's face must have shown the surprise she had felt at his relenting so easily as he laughed out loud.

"Don't look so shocked, I'm not wholly bad." He got up from the settee and came back with two glasses of a clear liqueur and put one in her hand.

"Bottoms up!" he said and downed his in one. Sandy sipped at hers and coughed as it caught in her throat

"What is it? I've never had this before?"

"It's absinthe, heady stuff but it keeps the cold out." Sandy had a little more of the drink.

"Can I have some lemonade or something in it, it's a bit strong for me?" David took the glass and disappeared into the kitchen to dilute the drink. He brought it back to her in a larger glass filled to the brim with lemonade.

"Shame to spoil a good absinthe but here you are." Sandy took the glass and sipped it. The taste was mostly lemonade with a slight bite to it, a bit like vodka and lime which she had had before. It was quite pleasant though she would have preferred a cup of coffee.

"So, what was this Paul doing in the middle of Dartmoor in the middle of the night?" David settled himself comfortably, stretching his legs out in front of him.

"I thought Josie told you. He had been tricked into running away by the vilest man I have ever met." Sandy recalled the day when she had told Josie the whole story, and remembered that Josie had been more excited about the gory details than about the personal and emotional aspects in the tale. This was typical of her. It occurred to Sandy that she may not have faithfully recounted the facts. Maybe if David heard the true and honest account from her, he would understand better and it would touch his sensibilities as it had done to all who had been concerned. There *had* to be a decent side to him, and he *had* said he would consider forgetting what he knew. If he knew all the facts... She thought for a few moments and deliberated on the wisdom of giving him more information. David knew the worst bit; that she and her family and friends had lied to the police and sheltered a suspected murderer. But it appeared that what he didn't know, was the story behind it and the pathos of Paul's situation.

Knowing the full account would not make matters any worse, it could and should make things better. Sandy began her tale. David listened attentively and appeared to be moved by her desire to help the Down syndrome man.

"You missed your flight because you wanted to help him. Am I correct?" He leant forward with a gentle look in his eyes as she told him of the mist falling and her fear when she realised she was lost.

"Yes, I felt responsible for not paying attention on the road and then when the mist fell I got completely disorientated."

Sandy took her time in the telling, being sure to emphasise the vulnerability of Paul and his sweet nature. That night underground when Oliver had gone for help and Paul had poured out his tale to her in the darkness still clutched at her heart. Surely David can't help but be moved by it too. "So, you see," she wound up her account, "I couldn't let him go back to that dreadful institution. He had no one to speak for him and he wasn't able to express himself coherently."

David came over to her chair and put his arm around her shoulder.

"You are a very kind person Sandy. But didn't it occur to you to trust the courts to find the truth? It would have been better that way and you wouldn't have broken the law and dragged all manner of people in with you. You are kind but foolish and now responsible for the potential ruin of two professionals' careers should it ever come out, apart from your family and the farmer's family possibly facing prison. You will carry the guilt of that for ever."

Sandy looked near to tears. "I know, David, but what could I do? I wish you could have known Paul, you'd understand if you had."

"Maybe I would have. Anyway, thank you for telling me about it." He took her glass and his own to refill them.

"Can I have a coffee please, then I really must go or I'll miss the train."

"Coffee it is then, after we finish the last dribble in the bottle. I'll dilute it for you again. There's plenty of time before the train leaves."

"Alright, but please don't make it too strong I'm already feeling a bit woozy."

Sandy's hopes began to rise; she seemed to have got through to him, she was sure he'd not be cruel enough to pursue it now. David returned with the drinks and the coffee pot on a tray.

"Here we are, do you want anything else, a biscuit or chocolate?"

"No thanks, I'm fine."

"I still want to make love to you." he replied. "Are you sure you won't, just this once?"

"No, I told you, I love Oliver, I will not cheat on him, even once. I'm sorry David, but you just are not my type of guy. There must be loads of other girls who'd give their eye teeth to sleep with you, why me?"

"Because I've wanted to from the minute I met you." He placed his glass on the table and leaned over her to attempt to kiss her. Sandy pulled away.

"No please don't. David, can't we just be friends?" David took the rebuff and returned to his seat.

"If that's what you want. But I don't give up very easily."

It was definitely time Sandy got out of there. The situation was becoming tricky and she didn't want to fall out with David after they had made such good headway. She smiled at him. "I'm glad I've told you what happened. Thanks for being so understanding, now we can draw a line under it can't we?"

"I expect so, I'll think about it. I don't want to lose touch with you Sandy and I will not give up completely."

Why couldn't he just say yes and let it go? She desperately wanted to leave his flat knowing they were all safe from him. But he procrastinated every time she asked for a straight answer. Did she trust him? No, she didn't. His behaviour this evening had been understanding and solicitous, but the cruel manipulating David from Mauritius was still very alive. Sandy finished her coffee and glancing at her watch she saw it was going to be a rush to get to the station on time. She leapt up and immediately felt dizzy, her head swam round and round and she slumped back down on the chair.

"I feel dreadful."

"Maybe that last drink was one too many." David laughed.

"I need to be sick." She half crawled towards the bathroom and fell through the door. Then she passed out.

Sandy woke to day-light, her head was pounding and she felt nauseous. She was naked and in David's bed. What had happened? Had she had betrayed Oliver's trust and allowed David to seduce her? She couldn't remember a thing after she had got to the bathroom. She reached for the dressing gown which David must have left by the bed as he came in carrying a cup of tea on a tray. She frantically wrapped the gown around her nakedness.

"What am I doing here?"

"You passed out my dear, there was no way I could put you on a train in your condition."

"But where are my clothes? And what am I doing in your bed?"

"I couldn't just leave you on the bathroom floor covered in vomit. Your clothes are clean and dry, I washed them after I'd taken them off you." Sandy was panicking, she remembered nothing about the night, had she had sex with him whilst she was drunk? He placed the breakfast tray on the table and began to pour coffee.

"Don't panic, I didn't sleep in here. I slept in the other

bedroom. I don't go in for rape. I prefer a willing lover not a comatose one."

Relief overwhelmed Sandy. And a sense of disbelief. David was a complicated character. But she could understand it when he said he preferred a willing lover, he didn't need to take advantage of women, they threw themselves at him. It would be beneath his conceited pride not to have adoring eyes gazing up at him. However, she was very grateful that he had treated her respectfully, except...

"Why did you have to take *all* of my clothes off? Surely it was only my blouse and trousers that needed washing?"

"Well they sort of all slipped off together." David laughed "Have you ever tried to undress an unconscious person?" Sandy cringed with acute embarrassment further into the dressing gown.

"There's a bath running for you and I've just taken your clothes from the drier, they're in the dressing room. I'll leave you to it."

Sandy had a very quick bath in the foamy tub and dressed hurriedly. She found David in the kitchen frying bacon and eggs.

"I must ring Mum. She'll be worried sick."

"Of course. The 'phone's in the sitting room."

June answered on the first ring.

"Sandy! Are you alright? I've been on the point of ringing the police!"

"Yes Mum, I missed the train, I'm sorry I should have 'phoned you. I'm alright, I'll be home later this morning." She didn't tell her mother that she had been out-of-her-head on drink, swearing to herself that never again would she drink absinthe.

She ate the breakfast David had cooked although she was agitating to get away and kept her eyes downcast to avoid the amusement in his eyes every time he looked at her. In the end, she snapped

"Okay so you've seen me naked, I'm sure I looked much like any other woman so stop leering at me." David laughed

"I confess I did take my time putting you to bed." Sandy turned scarlet at the thought of him looking at her and touching her.

"I'm leaving now, I can walk to the station." She grabbed her coat and bag and opened the flat door.

"Goodbye David."

"Farewell Sandy, I'll be in touch." he replied.

June was quite angry with her when she got home.

"Don't you ever think?" she berated her.

"I've said I'm sorry Mum, it won't happen again."

"Well don't. You have put us through enough anxiety to last a lifetime."

Sandy stayed the remainder of the week with June and then as promised she returned to the farm and Oliver.

When he met her at the station her first emotion was pleasure at the sight of him followed swiftly by guilt and embarrassment. What an utter idiot she'd been to get drunk. But it was not something she was going to admit to in a hurry and with any luck no one need ever know.

They slipped into routine and Sandy once again relished the beauty of the countryside and the way of life on the farm. She took to her painting with a fresh heart and put David from her mind. He had tried it on and failed. Maybe he would let her be now. She had to admit that he had behaved decently by not abusing her. However, she suspected that he had got her drunk deliberately, possibly with the hope that she would willingly sleep with him when she was relaxed. But he had overdone his assessment of her ability to hold her drink and thank goodness, she had not done anything she shouldn't.

⌒ ⌣ ⌒

The weather was still raw and the wind still howled through the windows at night sounding like a pack of wolves outside. She and Oliver dressed warmly and took Lilly for long walks into the woods and selected trees which needed felling or cutting back. Oliver marked them with paint and Sandy turned the marks into faces with a deft flick of the brush.

"That one's you!" She shrieked with laughter as she put the finishing touches of splodged curls on the top of the head. "And that's me." On the next one she stuck pine needles into the paint before it dried.

"It looks more like a hedgehog. But I suppose that's a good likeness." Oliver staggered backwards as she shoved him playfully.

"What about Lil?" She grabbed the brush and painted a huge lolling tongue on the next tree.

"Hey that one's not for felling!" Oliver laughed.

"No one would dare fell it with that mush staring at them." Lilly came running up as if to share the joke and as she sat there panting with her tail thrashing, sensing the jovial atmosphere, they both knelt down beside her and hugged her.

"Oh Lil, you make me laugh even when I want to cry." Sandy gave her a kiss on the top of her hot little head. Oliver heaved her up and held her tightly.

"How about a kiss for me?" Sandy looked up into his green eyes and sank into his embrace.

"I love you Oli."

Sandy's sense of reprieve was shattered when a letter forwarded on by June arrived for her. On her way, back from walking Lilly she heard the distinctive sound of the leaky exhaust of the post van coming up the lane and she stood on the grass verge to let it pass. The postman waved to her and pulled up alongside her.

"Morning miss, are you on your way home?"

"Yes, do you want me to take the post?"

"It would save me a few minutes on the round if you could m'dear."

Amongst the letters for the Tregowans a stiff white envelope caught her eye and her heart sank. It had to be from David. She slipped the letter into her pocket before delivering the rest of the mail to the house. The envelope would have stood out from the run of the mill brown window envelopes containing invoices and statements and tax forms etcetera and though far from nosey, the Tregowans would have shown curiosity.

Later that day when everyone was occupied Sandy took the letter to her room and opened it.

The shock she felt when she removed the contents nearly made her faint. There were three photographs and a note. The note read 'I think we had better meet again. We have things to discuss. The next copies will be for Oliver unless I hear from you by Friday. D.' The photos were definitely of her. There could be no doubt of that. But the poses! They were obscene!

Sandy tore them in tiny pieces, anger seething in her chest. *I'll murder that bastard.* She took them to the kitchen wrapped up in tissue and as nonchalantly as possible she popped them in the Aga fire. Of course, that wasn't the end of them, there would be more and David would have the negatives. What on God's earth was she going to do?

Dinner time came and Sandy pleaded a stomach ache and stayed in her room. Alice tapped on her door to ask her if she needed any pain killers assuming it was monthly menstruation and Sandy accepted agreeing that it was and explaining that she always lost her appetite at this time. Alice nodded kindly but couldn't remember Sandy losing her appetite the last time or the time before. Oliver tactfully left her alone and she sat forlorn on her bed, the images of her body in those disgusting poses fixed indelibly in her mind.

To ignore David was to invite him to act.

Her life was ruined; she'd have to tell Oliver that she had willingly gone to spend the evening with a man she professed to loathe and then tell him he had got her drunk and then somehow took disgusting photos of her when she was unconscious. No man would believe that! He'd think she was making it up and that she had wanted it. It would be bad enough for Oliver to hear what happened but for him to see photographs of it as well was more than anyone could accept or forgive.

She should have told everyone what had happened in Mauritius and they could have faced it together. Now David had something else he could hold over her. She couldn't deny what had happened but how could she make it clear that she had been there against her will? Not only had she put everyone in the hands of a vicious minded man but she had been completely duped. He hadn't got her drunk to have sex with her, oh no, his plan had been far more cunning and damning than that. And, she noted, there was nothing to link the photos with David which would cast aspersions on his behaviour. He had made sure not to include any pictures on the walls and the bedding had been ordinary and commonplace. The pictures could have been taken anywhere, even in a brothel! She may as well face up to the fact that Oliver wouldn't want her after this and just go and tell him everything and get it over with.

But in the end, she couldn't bring herself to do it. Oliver's loving smiling face when he held her hand or kissed her goodnight were like hot irons burning into her conscience. Maybe, just maybe she could avoid the *coup de grace* and not lose Oliver. If, somehow, she could get hold of the negatives and destroy them she would then tell everyone about David knowing what they had all done with Paul and to hell with the consequences.

When Oliver and George were out in the fields and Alice milking the goats, Sandy made a very quick call to David.

"I'm coming on Saturday."

For the remainder of the week Sandy managed to find things to do which were away from the company of the family. Oliver invited her to go for a beer with him but she refused saying she had a drawing she wanted to finish. He went to the pub alone and sat pensively in the corner wondering what he had done wrong.

Saturday arrived and on the pretext of visiting a friend from college Sandy caught the train to London.

When she waved goodbye to Oliver and the train sped away she felt desolate, she was lying to him already and they weren't even engaged yet. Sandy had an overwhelming desire to throw herself off the moving train.

Oliver drove back from the station in a low frame of mind. He couldn't put his finger on it but something wasn't quite right. Instead of Sandy being her usual bouncy self, she had been near to tears when she said goodbye. Surely, she didn't have to visit her girlfriend if she didn't want to. No, it wasn't that, something was eating her and he wished he knew what it was.

Oliver rang June on his return from the station. He couldn't relax owing to his feeling that something was wrong between them. The only thing he had done which he didn't do every day, with her was to ask her to marry him at the New Year. She had said yes, but he worried that she had not seemed very enthusiastic, and why did she hurry off to stay with a friend she had never even mentioned before? His conversation with June was not particularly reassuring; she congratulated Oliver on his unofficial engagement but had no idea Sandy was intending to visit her friend again and neither did she know who this friend might be.

"Oh, I didn't know she had visited her friend before, she didn't say. Is it the same one?" Oliver felt a small clenching in his stomach; why hadn't Sandy mentioned it?

"I assume so Oliver, though she didn't say." Oliver told himself that it must have slipped her mind to tell him because the visit hadn't been of any importance, just a catch-up between old friends. The clenching didn't go away though.

Just before they said goodbye June mentioned that a man called David had descended on them over Christmas and that Sandy had been very angry and thereafter very withdrawn. Had she not mentioned it? June remembered quite clearly that Sandy had told David she had a boyfriend and that she didn't want to go out with him but he had been very persistent. Oliver burned with anger.

"Where does this bloke live? I'll knock his teeth out if he doesn't leave her alone!"

June said he had left his card behind and if she could find it she would ring him. She didn't like the idea of her daughter being pestered like this and hoped she could rely on Oliver to sort it out. June searched the house, in Sandy's room and even in the waste bin but neither his greeting card nor his visiting card was there. Sandy must have thrown them both in the fire.

After a lot of heart searching Oliver decided to speak to Tim. He didn't really know what he was worried about but it was there; that nagging at the back of his mind that all was not well with Sandy. He drove over to Tim's cottage where Tim was busy completing a client's tax returns. Tim glanced up with friendly nod as Oliver let himself in.

"If you just hang on a tick I'm nearly finished. The kettle's hot if you would like to make us both a coffee."

Seeing the paperwork all over the desk Oliver apologised for interrupting his work and offered to come back another time.

"No, it's fine honestly, I was just totting up, won't be a moment." Oliver proceeded to make coffee, coinciding nicely with Tim putting the papers back in the file and turning off the angle-poise lamp over his desk. "Now you've got my full attention." Tim took the proffered coffee and swivelled his office chair towards the easy chair which Oliver had taken. "You look very serious Oliver, is there something wrong?" Oliver blew on his hot drink and took a small sip before answering.

"No everything's fine thanks." He didn't want to worry Tim

unnecessarily so he talked vaguely about Sandy and her friends from college and how he hoped she was having a good time over the weekend, hinting gently that he hadn't met any of them and had Tim met them and what were they like etcetera. Tim chatted along quite happily and told Oliver some amusing anecdotes about Sandy and her friends and what dare-devil things they had got up to whilst at college. He mentioned various girls and boys by name and Oliver wondered which of them Sandy was staying with. Now was the time he could find out if Tim knew where she was without alarming him or letting on that he was concerned.

"No idea I'm afraid, Sandy was never much good at planning or keeping us informed – much to June's chagrin. Didn't she mention a name to you?" Tim looked closely at Oliver who had become rather pink in the face. "What's eating you? I can tell there's something wrong, come on lad, out with it." Tim's immediate thought was that they had fallen out just before Sandy had left and Oliver was upset. Tim knew how Sandy could speak her mind, sometimes inadvertently hurting someone she cared about, she never meant to wound and often was unaware that she had. Oliver sighed and tried to put into words his misgivings.

"I thought everything was fine, Sandy did agree to marry me but she was preoccupied and when I saw her off on the train yesterday she was sort of tearful and a bit distant from me. Surely if she was going to have a good time with friends she wouldn't be unhappy, would she?" Tim was surprised at this, as far as he was aware Sandy had had a pleasant time with June and had been happy over New Year, what with their unofficial engagement and what not. He couldn't think what had upset her.

"The thing is," Oliver paused wondering whether Sandy had said anything to Tim about David's arrival at June's, she hadn't told Oliver which in itself upset him by its lack of confidence. Why hadn't she told him? He continued hesitantly "the thing is, this David tracked her down at June's and apparently, there was a very heated argument between them, according to June. But he had left after a short while and no more was said about it." Tim bristled with annoyance firstly because David had descended on Sandy without being invited and secondly that June had not told him about it. He would have tracked the slimy fellow down and given him a talking to had he known. So, the two men sat in Tim's cottage seething and worrying about Sandy and wondering what they could do to get David off her back.

Sandy sat in the far corner of the carriage and as she was joined by a woman who looked the chatty sort, dug into her bag and pulled out a book which she tried to read. She felt like a condemned person on her way to the gallows. If she could have got away with it and if she had the courage she would happily murder David. But crime fiction stories featuring unlikely killers were all very well, she knew that it took a particular type of person who could kill in cold blood and she wasn't one of those. No, she had to try and be as scheming as David. This was the only course she could take. Primarily she had to get the negatives and any copies of those pictures. Once that was done she would tell him to go to hell and go back to the support of her loved ones.

David was waiting for her on the platform and standing well back from the edge as if he could sense her desire to accidentally push him under a train. He took her arm possessively and led her to his car. Neither spoke. There were no pleasantries this time, just a business meeting, so to speak. Sandy felt so much hatred for him she was amazed his hand didn't catch fire with the heat of her anger.

As David closed the door of the flat behind them Sandy broke the silence

"You are an utter shit!"

"Yes, I know." David replied smugly. "I always get my way by some means or other so let's get down to business, shall we?"

"Give me the negatives of those disgusting pictures now!" Sandy's voice shook as she saw in her mind the pictures of herself spread-eagled on the bed. Never, not even for Oliver, would she have posed for pictures like those. They were depraved and pornographic, even featuring a sort of bondage with silk scarves. She felt sick at the thought of them.

"Sit down and I'll fetch the rest of the pictures to show you. You look very enticing in them, I could get a few bob for them from top shelf magazines." Before she could reach him to slap his face he had side-stepped and gone to the safe. He returned with a packet containing what must have been a full film of photographs.

"Twenty-four pictures and all of them good quality. Do you want them?"

"Yes, and I want the negatives as well."

"Oh, I daresay I can oblige but of course I do have other copies as well."

"For Christ's sake David, why are you doing this? I don't deserve this sort of treatment. Please don't do this to me!"

"You know why I'm doing it Sandy, I told you I want you to fuck me and to enjoy it. Then I will give you everything I have and we can carry on with our lives."

"I don't trust you. You are a complete bastard. I hate you. How could I even have sex with you without vomiting let alone enjoy it?"

"Suit yourself. But if you don't you will see your picture on the front of every porn magazine ever published. Look I have an example of one." He reached under the coffee table and drew out a glossy magazine. The cover showed a woman posing naked revealing everything. He opened it up to the centre page and Sandy turned away in disgust at what she saw.

"Now, will you discuss our arrangement?"

Sandy sat white faced with her eyes closed against the images he had shown her. How could any woman willingly pose like that? She was disgusted with her own gender and terrified that she would be joining them. If she had sex with him he probably wouldn't keep to his word. If she didn't have sex with him he would most definitely publish the pictures. She was damned if she did and damned if she didn't.

She sat and sobbed quietly whilst David looked on smiling his superior smile.

Finally, she decided.

"If I say I will have sex with you I want you to destroy all the copies and negatives in front of me now. When that is done, I will go to bed with you once. And then I want never to see or speak to you again. I don't care about what you do about Paul, do your bloody worst and we will all cope with it as a team just as we were when we were doing the decent thing. Unlike you, vile piece of shit, I keep my word."

"Done!" David agreed immediately which gave Sandy a moment's doubt, why had he agreed so readily? And the biggest question of all was why he was going to so much trouble to have sex with someone who so obviously despised him?

Whatever it was she would have to endure it then she would go home and confess everything to Oliver who would probably dump her on the spot. But at least the photographs will have been destroyed and even if she had to tell Oliver they were obscene he wouldn't have to actually see them. Then she would have to rethink her life without Oliver and he would have to rethink his without her.

"Get them." Sandy snapped. "I want to see all of them burned before I do anything."

"Of course you do." David went back to the safe and took out the roll of negatives and a further packet of pictures. He invited Sandy to check the remaining contents of the safe to be sure he had no more hidden away. She went through every piece of paper and envelope and finally, satisfied that there were no more she took the negatives from David and holding them up to the light she checked that they were the ones.

"Okay now burn them, all of them." David, watched carefully by Sandy, took them to the beautiful Georgian fireplace and set light to them. The photographs curled then flared. The negatives scorched around the edges and them with a whoosh of flame they were gone.

"Now!" David grinned at her. "Your side of the bargain if you please." For a moment, Sandy thought to run out of the flat and renege on her word but David was standing in front of the door.

"Just in case you have had second thoughts, I am much stronger than you and we don't want to get into a futile fight, do we?"

"David, will you leave us alone after this please? I intend to keep my word but it's the last thing I want to do. Please just this once give me your word that this will be the end of everything?"

"Of course, I will. I give you my promise." David replied with a smile. "You can go back and marry your farmer if you want to but once you've been loved by me you may decide to stay, I do know how to please my ladies. But first let's relax a little, you look like a cat trapped in a corner by a pack of dogs."

That's precisely what I feel like, thought Sandy.

"I'll make us some coffee to calm your nerves." Sandy nodded dumbly.

The percolator bubbled furiously from the kitchen, the smell of coffee was appetising and Sandy felt in need of it. David left it to infuse and returned to sit beside her.

"If you moved in with me you wouldn't have to work, just paint as much as you want and I'll bring home the money." To many women this would sound appealing but to Sandy it sounded like imprisonment; no long walks in the open air across the fields or on the moor, no goats or cows or Lilly, he wouldn't let her into this posh place, she shivered at the thought. She pushed thoughts of Oliver as far back in her mind as possible. Once it was all over she could tell him what she had done and why she had done it. It was then up to him as to whether he could bear to even look at her let alone love her any more. David wasn't going to hurt her physically, if she refused at the last minute he wouldn't harm her just throw her out and report them all to the police. The photos were gone, he had burned them all in front of her. Now she had to trust that he would keep his word about Paul. *Christ I feel like a prostitute! I'm selling my body!*

To be just a little bit fair to David, he didn't treat her like a prostitute, he cooked some food and opened the best wine as though he were courting her. However, this made Sandy feel worse than if he had just taken her to bed there and then.

Finally, it was time for bed. David insisted that they keep the light on and refused to be persuaded otherwise. Sandy had thought that she could perhaps try to imagine it was Oliver making love to her not David which would make it more tolerable; now that was impossible. She had drunk a lot of wine to physically and mentally anaesthetise herself and when he took her to bed she was nearly able to shut herself off from it all.

David appeared to sleep soundly but Sandy lay awake for most of the night. She had taken the final step and David had had his way. Had she not been in love with dear Oliver, and had she not been betraying his love and trust in her she might have been able to live with what had happened. After all, this wouldn't be the first time she had had a one night stand. College days had been a bit wild, it had been the age of free sexual expression and no-one thought badly of you if you had casual relationships.

The sense of freedom after she and Tom had split up and she had broken away from his controlling nature had made her reckless and she had been lucky not to get into trouble. But she had matured since then and one night stands were a thing of the past. Especially with a man whom she despised.

He had watched her during the night as she had paced the room thinking he was asleep and later when she had sat on the window seat staring out over the London night he had roused himself and draped a dressing gown over her shoulders.

"There's no point freezing, come back to bed and I'll warm you up." He slid his hand inside the gown and cradled her breast. "I need to think, leave me alone." She angrily pushed his hand away and pulled the gown tightly around her.

She wished she had made love to Oliver just once and told him about David's knowledge whilst she lay in the comfort of his arms. He would have understood and they would have all worked together to succeed or be damned. At least they would have been a team and whatever happened to them all their loyalties would have been intact. Now she would never have him, how could he want her after she had been with David?

David's naked body as he moved, reflected the hours he put in at the private gymnasium, not over-muscled but taut and fit, his suntan and his physique giving him the look of a bronze statue. Sandy was unmoved by his beauty and would have given anything for it to have been ginger freckled Oliver standing there. David got back into bed saying

"Suit yourself" and very soon went to sleep.

It was hard to believe that anyone had so little conscience that they could so cruelly manipulate others and sleep untroubled. Sandy had tried to reason with him to get him to back off and to forget what he knew. She had kept to her side of the bargain, if that's not too kind a word for what was basically blackmail and it appeared that he was keeping to his, she prayed that this was so. After some time shivering on the window seat Sandy gave in and crept quietly back into bed, lying on the far side so as not to touch him.

She must have dropped off because when she was woken by the sound of pigeons on the window sill it was daylight.

David entered carrying a breakfast tray.

"I'm not hungry." She turned away from him feeling the shame of what had happened. David placed the tray on the bedside table and began pouring the coffee.

"All in good time. Have some coffee at least." He handed her a cup.

"I'm getting up David. I don't want coffee or food. I just want to go home."

"As you wish." He took the cup from her and placed it on the tray. He remained seated on the side of the bed drinking his own coffee.

"So, shall we make another date for, say two weeks' time?"

"What? You said just this once!"

"Yes, I know I did, but I lied. You see I want a bit more than that. And I think that the information I have on you and your friends is more valuable than that, don't you?"

"You know David, I don't bloody care what you do about that. We'll all stand together and you will be on the outside. You may win and we may all be locked up but we will have each other and you will have no one. I hope you enjoy your victory!" Sandy threw back the covers heedless of her nakedness and began to fling on her clothes.

"Ah. Now there's just the little problem of the photographs."

"Don't try that on. I saw you burn the negatives."

"Yes, but I did take the precaution to have them copied. You can never be too careful you see. I'm amazed, quite frankly that you were taken in by the sacrificial burning. I thought you were brighter than that."

"You bastard!" Sandy grabbed the tray from the table and threw it across the room, butter and marmalade and coffee splattered against the wallpaper. "You're an utter shit. You never intended to keep your promise, did you? Now I'll have lost Oliver and all for nothing." David looked at the mess and anger flared in his eyes, Sandy was prepared for him to hit her and she almost wished he would just to prove what sort of person he was.

"Sandy, I wish you hadn't done that but no matter the room needs redecorating anyway." He looked around at, to Sandy's eye, the pristine bedroom and continued "My ex chose this wallpaper but I'm sure with your artistic eye you could find something better – more to your liking." What the hell was he talking about? Was he suggesting she redecorated his flat and move in? She couldn't stand any more of this man's taunting sarcasm; she was out of her depth. With a final tug, she pulled the zip up on her boot and standing as tall as she could she looked him straight in the eye and in a voice flat with defeat said

"Do your worst. I can't fight you anymore."

"You do realise don't you that if you married me you would be safe?" He picked up her packed bag and opened the flat door. "I could hardly have a wife of mine involved in a scandal."

"Stop playing games with me David, Hell would freeze before I'd agree to that and you know it so just shut up will you. Fuck you – you've ruined my life already so I don't give a damn what you do."

"Actually, you're quite wrong Sandy. I would marry you tomorrow; I am in love with you."

"Bollocks!" Sandy spat the word in his face. "Just get out of my way. I can walk to the station." With that she grabbed her bag and with head bowed and tears running unchecked down her face she ran down the stairs and into the street.

Sandy, wan looking and pink eyed arrived at June's house and attempted to put on a cheerful countenance before entering. She had had a good weekend with her friend, catching up and sleeping very little – hence her appearance...

June took one look at her and by her expression Sandy knew

she couldn't carry off the planned lie. But what could she tell June? Sandy very nearly turned around and ran straight back out of the house again. June took her by the arm and led her firmly into the sitting room where a log fire crackled homely in the grate. Oh, how she wished she could pour it all out to her mother but she was so ashamed of what she had done. It seemed as though she rode a rollercoaster which was never ending and which threw mud on her at every turn of the track. It had been so stupid to think that she could nip David's threats in the bud, so stupid to not admit that she had told Josie about Paul just because she was too embarrassed to admit her indiscretion. Now she had compounded this indiscretion with one which was not only impossible to admit but which was doomed to be an ongoing betrayal.

"What on earth's wrong?" June cried "You look dreadful!"

"Nothing Mum, honestly I'm fine." Sandy fought back tears and the overwhelming need for her mother's arms.

"No, you are not!" June almost snapped at Sandy, "You forget that I am your mother and I know you inside out Sandy. There is something upsetting you. Tell me darling what's wrong, is it Oliver? Have you fallen out?"

"No Mum, we haven't fallen out – yet."

"What do you mean by 'yet'? Darling you can talk to me, I may be old but I have been in love you know," she added quietly, "and I still am." Sandy refused to admit there was anything wrong just that she was tired and giving June a hug she climbed despondently up the stairs and quietly shut herself in her room. Lying on her bed staring up at the ceiling she wished she could cocoon herself there for ever and never face anyone again. After all the mental arguments, back and forth that she had done since David had come back on the scene she had got nowhere near to a solution. Instead she had ended up making the wrong decisions and stepped beyond the boundaries. Who was she trying to protect – herself? No, not altogether, she had been trying to protect all of them from a manipulative insensitive man. *What a bloody fool I am!* She was drained. Drained of all emotion and any enthusiasm for life, for painting and most of all for her and Oliver's happiness together, it had evaporated like their breath on that frosty evening by the pond.

Downstairs, June busied herself preparing supper whilst worrying about her daughter who had been behaving so strangely. She couldn't make sense of it. All June could think was that Sandy was regretting having become emotionally involved with Oliver and was worrying about the inevitable moment when she had to tell him.

Sandy came when called for supper and, June noted, looking a bit brighter.

"You look better than when you came in," she put Sandy's favourite meal of 'beef stroganoff á la June' on the table "you must have had a hectic weekend, you looked shattered." It was no good June fishing; Sandy didn't want to be forced into telling yet more lies. Instead, she took a mouthful of food.

"Mm this is one of your best Mum." They ate mostly in silence, savouring the meal and Sandy mopped her plate much to June's pleasure. Sandy carefully steered the conversation away from her weekend and June let it be, knowing it was no good pushing her.

Oliver 'phoned later that evening and June discreetly eavesdropped hoping to hear them make arrangements for Sandy's return. But although the tone of the one-sided conversation appeared relatively light and friendly it was not a lengthy call and nothing pertinent was said to June's knowledge. Sandy rang off with a promise to ring after the weekend and 'love you too'. Well, that boded well June thought but when she saw Sandy's face as she entered the sitting room she had second thoughts. Sandy was flushed and her blue-green eyes, the colour of a winter sea were watery. June tried again to get her to tell her what was wrong but Sandy swore that it was nothing, she just needed some space.

Strangely, after longing for Sandy to live with her, June tried daily to persuade her to go back to the Tregowans.

"Sandy why don't you go down to the farm? You love it there, don't you? You don't have to stay here for my sake you know."

"Mum stop nagging me! I'll go back when I'm ready okay?"

⌢ ‿ ⌢

One week stretched into two and Sandy still refused to return to the farm or to talk to June about what was wrong.

"Mum, I think I'll stay a bit longer I don't feel like going back to Oliver just yet. In fact, I'd like you to tell a little fib for me. Can you say you want me to go with you to a hospital appointment or something? It needn't be serious, an ingrowing toenail or something." She looked pleadingly at her mother. June was very reluctant to tell outright lies without good reason and initially refused.

"No Sandy, it's tempting fate to say that and anyway why do you have to lie to Oliver?"

"Please Mum, just this once?"

"I'll do it this time Sandy, but I'd like to know why."

"I can't really explain Mum, it's just that I need some more time to think things through."

"Well just tell Oliver that, he's an understanding man, it's better to be honest my love."

"I know it is!" Sandy nearly snapped at June but held her frustration back, "I just want a week or so and then I'll talk to him, I'm not ready at the moment, please Mum you must understand it's not all black and white in relationships, is it?" So, June agreed that it could be an appointment for something relatively minor like varicose veins or haemorrhoids.

"But you must promise me that this is a one-off and that you will tell Oliver one way or the other how you feel."

"I *know* how I feel Mum, it's more complicated than that but I promise I will talk to him."

"Well don't leave it too long or you'll lose him!" June replied sharply; already Oliver's 'phone calls had become less frequent and Sandy never appeared to make one back unless she did it when June was out.

Sandy rang Oliver at the farm on Sunday afternoon; she wouldn't be coming back yet – her reason being that June had asked her to accompany her to an appointment. She was apparently in a hurry to catch a train and didn't stay to chat or to tell Oliver where she was or when she would be returning. She sounded cheerful enough, he told himself. Sandy put the 'phone down resignedly. She had told Oliver yet another lie.

Sandy had lain awake most of the previous night trying to find a way out of the maze she was trapped in. As it stood, David had all the trump cards. He had information on all of them which could ruin them and he had the photographs of her taken when she was drunk and out cold. Any day now the police could come knocking. Any day now Oliver could receive one of the photos by post. And any day now she could appear on the cover of a top shelf magazine. Sandy knew she could never expect Oliver to understand why she had gone blindly into this intrigue without talking it over with him. Had she done so at least the photos wouldn't exist but knowing Oliver's temper he might have attacked David and ended up in prison, he may even have killed him! Oliver had been Sandy's protector and friend throughout their horrendous time on the moor, his loyalty to her had turned to love and Sandy knew his instincts would be to fight for her.

She thought she had been doing the right thing trying to de-escalate the situation verbally but she had underestimated David's scheming mind and had made the situation twice as bad.

Should she tell Oliver what she had done with David? Yes, she should and then he would be free to find another love. But even if she did, it wouldn't solve the main problem: David's hold over them.

She thought over the last words she and David had exchanged, was marrying him an option? No, he was just playing with her, giving her an out so that he could snatch it away again, enjoying the pain he was inflicting. But supposing he meant it? If she did marry him he would definitely have to destroy the pictures and drop his threats. Should she sacrifice herself to save the others? She owed it to them all, there seemed no other option.

Sandy decided that she would have one last try at persuading David to call it off. She crept quietly downstairs and rang his number.

June wasn't sure if it was her pestering that made Sandy decide to go away for the weekend but over dinner that evening Sandy, looking down at her plate and not meeting June's eyes, announced

"I'm going to visit my mate again this weekend Mum and then hopefully I'll go back to the farm the following week. Is that okay with you?"

"Of course, darling, where does she live in London?" adding "Just in case I need to get in touch with you." Sandy caught her breath and prolonging a small coughing fit to give herself time to think she finally spluttered

"I'll ring you when I get there and give you the number."

CHAPTER 11

OLIVER WANDERED SADLY across the rough ground and hoisted his back-pack higher. Lilly had run out with him but he had sent her back; he wanted to be quite alone. It was hardly the time of year to go trekking, especially on the moor but his emotions were in turmoil and he needed time to think. The carpet of heathers which only recently had still held its bloom was now turning to a dull and brownish green, stunted windswept naked trees stood starkly against the grey sky and the granite rocks of the tor glowered like malevolent giants. He had left at sunrise, his father's gun in its case slung across his shoulders and his first meal in the pack. Thereafter he would do his usual: foraging and hunting whilst he tried to make sense of what was happening between him and Sandy. Gradually the grey wisps of early morning mist had dispersed and a pale sun attempted to break through the cloud only to be ushered back in again like a wayward child. The January days were short and probably the most miserable days of the year and now the more so as he thought of first Susie and now Sandy both appearing to reject him. What was wrong with him that neither of them could commit themselves to him? When Sandy had told him she wasn't coming back yet, his immediate first thought was what had he done to upset her? Following on from this thought was the uncomfortable feeling that the presence of David had something to do with it. She had made it very clear that she didn't want to see him but why? And what had she done with him when she was in Mauritius? Oliver couldn't bear the thought that she had had a relationship with David or that she still had feelings for him, were her protestations to June lies? Tim had told Oliver about the man and his pursuit of Sandy on the island, he had re-assured Oliver that Sandy couldn't stand him however good looking and rich he was. But was she secretly seduced by his money and his looks and the fact that he could give her a better lifestyle than Oliver could? If that was what she wanted, then she'd better just get on with it and stop torturing him!

On reaching the first of his planned resting places at the foot of a small tor he slung his pack on the ground and slumped down beside it. As he unwrapped his sandwich remarking to himself that the only blessing the winter held was the lack of mosquitoes, a little field mouse scuttled past his feet. He threw it a crumb but it darted off as quickly as it had come. *I'll call it Sandy* he scowled. Maybe it would have been better had they just remained mates. He almost wished they had – almost.

Oliver didn't intend to trek far into the moor or to stay away for long as there was work to be done on the farm and now he had taken on more of the running of things he took the responsibility seriously. Just a few days away to get his head straight and then hopefully Sandy would be back and he could find out what if anything was wrong with her. However, the moor drew him, as always, into its spell and after eating his lunch he heaved the pack on to his shoulders and set off once again. As he strode on his spirits rose slightly as the dull light which coated the moor in a grey gauze soon brightened and a slightly cold but refreshing breeze shooed the remaining clouds over the horizon to drop their rain elsewhere. Gradually the sun rose to its low winter height and shadows, though still elongated, gave emphasis to the sunlit grasses and heather and relinquished to the moor its tableau of subtle hues. Glancing up at the tor, Oliver watched the quartz and mica in the granite fissures sparkle against the blackness of the tourmaline as the rays fell on the rock; jewellery for giants and made by nature alone. He had planned his route to take him nowhere near the places which had unpleasant memories and initially following the clear stream of the Dart he had headed north, away from the high ground of Dartmoor from whose treacherous, sodden mass of bogs the major rivers flowed. The Fox Tor Mire was one in particular he wished to give a wide berth to, it being probably the most dangerous area of the moor. Oliver's path led him to where the ground was firm with rocky outcrops and scrubby grasses. In the distance, Buckland Beacon surveyed a 360 degree panorama. He finally flopped down to rest just before the sun began its all too rapid descent. Having reached higher ground not too far away from the beacon he was able to see the vastness of the moor as it seemed to roll on and on as if it had no end. The small clouds scudding along in the fresh breeze created a moving picture on the heath as mauves turned momentarily to charcoal grey and then back to a seemingly brighter mauve. In the distance the bright green of sphagnum moss glowed in the sinking sunlight, its inviting colour belying its cruel contents. Oliver unpacked his tent and lit his cooking fire. As he settled down to his usual routine he felt the stresses of the past few days recede, wrapping his parka closely around him and pulling up the hood over his woolly hat he skewered his small game bird; an early morning shot had nabbed him his supper, and rotating it slowly over the fire he blanked from his mind the rest of the world.

George and Tim sat in the barn on the bales of straw in the same positions as they had when both apologising for their wives' behaviour; it seemed a lifetime ago that June and Alice had nearly come to blows over Paul. This time it was their children who were causing the anxiety. Tim told George of Oliver's visit and of his own concern for Sandy.

"I don't know what's got into her except that I think it's something to do with that damned David."

"Oli's pretty low, he's gone off for a few days, it's been quite some time since he's felt the need to go out on the moor. But I must say I think he's over-reacting, I'd be surprised, very surprised if your Sandy was playing him along or two-timing him. I'd say that was well out of character, though of course I don't know her as well as you do."

"No, you're right, I'd stake my life on it. Sandy's straight."

"Yes, that's what I like about her, you get what you see." George threw away the stalk of straw he was chewing, shivered a little in the cold open sided barn and pulling his coat around him invited Tim to come and help milk the goats. "You know, I reckon old Daisy's missing Paul, she hasn't been giving so much milk recently. Silly old fool, aren't I?"

Ever since Sandy had told them all about June's revelation and her regrets over her treatment of Paul, Tim had been uneasy. Their relationship had ended in a vitriolic way and he had walked away with relief to be free from June's callousness. However, now that he knew her reasons he needed to speak with her and to try to understand why she had kept her fears to herself all these years. Also, he asked himself, do I still care for her or have we between us destroyed all that we had for over thirty years? Then there was Sandy; what was going on with that girl? Tim decided to invite himself to June's over the weekend that Sandy would be away. This would allow them to be honest and more open with each other than if they had an audience, albeit an empathetic one. They could also discuss their daughter and why she was behaving so cruelly to Oliver. Tim felt a surge of annoyance with June when he thought of Sandy. She had not told him about David's visit and Sandy's reaction to it. He had had to get that third hand when June had mentioned it casually to Oliver almost as an afterthought. Honestly, sometimes that woman was so vague at times!

June's reaction to Tim's suggested visit was double edged; she knew that she still loved this big cuddly man but was frightened that she would be unable to stop herself begging him to come back. He was visiting purely to put things straight in his mind and to heal a few wounds, she knew that. He was not coming for reconciliation. She wondered whether it was such a good idea, she did not need to be hurt again and that was what would surely happen either way.

He arrived on Saturday morning instead of the Friday evening that she had hoped for. He parked his car in the driveway and she saw him smooth his hair in the driver's mirror – his blonde wavy mop which was sadly turning white, and just as she had when Sandy came for the first time, she found that she was trembling. Tim didn't unload any luggage. So, he obviously was not intending to stay. June forced herself to be calm and smiling a welcome she invited him in. They sat drinking coffee in the sitting room in front of the fire, neither saying very much other than the usual enquiries as to their wellbeing.

It wasn't exactly an uncomfortable meeting but neither was it very relaxed. June hopped up every few minutes to get more biscuits or to refill the percolator until Tim said

"For goodness sake woman, can't you stay still for a moment?" Momentarily June was hurt by his apparent impatience and flushed with embarrassment she resumed her seat. "You always were a fidget, just like your daughter." He continued with laugh.

"No I haven't changed much in that aspect over the last year, except," she paused, searching for words, "except that in other ways I am a completely different person." Tim knew what she was referring to and was pleased that she had introduced it rather than him.

"Yes, Sandy told me. You have no idea how much it matters to everyone, even though Paul is no longer an issue the fact that you were able to admit to your mistakes takes a lot of courage."

"I was wrong, so terribly wrong. I just couldn't back down, it was as though I were possessed or something, I don't want to think about the bitch I was then," she dropped her gaze as Tim looked to be about to agree "don't say it Tim, please." Tim pondered how to approach her anguish when Sandy was born and why she hadn't confided in him. But there was no need as June, pre-empting him continued "I wish I'd told you at the time but I was so frightened that you'd think I was to blame if Sandy hadn't been normal." Tim started to speak but she held up her hand and stopped him "I know she was perfect and that silly nurse had frightened me unnecessarily but it lodged in my mind and I couldn't shake it off. I loved you so much I couldn't have coped if you had turned against me. But in the end, you did, didn't you and not for the reason I had feared, but quite the opposite!"

"I'm sorry June, sorry for all the hurt that has been inflicted on us all. But if only you'd trusted me and talked to me..."

"Is it too late?" June asked querulously. "Is there any way back?" She bit her tongue, she had been determined not to ask him and immediately a chill crept over her for she knew his answer.

"I don't know." He tried to see her as the woman he had loved but the anger and spite he had witnessed remained fixed in his mind. "Our feelings are still too raw, give it time." It was all the reassurance he could manage to give her. He wanted to leave but didn't want to hurt her any more than he had already, so he suggested they went for a stroll in the park. He just needed to get out in the open and away from June's home whose contents spoke of their years together, the furniture they had bought, the pictures on the walls – everything spoke of a married couple but like a photograph from which one person had been torn the scene was incomplete. June excused herself purportedly to visit the bathroom but Tim saw a glistening in her eyes as the firelight flickered across her face when she rose from her seat. Pushing his own sadness to the back of his mind he cleared the cups away and had his coat on when she returned.

They walked side by side, unspeaking and with a pertinent gap between them, until they reached the benches by the duck pond where Tim beckoned her to sit.

"June, what is going on with Sandy?" She gave a small start and without looking at him directly she answered.

"Nothing as far as I know. Just that she wants some time to herself." Tim had known June long enough to know when she wasn't being wholly truthful and this time he wasn't going to let it pass. Sandy was both of theirs and not June's sole domain. Tim replied angrily

"You didn't tell me about David, did you? Is Sandy seeing him?" He stood up and faced June. "Don't you think Oliver deserves more consideration from Sandy? What the hell is she playing at – cock teasing?!"

"Hang on Tim, that's harsh. You know Sandy has never been like that, she either likes or doesn't like a boy and she doesn't play them off against each other." Although June was concerned about Sandy and her sudden retreat from the farm and Oliver she jumped to her defence immediately.

"Has she talked to you about Oliver? He was very disappointed when she said she had to stay with you longer than she had promised but being a decent bloke he didn't make a fuss. Come to think of it, what was your hospital appointment for?"

"Oh, nothing much, just my varicose veins." June flushed as she lied yet again "No, forget I said that. I can't keep on telling fibs for Sandy, she asked me to make up some complaint as an excuse for her staying longer and though I said I would I wasn't happy about it I can tell you. To be quite honest I am as much in the dark as you are about her feelings." June shivered; a light but cold wind had blown up and she tucked her hands deeper into her pockets.

"Let's go back home, I can't have this conversation here when I'm freezing half to death." Tim turned his collar up and rubbed his hands together.

"You're right. It was a stupid idea when you've a log fire at home." They walked back in near silence stopping at the corner shop for a few things June needed and Tim bought a bottle of wine to have with lunch. He was relieved that June's move to her new house was well away from their old home as the last thing he wanted was well-wishing neighbours' assumptions and knowing glances.

The fire was indeed a welcome sight and Tim suggested they had a sherry as an aperitif. June had hardly sipped her sherry before Tim launched into his cross-questioning again.

"Okay, so when's she due back? I need to talk to her and so does Oliver. George thinks the sun shines out of her backside but I am bloody furious; that lad is the best boy she's ever met, he has looked after her without making any demands and she's treating him with contempt!"

At that moment the 'phone rang in the hall and June hurried to answer it hoping it was Sandy.

"Mum?" Sandy's voice shook as she spoke. "Is Dad with you?"

"Yes, love and he wants to speak to you." There was silence. "Sandy, are you still there?" The pips went on the line and June waited for Sandy to put more money in but the dialling tone cut in and the connection was lost.

"She'll probably 'phone back and when she does, get her number so *you* can ring *her*." Tim instructed June as she hovered in the hall. Somehow, she knew that Sandy would not ring again until she thought Tim had left.

There was something very wrong about Sandy's visits to this invisible friend of hers and Tim was sure June knew more than she was telling.

"Do you actually know who she is visiting? Is it someone we

have met?" He held June's gaze as she had to admit that she hadn't asked. Why hadn't she asked?

"Is she seeing David?"

"Oh, Christ Tim stop nagging me. I don't know. I'll ask her when she comes home." She added heatedly. "She can't stand the man so why on earth do you think she's seeing him?"

"If it isn't him why hasn't she told you where she's going and who she's with? My God woman you haven't even got a 'phone number for her."

"She said she'd let me have it when she got there, she's an adult Tim and I've already learned my lesson for trying to control her haven't I?!" June was very flushed both with anger and embarrassment. "Just leave it will you, I will do my best to find out what's going on but it's probably absolutely nothing and she's just having some time to think and to make sure she's doing the right thing with Oliver." The tension was steadily growing between them and Tim began to regret taking June to task over Sandy, her last comment had pulled him up short. She wasn't Sandy's warder and what Sandy did with her life was her own affair. However, he still couldn't understand why she was treating Oliver so badly. To lighten the tone of their conversation he suggested that they might have lunch at the local before he left saving June the trouble of cooking. June was near to tears, she had thought Tim was coming to ease the hurts and hopefully, to renew their relationship albeit on a platonic level but he had hardly addressed it, merely crashed in with questions and accusations as though he were talking to one of his employees who had failed to complete an assignment.

"No I don't feel hungry, if you want to get home before dark you'd better be off soon." She rose abruptly from her chair and left the room before he could answer.

June was washing the coffee cups in the kitchen when he found her, she barely turned from the sink as he spoke.

"June, I'm sorry, I didn't mean to put you through the third degree but you must agree that Sandy is behaving out of character and surely you want to know why as much as I do?"

"Yes of course I do!" She spun round spraying water from the dishcloth in her hand. "I said I'd find out if I can, is that enough? Now I've got things to do, so unless you have anything more to discuss maybe you'd better go." Tim saw himself out with a heavy heart knowing he had made a complete mess of the whole meeting.

⌒ ◡ ⌒

Sandy put the 'phone down when she heard the pips. It wasn't that she had no more change but she couldn't bear to talk to Tim – what could she say? He was the man she loved most in the world but he was angry with her, she knew that her behaviour seemed callous and unreasonable to everyone else but she couldn't explain it to them. She made her way slowly to David's flat and rang the bell.

"Welcome back." He grinned at her. "Have you seen sense yet?"

Sandy had to try one last attempt to find some tiny bit of decency in him, she had considered many approaches from anger to pleading. But in her heart, she knew that he would not let go no matter how she presented her case.

"Would you like to eat out tonight or shall I cook you one of my splendid meals?"

"David, I don't really care about eating. All I want to do is to beg you to let me get on with my life and to drop all the threats you've made. Please?"

"And why should I do that when you've only given me one night of you? My price is higher than that."

"What is your price David? To have me prostituted to you? I made the mistake of trusting you once, no, twice, and both times you have manipulated me and then double crossed me. I don't want to make any more bargains with you. I just want you to stop!"

"I don't want a prostitute, I want a wife. That is your only solution, marry me."

"But why? Why do you want to marry me when you know I hate you?"

"Because I love you. Do you think I would waste all this effort just to get you to sleep with me a couple of times?"

"I repeat, bollocks! You don't love me, you're just messing with me and enjoying every minute of it."

"No, I'm serious, if you agree to marry me everything I have on you would be obsolete, I can't have scandal linked with my family name."

Sandy didn't know what to say or do. How could she marry David when she loved Oliver? But would Oliver still want her after this? No, he definitely would not, she was defiled and had deceived him. He would never trust her again. When she assessed the reasons for her actions they sounded feeble and immature. Oliver would immediately ask why she hadn't told him about David's threats, and then those pictures, how would she ever be able to face him again after he'd seen them? Whatever way she looked at it, she had destroyed everything. She had to get away now, somewhere to be alone and to think about what to do.

"I'm leaving."

"You've only just arrived. Surely you're going to stay the night?"

"No, I must go now." Sandy shrugged his hand from her arm and walked out of the door. She didn't take the train immediately but wandered around Hyde Park in a dreamlike state. Was all this really happening? Sandy's initial distrust of his professed 'love' for her was as strong as ever. She very much doubted if he was capable of loving anyone. As for that weird offer of marriage; Sandy couldn't think why he had made it other than to tease her into considering the safety it would give her only to withdraw it with a sneer. Sandy sobbed a laugh; trusting David was like trusting the troll under the bridge.

She rang June from the station saying she would be coming home that night but not to wait up as it would be the late train. She sat on a bench in the park and huddled in her coat against the damp chill in the air she tried to think what she should do. The night began to draw in and still she remained as though frozen in time on the bench, a decision had to be made and she had to decide what it was going to be. Finally, she wandered to the station and caught the train to take her home. Her home station was quiet and deserted and as the carriages rolled away into the distance she stood for a while in the silence left by their absence. Her life had to be rewritten. There would be no more Oliver or the farm, she would have to tell him it was over, he did not deserve to be hurt any more than she had already hurt him.

CHAPTER 12

AT HER HOME, HILDA HAZLETT was deciding whether to visit the cemetery and chance meeting the unpleasant neighbour or whether to give it a miss for a week or two in the hope that it would put an end to her being scrutinised. *I'm so sorry Sally*, she thought, it would be the first week since her friend's death that she hadn't taken her flowers, with the exception of the time when they had become ruined in the storm. No matter what the weather she had religiously visited the graves and spent a minute or two talking to the mother and son who over the years she had come to love so much. Instead, she wandered into her garden and picked the flowers she would have taken to the graves and placed them in a vase on her table. "There," she said "I haven't forgotten you."

At the cemetery, a man and woman stood by the graves. The man nodded, noted something in a book and left. The woman stayed for a while, a satisfied expression on her face, then she too turned and left.

Oliver returned to the farm with his mind made up. He would visit Sandy at June's if she did not come back to the farm this week. He must know one way or the other what she wanted. Throwing himself back into work he tried to put all thoughts of her from his mind. What a fool he had made of himself, they should have remained mates and then she could do whatever she wanted to in her private life. Once two people have taken that short but vital step into a relationship everything between them changes. Becoming mates again was not an option. If she didn't want him then they would have to part completely. The thought of Sandy staying on the farm again without a commitment to him was unbearable. He felt the warmth of his own tears as they fell.

Early Monday morning the 'phone rang, Sandy had been awake for hours but remained in her bedroom feigning sleep; she didn't want to face the day. June called up the stairs

"Sandy love, it's Oliver on the 'phone. Are you awake?"

"*Oh Christ*!" Sandy buried her head under the pillow, *I can't bear it!*

"Sandy?" June called again.

"Alright, I'm coming Mum." She flung on her dressing gown and stumbled down the stairs, taking the receiver from her mother she indicated with a look that she wanted privacy. June took the hint with a little smile and went upstairs to make the beds. *Oh, Mum how wrong you are.*

"Hello Oli, how are you?" She grimaced at her banal greeting.

"Sandy when are you coming home?" Oliver went straight to the point. "I thought you wanted to be with me."

"Oh Oli I do – but..."

"But what Sandy?"

"But I can't Oli. I'm sorry." Sandy's throat ached with restrained grief.

"Why can't you? What's happened to you?" Oliver's voice was thick with emotion and a hint of anger. "No don't answer me now, I'm coming to see you." Oliver rang off immediately without allowing her to reply.

Oh, Jesus bloody Christ! The time had come as she knew it would when she had to tell him goodbye.

Oliver placed the receiver back on the hook and slumped down on the chair his head in his hands. On hearing Sandy's refusal to come back his stomach had clenched and nausea swamped him. She wasn't coming back to him. She must have had second thoughts, or was there someone else? Oliver couldn't believe that Sandy could double cross him, everything about her character up until now had been blatantly on the surface. If she was angry everyone knew and kept out of her way. If she was sad the clouds enveloped all around her. But since she had gone to London to meet her friend she had been closed to him, there was no doubt in Oliver's mind that these visits were the cause of this and he was going to find out what was going on, whether it hurt him or not, even if it completely destroyed their friendship. His grief mixed with anger and he stormed out into the overcast day and made his way to the barn where they had kissed deeply and recognised their love for each other.

It had seemed too good to be true. If only I could put the clock back, I'd never have kissed her. First Susie and now Sandy had rejected him. He knew that was what was going to happen when he saw her. Maybe he should just ring her and spare the pain of a face to face for both of them. *No damn it, I deserve better than that, why should I let her off so lightly?*

A little cold wet nose and a gentle lick on his hand made him jump.

"Oh, hello Lil' have you come to find me?" He ran his big hand over her hot little head and tickled her behind the ears. "I shall be losing you as well won't I? Not that you've seen much more of your mistress than I have, I wonder if she remembers she owns you at all?" Again, this was so out of character for Sandy; Lilly was her special friend, she hated being away from her but it had been weeks now and she never mentioned Lilly in their 'phone calls or asked how she was and was she missing her? Oliver stood up with firm resolution; he was going to pay Sandy a visit and take Lilly with him and he was going today.

⌢ ‿ ⌢

After a few weeks had passed, Hilda decided that she would once again visit the cemetery and hope this time to be left alone. The same bus driver welcomed her aboard with a wide smile.

"Haven't seen you for a while, have you been away?"

"Oh no, nothing as exciting as that." As she took her seat near the driver she pondered over what she wanted to ask him. Then, leaning round the partition she said "Did you ever notice a woman in a raincoat getting on and off at the same time as me?"

"Hmm, let me think now, it's a pretty quiet route this one so I should remember." Indicating to let a lorry overtake him his attention was distracted for a minute or so, then "Yes, where was I?" Hilda was by chance the only passenger on the bus as it was nearing the end of the route and the driver was curious about her question, why did she sound so worried? He pulled into a lay-by and turned off the engine.

"We're early. I can spare a few minutes." He left his seat and sat across the aisle from Hilda. "Now m'dear, let's start again. You asked about a woman who travelled with you."

"No, not *with* me but at the same time as me. She got off when I did and back on when I did. But you wouldn't know about the return journey, your other driver does it, doesn't he?"

"Yes, that's right. But I do have some idea of the woman you mean. I remember seeing her go in through the gates behind you just as I was pulling off. I didn't pay it any attention, why should I?" He looked kindly at the elderly lady in her neat suit and grey hair worn in an immaculate bun. She had her little brooch pinned to the lapel, as always and her hands were clad in soft grey leather gloves which matched her shoes. *He thought she must have been quite a little beauty when she was young.* He wondered if she were widowed as she always came alone, were there any children to care for this woman to whom he had taken a liking. She reminded him of his paternal grandmother, the one who always laid the tea table with damask linen and napkins and who made him and his brothers sit up straight for tea. Unlike his other gran who was big and buxom and cuddly, easy going and fun loving. He had loved them both in completely different ways. This lady sitting in the bus with him was elderly and vulnerable, but she commanded respect and, he noticed, she spoke in an educated way and didn't drop her aitches the way he did. However, he could see that she was nervous and he wanted to pick her up in his big arms and care for her.

"I know it's none of my business but why do you want to know if I've seen her?" Hilda didn't really know how to explain to this chubby gentle man why she had asked.

"To be quite honest I can't explain properly it's just that I wondered if you had seen her coming here whilst I've not?"

"Yes, indeed I have!" She was here the first week you didn't come. She had a younger man with her, I assumed it was her son maybe visiting the husband's grave or some other relation."

"Hmm I see. And was that the last time she came?"

"Yes, to my knowledge she's not been again." He glanced at his watch "Crikey, look at the time, I must get going. Are you alright?" Hilda had gone a little pale but she nodded her head and assured him that she was fine.

"Thank you very much, er, I don't know your name."

"It's Bob luv, and you are?"

"Hilda, Hilda Haslett."

"It's a pleasure meeting you m'dear. Anything I can do for you just ask." With that he clambered back into the driving seat and a hiss of brakes they continued on the journey.

On the one hand Hilda was relieved that the neighbour no longer haunted Paul and Sally's graves, but on the other, the presence of another person disturbed her. Whatever was the woman up to?

⌒ ‿ ⌒

"Dad can you spare me for the rest of the day?" Oliver sought out George in the goat shed. "I want to drive up to see Sandy."

"Oh course, just a tick and I'll pack you some meat and cheese to take for them."

"Thanks Dad, but I don't think it's going to be that kind of visit." George looked up and noticed Oliver's troubled face, *Oh dear, not Sandy as well as Susie.*

"I don't think I'll be staying long. I'm just giving Sandy a chance to break it off. I'll take Lilly with me and leave her there."

"Don't be too hasty my lad, there may be other reasons why she's keeping away. Give her a chance to explain herself before you write it all off."

"Okay Dad, but I'm pretty sure that's what she wants."

Oliver, with Lilly sitting alertly on the passenger seat beside him set off to seal his fate. As he drove across the moor he recalled all they had been through together and how they both had promised to remain mates for life. But that had changed now. In spite of, no, because of his newly found love for Sandy they would part for ever.

Sandy skulked in her room all morning refusing lunch and pleading with her mother to leave her alone as she had a headache. This was the wrong move as June fussed over what sort of headache it was. Was it behind her eyes? Did she have any flashing lights? Did she want some pain killers? In the end, Sandy shouted

"For the last time, Mum just leave it, you're just making it worse!"

June returned downstairs hurt and worried. This wasn't right. Sandy wasn't the girl she knew any more. For the last few months she had been un-communicative and rarely laughed or even smiled. She seemed to have lost her spark, she didn't even want to paint. June started to worry that Sandy was ill; her lack of energy and her decreasing appetite could be symptoms of glandular fever or any number of illnesses. She would speak to Tim and probably ask Mike to pop in, just to give her the once over. Sandy would be angry but she couldn't help that, her daughter's health was more important.

Oliver didn't say when he was coming and Sandy was frantic with trepidation that he would come immediately. However, he usually thought things through before acting on them so maybe she would have a day or so to gird herself up to the ultimate goodbye. With that in mind she finally came downstairs into the kitchen and poured herself a glass of milk which she took outside into the garden. Although the air was chilly little green shoots were poking out of the ground and the buds on the trees looked ready to open, the snowdrops were already going over making way for crocuses and daffodils. She wandered over to the seat beneath the laburnum and brushed a few leaves from it then sat turning her face to the mild warmth of the thin sunshine. How was she going to look Oliver in the eye after what she had done? How was she going to tell him to go when she loved him so much? She watched the goldfinches and blue tits flitting back and forth from the feeder to the hedge and the sparrows gathering grass and twigs for their nests; spring was the season for re-birth, but for Sandy it was the winter of her life.

From the garden, Sandy heard a car door slam and her heart leapt. A few moments later June called through the back door "Sandy, Oliver's here!" *Maybe that will perk her up* she thought. "Come on through Oliver, Sandy's in the garden. I'll put the kettle on. You are staying for dinner – yes?" Sandy heard Oliver's quiet voice thanking June for the offer of coffee and then there he was, standing in the doorway. They looked at each other without speaking and Sandy desperately wanted to throw herself into his arms, but what would be the point of that other than to increase the final hurt? His face was flushed and his expression stern. He didn't smile or greet her but walked over to the seat and sat beside her.

"Hi."

"Hi." she answered. Neither knew where to start, they remained seated in silence until June came out smiling bearing three mugs of coffee and biscuits on a tray.

"Mind if I join you? It's a lovely day, isn't it? Good to see you Oliver." She plonked herself down on the seat next to them her face wreathed in smiles. "No doubt you'll be going back with Oliver won't you darling? Oh, look here comes Lilly." The little mongrel had put her tummy first and gobbled up the scraps June had put down for her and now she was all wags and 'I love you, play with me!'

Oliver bent down to smooth Lilly's head and quietly said in Sandy's ear

"Shall we take her for a walk?" Sandy nodded, there was no chance to talk with June there and it was going to be a difficult enough time even without an audience. They finished their coffees while June chatted on oblivious to the subdued mood of Oliver and Sandy. Putting the mugs back on the tray Oliver politely thanked June and in as cheerful a voice as he could manage said

"Come on then you two let's go for that walk in the park."

Lilly charged after the ducks as soon as she was off the lead and Sandy and Oliver trailed along behind her. Oliver broke the silence finally when they had reached the bench under the chestnut tree. Looking near to tears he took Sandy's hand in his and held it tightly.

"What's wrong my love? What have I done to upset you?"

"Oh Oli, you haven't done anything wrong. You've no idea how good it is to see you but it breaks my heart to look at you." Oliver frowned with confusion, this wasn't what he expected; he was sure that Sandy had gone off him completely yet here she was saying how good it was to see him. However, what did she mean by her heart breaking?

"I don't understand, why are you staying away from me? I miss you so much and so do Mum and Dad." Sandy looked away from him trying to control her shuddering breathing as she held back the desire to cry her heart out.

"Oli, I can't come back. I just can't. I'm sorry, truly I am so sorry." Oliver released her hand and stood up.

"I knew you were going to say that but why did you say you were pleased to see me when you obviously were not?" He walked away and rested his head against the rough bark of the chestnut, Sandy could see his shoulders heaving as he wept silently. She too allowed her tears to finally come; she wanted to hold him close and play with his curls again. She wanted to tell him everything and throw herself on his mercy, on his love for her, but that would be even more cruel than just telling him it was over, that she didn't love him. Oh how can she bring herself to utter those words?

"Oli, I'm sorry but I don't love you." she blurted out. Oliver spun round from the tree his eyes red and desolate.

"Obviously not!" he snapped, "No one does, apparently!" He scrubbed his hands across his face to wipe away the tears "What's wrong with me that both you and Susie dumped me before we had even made love?" On speaking those words, he broke down and sobbed. Never in her life had Sandy felt so responsible for someone's pain and grief and been so helpless to ease it. She wanted to retract her words and tell him she loved him and it was all a mistake but either way she knew she had lost him.

"Have you... have you met someone else?" Oliver managed to say amid his tears.

"No, I don't love anyone else Oli." She managed to sidestep the question, it was true, she didn't love anyone else in fact she hated the other man; that bastard David. She should confess everything to Oliver and their two families and maybe they would understand that she had only been trying to protect them all. It would make no difference now because she and Oliver could never be the same again but at least he would know that she did love him and would always do so. He would probably be disgusted with her but that would be better than him thinking it was his fault and that he was unlovable. Yes! I should tell him everything right now; her mind was made up. Looking at his strong back with the ginger curls spilling over his collar the urge to hold him in her arms became irrepressible and she gave into it. Reaching out to him she touched him gently on the shoulder

"Oli..." she began, but he stiffened at her touch and pulled away "Don't Sandy. Don't touch me I can't stand it. I'm going home."

"But Oli please just listen I want to tell you everything."

"If you're going to tell me that you're sorry but you have met someone else don't bother, it's quite obvious to me. It's over isn't it Sandy?" He strode away back towards the house.

"Oli please wait, I have to get Lilly. Please wait!" She called for the dog who was busy in the undergrowth "Lilly come here now!" But by the time she had fastened the lead on her collar Oliver was gone. He reached the house without waiting for her or saying goodbye to June and got in his car and drove away.

George watched the car drive slowly up to the house. From the window, he could see that Oliver was alone, no Sandy and no Lilly perched up beside him. His heart sank for Oliver, it appeared that he was right after all and their relationship was over. He dug deep to find a small inkling of hope, maybe she would come down later, maybe she had a commitment back at June's. But one look at Oliver's blotchy face as he approached the house told him that this was a futile hope.

"Don't say anything Dad." Oliver begged him as he entered. "Just pour me a beer would you?" They sat quietly together for some long time before Oliver spoke again. "I've had it with girls, I just don't know what they want anymore. I feel like I've been punched in the stomach, she told me in no uncertain tones that she didn't love me – there's no answer to that is there?"

"I suppose not, but didn't you talk it through? Did she explain anything about what had made her change her mind?"

"No. Well, she started to, but by that time I was beyond listening and quite frankly I really didn't want to know." He put his head in his hands and groaned "What's the matter with me Dad? Why can't anyone love me?"

"Son, there's nothing the matter with you." He got up and put his arm around Oliver's shoulder "Sandy is a great girl and we all love her but perhaps she's a bit too independent to settle down just yet. Don't break ties with her altogether, give her time." Oliver looked up at his father and his look of pain was so deep that it brought tears to George's eyes.

"Okay Dad, I'll give her time but I don't want to see her for a long while yet. If she wants me, and genuinely wants me, I'm here but I'm not chasing her." Oliver put his glass on the table. "I'm going for a bath, I feel dirty."

June heard the car drive off and assuming they were going for a drive or popping to the shops to get wine for dinner she took very little notice. However, she did think it a little inconsiderate of them not to ask her if she needed anything. Glancing out of the window she was surprised to see Sandy running up the road half dragging Lilly on her lead as she tried to stop at every doggy smell. She went out to meet her but Sandy had stopped short of the empty drive and was standing staring down the road. She then turned around and walked slowly away from the house.

"Sandy!" June called after her, "Where are you going and where's Oliver?" Sandy ignored her and continued back in the direction from which she had come.

By late afternoon Sandy still hadn't returned. June paced the house anxiously. It was obvious that something had gone wrong between them; Oliver leaving abruptly and Sandy's behaviour gave credence to this. Oliver was not the sort to not bid her goodbye, he was a well-mannered young man. Whatever had gone wrong? June put on her coat and went in search of her daughter. There were very few places Sandy could go on foot which were away from people, which June guessed is where she would want to be. Knowing how Sandy needed space and solitude when she was upset June made for the park. It didn't take her long to find Sandy, she saw a little figure huddled on the bench under the chestnut tree where she and Tim had sat on his visit. It was the quietest place in the park and gave onto a small copse behind, where the old Lebanese cedars spread their dark branches and the Scots pines stood tall and thin against the skyline. Sandy looked up as June approached but made no move to meet her. Lilly was sitting beside her and gave a little wag as June, puffing a little from her hurried walk sank down onto the seat. She expected to see Sandy in tears or with some evidence that she had been crying but her eyes were dry and her expression hard.

"Sandy my love come on home, it's getting cold." June took Sandy's hands and rubbed some warmth into them as she used to when Sandy was a child and had played in the snow for too long. Sandy allowed her mother to take her home. She was walking in a trance, uttering not a single word. What was there to say? Everything or nothing?

June prepared the evening meal, which they ate in silence. June for once didn't probe but allowed Sandy the time to talk should she want to. After Sandy had moved the food around her plate a little, taking one or two morsels of food she put down her cutlery.

"Oli and I are finished Mum. If you don't mind I'm going to bed."

June waited for an hour or so until she thought Sandy would be asleep then she 'phoned Tim.

"I was on the point of ringing you." he said as soon as she

spoke, "I've heard it from George, Oliver is desolate, whatever happened?"

"I have no idea Tim, she disappeared for ages after he had left and she's hardly said a word since."

"Well she's done it good and proper this time, George says that Oliver has sworn himself to bachelorhood unless she comes back to him. I don't suppose there's any chance of that is there?" Tim's voice rose hopefully as he asked, he had found true friendship with the Tregowans and was extremely distressed that his daughter had hurt them so much. "I'm going over there later and I'll pack up Sandy's things, her easel and paints etcetera and bring them up at the weekend," he added "that is unless I hear otherwise, you never know, they may have made up by then."

Sandy wasn't asleep. She lay on the bed trying to decide what to do. Her emotions seemed to have atrophied; she felt neither sadness nor anger, just a flatness over which she had no control. When Oliver had turned away and left her behind Sandy knew that she had destroyed any feelings he had for her. He had turned up before she had thought what she should do. If only she had told him everything and admitted what she had done he might still have walked away but he would have known why she had done it and that she still loved him. Now it was too late.

She heard her mother getting ready for bed and hoped she wouldn't come in to see if she was alright. However, when June's footsteps continued past her door she felt a surge of regret.

Sandy quietly crept downstairs and from her mother's bureau she took a pad of writing paper and a pen. 'Dear Oliver,' she began. For the next hour or more she wrote everything down. From the beginning to the end. Sandy re-read the letter and when she reached the account of her drunkenness and the subsequent photographs she scrubbed it out over and over so that no one could possibly decipher it. She knew that without this final blackmail her reasons for doing what she did would appear tenuous and implausible but she just couldn't bear to tell him in writing. She couldn't bear to tell him at all. It was an inadequate letter but it was all she could do. She would post it on her way to London Saturday morning, he would probably get it on Monday or Tuesday. She then 'phoned David.

Tim and Alice sadly packed Sandy's things in the car, Oliver was nowhere to be seen.

"This isn't goodbye," Alice hugged Tim "you know you're welcome any time. I know Oliver would agree." Tim thanked her and set off. He was hoping to have some time with Sandy to talk things over and to help to put her life in order. She needed to get on with her career and she needed to find work. He already supported June completely and funds were tight, that was the reason he only bought the tiny cottage for himself after all the money from the sale of their old house had gone on June's new one. *What a damned mess our lives are!* He arrived as early as he could as June had told him Sandy was going away that weekend and if he possibly could, he wanted to persuade her to stay home and have a sensible talk. But June had told Sandy he was coming and she had left early saying she and her friend had something planned.

"Damn that girl!" Tim exploded, "I know she's avoiding me. Why did you tell her I was coming?"

"For goodness sake Tim, don't start badgering me before you even come indoors!" June hadn't forgotten the way he had cross-questioned her on his last visit.

"I need to know when she's going to get a grip and start earning her living. Apart from the fact that I would dearly like to know why she's been so cruel to Oliver."

"I don't think their relationship has got anything to do with us Tim, I haven't interfered and neither should you. But I agree she should get a job of some sort, it might settle her if she's got something to focus on." Together they unloaded the car and took things up to Sandy's bedroom.

"What's this?" June picked up the letter from the bed. "It's addressed to Oliver." She turned it over and saw that the flap was unsealed. As she lifted it to her lips to lick the gum Tim cried

"No don't seal it."

"It's private, Tim, I've never read any of Sandy's diaries or letters and I'm not going to now!" She licked it and sealed it. "I'll post it later when I've bought a stamp." She added as she tucked it into her apron pocket, "If it's of any interest to us no doubt George or Alice will tell us." Tim shrugged resignedly.

"Okay, do whatever you want, I am on the point of not caring anymore."

CHAPTER 13

"OH SHIT!" SANDY EXCLAIMED as she stood in the queue at the post office near the train station.

"I beg your pardon young lady!" An elderly man gave her a stern look, "That's not the language for a lady to use!"

"Sorry!" Sandy snapped back at him. She left the queue and rummaged deeper in her bag but the letter wasn't there. Had she dropped it on the train? Oliver had to know why she must do what she was about to do. She stormed out of the door swearing under her breath. Where had she left the bloody letter? *Oh Christ I think I left it in my room!* She had been undecided over which bag to take. Bearing in mind the amount she needed this time her usual back pack for weekends was too small. She remembered emptying everything out on the bed and re-packing it in the larger one. *I hope Mum doesn't find it.* Then with a start she remembered that she hadn't sealed it just in case she wanted to add more. With any luck June would post it without reading it first. The post would take a couple of days thereby giving her time to marry David at the registry office and then they would all be safe. But if she *did* read it and showed it to Tim it was a certainty that he would banging on David's door before the night was out.

Tim stayed for lunch, after which he mowed the lawn for June and did a few maintenance jobs, all the while thinking about his daughter who was avoiding him. They had been so close in Mauritius and all the time whilst she was at the farm. But since Christmas she had changed, become secretive and un-communicative. It didn't take much imagination to link this with the appearance of David and he wondered if in fact she *had* formed a relationship with him in Mauritius and on meeting him again her feelings for him had re-surfaced. If this were so she was a very dark horse as she had implied very strongly that she disliked him. Perhaps he had hurt her and had come to make it up? If this was the case why hadn't she come out with it and introduced him properly and why had she given Oliver to believe that she loved him? He found it hard to believe that Sandy was so callous as to lead Oliver on and then drop him, it was so unlike her. *Damn it all, we don't even know the bloke's surname!* Tim was sure that Sandy wasn't meeting a female friend on these weekends and he was annoyed with June for not pushing her for a contact 'phone number or an address. When he had finished the chores, he sat with June in the garden and drank tea in the early spring sunshine.

"I don't suppose you ever got a 'phone number for this friend of Sandy's, did you?" He didn't want to harangue June but he found it hard to keep the accusatory tone from his voice.

"No I didn't. She kept promising but never gave it to me. I'm sorry."

"I know she's been very secretive, it's not your fault." Tim softened his approach. "I think we have to do a bit of investigation. I know you don't like to intrude on her privacy but I do think we need to know where she is and why she is keeping it from us." June nodded in agreement.

"I think some of her college friends are in the address book, I'll get it and we can ring around."

"That's a start" Tim smiled at her, "but I think she's seeing David er... whatever his name is."

"But she was furious when he came here!" June exclaimed. "She sent him packing!"

"So she says, but I reckon there's more to it than meets the eye." Tim's face clouded when he added "What the devil has happened to that girl? She's damned near broken Oliver, he's been the best friend she's ever had, how could she treat him so badly?"

"*I* know!" June grasped his arm in her excitement of a possible line of enquiry "Why don't we contact Josie, she'll know whether Sandy and David are involved."

"Good idea, I'll ring her, hopefully she's at the same address. I'm sure I wrote the 'phone number down in my book when Sandy stayed on."

"What time is it in Mauritius? I don't want to ring her in the middle of the night." Tim tried to remember the time zones but he wasn't sure if he had them right "Oh never mind, I'll ring anyway she can always tell me to go away." He went to the car and brought in his brief case. He was a methodical man and even his briefcase was in order. "Ah here it is." He rifled through the pages and found the 'phone numbers for both the family planning office and Josie's flat. "I think I have to go through the operator" he said as he dialled 100. "Hello, I wish to place a call to Mauritius." He gave the number and after a little wait "It's ringing!" And it rang and rang.

"I'm sorry, there's no answer, did you wish to place another call?" the operator asked. Tim gave her the number of the office and waited whilst she attempted to connect him.

"Maybe she's at work, I've no idea what the time is there." The call was answered in French by a man with a strong Indian accent. Tim strove to remember his schoolboy French but other than 'bonjour' it had deserted him so he addressed the man in English and asked if he might speak to Josie Whitehouse who worked as an artist for them.

"I'm sorry but she has left," he paused and then he continued in a conspiratorial voice "there was a bit of, er, how do you call it – rumpty tumpty?"

"What do you mean – 'Rumpty tumpty'?"

"She was sexy with a married man!" he answered "You know – going to bed with him!"

"Oh, I see." Tim mouthed to June that she wasn't there. "Do you know where I can contact her?"

"No we don't have anything, sorry." The man rang off. Tim replaced the receiver with a crash.

"Well that's that idea gone for a burton! Your turn, try her friends." June 'phoned all the numbers she had but none of the girls had seen Sandy since she had left college. June and Tim exchanged despondent looks, Tim sighed "Any more ideas?"

Tim returned to his cottage later that evening leaving June feeling totally bereft, she went to Sandy's bedroom and suppressing her instinct not to look into her daughter's possession she began to search for any clues as to where she might be. She wished now that she hadn't posted the letter to Oliver when she took Lilly for a walk earlier, she would have opened it now and maybe the answer would be there. Tim had offered to deliver it by hand but she hadn't trusted him not to steam it open first. Having taken the moral high ground June now felt stupid. Tim only wanted what was best for everyone and yet again she had done the wrong thing. He must be exasperated with her. She wondered how he had put up with her all those years of their marriage.

Tim arrived back at the cottage with much the same thought. There was a time when he would have found June's daffiness endearing but now he found it just plain irritating. However, he recognised the fact that she was nervous around him now and consequently became flustered when trying to talk to him in case he became impatient with her. He resolved to be kinder when they next communicated, maybe in time they could get on again.

Sandy and David met with two of his friends as witnesses at the registry office, having procured a special licence and were married without ceremony. Sandy had refused to go with him to buy a new dress.

"I haven't worn a dress since that bloody cocktail party!" She stubbornly turned up wearing her jeans and boots.

"Well, Mrs Montgomery it wasn't that dreadful was it?" David led her to the Mercedes. "Now for the honeymoon!"

My God I hate you! Sandy would have cheered loudly were David to fall under a bus right then. The deed was done and her family and friends were safe. That was all she cared about now. As far as she was concerned, he could murder her tonight and she wouldn't try and stop him.

Now she had to tell her parents what she had done.

David said he had a surprise destination booked for their honeymoon which nicely coincided with his work. She didn't give a damn but she couldn't keep fighting him for ever. Marrying him had assured his silence regarding Paul and now she had to make the best of it. If she left him, his threat would still stand and all would have been for nothing. Though she still asked herself why he would want to marry someone who disliked him so much and what did he hope to gain by it? David was so devious that she couldn't hazard a guess at his intentions and when he had whispered in her ear at the registry office "now you belong to me" she had felt a shiver run up her spine.

The first thing Sandy needed to do when they returned to David's flat after leaving the registry office was inform her parents that she was married. Taking a deep breath, she dialled June's number. But June was walking Lilly and the 'phone went unanswered. Building herself up to a heated conversation with her father she then dialled him at the cottage, but he was driving home from June's and the 'phone went unanswered. David refused to let her keep trying and insisted that they go out to eat and 'celebrate' their union. By the time they returned home that night, he told her it was too late to ring them and she could do it in the morning.

"Come along darling we need to consummate our marriage!"

He almost forcibly dragged her into the bedroom.

By Sunday morning David had consummated their marriage more than once and he lay deeply asleep as she crept from the bed. Closing the door quietly behind her she rang her mother. *Why doesn't she answer?* Sandy began to feel very anxious about June, where was she? Was she alright? She should be up and about by now, it was past nine. Finally, she put the 'phone down; she wanted to talk to her mother before speaking to her father, June would be more understanding and prepared to listen and she hoped it would be an easier conversation. But, in reality, she knew that it was her father to whom she had become closest over the last two years and that it was guilt which was preventing her speaking to him.

David was stirring and she used that as an excuse to herself for not 'phoning Tim.

"Tomorrow we are going shopping for clothes for you. Nothing you've brought is suitable for our honeymoon." David faced her down. "No arguing. You'll need it when you know where we are going."

"Where *are* we going?" Sandy asked in a small voice. She didn't want to go anywhere, just hide away and hope it was all a bad dream. "I can't go anywhere until I've spoken to Mum. I have to let her know where I am and that I'm alright."

"You can do that later."

That evening Sandy tried to ring both her parents but neither answered and David refused to let her keep trying.

"I doubt they'll be that worried, you're not a child any more. Give it a break."

The plane took off at midday on Tuesday with the newly-weds on board in the first-class seats.

David was travelling as a diplomat on foreign business; just happening to take the wife along as well. There was no mention of honeymoon by the pilot as he welcomed him aboard, he nodded absently to Sandy and all but saluted David in the way that some men have of sucking up to other men in a position of influence. Sandy imagined how Josie would feel were she here as David's wife; she would be soaking up the glamour and clutching David's arm whilst smiling up at him adoringly. She sank further into her seat and turned her head to look out of the window as the plane taxied down the runway to take her to the bitter cold of Moscow.

Tim answered his 'phone late that evening to June who in a panicky voice told him that Sandy's passport was missing and that she seemed to have taken more clothing than she normally did for a weekend.

"Oh Tim, whatever is she doing?" June cried down the 'phone.

"I don't know but I'm going to find out. I'm sure she's with that David bloke, have you no idea where he lives?" June remembered him leaving his card with an address on it but Sandy had taken it and June's search of her room had revealed nothing other than the missing passport.

"All I know is that it was London but that doesn't help does it?"

"No, hardly!" he answered abruptly. "I'll spoil his pretty face when I catch up with him. And as for Sandy – well I can't understand her at all."

Was there no way they could find out firstly, what the damned man's surname was and secondly, where he lived? Tim could only think to enquire at the Foreign Office but they were very unlikely to give out information on one of their employees to a total stranger so he struck that off his list as an option. Then a thought occurred to him – Jeremy Small! Tim dialled Small's number and waited agitatedly drumming his fingers on the 'phone table. *Answer damn it!* Then finally a rather sleepy voice said "hello?"

"Oh Jeremy, I'm so sorry if I woke you but, good heavens is that the time?" He glanced at his watch – it was past midnight.

"Tim?" Jeremy recognised his voice, "Whatever is wrong?" Tim felt dreadful at waking him at such an hour but his anxiety and anger had taken hold.

"It's Sandy." He floundered as to where to start, "I'm sorry, look I'll ring you back later when you're up. There's nothing you can do at this time of night." But Jeremy was now wide awake and alert.

"No Tim, don't ring off! What's happened to her? I'm hardly going to go back to sleep now am I?"

"She's disappeared with her passport and I think I know who with but I've no idea how to find him. This sounds ridiculous I'm sorry." Tim took a deep breath, "May I come and see you tomorrow and explain everything properly?"

"Of course, first thing? Hang on, I'm free tomorrow. Why don't I come over to the farm and see you all, it's been a while since we all met up. The Tregowans will want to know if anything has happened to Sandy won't they?" Tim hesitated, "That could be a bit difficult, I can't explain now Jeremy, come to the cottage and in the meantime I'll ring George and ask if they would join us."

Tim rang June at seven o'clock when he was sure she would be up and explained his thinking that Jeremy may have links in the profession which could find out about David and his name and address and that he was expecting him and George and Alice later that morning.

"I haven't slept for worry." June sounded exhausted. "Please ring me Tim as soon as you know anything?" Her voice broke as she said goodbye.

True to his word, Jeremy turned up at the cottage at ten o'clock to find George and Alice already there. George had not mentioned anything to Oliver about Sandy, he merely said

"We're popping over to Tim's for coffee later, you can manage here on your own can't you Oli?"

"Sure, I'm fine." Oliver replied in a flat voice and continued with his breakfast.

Tim made coffee for everyone and began his plea for help. All Alice and George knew was that Oliver and Sandy had split up and although they were sorry that Sandy had made this decision they in no way had lost their affection for her. They listened in surprise as Tim recounted to them Sandy's regular trips to London following on from the one she had made shortly after agreeing to marry Oliver.

"I feel so ashamed on her behalf that she has treated you so thoughtlessly after all you've done for her." Tim said with downcast eyes. "I've lived for twenty-six years with those two women and I don't seem to have known either of them." He ran his hands through his hair which was already dishevelled from tossing and turning as he had attempted to get a little sleep. "I need to find her and get to the bottom of why she has been so secretive – she avoids even speaking to me on the 'phone and every time I go up there she disappears."

"That doesn't sound like the Sandy we know." George commented "So you think she's taken up with the fellow from Mauritius?"

"Yes and I've no idea who he is or where he lives!" He turned to Jeremy "This is where I need your help Jeremy, if it's in any way possible." Jeremy took a deep breath and blew it out slowly. "I don't know how I can help Tim, I never spoke to Sandy in any depth after she came back home."

"I was wondering if you knew anyone who might know this man." It embarrassed Tim to lean on Jeremy yet again but this concerned his daughter and he would go to any lengths to know she was safe. "We don't have a very sophisticated circle of friends and the Foreign Office, rightly so, won't hand out personal information to whoever asks for it will they?"

"You're right there, Tim. I'm just wracking my brains to call anyone to mind." He grunted and huffed as he thought, muttering

"No, he's dead... Oh he might... no debarred if I remember rightly... Hang on, there *is* one chap I was at university with, joined the Foreign Office as a sort of tea boy, father's influence... thick as pig shit. Hmm I wonder." His face brightened, "He used me as a sort of buffer; wasn't enjoying the course, found it too taxing for his tiny brain – just the sort for government employ!" he guffawed. "I can't recall his number as I haven't spoken to him since the last reunion a couple of years ago, but I *will* have it at home." He beamed at them all as though he had already solved to problem.

Just then there was a loud rapping at the door which made them all jump.

"Good God, who on earth is that trying to knock the door down?" Tim exclaimed "Oli do you think?" He hurried to the door thinking something serious had happened at the farm but when he opened it June was standing, Lilly on the lead beside her, in the little porch shaking like a leaf. Over her shoulder, Tim caught a glimpse of a taxi as it disappeared down the road.

"I caught the early train." she explained. "I couldn't bear it all on my own just waiting." She gulped back a sob "It took me back to those terrible months when she was lost." She suddenly looked angry instead of tearful "The cruel, selfish child!" Tim couldn't help but agree with her anger, he put his arm around her shoulders until she calmed down and then led her into the tiny sitting room where the others sat waiting. This was the first time that Alice and June had met since that night when they had rowed over Sandy going back onto the moor. For a moment there was a stiff silence, June stood in the doorway and looked about to retreat and Alice flushed with the awkwardness of the situation. George, as usual was the one to ease the mood, he got up and invited June to have his seat whilst he pulled a less comfortable dining chair from the table for himself.

"June, hello, let me introduce myself." Jeremy rose with an

exhalation of breath as he levered himself from the soft and very low armchair and extended his hand to June with a welcoming smile. "Jeremy Small, I'm very pleased to meet you at last." June took his warm hand and managed a small smile. Jeremy continued "Tim has told me what has happened and I'm going to try and help as best I can."

"Yes, Jeremy's got an old friend who works at the Foreign Office..." Tim began to explain.

"*Did* work, I'm not sure if he does any more." Jeremy interjected, "But if he can't help he may be able to put me on to someone who can, with any luck."

"Oh, Jeremy, thank you so much, I feel dreadful asking for help." June warmed to this giant of a man with a gentle hand-shake, "I can't understand what's got into her." She felt very small and humbled by the sight of Alice and George yet again rallying to help when in truth it should not be any concern of theirs. She thought back to the first visits to the farm when Sandy had been rescued by Oliver and found it hard to believe that she had been that person. She got up and trembling a little she approached Alice and in front of them all she reached out her hand to her saying

"Alice, I'm very, very sorry." Alice took her hand and held it for a few seconds then released it. Nothing more needed to be said; as their eyes met their maternal empathy allowed a line to be drawn through the past.

Jeremy looked on with a fond expression on his large face, to his chagrin he wasn't married and had no children, somehow it had just never happened. He noted the anguish of these parents and didn't envy them this but he envied the fact that they had children at all. He couldn't help that now; he was fifty years old and the chance had gone, instead, he thought in his big hearted way, he would be a big 'uncle' for them if nothing else. He pulled himself together, *soppy idiot*, and got back to the matter in hand.

"I'll get off home now and look up the number of dear old Scott and see what I can find out. But of course you have to consider that Sandy may not be with David but with an old friend from college, which is what she told you. And if she is with David she has obviously chosen to be so and she is an adult!" He looked apologetically at Tim and June "However, I will certainly try and help you track her down if only to know she's safe." He began to heave himself out of the chair, "Well I'll be off then."

Alice glanced at George who nodded at her subliminal message.

"Have lunch with us before you go, Tim, June, do you mind Jeremy delaying for an hour?" George asked. Then remembering that Oliver was in the dark at the moment he hastily added "Or perhaps we should go to the pub?" George would rather tell Oliver in private what was going on as he was low enough as it was and a great crowd turning up unexpectedly all talking about the girl he loved going off with some bloke would be extremely thoughtless.

"I wouldn't mind a pint and a quick snack if that's alright with you, I confess I left without my usual porridge this morning." Jeremy decided the matter for them and they trooped of to the King's Arms.

Bert served them quickly as he was expecting a large party for Sunday roast and needed the tables. They had a ploughman's and a drink each and then waved Jeremy off.

"Why don't Alice and I go home and have a little chat with Oliver, he needs to know, whether he wants to or not?" George suggested. "And no doubt you two have things to discuss as well." Tim and June went back to the cottage and the Tregowans to the farm. There to wait for news. As time wore on Tim and June ran out of conversation; their minds being focused only on Sandy there was nothing more to discuss. By tea time they were both fidgeting so much that June decided to leave.

"I'll go home Tim." June was aware of the accommodation in the cottage, there being only one bedroom they would either have to share or one would have to sleep on the settee.

"I'll run you to the station," Tim offered "I'd drive you back but I think one of us should be near a 'phone."

"I agree, it's alright Tim, I don't expect anything more from you." June had already once betrayed her longing for them to get back together and been brushed off, she had more pride than to let it happen again. Tim dropped her off at the station and hurried back home where he sat alone well into the night waiting for the 'phone to ring.

The following day passed with no contact from Jeremy or indeed Sandy. At eleven o'clock as he gave up hope for the day Tim rang June and told her to go to bed.

"Jeremy won't ring now, he knows we can't do anything tonight even if he did have any information." June sounded exhausted and Tim felt his anger at Sandy growing. After all that June went through during those months, thinking Sandy was dead, how could she do it to her mother again? The old Tim wanted to go to June and comfort her and love her as he would have done before, but he knew it was no good. Adversity might throw them back together but it had also once pulled them apart, he couldn't let that happen again.

"I expect we'll hear from him one way or another pretty soon. Try and get some sleep."

CHAPTER 14

"TIM, I'VE FOUND OUT HIS NAME AND ADDRESS! Have you got a pen ready?" Jeremy's voice boomed through the receiver.

"Yes, fire away." Tim scribbled the information down and read it back to check. "You're a star Jeremy, thanks so much." Already Tim was planning when to leave for London as he was saying goodbye. "By the way," he added, hoping Jeremy was still on the line, "did your man say anything about David, what he was like or anything, you know, whether he was in any way dangerous? I know that sounds preposterous but you never know do you?"

"No one ever *really* knows anyone Tim, but as far as I could glean from Scott, David is very pleased with himself and has contacts with influence. Clean slate, no wife beatings and a brilliant scholar. Oh yes, and he's very well off."

The quickest way for Tim to get to London was by train and he rang June to tell her that was what he planned to do. He persuaded her not to come as he wanted to meet David man to man. She reluctantly agreed after making him promise to be careful.

"Please Tim control your temper won't you? We don't know the full story yet." Next Tim rang the farm.

"Hello?" Oliver answered damn Tim thought, had George brought him up to date yet?

"Oli, it's Tim just to tell you I'm going to London." That seemed innocuous enough.

"I'm coming with you." Oliver answered immediately. George had obviously spoken to him. Tim was pretty sure this wasn't a good idea but didn't feel he was in a position to refuse him given his relationship with Sandy. However, he wished to go alone and Oliver's presence would immediately throw sparks into any confrontation with David. They were not even sure Sandy was with him and if accusations were thrown about and Oliver's temper got the better of him they could find themselves arrested. Jeremy had said David had contacts in high places and they had to tread carefully.

"Look Oliver, I'm coming over to the farm now and we'll discuss it then."

Tim was met by Oliver on his arrival at the farm, he had his coat on and was waiting on the doorstep.

"I'm coming with you Tim. It's as much my business as yours." he said abruptly. George came hurrying out and took Oliver by the arm.

"Come on Oli, let's look at this sensibly." Oliver shrugged himself free his face set and stubborn.

"Dad I'm going too." Tim was at a loss, he had no right to refuse Oliver but he feared Oliver's mood would disadvantage them. Apart from his animosity to David whom he had never met, what would his attitude to Sandy be when he got there? If he lost his temper with her he would lose her completely. The whole situation needed careful handling and Tim's anger would justifiably be at Sandy for her treatment of her parents not at David who could well be innocent of any knowledge of the chaos she had left behind.

Finally he spoke firmly to Oliver

"Okay Oliver you may come but for God's sake keep your temper." Oliver dropped his hunched shoulders with a sigh of utter sadness saying

"I wouldn't hurt Sandy no matter how she's treated me. I love her Tim." He turned away and walked to the car. "Let's go."

Jeremy had not been able to acquire a 'phone number for

David but even if he had Tim had already decided not to 'phone first. As Sandy had been deliberately avoiding him since these visits to London had started, she would probably not speak to him anyway. He and Oliver travelled to Paddington station with hardly a word between them. Oliver sat hunched in the corner by the window and gazed unseeingly at the passing countryside. Tim tried to keep his mind clear and relaxed by buying The Times newspaper and attempting the difficult crossword which certainly occupied his mind until he threw it down in exasperation.

"Who on earth compiles these things!"

As the train drew into the station Oliver's neck and face reddened, he opened the window and thrust his arm out in anticipation of opening the carriage door. Tim had to scurry a little to keep up with him as he jumped down and headed for the ticket collection.

"Hang on Oli, I'm not as young or fit as you." Tim puffed as he caught up with him. "Anyway you need me for the address. Let me look. Ah yes I think," he pulled his A-to-Z from his pocket whilst Oliver impatiently shuffled his feet, found the page and running his fingers along the marked streets nodded "yes we can walk, it's not far."

"Well?" George and Alice met them at the door looking hopefully over their shoulders to see if Sandy was with them.

"Gone away." Oliver pushed past them both and barely able to control his upset he went upstairs to his room. Tim followed George into the sitting room where he flopped down into the proffered chair.

"Apparently, according to the concierge, David and his 'young lady' went off this morning with suitcases. They didn't say when they'd be back."

"Maybe this will explain things." Alice held a letter in her hand. It came after you'd left."

"Oh, bloody hell!" Tim exclaimed jumping to his feet. "That

bloody letter – I forgot clean about it. What an idiot!"

"You knew about it?" Alice looked extremely confused, "I don't understand."

"Yes, Sandy must have accidentally forgotten it when she left on Saturday and June found it on her bed. I wanted to read it but June refused to let me, she said it was private and she would post it, which she obviously did."

"Well that clears that mystery up I suppose." Alice managed to give Tim a rather sour look before going in search of Oliver to give him the letter which he could have had three days ago, had it not been for June's new found respect for Sandy's privacy.

George gave Tim a large glass of whisky. "Don't mind Alice Tim, she's had the brunt of Oli's moods since he came home from seeing Sandy. I've tried to talk to him about not taking it out on his mother but he just storms off saying she won't leave it alone. She cares, we all care, that's the trouble."

Alice gave the letter to Oliver and without waiting for him to open it she withdrew and went back down stairs. Oliver stared at the handwriting on the envelope and his heart sank even further; this was the 'Dear John' letter he had been expecting for months now. It would confirm what she had said to him when he had gone to see her. With trembling fingers, he carefully opened it without tearing and took the page from the envelope.

'Dear Oliver,' he read 'I love you. And because I love you I have left you.' This didn't make sense, angrily he read on 'There is no going back from what I have had to do but at the time I felt I had no choice. When you have finished reading this letter I hope you will not hate me for ever and will understand.' Oliver felt the tears well in his eyes and dashed them away aggressively. He read on 'It all began in Mauritius...' He read Sandy's account of her outpouring of the whole episode of Paul and the breakdown of her relationship with June to Josie who, unbeknown to Sandy, had told David. It wasn't until David turned up after Christmas that she realised that Josie had done this. On reading the pursuance of Sandy by David and his later threats Oliver could barely contain his anger.

"The bastard. I'll kill him!" he shouted out loud. The three parents downstairs jumped at the sound, Alice rose to go upstairs but George pulled her back.

"Leave him love. Let him get it out of his system."

Oliver forced himself to read on. 'By the time you read this, dear Oliver, I shall be married.'

"Oh, bloody Jesus Christ!" he shouted again banging his fist against the wall. He couldn't believe what she was telling him, why had she been so bloody stupid? 'I couldn't tell you before or you would have stopped me and then David would have destroyed all of you.' Oliver hit his forehead over and over, *I walked away, I bloody well walked away when she tried to tell me.* Sandy's letter finished 'Please forgive me Oli, I should have told everyone what was happening and we could all have faced it together like people who love one another do, but I felt so responsible for having told Josie. I was ashamed that I had. And I felt foolish, like an immature teenager. But now my shame is compounded. I lost you that first weekend and once I had gone that far I knew you would never want me back. I am soiled and prostituted. Goodbye my dear Oli. I will always love you. Sandy.'

Oliver sat on his bed and wept. Huge gulping agonies poured from him. His beloved Sandy had given herself away to protect the ones she loved knowing all the time that the sacrifice she made would turn those very people against her. Thank God she had written the letter. Now it was their turn to rescue her and to hell with the consequences. Oliver dried his tears and washed his face in cold water. When he felt in control of his emotions which hopped from anger to despair he joined the others downstairs.

CHAPTER 15

THE COLD HIT SANDY like a blow in the chest as they exited the airport to the waiting diplomatic car. She pulled the fur coat David had bought her tighter and snuggled her face into its warm collar. The snow creaked under her boots like floorboards in a haunted house. The driver handed her into the back of the limousine and tucked her coat around her feet solicitously. David took his place beside her and squeezed her hand, she assumed, affectionately. But she didn't return the pressure.

"Take us to the hotel first." he instructed the driver who touched his hat in salute. "I want you to get in the warm whilst I go straight to a meeting." He removed his hand and placed his arm around her shoulders instead. "You're shivering." Sandy was freezing; never before had she experienced cold like the blast that met her, it had taken her breath away. "A bit different to the climate we met in isn't it?" he laughed.

"Yes." She managed to get her breath, "Why did we have to come here of all places? Do they actually have a word for spring?" David sighed

"I told you, it's work and I'm being paid for it."

"And what am I supposed to do with myself? It's too bloody cold to go out and I don't want to sit in a blasted hotel bedroom for however long you intend to stay here." Sandy wanted to cry, she hated the cold, hated tobogganing as a child, hated playing snowballs and hated playing hockey in sleet. "Why couldn't you have come on your own? I wouldn't have run away would I?

You've made sure of that."

"Because, my dear little wife, I want you here. I won't be working all the time and I promise you Moscow is a beautiful city. I'll show you the sights, we can go to the opera, see a play, whatever takes your fancy." Why was he being so bloody nice? Sandy was extremely suspicious, she thought of the over-used maxim 'a leopard doesn't change its spots' – no they don't, and neither does David!

They stopped outside of a large hotel and the driver carried their cases inside, returning to the car to await David. A porter took them and their luggage up to a huge suite equipped with every luxury imaginable.

"I'll get them to send up some refreshments and tea. I'll be back for dinner." David leaned in to kiss her but she turned her head ever so slightly and he kissed her ear instead. He appeared not to realise she had turned away deliberately and with a smile he left for the meeting.

Sandy immediately searched the suite for a 'phone. But there was none. How could she get a message to her parents to tell them where she was and that she was safe, at least she hoped she was? She paced the rooms, unable to settle and worrying. Oliver's letter may be lying undelivered in her bedroom, what if it had slipped under the bed when she was grabbing her bag to make her escape before Tim arrived? It may not be found for ages, Mum didn't clean under the beds every day of the week. She started when there was knock at the door and a maid entered carrying a tray of tea and cakes. Vacantly Sandy thanked her and left the food untouched on the table. David had given her no information as to how long they were staying or whether they were going straight back to England when they left here. All she could do was wait.

The sight of Oliver's face; a ghostly white with angry red suffusion across his cheekbones made Alice gasp.

"Oli whatever is it?" She rushed up to him and forced him to sit down. "George get him a brandy or something." Oliver, clutching Sandy's letter in his fist, exploded

"Your daughter is the stupidest bloody person alive!" he shouted at Tim. Tim got to his feet, his eyes blazing.

"There's no call to speak to me like that Oliver! Explain yourself!" Oliver too got to his feet and looked around at everyone

"Sandy bloody Williams is stupid and... and..." He burst into tears. "I can't." he stuttered through his tears "I can't handle this!" He thrust the letter into Tim's hands "Read it." He staggered out of the door and into the open air where he took gulps of air, then he walked off across the yard into the fields beyond. Alice attempted to follow but he waved her back "Just read the fucking letter Mum!"

George took the letter from Tim's shaking hand

"Hold your temper Tim. Let's read this first." George read the long letter aloud, his voice at times rising with incredulity and at others breaking with emotion. The last line hung in space in the horror struck silence which followed.

All Tim could think was if only he had read that damned letter they might have been in time to at least stop the marriage. What came after that they could have faced later. Now she was gone somewhere abroad and they had no way of knowing where.

"The silly, silly girl." he groaned.

"Silly maybe, but what a girl!" George loved Sandy like a daughter and the respect he had always had for her had multiplied tenfold as he read her words. "She is the bravest and the most selfless person among us." He shushed the others as they began panicking about what to do and where was she? "Right, the facts are: she has martyred herself and she is married, she has disappeared – temporarily. But we can find out where she is now that you're David's father-in-law; you'll have a bit more of a right to know than you did before."

"That's all very well George but that's only the surface problem. The main thing is the man's got a hold on us all and Sandy will never betray us. If she's gone this far she's not going to throw everyone in it now." Alice doused George's optimism. Tim leapt to his feet

"On that point, Alice, we must get in touch with Mike and Jeremy immediately. But firstly, I have to ring June."

The conversation with June began immediately with recriminations by Tim regards the letter and George cringed in his seat as he heard Tim's words. He attempted to get Tim to soften his approach by hand signals and shaking his head until finally Tim realised what he was doing and apologised to June explaining that he was overwrought.

"She's coming down by the next train." he said as he put the 'phone back. "I'm sorry but we can't leave her on her own; she's in a dreadful state."

"No thanks to you!" George said bluntly.

"Ring her back Tim and tell her to bring clothing and overnight things. She can stay with us." Alice insisted and George agreed with vigorous nodding. That done, the next call was to Mike who also declared he was setting off as soon as possible.

"Now for Jeremy." George took a deep breath "He's going to wish he'd never met my youngest son."

"Bloody hell!" Jeremy had exclaimed when Tim had briefly explained on the 'phone what Sandy had done and her reasons for it. "That just about takes the biscuit! Whatever next?"

"I'm so sorry Jeremy, you must wish you'd never got involved. It's just one thing after another, when is it all going to end?"

"I must say, I never thought it would turn into an on-going saga." He gave a grunt of a laugh. "Well it has to be sorted doesn't it – one way or another." He added that he couldn't get away until Thursday when he'd come over and in the meantime he'd try and find out from Scottie where they had gone.

"Other than that, my friend, there's not a lot we can do until they come home. And frankly I'm not altogether sure what we can do then."

"He didn't sound too happy, needless to say." Tim reported back "But what can you expect? The poor bloke's been drawn into something which could ruin him."

"Yes he has and I'm sad to say it was done by deceit." George added. "Where are the guardian angels when you need them? Everything we have all done for good has been turned against us. It's enough to make you atheist."

"I'm afraid I already am!" Tim admitted.

"It's your bloody fault then!" George managed a small laugh.

It was dark by the time Oliver returned to the house to find Mike's car in the drive and both he and June swelling the ranks indoors. He had walked for miles through the fields and the woods mulling over Sandy's letter. The thought that she had had sex with someone else tortured him, had she liked it? How often had they done it? He knew that Sandy had had previous relationships but that was before he knew her and certainly before he loved her. They didn't matter; it was life. But after they had declared their love she had abandoned him and left him in tatters. The dreadful question in his mind was whether David's hold over her had been the reason for what she'd done or was she in fact exaggerating his threats to excuse herself from doing what she wanted to do? Did he even make these threats? Did he really know about Paul? Would she tell those sorts of lies and scare them all just to cover up her true purpose? Surely not. Not the Sandy he thought he knew. He needed to read the letter again in a more rational frame of mind. He really didn't want all these people here, he knew they were all just as involved as he was but not in the same deeply personal way, she was his girl; *was*. Taking a moment on the step he inhaled deeply and entered. There was a hubbub of conversation in the sitting room, no one appeared to be listening to what anyone else was saying. As Oliver entered the room fell silent.

"Dad, may I have Sandy's letter back please?" He nodded a welcome to Mike and June and retired with the missive to his room. His small writing desk was situated in front of the window overlooking the garden and this is where he sat to re-read her account. His eyes straying often to the seat by the pond, he tried to discern whether her anguish was genuine. He read it through over and over then folded it carefully and put in his drawer. The memory of their last meeting was still fresh and he re-visited it, trying to view it from a third person's perspective. He had been too overwrought to think about what Sandy had been feeling or to see beyond her words. When she had blurted out those dreadful words 'I don't love you' his vision had gone red and he could no longer see or hear her. If only she hadn't said it. If they had tried to talk over what was wrong between them she might have been able to explain. She had attempted to in the end, but by that time he was off.

According to her letter there had not been anything wrong between them, just something which had *come* between them. Did it tear her apart when she told him she didn't love him? Oliver took his mind away from the present and right the way back to when he had first found her, injured and cussing at the base of the tor. He couldn't help but smile at the memory. All through their friendship she had been volatile, feministic, argumentative and most importantly, dependable, honest and brave. Could a person with such a strong character change just like that? Could she suddenly become deceitful and closed without there being a very good reason?

Oliver admitted to himself that he had not known her as anything other than a friend and that he had no idea what she was like when it came to boy/girl relationships. Was she a different person when sexual encounters were involved? Did she play around and set one man off against the other, was she a flirt? He had no answers to these questions. Finally he went down to dinner when Alice called him and sat quietly listening to the opinions of the others and their thoughts on what should be done.

At the end of the meal he had answered the questions in his head.

⌒ ‿ ⌒

David returned later looking very pleased with himself.

"Come on let's go for dinner." He looked again at Sandy "Haven't you changed yet?"

"What am I going to change into – a pumpkin?"

"Oh, yes very funny. I bought you an evening dress, it's in your case. You haven't even unpacked it! What have you been doing all afternoon?" He unpacked the case and handed her the dress and shoes he had bought and then he stripped off to his underwear and put on a fresh shirt and evening suit complete with bow tie. Sandy scowled at the dress. It was okay but not for her. She had never worn an evening dress before in her life. Some of the girls had dolled themselves up for the diploma presentation but, true to form, Sandy had merely changed her jeans for ones with less paint on them. "Come on darling, we'll be late." David chivvied her along and she had no option but to put it on. Glancing furtively in the mirror she wasn't too displeased with what she looked like. But it hardly went with her hair! She refused to flatten it however when David remarked that it would be nice were she to grow it a bit and have it nicely styled.

"No." she answered "If you don't like it that's tough. You've taken everything else away from me, leave me some of my identity." She battled between anger and tears "In fact David I'm not hungry. Go by yourself."

"Suit yourself." Another of his irritating stock phrases always said with a shrug and a sardonic grin. Sandy suddenly grabbed hold of him and he stepped back in alarm thinking she was about to slap him but she just held his arm and pleaded "Just let me go – please." She had been brave up until that point, shutting her mind to what was happening but suddenly she felt she couldn't go on, just couldn't go any further. He smiled down at her upturned face and gently ran his finger down her cheek and across her lips.

"Hush my dear, you don't mean that do you?"

"Yes I do. Please take me home." She pulled away from him and sat on the edge of the bed tears flowing down the cheek he had just stroked.

"I'm sorry my dear but I can't do that." He left her then and went to dinner on his own. She pulled off the shoes and flung them across the room, likewise the dreadful gown and digging into her own bag which she had packed herself she pulled out her jeans and tugged them on. Inhabiting the real Sandy again she felt something stir in her soul; it was called courage. It recalled the days on the moor when all had seemed doomed and how they had almost given up hope only to find hidden strength in all of them. She felt herself grow stronger as that old courage forced its way into her. She would find a way of getting out of this and making sure David couldn't hurt them. What it was she had no idea but she would find it.

So instead of pleading and instead of fighting David she would attempt to play him just as he was playing her. What she needed was just a bit more knowledge of the place and the currency and most of all the plane times back to England. She checked to make sure he hadn't rifled through her bag whilst she slept and filched her passport, luckily it was still there. She removed it and hid it under the wardrobe just out of sight but near enough that she could reach it. Then she went to bed and slept. David didn't come back that night. When she woke to find he was not in the bed Sandy wondered fleetingly where he had been but didn't give it any more thought and turned over and went back to sleep. She had half formulated her plans, she just had to make sure she played the part well.

Sandy was woken when David slammed the door shut.

"Come on get up we're going out." He gave no explanation of where he'd been and Sandy didn't ask.

"I need to bath first. What's the hurry?" she mumbled from the sheets. David merely pulled the covers off and repeated

"Get up." His face was unreadable and he looked a bit dishevelled. He stripped off and went into the bathroom and very soon Sandy heard the water running and the buzz of his electric razor. Not wanting to share the bathroom with David she got up and dressed in the warmest clothing she could find in the selection he had purchased, choosing fur boots and trousers over a skirt. David didn't seem to notice that she had forgone the bath or if he did he didn't care and seeing that she was ready to go out he slipped his fur coat on and together they left the suite. When they had reached the open air he seemed to relax a little and slowed his pace. Sandy took the opportunity to venture the question as to where he had been.

"So, what kept you out all night? Or is it top secret?" she mocked.

"Actually, yes!" David snapped back. "You know very well that I'm here to work as well as for pleasure."

"I haven't seen much pleasure in being here yet!" Sandy muttered "How long do we have to stay, it's so bloody cold I can hardly get my breath." David sighed loudly

"As long as it takes." He glanced behind him and without appearing to, he quickened their pace. Turning a corner he hailed an approaching taxi and surprising Sandy with his apparently fluent Russian he gave the driver instructions to their destination.

"What exactly do you do? I know you work for the British Embassy that's common knowledge but why do you have to come here, can't you communicate by 'phone or letter or something?" David replied quietly

"Shut up!" Sandy glanced at his profile as he studied the driver in the mirror. "Wait until we get out." he added.

The taxi pulled up in front of a large house and they got out. He turned to Sandy and with exasperation said

"My dear girl, are you so dim that you are unaware that there is a cold war going on, the Russians have spies everywhere. Yes, even taxi drivers!"

"But you're here officially and surely it isn't a secret that you're British and aren't you protected with diplomatic immunity?"

"Yes I am but it's as well to keep your mouth shut."

"But what *is* your job? Surely as your *wife* I'm entitled to know." She emphasised her title with sarcasm.

"Considering your obvious lack of enthusiasm for the role and your lack of loyalty to me I hardly think you have a case. And that's it – case closed."

They entered the building which was divided into apartments and climbed the stairs up to the first floor where David knocked quietly on a door. It was opened immediately by a slightly balding middle-aged man.

"I saw you arrive from my window." He smiled as he closed the door behind them.

"Good morning Hugh, may I introduce my wife Sandra." Hugh took Sandy's hand in a firm grip and shook it warmly.

"What a pleasure to meet you my dear." He spoke with a BBC accent and emitted an aura of superiority and power.

"Would you like coffee? I'm having some myself." He gestured to the sofa and chairs. "Please make yourselves at home." David followed him into the kitchen leaving Sandy alone in the small sitting room. She heard them talking quietly but was unable to make out what they were saying. She looked around the room. It was relatively sparsely furnished but comfortable with pictures on the walls, she got up and looked out of the window at the snow covered street below. The very sight made her shiver.

David and Hugh emerged from the kitchen with the coffee and some plain biscuits which they placed on the low table in front of Sandy.

"Help yourself Sandra." Hugh smiled at her. Then turning to David he raised his eyebrows "Much as I am delighted to meet your wife David, you are aware that the purpose of meeting *here* is the need for total privacy?" His manner changed and he suddenly looked stern and his dark eyes became hard. David flushed a little and looked uncomfortable.

"I'm sorry Hugh but I can assure you that my dear wife is totally unversed in the ways of the world and is no threat to security whatsoever. I have brought her with me because this morning I noticed someone loitering outside the door of our suite. I didn't want to leave her there alone." He took Sandy's hand and squeezed it in a gesture of affection.

"Very well. So be it." Hugh said dryly. "Right, David you are the one person in the embassy in whom I have complete trust, I gather you have some reports for me." David nodded and reached into his inner pocket to pull out a sheaf of papers which he handed to Hugh. Sandy butted in, she was feeling extremely uncomfortable and very resentful that David was putting her down as someone who was unimportant and dim to boot.

"I don't wish to intrude in your *private* conversations and quite frankly I don't want to be here." She rose from the seat saying "David, I'm going back to the hotel please give me some money for the taxi." Hugh turned his gaze to Sandy and she saw in it both mockery and something else which she found hard to recognise; it was almost seductive. She looked away quickly feeling the heat of embarrassment rising through her. He smiled to himself at her reaction and reached for his coffee. Leaning back in his chair he scrutinized them both without speaking.

"Sit down my dear." he said to Sandy, "There's no need to be petulant." Sandy was taken back to being a school girl again standing in front of the headmistress and she realised that she was behaving like one. She felt totally out of her depth with this man who on first meeting had seemed charming and welcoming but in a flash could change into a cold inquisitor. "David, perhaps we could meet again at another time, there are some quite nice shops in Moscow and no doubt Sandra enjoys shopping as most ladies do, tomorrow perhaps?" Sandy had thought David was patronising but this man took the prize. David had remained silent throughout this exchange looking as uncomfortable as Sandy felt.

"Yes Hugh, I'll give her a little tour when we leave here so she will know where to go and where not to go."

"In the meantime, you two newly-weds, I think it would do no harm to tell Sandra a little of the purpose of secrecy if only to put her on her guard should any questions be asked of her."

Sandra's interest was piqued, she had experienced the Russian sailor's drowning in Mauritius and the other sailors' strange behaviour when offered refreshments and help. As for the Cold War, she had heard it talked of but had no real idea of what it was all about. It didn't affect her way of life in any tangible way and thus, like most ordinary people, she paid it little attention.

"Are you sitting comfortably? Then I shall begin." Hugh mimicked the 'Listen with Mother' introduction, again underlining her immaturity. "But first I would like you to tell me why you decided on Mauritius as a holiday destination when most people of your age would, I'd have thought, opted for Spain or the South of France where the night life is good."

"I don't like discos and 'night life' and the only reason I chose Mauritius is that my friend from college was already there working for The International Voluntary Service" Sandy answered promptly.

"So that's where you met your husband?" Hugh didn't wait for affirmation "Did you have any idea what David's job was in the High Commission?" David shifted uncomfortably.

"Not really except it was something to do with the Russians." Sandy heard David give a sharp intake of breath.

"Hmm I see." Hugh replied. "I suppose that wasn't hard to work out. Did he tell you anything about his work?"

"No but he talked to Josie, my friend, about it a bit I think." Sandy knew she was doing damage to David's credibility with this man and she enjoyed a brief moment of pleasure from it.

"And where is this Josie now?" The questions were coming faster now and Sandy watched Hugh's face; it was inscrutable.

"Still there I assume." Sandy wondered where this was going. "She loved Mauritius and was hoping to stay as long as she could. She worked for Family Planning."

"Actually," David interrupted "she was sacked." Before she could help herself Sandy spun round on him

"You bastard!" she cried. "You evil manipulating bastard!" Hugh questioned David with a look, and his struggle to explain Sandy's outburst was plain on his face. At last he said bluntly.

"She was unsuitable and unstable." He appeared to bite his tongue as he uttered the last word.

"Unstable? In what way?" Hugh leaned forward in his chair to look directly into David's eyes.

"Well, not unstable as such…" David floundered a little, "just, how shall I put it, a little generous with her favours." Sandy actually shrieked with laughter. Hugh patiently waited until she had stopped and was about to speak when David cut in "I think I'll take my wife back to the hotel."

"No David, I want to hear more about this 'loose' woman. Go on Sandra, what's so amusing?"

"I hardly think any of this is relevant Hugh, Sandra and her friend were just having a good time and Josie probably got carried away, what with the parties and the heat. I fell for Sandra the minute I saw her and I think Josie was jealous, that's all." David chanced a warning look at Sandy which she chose to ignore.

"I don't know about loose women, Hugh, but my husband took the biscuit where that behaviour is concerned."

"So why did you marry him Sandra if he was such a Lothario?" Sandy fell silent, what could she say? She had pushed herself into a corner in her pleasure at deriding David to his superior and now she was in the hot seat. David smirked at her

"Yes, why did you marry me Sandra?"

"I've absolutely no idea!" Sandy reposted, "I certainly wouldn't have had I known our honeymoon would be in the Arctic!" Hugh laughed, the moment had passed and Sandy breathed again as Hugh poured more coffee.

"Now, I was about to give you some idea why security is such a big issue especially here." He once again darted a hard look at David. "You may know the saying used in the war 'careless words cost lives', well that is still apt now even though the war is over. Regarding Mauritius and the presence of so many Russian ships in the area I will give you a brief history. Ever since the seventeenth century the islands in the Indian Ocean have been important for shipping, originally for goods to and from the east, all the major powers have wanted a foothold on them from Madagascar to the Maldives. When the Suez Canal was opened in 1869 they became slightly less important for trade as the canal provided a shorter route." He paused, "Am I boring you?" Sandy shook her head, they had covered some of these aspects in history at school but she politely replied

"No not at all, it's very interesting." Hugh nodded and continued.

"However, during the early twentieth century the Suez Canal had two opposing effects, on the one hand it enabled us, the

British, to maintain the control we had over the Indian Ocean and on the other, it also enabled the other European powers easy access to the area. The Russians in particular wanted the warm water ports. Even the United States attempted to gain supremacy as did the Japanese but our navy was very strong and we retained control." He pushed the biscuits towards her "Do have some, they are particularly tasteless and I'm trying to get rid of them." He allowed himself a smile at his joke. "To continue, you as an ordinary young person are probably unaware that this battle for control is still going on and although we granted Mauritius independence in 1965 there were provisos which I won't bore you with. Suffice it to say they consisted of maintaining control of the area mainly keeping the Russians out. This was when the Crown Colony of the British Indian Ocean Territory was formed. Would you like to continue David? No? Very well I shall." He addressed Sandy once more. "The Americans had, with British consent, deployed ballistic weapons in the Pacific Ocean in 1964. The Russians were worried as they foresaw a military build-up by the west in this desirable area." He paused. "Are you following your history lesson?" Sandy nodded again.

"Thank you for the information but why are you telling me all this?" Sandy was very puzzled as to why Hugh was giving her a concise history of the British Empire, was it really necessary? Hugh continued.

"I am coming to the purpose of this little lecture, what an impatient young thing she is isn't she David? Where was I? Oh yes, when the Suez Canal was closed in 1967 due to the Arab-Israeli war the Indian Ocean islands became once again important ports as the closure meant that shipping had to take the longer way around the Cape of Good Hope and those in control of the islands could control the Cape route. The Canal was closed for seven years and in this time many companies had built bigger ships to handle the Cape route and when it re-opened they were too big for it. Thus the importance of the islands remained. So you see, that is why we retain a High Commission in Mauritius and employ people like your husband to supervise the running of them and to report back to us any Russian activity."

"So the Cold War is just powers playing a sort of game of chess, not a war as such?"

"Got it in one." Hugh smiled at his pupil, his eyes softening again with that vaguely seductive look. "I haven't given away any government secrets Sandra, just brought you up to date with your husband's role. The reason we are here to talk is that all the hotel rooms and possible half the Embassy rooms are bugged. I have sole access to this flat and have had it totally checked; here we can speak openly. However, that side of things is not for your ears and David and I will meet tomorrow whilst you are shopping."

After they had left the apartment David grabbed her by the upper arm so hard that she cried out. He tightened his grip and hurried her down the stairs and out onto the street. It was at this point that his temper flared.

"What the hell do you think you were doing? Have you any idea what damage you've done to my career with your blabbering?"

"I only told the truth. You slept around all over the island and then you had the audacity to get Josie sacked. How could you be such a bloody hypocrite?" Sandy yanked her arm from his grip. "I don't give a damn about your career or you. Let me go and send me home and do your bloody worst. I don't care anymore, all I want is to be shot of you." Sandy stood facing him defiantly, bristling with anger and shaking with the cold. Her slight figure was dwarfed by the huge fur coat and hat and she looked like a child in her mother's clothes. But her anger was that of an adult; a wronged adult. "Why did you bring me here? Why did you marry me? Why did you take me to your meeting?"

"I took you because I didn't dare leave you on your own. God knows what you might have done. I know you. You're just waiting for a chance to screw me and to run off home but I can't let you do that, I need you here."

"What do you mean, you need me here?" Sandy thought back to her own questions she had asked herself. *Why did he want to marry someone who disliked him so much?* She had always distrusted David but by marrying her he had protected her and her family and friends from himself. Confusion swept over her. David calmed a little and in a gentler voice he said

"I'll take you home when we're done here." He attempted to put his arm around her shoulders but she shrugged it off. He took her arm instead and began leading her along the street. Something made her glance back to the entrance to the apartments. Hugh was standing quietly in the shadows and had probably heard every word they had said.

CHAPTER 16

AT THE HOTEL lunch was being served and Sandy realised how hungry she was having missed dinner last night. They sat at a table in the corner and ate in silence. David handed some roubles over the table to Sandy

"There you are, go shopping." Sandy slipped the cash into her purse. She had no intention of shopping, this was the start of her plan. It could take some time but she was determined to stash away as much money as she could in order to make her escape. "I'm going into the embassy this afternoon, make your own way back to the hotel after your shopping." David pushed back his chair and without looking back he left the dining room. Sandy leaned back and breathed a sigh of relief now she was alone. She ordered coffee and drank it slowly as she thought. She gazed out of the window at the cold unwelcoming street, the snow was beginning to fall again and she had no inclination to venture out in it. Her coffee drunk, she signed the bill and went upstairs to her suite. The first thing she did was to check that her passport was safe and felt a glow of pleasure that it was in her own name and that she had managed to hide it from David. He was unaware that she had her own with her. She sat at the little writing desk and pulled towards her the hotel notepaper. 'Dear Mum.' she wrote. She would take the opportunity to let them all know she was safe and where she was. If she hurried she could complete the letter and take it down to the reception for posting before David returned. She had written no more than a few lines when there was a quiet tap at the door. *Bugger, room service I suppose*, she sighed and got up to open the door to tell the maid or whoever to come back later. However, it was not the maid at the door but Hugh. *What the hell does he want?*

"David's not here, he's gone in to work." She didn't invite Hugh in and was about to close the door when he gently but firmly pushed it further open and came in.

"It's you I've come to see." Hugh closed the door behind him. "Shall we have a little chat?"

"I can't. I have to write a letter home." If she didn't do it now she had no idea when she would get another chance.

"I can wait my dear, I'll just sit here whilst you write it and I can send it for you by diplomatic mail if you like." Sandy hesitated, the offer seemed a good one but how could she write what she wanted to write with him sitting there, what if he came and stood over her and saw the content? In the end she decided that she *would* write her letter but make it clear to him that it was private. He should respect that after the lecture on secrecy he gave her earlier. She did not write at length as she had intended but explained briefly where she was and that she hoped to come home soon. As she was writing she realised that there was a possibility that her letter to Oliver had not been delivered, June may not have found it or worse still Sandy may have dropped it on the way to London. If this was the case then they would all still be in the dark and worried out of their minds but with Hugh sitting there waiting she had no time to explain in depth. Instead, she very quickly wrote that she had written to Oliver explaining everything but had not posted the letter and hoped that she had left it in her room and that June had found it. Just in case the letter had not been found she wrote 'David knows everything about Paul that is why I've had to do what I've done.' She folded the paper and slipped into the envelope ensuring that it was tightly sealed.

"Thank you for offering to post it for me Hugh, at least I know it will arrive safely now." He tucked it into his inside pocket without even glancing at the address and replied

"It's safe with me. Now Sandra, that little chat." Sandy was sure it was related to her comments about David and the subsequent eavesdropped conversation they had had outside the apartments. She was not mistaken. Hugh launched directly into his cross questioning technique.

"You do not love your husband do you?" There was no problem with the answer to this but should she tell him the truth? No she wouldn't.

"Well, we sometimes don't get on but I suppose I do love him." She lied.

"Don't tell me untruths Sandra. I haven't the time to banter and I assure you I will know what are lies and what are truths." He fixed her with those dark eyes and asked again.

"You don't love your husband do you?"

"No." she answered but made no move to enlarge on why for obvious reasons.

"So, I ask you the same question I asked you earlier, why did you marry him?" Sandy was flummoxed, there was no way she could tell this official man the truth about sheltering Paul and David's subsequent blackmail, and she certainly couldn't tell him the most humiliating thing of all: the photographs. She still was at a loss as to why David had in fact married *her*.

"It's a long story, I can't explain..." She knew this answer would not suffice and indeed it did not.

"I have the whole day at my disposal Sandra. David will not be back for a while, I have sent him on a small journey." He sat back and crossed his legs and waited. Sandy said nothing for a while until she felt a surge of anger at this man's intrusion into her life and wished she had not given in to her impulsive character and made it so obvious that all was not as it should be between two newly-weds.

"Quite frankly Hugh, our personal relationship is nothing to do with you."

"Oh but it is. David is in my employ and that of the British government, everything about him is of my concern." When Sandy still didn't answer his question he changed tack. "Tell me about your holiday in Mauritius, who did you meet and who did your friend Josie sleep with?" He added, "And tell me about David's behaviour there." There was no escape from this man's scrutiny. She had no worries about telling him about her holiday; she went for the experience and for the love of the sun and she'd talk about it all night if it kept the subject away from why she married David. So Sandy took a deep breath and began.

"My father booked it for us as a surprise after I'd finished college. We enjoyed the month there but when it was time to go home Josie suggested I stayed with her and renewed my visa. I agreed because I was having a nice time swimming and painting."

"Yes, it is a lovely island isn't it? But let's move on from the holiday snaps and try to answer my questions." Hugh prompted her impatiently.

"I went to a cocktail party and met loads of people who I can't even remember. Josie had been there longer than me and had been going out with David and went to lots of functions with him. I don't know the name of the man she had an affair with but I do know that David stepped in and thwarted his promotion. But she had been seeing this man before David even came to Mauritius and it was all over and no harm was done until David took out his spite on them all."

"Why did he feel spite?" Hugh shot the question at her. There was no way out of this questioning, whatever Sandy said Hugh picked up on and dug deeper towards the one truth that Sandy couldn't tell. She thought quickly.

"Josie dumped him because he was sleeping around." Phew,

she had sidestepped that one.

"But he said that she was jealous because he fell for you. He would have had no need for spite were it his decision to date you would he?"

"You don't know David very well do you?" she shot back at him. "He is spiteful and manipulative and I wish I'd never married him."

"Ah, now we're getting down to it. You said David talked to Josie about his work, did he also tell you what he was doing?"

"No I wasn't particularly interested, I went there for a holiday and to paint, I couldn't give a damn about what he was doing. And I have no idea what he said to Josie other than what I said earlier about the Russians."

"Did you ever meet any Russians when you were there?"

"Well yes, sort of." Sandy replied, "One of the sailors drowned on the beach near where we were having a party." Hugh sat up interestedly

"Tell me what happened."

"They are strange, aren't they?" This had been an experience that Sandy had recounted at home to Oliver and family, they had been amazed at the sailors' behaviour. "They had come on to the beach further up at Grand Baie and gone swimming and one of them drowned. When a doctor at the party tried to see if he could save the man they wouldn't let him through and when we offered them warm drinks and invited them into the house they refused and wouldn't talk to us. I don't know what they said to each other because they didn't speak in English. They took the dead man and went straight back to the frigate."

"Interesting that you were there, we did have a report about it if I remember rightly. Did you or anyone speak to them alone before the incident or give them anything? Are you sure the man was dead?"

"He looked pretty dead to me but I'm not a doctor and I don't think anyone went near them. Josie and I were heading their way to have a bit of a snoop when the accident happened."

"Hmm, I believe you are telling me the truth. You do understand that anyone involved with a government employee is bound to come under scrutiny especially at this time and place. After all," he added with a smile "you could be an agent for the Russians; you could have been approached whilst you were at college, especially if you showed any overtly communistic or left wing beliefs, they are very good at recruiting young people who think they know it all."

"So all this is about me and whether I'm a spy?!" Sandy almost laughed at the ridiculousness of it.

"Not entirely about you my dear. I now want to know about David's behaviour and I ask you again why you married him when you obviously dislike him and it would appear that you have always disliked him." Sandy felt her heart lurch, she thought he had left that behind but that bloody smile of his hiding his cold look sent shivers up her spine.

"Why do you want to know? You've already said that you have dismissed the idea that I'm some sort of Russian agent. What does it matter why I married him?" A thought sprang into her head and she smiled inwardly, he couldn't disprove this – "Okay it was for money, satisfied?" She sat back pleased with herself. What David does when she buggers off from him is in the future and they'll all hack it together when it happens but why pre-empt it by telling Hugh. He could have her arrested on the spot and sent home in handcuffs.

"Alright, if that's what you say but you don't seem to me to be a gold-digger. Rather more of a country girl, look at your hands?" Sandy glanced down at her fingers, scarred from various Stanley blade wounds and still showing ingrained stains from oil paints. Her nails were short or broken, no nail varnish or signs of manicure on them. They were not the hands of a flashy social climber.

"I like gardening." she replied lamely.

"And your preferred choice of clothing – jeans. And your haircut – like a little urchin. Come along Sandra it wasn't for money was it?" *Oh Christ does he miss nothing?*

"Yes it was! You shouldn't judge me by my appearances. I married him for his money, I'm not proud of it but I thought he would give me a better life." She grimaced "So far that hasn't been the case and I'm leaving him as soon as we get home."

"A divorce settlement? What a cunning plan." Hugh commented. "But shall we see what you have written to your mother? Was she in on the marriage for money idea?" He reached into his pocket.

"No!" shouted Sandy, "That's private, give it back!" Hugh calmly held it out of her reach and ripped the flap open. Sandy sank back into her chair, her energy spent. Hugh settled himself on the opposite chair and calmly withdrew the letter from the envelope.

"So, from the first sentence I see that your mother didn't know where you were. Why's that I wonder." He read on. "Innocent enough so far other than that. Hello, who's Oliver? Is he your lover?" He didn't expect a reply and Sandy gave none. "Ah, here it is, the crux of the whole matter!" He must have reached the last sentence. "What does David know?"

"What?! Russia?" Tim couldn't believe what Jeremy had just said. He shook the 'phone receiver as if to clarify his hearing. "What the hell is she doing in Russia?" Jeremy's voice echoed into the silent room where they were all waiting the news. "David has been sent to Russia for work apparently. That's all I could get out of Scott. Anything to do with the Soviets is top secret these days as you probably are aware. There's not a lot more we can do until they return."

"Did he give you any indication when that might be?" Tim rubbed his hands over his face, he had hardly slept since Sandy had gone and his face felt taut and old.

"No, I'm sorry Tim but at least you know where she is and that she is under the protection of the embassy there."

"I'm going to find her." Oliver took the 'phone from Tim and spoke

"Jeremy, hi it's Oliver here. Where in Russia is she? I'm going to get a flight and bring her back."

"Well, the embassy is in Moscow so I assume that's where she is but as for getting there I'm not so sure."

"I'll ring the airlines and make enquiries then. Thanks Jeremy for all your help." He replaced the receiver and lifted it again to ask the operator for the 'phone number of Heathrow.

"Oli, leave it. You'd have to apply for a visa and that can take weeks if you get one at all and by that time she'll probably be back." George took the 'phone from his resisting grip and placed it back on the rest. "Let's be honest, there's nothing we can do at the moment. But what we must do is consider the possibility that this vile man may land us all in the shit." He swept his arm across the gathered company. "What in heaven's name do we say?"

"For a start we have forgotten Hilda and her knowledge which in itself implicates her. She has to be told of the threat and we still haven't solved the riddle of the watcher at the cemetery." Tim reminded them.

"Gosh yes! But as far as I could gather from Jeremy she hasn't been followed since the confrontation, but he did say that the bus driver saw the neighbour and a man going into the graveyard on one of the weeks when Hilda stopped going. Though whether that has any bearing on the matter I can't say." George paced about the room. "Any thoughts anyone?"

Alice joined them with a tray of coffee.

"It could be just coincidence, but that woman does sound like a thoroughly horrible person all the same. George, ring Hilda and update her, it's the least we can do to forewarn her." She poured the coffee and added "I do feel sorry for her all alone and feeling threatened like that at her age." As they drank their coffee in a very subdued manner George rang Hilda from the 'phone in the hall.

"She's made of strong stuff that woman." He commented on finishing the call. "She didn't throw a fit or anything, just took it in her stride and asked to be kept informed."

"What are you going to do now, Tim, June? Do you want to stay here June? You're very welcome and at least we'll all be together as and when news comes."

"Or the net will catch us all in one throw when the police come knocking!" George attempted to throw a little humour into the humourless situation.

"I think that's a good idea, thank you Alice. I'll go back to the cottage as it's close by and June you should stay here, I don't like to think of you on your own worrying." Tim put his arm around June who had not said a word but had sat curled in on herself in the corner seat with silent tears rolling down her face. "Come on old girl, she's safe, at least we know that."

"Come along Sandra." Hugh moved closer to her and reached out to take her hand. "It's time to put all your cards on the table." He played with her fingers, lifting them up and inspecting the nails, he gently turned her wedding ring round and round her finger "So there was no engagement then?" His voice had become gentler and his hands were warm and tanned, had he been there in Mauritius as well? She was sure she hadn't ever seen him before but there had been scores of people at the one and only cocktail party she had attended and she couldn't remember any of them. "Was it a hasty marriage? Are you pregnant? No I don't think so. I have two children and I know the signs in a woman very well." Sandy looked into his eyes and they were smiling, not the insincere smile he had worn before but a genuine smile. "You don't have to fear me Sandra, all I care about is the security of our country. Whatever you tell me will be between just us." Sandy had never had experience of a man like Hugh, she didn't know whether to trust him or not. She could not tell him all that had happened, apart from the illegality of sheltering Paul and she was ashamed of herself for what she had done with David. How could she look this man in the eye and tell him about her drunkenness and the subsequent photographs? About how David had tricked her into trusting him only to find she had given herself to him for nothing? She flushed with embarrassment at the memory. She wanted to run away and her eyes strayed to the door.

"It's locked." Hugh rose from his seat and lifted her up from hers. "I can see why David desired you, you have a feistiness which is hard to resist putting to the test. But I need to know why you married him." He stroked her hair and let his hand fall to her breast. "Come along tell me all about it." His gentleness began to break down Sandy's defences and she felt tears pricking behind her eyes. She disliked him touching her breast but as he made no other move she excused it as an accidental brush. He saw her tearfulness and reached into his pocket for a pristine white handkerchief with which he dabbed her eyes. "There, let it all out my dear, you will feel better when you have and I can assure you that if David has wronged you in any way he will answer for it." She could hold back no longer, she sobbed into his handkerchief and then she cried in his arms. For a moment she imagined she was in her father's embrace and an immense feeling of safety came over her. After a while he fetched her a glass of water and watched her drink it. Then he took her again in his arms and held her close to him making comforting noises while she controlled her crying.

"Come and lie down for a while in the bedroom, I won't hurt you and you can tell me what he has done to you then you can relax knowing I'll take care of things." As if in a hypnotised state Sandy allowed him to lead her to the bedroom where he pulled back the bed covers and gently laid her down. He sat on the side of the bed and stroked her face and hair. "Start right at the beginning, I won't interrupt you."

"Right at the beginning?" she asked croakily, her tears still clogging her throat. "It's a very long story."

"Right at the beginning."

Sandy finished the account of her life from the trip across the moor to the present day and on the last words she fell abruptly asleep as though a huge weight had been lifted from her consciousness. Hugh continued to sit on the side of the bed whilst he digested all that she had told him. He felt utter disgust for David, what he had done to this young woman was unforgivable. But why had he done it? That was where the conundrum began. David had always had a reputation for being a womaniser but it had always been with a willing recipient. This account just did not make sense.

As Sandy began to stir he shushed her gently and lay down beside her "I'll keep you company for tonight, if you like." he whispered in her semi-conscious ear. "David won't be back until tomorrow at the least." He slipped her jeans and top off and laid his clothing on the chair beside the bed. When she began to protest he reassured her that it was only for comfort and he was not going to molest her. With those words, Sandy fell asleep in his arms.

Sandy woke to a bright white light. Hugh had drawn the blinds back and the sun was actually shining. The reflected light off the snow-covered rooftops was dazzling. He sat partially clothed in the chair by her bed. She scrabbled for the sheets and pulled them up over herself. She frantically felt for her underclothes and was relieved to find that she was still wearing them.

"Good morning Sandra, would you like a cup of tea? They do very good tea here." She mumbled a 'yes please' and tried to put together what had happened. With a jolt, she remembered that she had told him absolutely everything. Yet here he was offering her tea as though he were her father. The police weren't waiting for her with handcuffs and David was still missing. Hugh had come to her suite in the middle of the afternoon, where did the evening go? She was ravenous, they hadn't eaten anything and all she had had to drink was that glass of water. Somehow the realisation that she had 'laid her cards on the table' as he had put it, didn't alarm her as much as it should. She was beyond caring any more whether she could trust Hugh, all she felt was a huge sense of relief. He returned with the tea and plumped the pillows up for her solicitously then retired to his chair and watched her, a gentle smile hovering around his lips.

"My word, what an adventurous time you have had over the last couple of years. I'm surprised you still have some fight left in you." He got up and sat on the bed, taking her empty cup from her hands he leaned forward and kissed her on her brow. "Do you feel like getting up or would you like to stay there for a while? Oh don't worry about David, he's otherwise engaged. I could join you if you like, I didn't sleep too well." All Sandy's instincts told her to get up and to try to ascertain what Hugh was going to do with the information she had given him. Why was he still here and where was David?

"I'll get up. I need to think."

"Of course you do, you need to think how you're going to get away from David and back to your family. I can help you if you will let me. David's blotted his copybook too many times and I've arranged to interview him next week when he returns from Warsaw. I sent him there on a bit of a fool's errand so that we could have our little chat." Sandy's hopes rose, would David be sacked? But if he was sacked how would that help her? On the contrary he would blame her and be out for revenge. And she knew what that would entail. She had to get home and rally her family and friends to formulate some sort of defence.

"How can you help me Hugh? If you dismiss him I'll still be in the same position as before only worse because he'll know it's my fault?"

"No he won't because I am not dismissing him."

"But I thought you said he'd done something wrong?"

"Oh yes he has but I need him to stay in the service a while longer, I'm keeping him here but sending you home. He will have no say in the matter."

"Are you really going to send me home? What about Paul and what we did – are you going send me home and then have us all arrested?"

"My dear little girl, I would not do that to you. You see I have quite fallen for you. I don't have any daughters and if I had I would want them to be just like you." He moved to the side of the bed and lay down beside her gathering her in his arms he hugged her tightly. She relaxed into his embrace, finally feeling at peace and safe. They remained like this for a long time, she breathed in his slightly salty smell as if he had been in the sunshine and he caressed her hair fondly. Finally he got up and pulled on his trousers and shirt.

"I must be going now, order yourself some breakfast and I'll pop in later to check you're alright. I want to arrange for your flight and to get you out before David comes back. Goodbye for now." He kissed her lightly on the lips before picking up his jacket and leaving the suite.

Sandy lay for a while in the bed which still carried his scent and couldn't believe what had happened. This complete stranger had come to her rescue and in spite of what she had told him he was still going to help her. What luck to have met him! She hummed as she ran a bath and soaked in it for some long time. Then she dressed and ordered room service. The breakfast came and she tucked into it with relish. Remembering her passport she retrieved it from under the wardrobe and put it back in her bag. Then she waited.

The knock came at about six pm. Hugh entered dressed in a smart suit.

"I'm treating you to dinner, no don't change you look very lovely as you are." Sandy was wearing her jeans and although they were new they were still a bit scruffy compared to his suit but if he was happy then so was she. There was an official car waiting below and a driver in uniform. They drove out of the city for half an hour or so until they came to a small inn of sorts. The owner welcomed them warmly and addressed Hugh by his name. Hugh introduced Sandy as a very dear friend. They were seated by a huge open fire and given the menu. There were no other guests.

"I can't read this it's gibberish!" Sandy laughed as she turned it over and over not knowing which way up it was meant to be.

"Shall I choose for us? What don't you like? That will be a start." Hugh ordered them a vodka each as an aperitif and suggested to Sandy that she might like it diluted as it was strong stuff.

"Yes please." she gasped after she had taken a sip, "Some sort of juice please." They chatted about many things over dinner, never once referring to David or Paul. She talked about her college days and her milk round and the friends good and not so good she had made whilst there. The meal was very tasty and between them they drank a bottle of wine, again very strong stuff. By the end of the evening Sandy felt warm and relaxed and increasingly fond of Hugh. The owner cum chef cleared their plates away and asked Hugh if he would like drinks taken to his room. Sandy gave a little start, "Are you staying here? Will the driver take me back?"

"My dear girl, you can stay here as well. They have plenty of rooms." He thanked the owner and agreed that he would like some brandy and some water taken to his room.

"But I haven't got my toothbrush or anything with me!"

"All is provided even a nightdress if you wish." He tucked her arm under his and they followed the man upstairs to Hugh's pre-booked room. "You will join me for a nightcap please Sandra, I've very much enjoyed your company this evening and am loath for it to end." In the room another warm fire was burning and the glasses laid out on the table. There was a small sofa next to it. They sat side by side and stretched their toes out to the warmth of the flames, Hugh closed his eyes and sighed

"I can't think of a better way to spend an evening." With his free hand he took Sandy's hand and held it close to his chest. "You are very kind to an old man, you make me feel young again."

"You're not as old as my Dad." Sandy felt a little tipsy and began to giggle.

"Perhaps you've had enough to drink my dear." Hugh took the glass from her hand and put it on the table. "Me? I can drink most men under the table but I don't make a habit of it as it's not good for the British reputation here, as it is they think we're all drunks in the embassy and there are one or two diplomats I'd like to be shot of. But let's not talk shop." He took a large sip of his brandy and put it on the table.

"Tell me more about yourself Sandra, are you in love with your Oliver? Do you intend to marry him?" Sandy felt her short lived happiness at Hugh's offer of rescue drain from her as she recalled the last meeting with Oliver and what he must be thinking of her if he had ever received her letter.

"Yes Hugh I do love Oli but I doubt he still loves me."

"I would bet on it that he does. Who couldn't?" He pulled her to him and kissed her very softly and then quickly pulled away.

"I'm sorry I was overstepping the mark."

"I'm already defiled Hugh, Oliver won't want me back now. I

was to be his first, you know, his first sexual relationship, how can I go back to his purity when I have been a virtual prostitute?"

"From what you have told me you have been more of a martyr than a prostitute. That bloody David has been a thorn in my side for years. He loves high living and spends money like water. According to him he was left some inheritance but it won't last long the way he lives it up." He stopped suddenly. "I should not be talking like this, after the lecture I gave you about careless talk and here I am blabbing away like a lovelorn fool." He thought for a moment then slapped his hand on the table.

"I know what's been bothering me. It's not just why you married David, which you have already explained to me, but why he married you when he already had a hold on you. By marrying you he negated his threat didn't he? It's obvious that he doesn't really care about you, he doesn't care about anyone but himself, so why marry you?"

"I've tried to work that out myself and I really can't find the answer, by marrying me he's shot himself in the foot hasn't he?"

"Yes, so it would appear. Hmm this needs to be thought through." Hugh downed the last of his brandy and yawned.

"It's time we slept my little one. Will you stay with me let me keep you warm?" He turned to her and his dark eyes twinkled as he added "Just to keep you warm nothing more." The fire was already dying down and the air cooling rapidly, she imagined sleeping on her own in a freezing Russian inn in the middle of nowhere, shivering all night. After a few moments of deliberation Sandy said hesitantly

"Okay. But just supposing I'd said no. Would have abandoned me and refused to get me home? Would you have reported me to the police? I've been blackmailed before Hugh, please don't do it to me again." She ended her sentence with a catch in her voice and before she could continue he caught her to him saying

"Hush hush my little one, I am a man of my word, I will get you home." They began undressing before the fire died completely and when Sandy was down to pants and bra and Hugh to his underpants they pulled back the covers to find an old fashioned warming pan had been placed between the sheets.

"Good old Yuri, he knows how to look after his guests." Hugh chuckled as he pulled it out and laid it in the hearth. Sandy lay in Hugh's arms and absorbed the warmth of his body, unlike David he had no hairs on his chest so she wasn't for ever tickling. He held her closely but demurely and at no time attempted to go any further. Just as Sandy was dropping off Hugh asked her if she would like to take off her bra as it couldn't be comfortable sleeping in it.

"I just would like to feel your skin against mine. Nothing more." He reached round behind her back and with a deft flick he undid the hooks and slipped her bra gently away from her.

"That's better." he sighed and cupped her breast in his hand and promptly fell asleep.

Sandy lay awake, she was totally bemused. Whatever was she doing cuddled up to Hugh? She made no attempt to remove his hand and strangely felt no guilt over Oliver. Never had she been in such a strange position. In bed with a man who wasn't her boyfriend with no fumbling attempts to seduce her was not a usual occurrence. If a man went to bed with a woman it was a forgone conclusion that they would make love. This was a different feeling, vaguely sexual but sort of fatherly as well. Not that she had slept in her father's bed since she was a teething baby and he certainly had never touched her breasts but Hugh's presence felt comforting and safe. Maybe it was just because he was an older man who exuded authority and strength. She moved closer and he stirred and pulled her gently to him so that her head rested on his chest.

"Goodnight my little one." he whispered softly in her ear.

Sandy woke to find that neither of them had moved from their original positions. Hugh appeared to be still sleeping and she snuggled into his warmth and breathed the salty smell of his skin. She had noticed before that he wore no aftershave and the only other scent she could discern was that of soap. The evocativeness of smell is the strongest of all the senses; she remembered her grandmother's smell of face powder and her grandfather's smell of pipe tobacco. She thought that she would remember the smell of Hugh's skin for ever. Hugh opened his eyes and smiled at her.

"Good morning my little urchin." He rose on one elbow and looked down at her then ran his hands through her hair, once, then again.

"Is your hair always so wild?"

"Always has been. Mum says it was because I was born in a thunderstorm." Hugh chuckled, "I wouldn't be surprised if I could run my razor off it."

"Kids at school were always attaching balloons to my head, they thought it was so funny."

Hugh ruffled it once more and then he rolled back down beside her.

"I am such a lucky man to have spent two nights with you Sandra, I could happily throttle David for using you so badly." He sat up suddenly and his face was dark "Was he a good lover? Did you enjoy sex with him?" Sandy, surprised at this change of mood, was for a moment speechless. She had put David completely out of her mind, Hugh's attentions had been so nice after David's cruel taunting. She spluttered a little before replying

"Yes Hugh, he was a good lover..." Hugh swung his legs out of the bed and turned his back to her.

"And did you enjoy it?" he asked sharply.

"Actually, Hugh I hated every second of it. Being a good lover doesn't make you a good person or even a very nice one. All the time I was trying to pretend I was somewhere else or someone else." The tension in Hugh's back relaxed a little but not completely and he remained with his back to her.

"If he was a good lover he must have pleasured you in spite of your wishing to be elsewhere." He turned to face her and his eyes were hard again like they were in the apartment when he was questioning her and it alarmed her.

"How do you want me to answer that question? Yes, he did give me sexual satisfaction because he is a practiced fucker!" She could think of no other word which described David better. "He gave me the same pleasure I would have got from masturbating! Does that satisfy you Hugh?" Sandy didn't want to recall the memories of David taking her two or even three times during the night so that she was exhausted in the morning. To her surprise Hugh burst out laughing.

"You have an interesting turn of phrase my little girl, especially for one so young. I noticed you were not afraid to let rip in my apartment when you swore at David. I thought then what a strong minded little madam you were. Come here and take that look off your face, come and give me a hug." He was back to the gentle Hugh she had cuddled all night. Sandy grinned a little sheepishly.

"Mum gave up with me ages ago, she said I was always uncouth and art college had made me worse." He held out his arms to her and she snuggled in close.

"I'm sorry if I upset you I suppose I'm jealous that's all." Hugh sighed.

"You mustn't be jealous of David, I loathe him, I have from the first time I met him. He's the last person on earth I'd have slept with if I had had a choice." They lay together quietly, their small altercation had, if anything, brought them closer in their mutual dislike of David. Hugh traced his hands over Sandy's body caressing her gently and lovingly. "You are so petite I fear I could crush you if I held you too tightly Sandra."

"Hugh, please call me Sandy, all my friends do."

"Sandy, I shall call you Sandy. But to me you are my little urchin." Hugh sighed again, a long, long sigh, then very gently he asked

"Sandy, would you let me love you?" He held her away from him and watched her face as she fought with herself. He watched her closely, locking eyes with her as though he were reading into her soul. "I will be gentle and if you want to stop I will stop." Sandy began to tremble, she was unable to control it. Not trembling from the cold but, she realised, from desire. She lowered her eyes from his and very quietly said

"Yes."

They were picked up later that morning by the same driver who had brought them and Hugh accompanied Sandy back to hotel. Hugh held her hand in the back seat of the car and only released it when they arrived.

"I'll just see you to your room and check all is in order then I must go to work. I'll pop in later if you'd like me to." Sandy nodded shyly

"Yes I'd like that." Hugh took her key from her and opened the door to the suite and entered first. His sharp eyes took everything in instantly and he nodded to himself, satisfied with what he saw.

"No sign that anyone's been here, by that I mean David. I left instructions with Warsaw to let me know if he left before the end of the week." He closed the door behind them and gave her a hug and a kiss goodbye. "I'll be here at about six. We'll eat in if you like and then we'll have more time to ourselves."

"Oh Hugh, did you do anything about my ticket home?" Sandy asked, but at the same time she felt a reluctance to go home. What had happened to her? She felt an overwhelming desire to be with Hugh which was all wrong. He was married or so she assumed as he had children, and she loved Oliver didn't she?

"It's all in hand, don't worry." he added with a smile "But there's no hurry is there, not now?"

"I just worry about Mum and Dad not knowing where I am. If they knew I was okay I could relax and stop worrying." Hugh chuckled

"No need to worry, I've sent a telegram to your father, they know you're safe."

"Oh! But how did you know his address?"

He tapped the side of his nose. "You'd surprised what I can find out in a very short space of time."

"Did you post the letter to Mum?"

"No need, you'll be home before it arrives. It's okay I still have it. Hugh pulled the letter from his jacket and gave it to her.

"By the way did you travel as Mrs Montgomery or Miss Williams? We must make sure the ticket name matches your passport must we not?"

"I travelled as Mrs Montgomery and David kept the passports, but," she dashed off to fetch her bag from the bedroom as Hugh grumbled

"Damn, that will delay things if I have to get you a replacement."

"Tada!" She waved her own passport at him. "He doesn't know I've got it."

"Clever girl. I'll keep that in my safe then we'll know it's secure." Sandy hesitated a little before handing it over. "Don't you trust me?" Hugh asked sharply.

"Yes, yes of course I do it's just that it has been my safeguard and my ticket to freedom and I have sort of got attached to it. But yes, you're right, here take it and lock it away just in case."

Hugh gave her a rather hurt look and took it from her. He tucked it deep into his inner pocket.

"You can always ask to look at it from time to time just to reassure yourself." He smiled as she blushed with embarrassment that she had appeared to distrust him.

"I won't need to do that, I do trust you, honestly."

"See you later on then." He kissed her goodbye once more and lingered for a while then pulling himself away he left abruptly.

When he had gone Sandy re-read her letter and then screwed it up and put it in the waste basket. Hugh had thought of everything, she had no need to worry anymore.

The day dragged for Sandy, she fidgeted and paced, unable to relax. She opened the book she had brought with her and tried to read but her thoughts kept returning to Hugh and the feelings she had for him. Her conscience kept telling her it was all wrong, he was too old and she loved Oli. But every time she tried to summon Oli to her mind all she saw was Hugh's eyes, seductive and loving, protective yet dangerous all at the same time. She had never liked David's dark eyes and his permanent five o'clock shadow but Hugh's eyes were different; they changed, sometimes black and sharp and scrutinizing and sometimes soft and gentle. He was always clean shaven and his skin was smooth, no scratchy stubble and no coarse black hairs on his arms or chest. She found it hard to contain her impatience for his visit later. To pass the time she ran a deep bath and soaked in it until the water cooled, then she dressed in clean clothes and went down to the restaurant for lunch. The snow had stopped falling; a short respite in this miserable place, and she returned to her room to fetch her coat and hat, she would go for a short walk just to get some exercise and some air as so far she had spent most of her days indoors. She may as well have a look round the immediate vicinity of the city whilst she was here after all. She had the few roubles that David had thrust at her the day they had visited Hugh and now that her flight home was in Hugh's hands she didn't need to worry about spending it. She pulled her hat over her ears and did her coat up to the neck. It wasn't snowing but it was still very cold.

After wandering not too far away from the hotel so as not to get lost, she found a little shop which sold small wooden carvings and after struggling to communicate with the shopkeeper she purchased a small carving of a wolf. It was the nearest they had to a dog and she missed her little Lilly, it was a small comfort to her and she tucked it in her bag and wandered back to the hotel.

There was a note in a sealed envelope propped on the writing desk, it was in the same sort of official envelope that David had used to send his card and her heart missed a beat. Was he back already? Hugh had said that he would be away for the week. She picked it up and with a trembling hand she opened it. Thank goodness, it was not from David, it was just a quick note from Hugh telling her that a car would pick her up at six and take her to his apartment instead of him coming to her. He hoped she didn't mind the change of arrangements but explained that they could talk freely there. No, she didn't mind, she didn't mind where she met him as long as she could see him.

At six the driver entered the foyer where she was waiting and she went with him to the car. Ten minutes later she was being greeted by Hugh at his apartment door.

"Thank you Michael, that's all for today." He dismissed the driver and led her indoors. "I hope it's not too presumptuous of me to hope you will be staying the night?" He grinned as he took her coat.

Hugh cooked dinner for them and played some modern jazz records.

"I don't suppose you've ever been to Ronnie Scott's have you?" he asked as they ate. "I'd love to take you but it's too near home."

"Talking of home, when am I due to leave?" Hugh laid his hand over hers as she rested it on the table

"Not for another week I'm afraid. You see, I have to go back to London then and I thought it would be a good idea to travel together. Then I can look after you."

"But what about David? He'll be back by then. What am I going to say to him? What if he refuses to let me go?" Sandy was dreading meeting David again. He must hate her.

"Leave him to me." Hugh squeezed her hand and continued eating. The evening finally moved into night although it had already been dark when she left the hotel at six o'clock. Sandy and Hugh relaxed on the small sofa, his arm around her shoulder. They leaned into each other and kissed, his kisses were so gentle, not like David's hard mouth.

Admittedly David hardly ever kissed her, his feelings were not of love and tenderness, merely those of sexual gratification. She responded to gentleness and Hugh couldn't be more gentle. His love making earlier that morning at the inn had been just that – making love, and his offer to stop should she wish was something she never thought a man could make.

They left the dishes on the table and in turn used the bathroom to clean their teeth and in a calm and mature way prepared for bed. There was no mad struggling out of clothes to get to each other as soon as possible, the night was long and they had all of it to themselves.

Sandy stayed at Hugh's apartment for the remainder of the week. Some days he didn't go into the embassy and they took the car on random trips out of the city and into the Russian countryside. At other times when he was working Sandy stayed in and read. Hugh had a large collection of books, fiction and non-fiction, biographies and travel books. He left her the run of the place but his safe, of course, was always locked. Out of curiosity one day Sandy did give it a little tug but was pleased that it didn't open and she wouldn't be tempted to pry into private things. Although she wanted to know more about Hugh and his private life Sandy didn't want to hear about or see pictures of his wife who was probably beautiful and elegant, it would only make her feel jealous and inadequate. Their conversations instinctively veered away from this topic and Sandy happily chatted away about her family and her life and her painting. It was only after one evening when he started on one of his inquisitional phases that she realised that he knew everything about her from her shoe size to her diploma grade and she knew absolutely nothing about him. She didn't even know what position he held at the embassy although she had worked out that it was pretty senior right at the start. When she asked him what his title was; High Commissioner or something important like that? He laughed and replied

"Mister!"

One more week with Hugh and then she would be going home. How was she going to face Oliver? Though he probably had already wiped her out of his life anyway. No doubt she'll find that he was back with Susie and there would not be any reason to tell him about Hugh. Half of her hoped he had found happiness and half longed for him still to care.

CHAPTER 17

THE TELEGRAM ARRIVED. Tim was surprised to receive a telegram; the 'phone had taken over from telegrams these days. He couldn't remember ever having received one before. He tore it open and read the message.

Mr. Williams. Your daughter is safe and under the protection of the British Embassy. Due home end of March.

It was signed: H.G. British Embassy Moscow.

Tim breathed a sigh of relief. He immediately rang the Tregowans and spoke to June. She burst into tears and called out to George and Alice the good news.

"Did it say anything else?" George took the 'phone from June. "Was it from David?"

"No it's just signed H.G. I've no idea who that is. I suppose it's genuine, not some weird hoax."

"We'll reply to it then we'll know." Tim was already putting his coat on to go to the post office as he rang off. He sent a reply for confirmation that this was truly from the embassy and received one back almost immediately stating that it was. Again signed H.G.

All they could do now was wait for Sandy's safe return and then they had to sort out the dreadful fix they were all in.

Hugh arrived home early to find Sandy asleep on the bed, she looked so like a child that he hardly dared touch her. Her hair was as spiky as ever and he wanted to touch it and feel the sparks of electricity run through his fingers, as they ran through his body when he loved her. Instead he sat softly down on the bed beside her and watched her sleep. *She's young enough to be my daughter.* He fought with the guilt and won. Sandy was twenty-five years old, she could easily be a mother by now. She could even be his wife, other men he knew had married younger women and been happy. He had married at twenty-three, swept off his feet by Angela whom he had met in his early days of government employment. They had been happy enough and he had been faithful although he knew that this had not been the case for her. He had turned a blind eye to it because the children were still young and to his knowledge it had only happened the once. Angela was still very lovely even though she had just turned fifty, the same age as him, and she was still pursued by many men on their various postings around the world. She had cried off this posting because of the cold monotonous life and had instead taken a cruise with a friend around the Caribbean where the sun shone constantly. He wondered if her friend was male or female and found that he didn't care.

Sandy stirred and stretched like a little kitten and yawned like a child. Then as she opened her eyes and saw him she blushed and covered her mouth with her hand. He couldn't resist her.

"Make love with me – now!" he commanded her as he stripped off. "I'm sorry my little urchin but I love you, I want you for myself." Their time together was running out and he ached with the thought of saying goodbye. Sandy reached out for him with the same look of pain in her eyes as he felt in his heart and welcomed him in.

"I think I love you too." she whispered to him as he took her in his arms.

Sandy returned to the hotel to pack her bag to take back to Hugh's apartment for their last night together. They were leaving for England the following morning. They had had a rather subdued evening and Sandy had shed a few tears into his chest as he held her tightly all through the night.

"I don't want this to end. I want to hide you away somewhere just for me." Hugh held her even tighter as though he would never let go.

"Does it have to end? I have nothing to go back for, Oliver won't want me and I love you so much."

"I'm a married man my love, I should never have done this to you. We have to go back to our own lives now. I shall treasure your memory until I die."

"Will you keep in touch with me please, just sometimes?" Hugh sighed and shook his head

"I dare not. If I do I shall never be able to let you go. You go home and marry that nice lad Oliver and be happy." He kissed her tears away. "But I shall never be happy again."

Hugh arranged for the car to take her back as he had some last-minute things to attend to.

"I'll tell Michael to come back for you in say an hour, you should be packed by then. He'll bring you straight back and we'll have our last night together. I can assure you I shall make it one we will remember for ever."

As Sandy opened the door to the suite she knew immediately that David was there. She smelt his aftershave and her stomach heaved at it. He must be in the bathroom as she could hear water flowing. If she was quick she could just grab a few things and get out again before he saw her. There was nothing very much that she wanted, just the few bits of her own clothes. The rest that David had bought he could shove up his arse. Very quietly she tiptoed into the bedroom and gathered up an armful of clothes and her suitcase. Leaving it un-latched for fear the sound of the clips would reach him she made for the door with the case clutched to her chest.

"Going somewhere?" David emerged from the bathroom, strode across the room and slammed the door shut. Sandy dropped her case as he grabbed hold of her. "Pack it properly, we're leaving now."

"No, let me go you bastard. I'm not going anywhere with you."

"You are or so help me I'll throttle you now and to hell with the consequences!" David flung her on to the bed and locked the door pocketing the key.

"I'll scream if you touch me again. Hugh's driver is only downstairs and he'll break the door down."

"He won't hear you it's a long way down to the foyer. I warn you, I'm not joking, I *will* kill you!"

His face was suffused with blood and the hatred in his eyes was terrifying.

"Where are we going? Why do I have to come?" She began to plead. "You don't love me, you never have."

"No I don't and I never could love a scruffy bitch like you. But I need you. Get a move on and don't think you can get away from me, I have diplomatic status and these peasants would hold you if I ordered them to."

David forced her case shut ignoring half of the clothing which had fallen on the floor grabbed her by the arm and half dragged her out of the room. He didn't loosen his grip on her until he had pushed her into the waiting taxi and slammed the door shut on them. Sandy wept with anger and fear as they drove out of the city.

"Shut it!" David snapped. Sandy tried to open the door of the taxi when it slowed at a junction but David flung his arm around her throat and gripped hard until she thought she would pass out. "Don't be bloody stupid. Just do what I say and I won't hurt you." They arrived at the airport and with David still holding her by the arm they entered and approached the desk. The attendant checked the passport and then asked for the ticket. David handed him Sandy's ticket saying something in Russian which she didn't understand. When the attendant handed back the boarding card David took her through to the departure lounge.

"You are going to Warsaw. When you get there, you must stay in the arrivals until I join you. This is a one-way ticket and you haven't got any money. I'm keeping your passport so you won't be able to get out of the airport without me. Got it?" Sandy nodded dumbly, she could scream and fight but with his authority the officials would take his side. He spoke their language and he could tell them she was a runaway or a criminal, anything, she didn't stand a chance. David waited until the flight was called and then he shot her a vicious look saying

"Don't try anything foolish, their prisons for mad people are pretty vile."

"You told them I was mad?!"

"Yes, and they promised to watch you for me." He pushed her towards the gates and then turned around and left.

Michael had waited for more than an hour for Sandy to come down with her bags and in the end, he went up to her room to chivvy her along. The door was open and clothing lay scattered on the floor.

"Hello? Miss?" he called as he entered. There was no answer. He looked in all the rooms and she was nowhere to be seen. He hurried back downstairs again and enquired at the reception whether she had gone out.

"Yes sir, she left with her husband about an hour and a half ago." He grabbed the 'phone on the desk and without asking permission to use it he rang the embassy and was put through to Hugh immediately

"Sir, Miss... er Sandy has gone. Mr Montgomery has taken her somewhere. It looks as if they left in a hurry there were clothes all over the floor and the door was open."

"Bloody hell! Where in God's name has he taken her? Michael find out as much as you can, whether they walked or went by taxi... anything." Hugh then rang security. He told them to search the train stations and the airport and to arrest David on sight. He hoped they were not travelling by road as they could be anywhere by now. Michael rang again.

"Sir they went by taxi so they are probably going to the airport. I'll see if I can find the driver who took them. I'm off now to their office."

"Good man." Hugh then rang Domodedovo Airport which was the nearest and asked them if there were any flights with David and Sandy's name on the passenger list. He waited impatiently as they went through their lists and groaned and nearly sobbed as they told him that the plane had taken off fifteen minutes ago, but only Mrs Montgomery had been booked on the flight.

David hadn't looked back as he left the departure lounge he was confident that he had subjugated Sandy enough that she would obey him, he was pleased that she was scared of him, it made it all so much easier. However, as soon as he exited the door Sandy looked around for a means of escape. She didn't dare ask the attendant to use the 'phone to ring Hugh as she didn't know what David had said to them and didn't want to draw attention to herself in case he was lurking outside. Instead she looked for the toilet. Finally, she judged that the room with women going in and out was the female toilet. The sign over the door had no image just writing which didn't resemble any letter in the English alphabet. She nonchalantly joined the small queue and clutching her case and bag she went to the far toilet and locked herself in. A couple of times someone tried the door and there were mutterings outside which she assumed were women complaining that she had been in there too long. What she couldn't understand was why David was sending her on alone. It just didn't make sense.

Hugh sat at his desk in despair, whatever was going on? Had he misjudged Sandy, had his powers of deduction failed him because of his attraction to her? Was she an agent working with David after all? He had suspected that David was up to something for some time but had been waiting for the chance to trap him. David was cunning, he covered his tracks well, Hugh couldn't help admiring this aspect in him but wished that he had used his wiles for his own country and not for money. He felt like crying, he loved that little urchin – had she been playing him along all the time? He couldn't bear to think that. He considered what Michael had said about the state of the room, it didn't sound like a well-planned exodus. It sounded more like an abduction but why had she boarded the plane without David? He put his head in his hands and nearly wept. "If David has harmed her I will personally kill him!" he said out loud.

Sandy heard the loudspeakers announcing something but she couldn't understand. She didn't know what time the flight was meant to take off but she was determined not to be on it. She sat on the toilet seat until her backside was numb, how long had she been in here? Her watch told her she had been there for an hour or more, surely the flight would have left by now. But still she didn't venture out, David said he was catching a later flight but how much later? If she walked out now she could bump straight into him. Sandy realised that her stay could be a very long one and using her fur coat as a cushion she made herself as comfortable as possible and waited.

Whilst she sat cowering in the toilet the embassy security guards had arrived at the airport and were told that the flight had taken off without one of the passengers. An English woman called Mrs Montgomery. Hugh answered the 'phone and on hearing the news he summoned another driver and set off for the airport praying that David hadn't hurt her, praying that they wouldn't come across a body by the side of the road.

The security guard under Hugh's instructions negotiated with the airport managers to close the doors and to prevent anyone from leaving or entering whilst they searched the building. Hugh wanted David caught and preferably hanged. But unfortunately, it would only be imprisonment for him if they ever caught him.

They found her curled up on the floor trembling and scared. She had refused to open the door and they had to force the lock. Kind strong arms lifted her to her feet, she looked up into his eyes. She cried in his arms as he half carried her to the car.

"My darling little girl thank God I've found you."

They drove back to Hugh's apartment where he ran a hot bath for her and coaxed some life back into her limbs as he gently washed the warm water over her body. She sobbed almost continuously. Hugh lifted her from the bath and wrapped her in a warm towel like a child and carried her to his bed where he tucked her in with a hot water bottle.

"You are safe now, my little one. Rest now and you can tell me all that happened when you feel up to it."

"He threatened to kill me!" she cried. Hugh clenched his fists by his side and his eyes flashed with anger.

"I'll finish him. I promise you even if I have to shoot him!" Slowly Sandy's eyes began to droop as the warmth made her sleepy, she fought against it and reached out to him.

"Don't leave me, please don't leave me alone."

"I will be in the next room my love, just call for me and I'll come." He held her hand until she breathed the steady breath of sleep and then gently extracting his fingers from hers he went immediately to the 'phone.

"I want that man caught, scour the area and find him!" He rattled off instructions to his colleagues and security guards. "Contact Warsaw, get them posted at the airport." Every time the 'phone rang he snatched it from the cradle hoping for good news. There was no news, no sightings and the oddest thing was that David had not been booked on any other flight either to Warsaw or anywhere else. The same reports came back from Sheremetyevo, Pulkovo and Vnukovo Airports; David had not booked or taken a flight from any of them.

"The swine is still here then!" The orders went out to check every train station in Moscow and stopping points along their routes. He dared not leave Sandy alone, if David realised that she had not gone on the plane he would very quickly work out where she was. He increased the guards on the apartment and double locked the door. He then opened the safe and took out a gun which he loaded and slipping off his jacket he strapped on a shoulder holster and placed the gun in it. When he had done all he could to organise the search for David he returned to the bedroom where he sat quietly in a chair and tried to work out exactly what David had been planning. He needed to question Sandy but was loath to disturb her, he sat and watched her and waited for her to wake.

Sandy opened her eyes and shot up in bed looking frantically around her. Then, seeing Hugh she fell back onto the pillows.

"I'm here." Hugh went to the bedside where he sat and held her hand.

"My little girl is safe now, don't worry anymore." She gripped his hand and said again

"He was going to kill me if I tried to get away, I was so frightened. He hurt me Hugh, my throat hurts." Hugh had noticed the bruising to her arms and throat as he had bathed her and his anger had surged through him like a raging fire.

"Start at the beginning, tell me everything."

"He was there, in the bathroom, I could smell his aftershave. I thought he hadn't heard me come in but he must have. He was so angry and so vicious, I tried to get away but he threatened me – he meant it Hugh, he really did! I looked for Michael but he wasn't there." She gripped his hand tightly, "He nearly choked me when I tried to get out of the taxi." Hugh wanted to hold her close and comfort her but instead he questioned her ruthlessly – he had to know the whole story, the whole truth. He was in no doubt that Sandy was an innocent victim but what David needed her for was still out of his grasp.

"Do you know why he wanted you to go on alone? What were you meant to do when you got there? Did he give you anything, a package or a letter, anything at all?"

"No, nothing. He just told me to wait for him." Panic spread across her face, "It was a one-way ticket Hugh, and he kept my passport, I didn't have any money and you had my other one in your safe. He said he told them at the booking desk that I was mad and irrational and to watch me. I don't know whether he said that or not – I can't understand their bloody stupid language, I didn't know what to do."

"David didn't catch another flight. He's vanished."

"Oh God, he was going to leave me there!"

"It appears so, but I can't understand why he went through all the bother of doing that when he could have just disappeared quietly." There was more to it than just spite, Hugh was sure. David might have wanted to hurt Sandy and pay her back for her betrayal of his behaviour but this surely was the punishment of a twisted mind. David's anger seemed to have overridden his smooth urbane front which he showed to everyone whilst he double dealt behind their backs. But by allowing this to happen he had exposed himself and now he was on the run. Hugh thought it over, this wasn't David's *modus operandi*, there must be a reason and it wasn't a personal one, Hugh was sure.

"My bag, did you bring my bag?" Sandy looked urgently around the room, "It had Mum and Dad's photos in it and a present for Lilly, well not for her exactly, it's a little wooden carving of a wolf."

"You amaze me my little one. Here we are talking about your life being in danger and you are worried about a present for your dog!" He ruffled her hair and she grinned wanly up at him.

"I miss my little Lil' she probably thinks I've abandoned her."

"I've got your bag and your case, you were huddled round them like a cat with its kittens. We had to prise them out of your grip."

"I don't care about the case that much, it was only clothes but my bag was personal."

"You realise now that I won't be able to go back to England at the present?" Hugh was not only duty bound to find David and to discover what he was up to but his personal interest would not let him just turn his back on the whole affair and leave it to his successor.

"I'm not going without you. I'm scared Hugh. Please don't put me on a plane on my own. He will find me I know he will."

"You'll be safer in England than you are here. David will be picked up as soon as he lands at any airport in the British Isles. All the ports are aware he's wanted and anywhere he produces a passport, even a forged one in a different name, he'll be arrested. He knows we're on to him he'll go to ground here I suspect. Anyway, I would not send you alone, I was intending to give you an escort."

"No I don't want an escort I want you!" She flung herself into his arms "I'm not going without you."

"But my little girl, I can't be with you all the time, I have to solve this and I can't do it all from behind my locked door."

"I'll come with you to work, I'll sit quietly in a corner you won't know I'm there." Hugh looked at her blue grey eyes which were filled with fear and her plea went to his heart.

"Very well, you can stay, but if things drag on too long I must honour my promise to your father and send you home." He levered himself wearily from the bed, "Are you hungry? I can rustle us up an omelette or some cheese and biscuits, I'm afraid it's far too late for the splendid meal I had planned for you." This was true, the grey wisps of dawn were already filtering through the blinds. "Or maybe breakfast would be more in order." he added.

"I'm a bit hungry but don't make breakfast yet." Sandy pulled back the cover and invited him in. "Just for a cuddle." Hugh discretely unbuckled his holster out of her sight, laid it on the floor beside the bed and shed his crumpled suit which was still wet from Sandy's bath water.

"Just for a cuddle then." He grinned wickedly and climbed in beside her.

Until Sandy regained her usual spirits Hugh remained in the apartment as much as he could and ran the operation over the 'phone. Messengers came to and from the flat with any information which they didn't want to relay over the 'phone but after a week of this he told her that he had to leave her in the care of one of his colleagues as he had to attend a private meeting.

"Who is it? Have I met him? Can Michael be here as well?"

"Stop, stop, stop!" he answered crossly, "I have to go so just accept that you will be safe. If you don't I shall have to bundle you off home!" Sandy stopped whining immediately.

"Sorry. I'll be fine, don't send me home yet." She pulled herself together, Hugh didn't need a grizzling child under his feet and she realised she was pushing his patience. Although he had been loving and kind since he had rescued her he was tense and sometimes snappy. Sandy cringed every time he cut her short or held his hand out to stop her chattering when he was thinking. Had he had enough of her? She prayed that it was only the stress which was getting him down. David had disappeared and though a few reports had come in of possible sightings nothing came of them.

"I'll have some dinner cooked for you when you get back if you like." she offered as an apology. Hugh smiled and gave her a little hug.

"That would be splendid. Send Michael out for whatever you need." He put his coat on and with a quick kiss said "I'll be back by five." Michael and a man she had briefly met called John were waiting outside and as Hugh left they came in.

The day passed with no problems, she got on well with John who was not a great deal older than her and who liked the same music and films she did. They chatted amicably and played a game of cards or sat reading quietly. Michael came back with most of the food she wanted and she set about preparing dinner.

Hugh returned at five o'clock and dismissed the two men.

"What have you got for me, other than your body?!" he said wrapping his arms around her waist as she peeled potatoes at the sink.

"It's not very exciting I'm afraid, Michael managed to get some chicken and I've made a wine sauce to go with it. Potatoes and some cabbage. I'm sorry, I wanted to do something really nice."

"I'm sure it will be lovely. Tomorrow I'm taking you on a little break, you must be fed up being stuck indoors all the time. I'm free for the next couple of days and spring is finally coming, the snow won't last much longer." Over dinner, which was quite edible, Hugh told her that the search for David had been relegated to a routine enquiry as he had disappeared and was most probably in a safe house for defectors. He wasn't a major threat to the Foreign Office as his post was a relatively minor one. Really important documents or information didn't come near him and what he passed on could quite easily have been found out by reading the British newspapers.

"He was probably being groomed for when he rose up the

ranks. No doubt he was paid well to keep him interested until he outwore his usefulness. He won't find life quite as cosy in Russia as he did in England. They don't value minor informers very much here. He'll be lucky to get an income." Hugh grinned. "These traitors think they're going to be lauded and covered in glory, given a mansion and a huge payoff. But I could tell you about many who have died destitute or from alcoholic abuse after being basically dumped by the Soviets. He'd probably have a better standard of living in a British jail than he'll get here," Hugh's eyes were twinkling with laughter "stupid young fool!" But in a more serious tone he added. "Poor David, what he didn't realise is that once there was a suspicion that he was an agent little snippets of false information inadvertently came his way, not so much as to make him wary but enough to undermine his credibility with the Russians. No, I'm afraid he will not have a good time here."

"What about all his money in England, can he get any of it?"

"It depends on whether he has thought ahead and already moved it knowing that he was going to defect on this trip. Or he may have been expecting to carry on accumulating for some while and didn't expect to be found out yet. In which case he's snookered."

"Good!" Sandy shared Hugh's glee at the thought of David without his flashy car and salubrious furnishings. "What will happen to it all, I mean his flat and car and everything?"

"Confiscated. He's a traitor and thus a criminal. Oh I've just thought, you are his wife, I'm not sure but I think you could go to court to try and claim them. I'd have to look into that for you."

"I don't want any of his ill-gotten gains. I'd rather set light to the lot of them."

"I love you my little urchin." Hugh pushed his chair back and pulled her to her feet. "You are gutsy, outspoken, bloody minded and adorable and... well I could go on and on. You married him for his money did you?! That's hilarious. Come here and let me kiss you, there aren't many women who would turn down the sort of assets David has, money has a way of making people forget their principles, but not my little girl!"

It was good to get away from the apartment and the city for the last few days of their residence in Moscow. They behaved like tourists, visiting interesting places and admiring the scenery. The snow was melting quickly now with the sun higher and warmer and Sandy could see that it was a beautiful country. Standing at the top of a waterfall and watching the sunlight change the colours of the spray as it fell, Sandy pulled off her wedding ring and threw it as far as she could into the deluge.

"That feels better." she said rubbing her finger as if to remove the taint of David's touch on it.

"That will probably be found in some fish's stomach in the South Sea Islands." Hugh laughed with pleasure as it flashed through the air into the abyss.

"Bit like 'Lord of the Rings', bringing bad luck to whoever finds it." Sandy said grimly.

Hugh was due to hand over to his successor before their departure for England, the tickets were booked for their return flight and this time they really were going. They were bitter sweet days as their fondness for each other intensified so did their sadness at the inevitable parting.

"Hugh?" Sandy lay in his arms on the last morning.

"Yes my love?"

"Hugh, what if Oliver doesn't want me anymore? What if I don't want him? Would you have me back? I could just be your mistress, your lover, I wouldn't ask for anything more."

"Darling, please don't tempt me. I am married, I have to go home to my wife. Oliver *will* want you if he's any sense at all."

"But what if I can't love him, I can't lie to him and pretend that I do if I don't. I love *you* Hugh, I have never felt like this before. I don't know if I can live without you." Hugh didn't answer immediately, he groaned and held her tightly.

"You will forget me, I'll be an old man before you're fifty and dead before you reach retirement age, think of the future, a young vivacious girl like you saddled with an aging octogenarian, wishing you had married a man your own age with whom you could grow old. You'd end up resenting me and I couldn't stand that."

"I wouldn't resent anything, I'd love you no matter how old you were."

"It's a lovely sentiment my dear but reality is not always as nice as dreams and though you may mean to honour your promise it would be very hard to do so."

"So this is the end. You will never see me again?"

"I dare not. I should never have given in to my feelings for you, I have blighted your future with Oliver and given myself enough pain to last me the remainder of my days. Forgive me my love, try and forget me and be happy." Sandy cried uncontrollably, she pushed herself closer to his smooth body as though she were trying to get inside the skin. Hugh dashed tears away from his own eyes as the bleakness of life without Sandy finally asserted itself in his vision of his future.

He could stand it no longer, he kissed her with passion and loved her tenderly. He locked the memories of this moment deep in his heart where he could call them back when she was no longer his.

"I will make one promise Sandy, and that is that once a year I will contact you to know you are well and happy. Knowing you are happy with Oliver, will torture me but I will be happy for you, you deserve better in life than being the other woman." Sandy had to be content with this but she still harboured a hope that maybe, just maybe, Hugh's wife would leave him and he would drive up to her home and sweep her away to marry her.

Sandy packed the few belongings that she still had in five minutes, Hugh had already sent his books and larger items in a crate to be delivered to his home where he would reside until his next posting. The atmosphere was charged with sadness and for Sandy with foreboding. She had no idea what she was going home to, or even if she wanted to go home. Later that day Michael knocked at the door and Hugh opened it to him and another driver.

"It's all there Michael, thank you." Hugh indicated the suitcases in the hallway and Michael and the other man carried them downstairs and stowed them in the boot. Hugh and Sandy stood in the empty apartment and with empty hearts they kissed for the last time within these walls where she had felt so safe and so loved.

As they entered Domodedovo Airport Sandy nearly panicked, she half expected David to appear and she had an image in her mind of him pulling a gun and shooting her and Hugh as they were standing at the check-in. Hugh put his hand gently on her arm as he heard her intake of breath.

"It's okay, don't worry." he said quietly.

They boarded the plane and settled themselves in the first-class cabin where the seats were larger and more comfortable and waited for take-off. It was a three-and-a-half-hour flight to London but to Sandy it seemed less. Why did time travel so fast when it was taking you somewhere you didn't want to be? It had been a ten o'clock take-off and against her will Sandy dozed off about an hour into the flight, her head resting on Hugh's shoulder. She woke as the plane began its descent with a sudden plunge which sent her stomach into her throat.

"Oh, we're here." she muttered "Shit!" Hugh couldn't help laughing at her succinct way of expressing her displeasure.

"I couldn't agree more." he replied.

They disembarked and by the time they had waited for the cases to be unloaded it was nearly midnight. Hugh's case came by and he heaved it off and they waited for Sandy's to appear, and waited and waited. In the end, Hugh was about to go and complain when Sandy said

"Oh, bugger the case there's nothing in it I want, let's just leave it, I'm knackered standing about here. It's probably gone to Timbuktu by mistake!"

"Language!" Hugh gave her a small slap on the hand as one would to stop a child touching things it shouldn't. He tried to stop smiling, there was he with his posh accent and beside him a little urchin with a vocabulary of which Hugh was sure he had only heard the scrapings. He felt a bit like Professor Higgins with Eliza Doolittle. They waited a little longer as Hugh was loathe to let the airport get away with losing someone's luggage but he was also tired of waiting.

"Are you sure?" he asked

"Positive." she replied. As they approached the customs Hugh was beckoned through without scrutiny and Sandy's bag was given only a cursory inspection. Then at last they were outside in England.

Sandy looked around for Tim.

"Sorry, I forgot to send him the arrival time." Hugh took her hand and led her to the taxi rank.

"It looks as though we will have to stay in a hotel tonight."

"You did that on purpose!" Sandy turned to him her eyes sparkling, "Is that why you booked such a late flight?"

"Maybe..." Hugh chuckled as they climbed into a cab. "Dorchester Hotel please driver."

CHAPTER 18

THE DAY HAD FINALLY COME, Sandy had to accept that there were to be no more postponements and allowed herself to be led to the car Hugh had booked.

"I am not coming with you." He gently pulled his hand from hers. "Farewell my little urchin and may you find happiness." His eyes were full of tears and Sandy reached up and touched his face tenderly.

"Goodbye Hugh. Don't forget me." Hugh slipped a card into her hand.

"Don't use this unless you are in real need. Promise me." Sandy nodded mutely and held it tight in her hand.

"I'll contact you a year from today. Goodbye my darling." Sandy watched him through the back window standing at the kerb, his hand raised in farewell until the car turned the corner and he was gone from her life for ever.

Hugh returned to the room with its scattered sheets and towels and absent-mindedly gathered them up. He found a single hair from Sandy's head on the pillow and tucked it in the innermost section of his wallet, placing it in his breast pocket, next to his heart. He then picked up the 'phone and pulling a scrap of paper from his pocket he dialled Tim's 'phone number. Sandy had requested that she be taken to her mother's house rather than Tim's, she couldn't yet face the Tregowans and, in particular, Oliver.

June had returned home after hearing that Sandy was being

cared for by the British Embassy and was safe. Though no other information had come their way as to why she had to be kept safe June relaxed a little knowing that she would soon be seeing her daughter again. However, the problem of David's knowledge was still unsolved. Hopefully when Sandy returned she would explain properly and they would know what, if anything they could do to protect themselves. Tim rang her during the morning with news that Sandy was back in England; he had received a 'phone call from someone called Hugh who told him that she was on her way to her mother by private car, courtesy of the government. Hugh had refused to discuss anything else with him and had wished him well and rung off.

Once again June paced the house waiting, just as she had done before Sandy's first visit, looking out of the window every five minutes to see if a car had pulled up outside. Finally, a large black limousine stopped and backed into the drive. The driver opened Sandy's door and out she stepped. He acknowledged June, with a small salute as she came rushing out of the door, and climbed back into the driver's seat and drove away.

"Don't start asking questions Mum. Just let me get indoors." Sandy forestalled the inevitable rush of words from her mother and looking very small and very sad she preceded June inside the house. "Where's Lilly?" She looked around for her little dog.

"I left her with Tim, she likes it there. Just go on in to the sitting room darling and I'll make some tea." June resorted to the usual safety plan of putting the kettle on. She called out from the kitchen "Your father is on his way, he should be here any moment, I expect he'll have Lilly with him." Sandy jolted out of the seat where she had thrown herself.

"He's not bringing Oliver, is he?"

"I don't know darling but I expect he might. Oliver was all set to go to Russia to find you he was so worried about you."

"Oh Christ! Not yet, I've barely got home and I can't face hordes of people asking questions and hugging me. I just want to be left alone!" She buried her face in her hands. "I'm sorry Mum, I'm exhausted and so miserable I could die. Please keep Oliver away from me, give me time, please!"

"But darling you're home now and everything will be alright."

"Ha!" Sandy replied, "How the hell do you know that?" June backed away from her daughter's anger and sarcasm, hurt and uncomprehending. She had imagined Sandy throwing herself into her arms and pouring out the whole story and crying how glad she was to be home.

"I'm sorry Sandy, but didn't it occur to you how worried we have all been? And when we read your letter to Oliver we just didn't know what to do. Tim and Oliver went all the way to London to try and find you but you had just up and gone without a 'phone call or anything."

"I explained in the letter Mum. David blackmailed me, I had to try and protect everyone." She ran her hands through her hair and then slamming her hands on the table she cried "Oh Christ, I can't go through it all with you and then all through it again with Dad and then again and again with everyone else. Let me just get used to being home again and then I may be able to talk to everyone about what has happened to me." Sandy's eyes were red and she looked as though she had been crying, June took a chance and put her arms around her, expecting to be shrugged off. But Sandy returned the hug and buried her face in June's shoulder and let her tears fall.

Once she had stopped crying she pulled away from June's arms, "I'm so sorry Mum, I don't mean to be unkind. I'm just trying to get my head around things, personal things, I can't talk about them, not yet, maybe one day."

The sound of a car in the drive signalled that Tim had arrived. Sandy heard one door slam and waited with horror for the second slam. When it didn't come, she breathed again: he had come alone. A sense of relief flooded over her, Oliver must have washed his hands of her, how could he still care after reading the letter she had sent? If he knew about Hugh he would never want to see or speak to her again, he'd be disgusted that he had ever considered marriage. Her behaviour would label her as a slut because no one would ever understand.

Tim knocked just as June opened the door.

"What's up? You don't look very happy to see her." He came inside and looked around. "Where is she?"

"Upstairs, she's very tired." June knew it sounded lame and that Tim would not be taken in by it. Sandy had avoided speaking to him for months before she ran away and it was going to be very hard for her to face him now.

"Okay, I'll leave her be. When she's ready she'll talk to me."

"I don't know why she seems so distressed, she's safely home and that David isn't banging on the door, maybe he's let her go, maybe nothing more will come of it all." June fished for a happy ending.

"We don't know anything yet. Hugh whatever his name is refused to talk about it. All he was concerned about was her safe return home. Until Sandy explains why she ended up being escorted home by a government official we can surmise until the cows come home."

"But surely she must know that we don't blame her."

"Far from that, everyone admires her. She put her loyalty to her friends before herself and chanced throwing away her happiness with Oliver just to protect everyone." Tim added sadly "Even if it was an error of judgement."

"It's Oliver, she's terrified of meeting him, which I can quite understand." June replied, "When I said you were coming she nearly had a fit in case you were bringing him with you. I suspect she thinks he's disgusted with her and she won't be able to look him in the eye."

"He wanted to come but I refused. I wanted to see how Sandy felt before throwing them face to face after the upset of their breakup. I wasn't sure how he would behave, he's been very quiet but angry, continually angry. Whether it's with her or with himself or, like the rest of us, with David I don't know, perhaps it's all of those."

June and Tim waited patiently for Sandy to make an appearance which she finally did after Tim had been there for about an hour. She entered like a little mouse

"Hello Dad." she muttered and sat down beside him.

"Hello my darling, good to have you back. Are you alright? Can you tell us what happened? Where is David?"

"Dad, one question at a time please. I am glad to be away from David, he's gone now for good, I think, and yes, I'm glad to see you both again. As for whether I'm alright, I suppose I will be in time but, at the moment, no I'm not." She looked so sad, Tim was at a loss, he glanced at June who shook her head saying

"If you don't want to talk about it yet, we understand. I can't imagine how terrible it must have been for you my love, just relax and get used to being home again and in time you'll find the memories will fade."

Sandy's eye filled with tears, she couldn't bear it, she loved Hugh desperately and she was never going to see him again. She didn't want his memory to fade. There was nothing left to live for.

"I'm sorry I can't do this. I can't go on like this." She leapt up and disappeared upstairs where she shut herself in her room.

"Leave her. She's suffering from shock I expect, goodness knows what has been happening to her, whatever it is she seems to be traumatised. We'll have to give her time. But," Tim looked worriedly at June, "keep an eye on her. I don't like this 'I can't go on like this' sort of thinking."

"You don't think she's going to do something stupid, do you?" June looked terrified, "She's not suicidal is she Tim?"

"I don't think it's quite as bad as that, no, but she's very, very, distressed, just be around for her, don't leave her alone for too long but don't crowd her either."

"How am I going to know if she's alright if she shuts herself away all the time?"

"Do you want me to stay for a while, maybe the feeling of a family unit again will help her settle?"

"Oh Tim, would you? I'll make up the spare room for you, you'd prefer that, wouldn't you?" Tim smiled at her and took her hand in his.

"Yes, for the time being let's concentrate on our daughter. We can sort ourselves out later."

Tim moved in to the spare room and they tried to behave as normally as possible whilst both keeping an eye open for any irrational behaviour on Sandy's part. It was almost a family unit but nothing like it had been in the past. There was a strange atmosphere between June and Tim who found the platonic friendship increasingly difficult to maintain after having spent so many loving years together. Neither wanted to plunge back into a relationship just because they were thrown together by the circumstances but as the days went by they slipped into their old routines. Tim would get up and make tea as he always had and take one to June. They drank their tea together, Tim perched on the bedside and June propped up by her pillows. A couple of times he attempted to take a cup to Sandy but she said through the door that she would get one later. Tim did the odd chores around the house and June cooked dinner which they all ate together, it was nearly normal except it seemed more like a stage set than real life. Sandy got up every day, she didn't skulk in her room but tried very hard to appear cheerful if no one asked her any questions. At the slightest enquiry, she would back off and they had to leave it be. She was annoyed with Tim as he had left Lilly behind at the farm, supposing that Sandy would want to go back to see them all.

"How could you think that?!" she snapped at him. He explained that they not only wanted to see her and thank her for what she's tried to do but that Oliver was agitating to speak to her. He tried to get her to tell him what the situation was regarding David, until they knew, they were left in limbo, not able to vanquish the fear of reprisals.

"Sandy, we do need to know whether David is still a threat. Where is he? What the hell happened Sandy? You must tell us, all of us." He became exasperated with her. "It's unfair to leave everyone at the farm and Jeremy as well not knowing whether they're going to get the police on their doorstep any day!"

"No, it's not an issue any more. David's defected to Russia. He's gone." And that was all she would say. Tim emphasised how much effort Jeremy had put into finding her whereabouts but she refused to ring him or to speak to anyone.

"Just thank him for me please Dad. I don't want to speak to him." Tim drove back to the cottage and then to the farm to pick up Lilly and to try to make them, especially Oliver, understand that she was suffering from shock and needed time to settle. But to put their minds at rest he told them that David was gone.

"So, she's free of him!" Oliver brightened considerably, "Is she divorced?"

"I have not been able to get any sense out of her Oli, I'm sorry, she just refuses to discuss it."

"But does she want to see me?"

"She doesn't want to see anyone yet Oliver, not even you I'm afraid. In fact, especially not you, I think she's finding it very hard to live with what she did to you."

"But she said she loved me in her letter, I thought she would want to make things better as soon as she came back. Did she fall for that shit while she was with him, is that the problem?"

"Oli, I really don't know, but from the way she spoke about him it sounded as though she despised him." It had been a difficult meeting, George and Alice were understanding but Oliver obviously found it very hard. He understood that she was unsettled but was desperate to make her understand that he still cared especially now that David was no longer apparent. "Can I come back with you Tim? Maybe when she sees me she'll realise that I don't give a damn what she did with that man, I must see her Tim, just to tell her that."

"I can't do that Oli, she's in a very strange mood, it might help if you came back with me but it may also make matters worse and I can't chance that. She could even send you packing for good because of her embarrassment. You must give her time." Oliver's face was full of thunder, he had been through so much with Sandy; he thought they had a deep understanding of one another, where had it gone? He accepted Tim's refusal with reluctance and, also promised that he wouldn't drive up to see her unannounced.

In the end, Tim promised he would try to get Sandy to ring him, she might be persuaded to do that.

However, though he waited impatiently for a call from Sandy, none came. Oliver begged Tim to let him visit her but Tim, desperate to protect Oliver from more hurt, persuaded him to wait until he had gone back to June's with Lilly which he intended to do the following day. Whilst he was there he was determined to make Sandy talk to him and find out once and for all, if Oliver still featured in her life. Thereafter, he would try to get her to meet Oliver to either reconcile their problems or to put him out of his misery for good.

His last conversation with June had not given him much hope; she said that Sandy was still very withdrawn and was losing weight, she hardly touched her food and spent most days in her room. She wasn't painting or doing anything much except writing in her diary, sometimes for hours at a time. June said it was as though she were trying to exorcize the demons by writing down what she found so hard to say out loud. The diary itself had been scrapped and replaced by a blank page notebook.

"Well that is a good thing, isn't it? It's a start. Maybe then she will be able to put it all behind her."

"Let's hope so." Tim had never felt so distant from his little daughter. Once they had been so close but especially so when he and June had split up and they had needed each other for support. Now he felt he hardly knew her.

Sandy wasn't really sure why she was writing everything down. Initially she thought she could just hand the whole account over to whoever wanted to read it and let them make up their minds about her without her having to even be with them or to look at them or to answer questions. Then she thought she would finish it then burn the whole bloody lot. Whatever she did with it was immaterial really, it was the act of putting down all her experiences, her thoughts and her agonies and her ecstasies on the blank pages in front of her which was the only way she could think to heal her wounds.

Whilst Tim was at the farm Sandy became a little less fraught. June wondered whether it was because Tim was her father and that it was the sexual aspect of David's blackmail which made her unable to talk to him. Girls usually confided in their mothers in these matters and not their fathers. And so, it proved.

"Mum?"

"Yes love?"

"Mum, I need to tell someone and I can't tell Dad or anyone else. You are the only one who will understand."

"You can tell me anything, anything you want. Just let it all out, you'll feel better when you have. Start right at the beginning, I won't interrupt you." Those had been Hugh's exact words when she had broken down under his scrutiny. She felt a shiver of longing for his touch which was followed by a deep emptiness.

Where to start?

"Mum, you already know most of what happened before I left but there's only one other person apart from David who knows all the reasons and for the moment I can't say who he is. Maybe when I get to him in my story I'll explain." She sat beside June and took her hand in hers.

"Mum, it was dreadful, I made all the wrong decisions, I don't know how I'm ever going to be normal again." June squeezed her hand gently.

"Just tell me my love, I know that whatever you did you did for the best. That was obvious in your letter. We all admire your courage and your selflessness and if you made the wrong decisions you are not to blame. All we want for you is for you to be happy again."

Sandy took a deep breath.

"Okay. When I met David in Mauritius he tried it on and I told him to get lost. He's a creep Mum and very clever. Bloody Josie was besotted by him and it's her fault he knew about Paul. When he turned up at Christmas he threatened to expose us all unless I slept with him." June controlled her anger and didn't interrupt. "Well, I went to see him to try to get him to leave us alone. I was never going to sleep with him. I told him I loved Oliver and begged him to forget what he knew." She turned her sad and haunted eyes to June and then looked down at her lap. "He said he would. He was really understanding and quite kind. He cooked dinner and then he must have put something in my drink. I told you I would be home, didn't I? But then I must have passed out."

"But darling," June did interrupt this time, "why didn't you just tell us he knew about Paul and let us all share the problem?"

"Oh, Christ Mum, do you think I haven't asked myself that over and over? I was so ashamed of myself for being a blabber mouth to Josie, after all we had done to keep it quiet I go and blurt it out just like that! I thought I could stop him if I talked to him, I tried to appeal to his better nature but, hah, the Devil has more kindness than David!" Sandy looked at June, her face full of hatred and anger. "Now I have come to the bit that trapped me. I couldn't tell Oliver in my letter, it was too horrible, even now I don't know if I can ever tell him. Even if he says he still loves me, he couldn't possibly continue to if he knows." Sandy fell silent and June held her hand and waited for her to continue.

"Mum, give me a minute, would you? Make a cup of tea or coffee, my throat's so dry..." She put her head in her hands and sobbed. June quietly left her and went to the kitchen.

When June returned, Sandy had wiped her eyes and assumed a determined expression. She took the tea and drank some, then in an emotionless voice continued.

"In the morning, David told me I had been sick and that I was very drunk so he washed my clothes and put me to bed. He hadn't molested me and he had slept in the other room so apart from the worry about you and the embarrassment of being sick in his flat I left feeling quite reassured. He had all but promised to let things be and for a stupid moment I thought it was all sorted out. I didn't tell Oli about my visit or about getting drunk because I hadn't told him about David. None of you knew anything because I wanted to sort it out myself because it was my fault. And I thought I had sorted it."

"I don't understand my love, why did he get you deliberately drunk if he wasn't intending to take advantage of it?" Sandy laughed, a derisive and hard laugh.

"Because he is much more devious than that. Mum, I never knew there were people like him in the world. He manipulated me and taunted me until I didn't know which way to go."

Sandy gripped her teacup so hard that June thought it might shatter, then placing it back on the table she finally told June about the photographs. By the time she had finished, her face was flushed and her eyes flashing with tears and anger.

"Mum, I can't go on any more now. I'm going for a walk is that okay?"

Over the course of the next few days Sandy told June all that had happened to her. There were moments when she broke down and others when she paced the room kicking at the furniture with barely controlled anger.

"I married the bastard Mum because I thought all my bridges were burned. It was the only thing I could do in the end. My life was fucked so the least I could do was to stop him fucking up everyone else's." June winced at Sandy's language but understood her need to use it.

"I don't know what to make of you my dear, you are the most foolhardy person I've ever known, but my goodness, you are the most decent and loveable person alive." She took Sandy in her arms and kissed her.

Bit by bit Sandy told her of David's strange behaviour in Moscow and how he had taken her to a meeting because he hadn't trusted her not to try and run away. She told her how she had run him down in front of Hugh, his superior and how David had reacted.

"I was scared of him, he wasn't charming any more but hard and cruel. Thank goodness, I met Hugh, he saved me Mum. God knows what would have happened to me had it not been for him!"

"David threatened to kill you?!" June's mouth fell open.

"Not just that but he intended to abandon me in Warsaw with no passport."

"But why? Why abandon you in Warsaw when all he had to do was send you home?"

"He was a double agent Mum. Hugh was laying a trap for him but he must have realised he had been uncovered so he disappeared. But I still don't understand why he was sending me there. All I can think is that he was going to catch me up and... I just don't know what he intended to do. And I still don't know why he was so desperate to have me as a wife. What a damned mess I made of everything!"

June, though horrified at what Sandy had just told her, kept calm and gazing at her thin, pale, haunted daughter she said

"You have nothing, absolutely nothing to be ashamed of."

"Oh, but Mum I have." Sandy had not for one moment put Hugh from her thoughts. She could see him now, his concern and love for her plainly written on his face. Would she ever see him again? Would she ever be able to forget him?

"Mum, I fell in love with Hugh."

ᴖ ᵕ ᴖ

Lilly arrived with Tim and leapt from the car to fling herself at Sandy who knelt down and succumbed to a furious face wash from Lilly's tongue. She glanced up at her father and smiled

"Hello Dad. Thanks for bringing her. Come on Lil' let's chase some ducks." She ran with Lilly on the lead beside her down the road to the park.

"I think that's the first time she's smiled since she got home."

"I was a fool not to bring the dog in the first place, I didn't think."

"Come inside Tim, you need to hear what she has told me."

It was hard to take it all in. Tim sat in a stunned silence as June updated him.

"Christ! Small wonder she's so disturbed." Tim pushed his hand though his hair and swore quietly under his breath.

"It's not up to us to tell Oliver or his parents Tim. We have to let Sandy do that unless she tells us otherwise."

"I suppose she realises that you will tell me?"

"No doubt about it. I think that's why she has gone out with Lilly. She has found it very hard Tim, some of the things she has been through are beyond belief."

"But where is that man? Is he still free? Will he come after her?" Tim was bristling with anger and anxiety.

"I don't think so. According to Sandy, he's probably hidden away in a safe house in Russia. And, so she tells me, he will not have a very good time of it."

"Who told her that? How can they be sure?"

"It was Hugh. He's a high-ranking diplomat or something. We owe him our daughter's life." She added "But that's the saddest thing of all, Sandy and he became lovers, serious lovers. She pines for him but knows she must try and forget him. I don't know how she's going to cope with it."

"Whatever is she going to do about Oliver?" Tim thought of him, waiting at the farm, hoping for good news on Tim's return and he felt deeply saddened.

"She loved, and I think she still loves Oliver, but, this relationship seems like a real passion. Oliver and Sandy sort of grew into each other didn't they, based primarily on friendship. But I don't think she ever felt the overwhelming surge of love for Oliver she seems to have felt for Hugh."

"Damn and blast it!" Tim felt hopeless and angry and sorry all at once.

"She didn't ask for any of this to happen Tim. Don't blame her please. Do you not remember what it was like to be in love?"

When Sandy returned from her walk she entered sheepishly to meet her father.

"I expect Mum's told you Dad?"

"Yes, love she has. I don't know what to say or think." He gathered her in his arms and spoke into her spiky hair. "I'm just glad to have you back in one piece. There's no need to talk to me about it if you don't want to, I quite understand." Sandy hugged him back. It seemed like years since she had snuggled up to his woolly sweater relishing the safety of her father's arms and poked his tubby tummy with her finger.

"Thanks Dad."

And so Tim had to return home with nothing new to tell Oliver. Sandy remained with June and tried very hard to get some feeling for life again.

She attempted to paint but nothing was successful. June thought that she was spending too much time alone and suggested she might approach the schools to see if they needed any extra help in the art classes or maybe she could do some private tuition? At first Sandy shrugged it off, she didn't want to teach anyone anything. But after thinking about it for a day or so she did apply for a teaching job with an art class for adults and apart from getting out and meeting people she earned a few pounds and she found that she almost enjoyed it.

CHAPTER 19

IT HAD COME AS NO SURPRISE TO HUGH when he found on his return to England that Angela had decided to prolong her cruise. Out of pure curiosity, as he really didn't care one way or the other, he asked a few discreet questions amongst his friends and found that his suspicions were not unfounded. Her companion was a man. His immediate thought was one of relief; he could divorce Angela, she would probably be amenable and happy that she no longer had to pretend that she still loved him. He was sure that she did care for him in her way but their relationship had been growing stale for many years and she took every opportunity not to accompany him on his postings. He didn't blame her as relocating every year or two was disruptive and as soon as she had settled and made friends they were on the move again.

He would be free to marry Sandy. Hugh was not impulsive by nature and this was what made him so good at his job. He gave everything deep consideration before acting and seldom made the wrong decision. However, on hearing the truth about his wife he grabbed the 'phone and rang Sandy's number. He slammed it down as it began to ring. He had no right to inflict himself on her, she was too young and her feelings for him were probably only the sort of infatuation younger women often had about older men. She had promised never to contact him unless it was an emergency and in time she would forget him and marry the young man whom she loved. She had kept to that promise and he hoped she had made it up with the boy Oliver. He removed from his wallet the photograph he had copied from her passport with the single short hair taped to the back and placed it on the table in front of him. He smiled as he looked at her scruffy hair and the cheeky grin hovering around her mouth, he would never forget her. Placing it back in his wallet he put his mind to the work he had in hand and opened the files he had on his desk. Life had continued as normal and he had carried out his duties by rote. He couldn't get Sandy out of his mind but he forced himself not to lift that 'phone or to jump in his car and drive to claim her.

Then one morning the 'phone rang, she needed his help.

The doorbell rang once; a long ring. June answered it still in her dressing gown, it was only seven thirty in the morning and Sandy was in the bath whilst June had been preparing breakfast.

Two men whom June had never seen before stood outside.

"Yes?" She half closed the door on them. They looked stern, almost sinister and June was glad to see one of her neighbours outside getting the milk in. She felt a little less vulnerable knowing the men had been seen and noted.

"Good morning madam. We are looking for Sandra Montgomery, née Williams. I believe this is her address?"

"Yes, but she isn't up yet. Who are you?!" June demanded. The men reached into their pockets and brought out identity cards which they showed her.

"Inform her we wish to speak to her please." They gently but firmly pushed June back inside and followed her, closing the door behind them. June ran upstairs to the bathroom and hearing the bath water begin to run away as Sandy pulled the plug she called through the door

"Sandy?"

"Won't be long Mum." she replied.

"Sandy, open the door a minute please." Sandy opened the door wrapped in a towel and took in the anxious look on June's face.

"What's up Mum?"

"Sandy, there are two men downstairs who want to speak to you. They are detectives I think, or some sort of government officials. Whatever do they want with you?" she whispered.

"I have no idea, unless it's to do with David. Maybe he's been arrested!"

"Well quickly get some clothes on and come down, will you?"

The two men had positioned themselves directly in line with the back and front doors and were standing with their hands behind their backs as though on guard. June felt alarmed. This was not a courtesy call.

Sandy came running downstairs still rubbing her wet hair with a towel.

"Sandra Montgomery?" the elder man addressed her.

"Well if you must call me that, yes, but I intend to get a divorce as soon as I can. I prefer to be called Williams if you don't mind."

"Sarah Montgomery, I would like you to accompany us to the police station. There are questions you need to answer."

"Why can't you ask them here?" Sandy replied.

"You can either come willingly Sandra Montgomery or I shall have to arrest you."

"Arrest me! On what charge for heaven's sake?"

"Treason."

"What?!" Sandy nearly fell over. She didn't know whether to laugh or scream. Was this some kind of practical joke? Was it April 1st?

"Okay, I'll come willingly, but I think it's a waste of time. I'm not a traitor, I wouldn't know where to begin!" She began to laugh but seeing no hint of amusement on their faces she realised that actually, it wasn't very funny.

"Wait. I'm coming too." June grabbed Sandy's arm.

"No Mum, ring Dad and Jeremy. Anyone. You'll be more help doing that."

"But where are you taking her? I need to know!" June was frantic.

"For the time being Mrs Williams, she will be held at the police station in Exeter, where she will be questioned."

"But what's it all about?" June cried. "My daughter's not a traitor!"

"I'm afraid we are not at liberty to tell you. Good day madam." June watched her daughter being escorted to a car between two large men who then sat either side of her in the rear seat before the driver took them away. She ran indoors and 'phoned Tim.

No one spoke to Sandy on the hour's drive to Exeter. When they arrived, she was put into an interview room with bars on the windows. It wasn't exactly a cell but it felt like one. Sandy wasn't particularly worried, it had to be something to do with David and she could soon put them straight on that. However, when the door opened a policeman entered carrying Sandy's 'lost' suitcase. Sandy sat up in surprise.

"Oh, my case. Where did you find it?" she asked innocently. The policeman didn't answer but left the room as two different plain clothes detective types entered. The elder of the two approached the table and sat opposite Sandy.

"Mrs Montgomery I have to inform you of your rights. He read her her rights and told her she was entitled to make one 'phone call.

"I don't need to ring anyone, I haven't done anything wrong!"

"Very well, that is your decision." He indicated the case with a wave of his hand.

"So, you admit this is your suitcase?"

"Yes. Why wouldn't I?"

"And where did you see it last?"

"At Heathrow. No, not at Heathrow, the last time I saw it was at the airport, Domodedovo or some such name. We hung around for ages for it to come around on the belt at Heathrow and in the end I gave up on it. There was nothing valuable in it only clothes and I got fed up with waiting." Sandy indicated the case which was lying open on the table. "Look, just a load of rubbishy clothes and, oh, that's where my book was, I thought I'd lost it." she added noticing her paperback amongst the sweaters and jeans. She was sure it hadn't been packed quite as badly as it now appeared. Everything was in a jumble and there was a huge tear down one side. "What's happened to it? It looks as though it's been run over."

"Mrs Montgomery, did you pack this bag yourself?" Sandy thought for a moment

"I never really unpacked it, my husband had stuffed it full of new clothes for me which I didn't like. He said the clothes I had packed were unsuitable. I just stuffed a few things in on top before I left to come home."

"So, you were aware of all the items in the case?"

"I think so. Look, what's all this about?" Her interviewer did not answer but persisted with his own questions.

"What was purpose of your visit to Warsaw?"

"Warsaw! I never went to Warsaw. David had booked me a flight but I hid and didn't go. I don't know what's going on here. I haven't done anything wrong."

"I have to inform you that papers of a secret and sensitive nature were found hidden in a false bottom to your case. During the baggage handling it had become entangled in the conveyor belt and as you can see it was badly torn. Whilst inspecting it to find its owner in order that compensation may be made, the airport customs found the papers which were intended for an address in Warsaw. Now please let us start at the beginning and tell me who you were meeting in Warsaw and what went wrong to prevent you making the drop."

Sandy was astounded. So, that was why David was sending her on alone. She was to be his carrier whilst he went underground. Was that why he had married her? He must have had it all planned months in advance. She was perfect: not only young and innocent looking but he had a hold over her that he didn't have over anyone else.

"I think I need to 'phone someone." she said.

June rang Tim in a dreadful panic.

"Sandy's been arrested!"

"Whatever do you mean? Why? Are they coming for the rest of us as well?"

"No, I don't think it's got anything to do with Paul, they weren't ordinary policemen Tim, they were MI6 or something. I can't remember. You must get hold of Jeremy!"

"Where have they taken her?"

"To Exeter police station but they said it was only initially, they might have taken her somewhere else by now. Oh, hurry Tim call Jeremy, see if he can get there quickly."

"I'll get on to him immediately and then I'll drive there myself."

Sandy was led into an office where she was given the 'phone.

"Just one call." the man said. She prayed that he would be there. His number was indelibly printed in her mind but she withdrew his card which she carried everywhere with her from her pocket and dialled Hugh's number. It rang and rang and just as the detective was about to tell her to stop it was answered. Sandy heard his voice and for a moment she went limp and had to ask for a chair.

"Hugh, is that you?"

"Sandy. Are you alright?" At the sound of her hesitant and breathless voice he knew she was in trouble.

"Hugh, I've been arrested on treason charges. Help me please."

"Where are you?"

"I'm in Exeter police station and they say I was smuggling papers or something. Oh Hugh, it's David, he's done this to me."

"Stay calm and don't answer any more questions. I'm on my way. Now give the 'phone to the most senior man there and I will speak to him." Sandy handed the 'phone to her interviewer who snapped

"Who is this? If it's your solicitor, he can go through the correct procedures." He lifted the receiver to his ear and listened whilst Hugh spoke to him.

"Yes sir. I understand sir." He put the 'phone down. "You have contacts in high places Mrs Montgomery!"

⌒ ‿ ⌒

Jeremy left his office immediately Tim had rung off.

"Take any messages Mary please. I shall be out of the office probably for the remainder of the day." He hurried up the steps and arrived slightly breathless at the police station.

"I am here to represent Miss Sandra Williams." he introduced himself at the desk. He was shown to an interview room and Sandy was escorted in by a policewoman.

"I would like to speak to my client in private please." Jeremy towered above her and his booming voice echoed in the room.

"Well Sandy, here we go again." He smiled at her and shook her hand. "Don't worry my dear I'm sure we can sort this out. Now, fill me in."

Sandy didn't know where to start. "How much do you know so far Jeremy? It's such a long story I can't go all over it yet again."

"All I know is that this David Montgomery blackmailed you into marrying him and going to Russia. Start from there." Sandy sighed. It was still too complicated to explain in the half hour or so they had been allotted.

"Basically Jeremy, David turned out to be an agent for the Russians and it seems that he was intending to use me to carry information for him."

"Hold it there." Jeremy interrupted. "Is this fact or surmise?"

"It's definitely a fact that he was an agent and he must have defected because he disappeared after dumping me at the airport. I didn't know he had put anything in my case. If I'd known he had, I would have told Hugh."

"Who is Hugh?" Jeremy was finding it difficult to follow Sandy's story. He needed more background information.

"Hugh was his superior in the foreign office in Moscow. He told me that David had been under surveillance and they had been on the point of trapping him but he must have realised and that's when he tried to send whatever those papers are to a contact in Warsaw," she paused then added "and to get rid of me in the process."

"Hmm I see. This is a tricky one for me as I haven't acted for anyone in these circumstances before. It's a government issue and I'm more attuned to common or garden criminals."

"Hugh said he was coming to rescue me. But he's in London and I've no idea when he'll be here."

"Oh, so you have made contact with him then? That was a smart move. I suggest then that you slowly and accurately bring me up to date and then I will talk to Hugh. What's his surname?"

"I don't know!" Sandy realised that after loving this man and spending weeks with him she had never known or even cared what his surname was. He hadn't offered it and it had not occurred to her to ask. He was Hugh and she loved him desperately and that was all that mattered.

"No matter, I expect he will tell me when we meet." Jeremy smiled at her worried little face with her hair sticking out all over the place. She had just rubbed it with a towel after her bath not realising she was going to be whisked off to a police station. "Don't worry Sandy, we'll get you home pretty soon I'm sure."

Whilst they awaited Hugh's arrival Sandy attempted to explain to Jeremy all that had happened in Moscow. He sat quietly throughout taking notes.

◠ ◡ ◠

Tim rang the Tregowans as soon as he had spoken to Jeremy.

"We'll meet you there." George was adamant that they all show their support for Sandy and would not be dissuaded. Oliver, however, hung back.

"No Dad, I'm not coming. Just let me know how things are and..." He added quietly "give her my love."

Thus, when Hugh eventually arrived at Exeter he was greeted by a room full of people who all wished to speak with him.

"I'm sorry, I cannot speak to anyone on this matter other than her solicitor. Is he here?"

The station sergeant showed Hugh to the interview room where Jeremy and Sandy were waiting.

His heart missed as he caught sight of her. He avoided her eye and strode forward to shake Jeremy's proffered hand.

"Jeremy Small, I'm her solicitor and family friend." Hugh nodded and seated himself beside Jeremy facing Sandy.

"Yes, Sandy has told me of you." He held Jeremy's eye just a moment longer then gave a slight nod. Jeremy returned the gesture.

Stemming from having spent many years in Iron Curtain countries Hugh was wary of the possibility of conversations being eavesdropped or recorded, even in England. This man was taciturn and Jeremy appreciated it.

Hugh tucked his emotions deep inside before looking at Sandy, his eyes, she noticed, held no warmth, they were the eyes of the man who first cross-questioned her in the hotel room. She let a small gasp escape her; what if he believed that she was working with David after all? Surely, he couldn't, not after everything that had happened. Hugh noticed the gasp and his instinct was to reach out and hold her hands across the table but he maintained his role as an investigative member of the Diplomatic Corps. He knew that she was innocent of any of these charges against her but his training and experience had taught him to listen to his head and not his heart. It was imperative that his emotional attachment to her was kept secret as any hint of his involvement could bring his integrity into question and put Sandy at risk.

"Sandra." He used her correct name. "I have to ask you if you were aware of what was secreted in your case."

"No of course I wasn't. You know what happened, you were there!" Hugh shot her a sharp look with a very slight shake of the head. Sandy looked confused for a moment and then she seemed to get the message. "No, I wasn't aware of what was in my case. Had I known I would have reported it straight away. I'm not a traitor. I wouldn't know where to start." She remembered having said those words before but it was true, she was a young artist, inexperienced in the world and as far as intrigue was concerned she had been, up until her experiences with David, naïve. Hugh nodded as if satisfied with her reply.

"Why were you in Moscow?" Sandy was bewildered. They had had this conversation before.

"I don't understand why you're asking me. I already told you everything, don't make me say it all again."

"I need to make sure all the facts tie up. So, tell me what did your husband require of you when you were there? Did he introduce you to anyone? Did you deliver anything for him? Anything, even a postcard?"

"NO!" Sandy shouted at him. "I didn't want to be there. I didn't like my husband, I regarded him more as my jailer!"

"Excuse me for butting in." Jeremy leaned forwards and looked Hugh in the eye. "But I was under the impression that you were here to help clear Sandy's name not to continue the grilling she has been having!" Hugh smiled faintly at Jeremy and gave him a subtle wink, just a flicker of the eyelid, nothing more.

"I have a duty to the Crown Professor Small and I intend to carry it out." He focused again on Sandy.

"Before I left London I made some enquiries as to the whereabouts of your husband." Sandy sat up.

"Where is he? Is he back in England?"

"No, he is not here, yet. But he has been tracked down and arrested, or rather, he handed himself in."

"Why? Why did he do that? He knows he'll go to jail!"

"Yes, he will. But he is determined to take you with him." Sandy's face lost all its colour and she looked about to faint. Jeremy stood up, towering about Hugh.

"I insist that Sandy be given some time with me alone. And I demand that she has a drink, water, tea, anything, the poor girl's in shock!"

"Yes, I think she needs some sustenance but I would ask you to hear me out and then I would like some time alone with her."

"Very well. But please get to the point. I am aware of your status Mr...?" Hugh did not supply the name and after a pause Jeremy continued "but I am representing Sandy and I know the limits."

"As I am no longer assigned to Moscow, some bureaucrat in the civil service deemed it unnecessary to inform me of events first before taking action. This is unacceptable as I was Montgomery's superior and instrumental in having him placed under surveillance. He is my case and no one else's. I could ask for their resignation should I so wish. However, because of this lack of communication my colleagues have acted without my authorization and that is why you are here under these circumstances. Do you follow me?" Sandy nodded mutely but Jeremy pushed him to continue.

"What exactly is Montgomery saying?"

"I'll explain a little. The point is this: David Montgomery has handed himself in, as life in Moscow was not all he expected it to be. He was found in a pretty destitute state in a rundown hotel and virtually penniless. According to him, Sandy's failure to deliver the documents to Warsaw lost him his final credibility and contrary to receiving the large payment he had been promised he was dismissed as a liability and cut off without funds."

"But, I was abducted! He was sending me there with no passport and no way of getting back! I could have been murdered. I didn't know what I was meant to do when I got there. He said to wait for him to come on later."

"But you didn't go did you?" Hugh looked kindly at her. "I was the one who found you hiding from him."

"What does he mean by taking me to prison with him?"

"He insists that you were a willing accomplice and that you had planned it all between you before leaving Britain."

"What! I, I, don't believe it! Or maybe I do believe it. His final bit of spite, his revenge. He is an utter shit. I loathe and detest him. I hated him from the first time I met him. He is selfish, cruel, greedy, violent and a fucking liar!"

Hugh couldn't stop himself. He burst out laughing.

"The same little urchin you always were." He wanted to hold her and kiss her angry little face. He wanted so much to take her away and make love to her. Instead he resumed his official demeanour and spoke to Jeremy who was looking slightly bemused at the change of mood in the interview.

"Unfortunately, the correct procedures have to be taken and he will be flown back here for trial. In the meantime, I will need to speak at length with Sandy to prepare her for a possible court appearance."

"Shit, no. Will I have to stand trial?"

"I doubt you will end up in the dock but you are a prime witness and will undoubtedly have to give evidence." Sandy looked anxiously at Jeremy who patted her on the hand reassuringly.

"Don't worry my dear, it will all be alright." Hugh nodded at Jeremy and continued.

"However, with any luck, when I get him in my grasp he will break and not only admit he is lying but I hope to debrief him totally and close a further hole in the network. This will not be the first time I have broken a spy." Sandy remembered his questions in the flat, coming fast and unexpectedly, changing tack and then later springing the original question, disorientating her and finding loopholes. He missed nothing, he was sharp and clever. Thank goodness he was on the side of right. She let out a long sigh.

"Thank you Hugh." She looked into his eyes which had now softened to the tone she remembered so well when they were laughing together or making love. "For everything." she added.

Hugh addressed Jeremy "If you would be kind enough to inform all Sandy's friends and relations or rather," he added *sotto voce* "'partners in crime', that I will personally take care of her and that they should all go home. 1 shall have to request her release from detention and that may take some time. I shall have to vouch for her whereabouts thereafter." He glowed a little as he saw a secret smile spread across Sandy's face. *Yes, my love I know what we are both thinking.*

Tim was a little annoyed at not being able to speak either to Sandy or to Hugh. June had told him about Sandy's relationship with this man and as a father Tim wanted to see him and assess him. But Jeremy and the others were unaware and that was how Tim intended it should stay so he had no option other than to ask

Jeremy to pass on their love and support before driving back to the farm. Jeremy took them all off to a small pub which was near his work place and they retired to the snug which was private. Here he updated them on what was happening and attempted to reassure Tim that even if Sandy had to go to court it would not be as a suspect but as a witness. He also told them that he suspected that Hugh knew all about their actions after Oliver had brought Paul and Sandy back to the farm.

"As far as I can tell he's uninterested in what we did. But it's as well to be on our guard and to keep on the right side of him."

"My God, I've just had a thought!" Tim burst out "If David is coming back for trial and is determined to have his own back on Sandy what's to stop him using that against her and us? After all that's where it all began isn't it?" The friends sat in silence taking in the implications of this, they still hadn't got to the bottom of Paul's neighbour and her interest in the case, they didn't need it to be exposed at a high-profile trial as well. They parted with Jeremy in a subdued manner and drove home. On his arrival, Tim rang June to tell her that Sandy was safe and that her 'friend' Hugh was taking care of things. He didn't want to tell her any more when she was alone and far away from emotional support.

"I'll drive up tomorrow and see you." He said kindly. June was grateful and he realised that he was grateful also; they needed each other just as they had in the past.

Sandy was taken to a waiting room which was more comfortable and less like a cell and Hugh instructed a woman police constable to bring her something to eat and drink. It was well into the afternoon and Sandy had had nothing since dinner the night before. She was relieved as she was beginning to feel faint. However, the food was very basic; a sandwich which had seen better days and a cup of weak tea was placed unceremoniously on the table. The constable then seated herself on a chair near the door.

"I'm not going to run away!" Sandy couldn't help saying to her. She got no response and shrugging her shoulders she attempted to force the stale sandwich down aided by gulps of tepid tea. Hugh had been gone for some time and Sandy fidgeted anxiously and began to walk about the room. The constable watched her coldly. When Sandy moved a little too close to the door the constable stood up and taking her by the elbow she escorted her back to her chair.

"Please remain seated Mrs Montgomery." Sandy sat back down and pulled her arm away.

"I don't know what you think I'm going to do!" she snapped at the woman. "I'm hardly dangerous!" The constable did not reply but returned to her own chair where she sat in silence until Hugh finally returned and dismissed her.

"You're free to go but I am to escort you to an hotel where you must stay until the paperwork is completed."

"Thank God!" Sandy replied, "I was going crazy just sitting here with that sour faced old bag watching me." Hugh grinned at her description which he couldn't help but agree with.

"This may take some time as you are still basically a suspect. They are within their rights to hold you here but I'm afraid I have used my influence and have vouched for you."

"Can we go now? I'm starving, that sandwich tasted as though it had been dug up!"

"I have your word then that you will not try to run away from me?" Hugh strove to keep the chuckle from his voice.

"I swear on my honour!" Sandy replied.

Sandy and Hugh signed various forms and then together they walked out into the daylight.

"I've booked two rooms at a decent sort of place which is just a few minutes' drive away." Hugh opened the passenger door to his car for her. "Hop in, I'm pretty hungry myself. We'll grab a meal and then we can relax a little. We have a lot to discuss and plan."

"Two rooms?"

"Two rooms but only one will be slept in!" Hugh reached for her hand and squeezed it. "We have to be a bit careful on home territory."

When Alice and George returned, Oliver was waiting for them.

"What's happening?" he asked looking over their shoulders as if expecting Sandy to be with them.

"She's sort of under house arrest from what I can gather." George explained. "That chap from the embassy in Moscow who looked after her there has come to her rescue and hopefully he will sort it all out." He sighed, "Come on in lad let's have a cuppa. I'm parched." Over tea in the kitchen George told Oliver what little information he had gleaned from Jeremy, finishing his account with Tim's comment about David possibly taking his revenge by spilling the beans about Paul.

"I'd like to murder that evil piece of shit!" Oliver's face had been getting more and more flushed as George was speaking. "He's wrecked everything Sandy and I had, and for what? Just to make money!"

"Well he's done for this time." George grunted with satisfaction. "He'll end up behind bars and all the money he's made will come to naught. Hopefully when all this is over Sandy will be able to put it behind her and become the girl we knew." Alice slid some cake across the table to them both saying

"That poor girl, what she has been through is unbelievable and all because of her consideration for others. Life is not fair, is it?"

"No, it bloody well isn't. Shame they don't hang traitors anymore." George took a big bite of his cake.

"Don't say that George, Sandy hasn't been let off the hook

completely yet!" Alice reminded him. "Anyway, I believe capital punishment for traitors hasn't actually been abolished yet!"

"Oh, I don't think anyone will believe David, especially with his superior taking on Sandy's case. Poor old Jeremy was a bit out of his depth, I felt sorry for dragging him along when he wasn't in fact really needed."

"Who exactly is this Hugh bloke? And why has he taken such an interest in Sandy?" Oliver's insecurities niggled at his insides and that familiar clenching gripped his stomach. "What's he like?"

"We didn't really have any time with him. He was very authoritative and refused to speak to any of us, even Tim. The only person he had any dealings with other than Sandy was Jeremy."

"But is he young? Is he good looking?" Oliver asked.

"Not particularly good looking and hardly young, I'd say he was in his late forties or early fifties, don't worry about him Oli he's just doing his job."

"Did you manage to speak to Sandy? Did she say anything about us?"

"I'm sorry Oli, we weren't allowed in. It was a bit of a wasted journey to be quite honest."

"Well at least she knew you were all there for her." Oliver remarked lamely.

ᴖ ᴗ ᴖ

After they had eaten Hugh took Sandy to the hotel and booked them in and they were shown to their respective rooms. A few minutes later Hugh knocked on Sandy's door and without waiting entered to be enveloped in her embrace. They kissed with a passion made stronger by their separation and made love with a desperation neither had felt before.

"I love you so much my little urchin, I don't know how I've managed to stay away. I'm so sorry, I've messed up your life, haven't I?"

"No, it wasn't you who messed up my life, it was David. But in a way, I'm grateful that he did or I wouldn't have met you."

"But what are we going to do my love? Your Oliver is the man you must marry, he is the one you chose before I came along. I have to let you go and you must return to him." Hugh turned away from her to hide the pain etched on his face.

"I can't. I love you Hugh, I can't pretend. I've hurt Oliver enough and it would be cruel and insulting to say the least if I went back to him on a lie."

"I'm afraid my darling that once all this is cleared up and David is securely locked away our ways must part. I shall probably be posted somewhere hundreds of miles away and I can't bear you to waste your life waiting for word from me or hoping I will one day knock on your door."

"I'd wait for you for ever, I can't feel like this about anyone again."

"But my little girl, I'm married and I am too old for you. I've said that before and I'll say it again, if you and I ever did marry, if my wife did leave me, you would spend a lonely old age as a widow. I am twenty-five years older than you. When you are forty and in your prime I shall be sixty-five and a retired old has-been."

"Sixty-five isn't old! When you get to eighty I shall be nearly a pensioner myself. Hugh please don't disappear from my life altogether, I beg you." Sandy clung tightly to him, her face buried in his neck. He clasped her to him and wished fervently that he was twenty years younger.

They didn't even discuss the pending trial of David or Sandy's role as a witness. They made love again without the desperation but slowly and lovingly, caressing each other with their hands and mouths until they fell deeply asleep in each other's arms.

CHAPTER 20

MISS HAZLETT STOPPED IN HORROR as she approached the graves. There were screens up all around them and men were standing around with shovels. A policeman stepped into her path and stopped her progress.

"I'm sorry madam this area is closed for the exhumation." She gasped and tottered back a step.

"Whose exhumation?" she asked faintly.

"I shouldn't be telling you this but," he was stopped in his explanation when an older man in plain clothes whom she took to be a detective in charge, called

"Constable!"

"Coming sir." He left Hilda standing there open mouthed and shaking. It was Paul's grave which had the boards around it. Why were they digging the poor boy up? She was going to find out what was going on. She may be old but she wasn't a shrinking violet.

"Excuse me officer, I wish to know why you are opening that grave. He was a dear friend of mine and I have a right to know." The detective was a little taken aback by this forthright little woman, he walked over to where she stood and taking her by the elbow he led her away from the scene.

"You don't want to be here my dear, it's not for public viewing." He shuddered and pulled his collar up and adjusted his hat. "It won't be a pretty sight and I am not too keen on witnessing it myself. However, the reason we're opening it is that it is thought to be empty so I might be spared the sight of a rotting corpse. I'm sorry, that was thoughtless of me." he apologised as Hilda blanched. "But even so my dear you are not permitted to be here whether you were a friend or not, this is police business."

Immediately Hilda thought of that damned neighbour and what she had said on their first encounter. But why did they believe her and why did they think it was empty and so what if it was? Even if it was a memorial and Paul wasn't buried there, which she knew he was, there was nothing illegal about that.

"I can assure you that it is not empty!" She drew away in shock as there was the sound of splintering wood and one of the men called out.

"There's a cadaver in the box sir." She heard one of the men retch and she cried out

"Leave the poor boy alone!"

"Go home. Leave this to us." The detective nearly pushed Hilda back down the path towards the road. "But firstly, tell me your name and address." He took out his note book and pencil and in a strangled voice Hilda gave him the details. As she staggered back down the path she heard instruction being given.

"Load it up in the van lads." *It*. Paul was not an *it*! With tears streaming down her face she found her way to the road and crossed it to wait for the bus home.

Jeremy had hardly got back to the office from seeing the Tregowans and Tim off when there was a 'phone call for him.

"Jeremy, they've taken Paul's body!" Hilda cried.

"Who have?"

"The police. They said something about suspecting that it was an empty grave and then they opened it and they've taken him away." Hilda's voice shook and broke as she tried to continue.

"Jesus bloody Christ!" Jeremy swore loudly. "It's just one damned thing after another. Stay home and wait for me, don't answer the door to anyone and don't speak to the police. Have you said anything at all to them?"

"Only that he was a friend and that I knew he was in the grave."

"That's more than enough. Don't say another word." He dialled Tim's number and instructed them *all* to, without exception, gather at the farm immediately and he would join them with Hilda. He grabbed his coat and called out to his secretary "Mary I've got to go out again. No idea when I'll be back." And muttering to himself about how his practice was about to go under, owing to the fact that he wasn't getting his work done, he set off for Hilda's home.

Through her net curtains, she saw him arrive and hurried to let him in.

"No, I'm not coming in, get your coat and lock up well. We're going to meet everyone at the farm." She scurried in and gathered her things and in less than five minutes they were on the road.

Tim waited at the train station for June with Lilly in tow to arrive accompanied by Mike Squires who had decided it was quicker than driving to pick her up and then coming by road.

Finally, it was evening by the time they were all gathered, with the exception of Sandy, who was still in Exeter. Jeremy had decided not to try to get a message to her as he wasn't sure, as yet, what to make of Hugh. He suspected that Hugh knew everything but, at this moment his priority was getting Sandy off the hook on the matter of treason. How much he would be willing to help regards defending them on an *actual* crime was something he didn't want to think about at the present.

"Well here we all are again!" Jeremy was agitated. "Let's hope we can have a more successful meeting than the last time!" Oliver began to apologise but Jeremy cut him short. "We do not have the time for that now." He sat at the head of the table in the kitchen and began.

"It appears that the nosey neighbour has managed to get the ear of someone in high places. They have taken Paul's body to the morgue where they will have no trouble identifying him. But that isn't why they've exhumed the grave. Hilda tells me that they expected it to be empty."

"Yes," Hilda agreed, "she implied that it was all a sham. I've tried to work out why she said that and now I think I realise what she meant and why she had that man with her the last time she went there. I suspect that she thinks that Paul is still alive and that we have been hiding him throughout and that is why they expected to find it empty."

"But now that they've found that he is actually buried there they surely will assume we have exhumed his body from the bog and given him a decent burial. What's illegal about that?" Oliver asked.

"That's the problem Oliver." Mike had for some years been a police doctor as well as running his own practice. "It's not uncommon to exhume a body if there's suspicion of foul play but in this case, it was thought he had drowned in the mire. But if they do an autopsy they will know he died of pneumonia and that will disprove the theory which we had everyone believe."

"Quite!" Jeremy took over. "Not only will it be obvious how he died but they will be able to ascertain approximately how long he has been dead. And that does not correlate with him dying at the same time as Jimmy. The question then will arise: where was he during that time?"

"We're snookered. How the devil do we explain that away?" George and Alice had been the people to hide him and to disguise him as one of their own to the extent of facing down the police with outright lies. No one had an answer to this. Alice put the kettle on the Aga for want of something to occupy her and the whistle as it boiled was the only sound in the kitchen. She made coffee and handed round biscuits which they all accepted absentmindedly.

"We have two choices." Jeremy broke the silence. "We either

come clean and throw ourselves on their mercy pleading human kindness or we concoct another set of lies which must and I repeat, must, be foolproof and unable to be challenged or disproved."

"That's a tall order. I don't think it's possible." George said. "I am prepared to take responsibility for sheltering him. I can swear that no one else was involved."

"Don't be ridiculous Dad. We, Sandy and I were the ones who brought him here and we knew all about him before we even introduced you to him. There's no way any one person can take the blame. It's all of us or none of us."

"You are correct there Oliver, it is far too complicated to half admit culpability, the police are not fools they would tear your statements into shreds. No, this needs a deal of careful thought."

Tim groaned "Oh Sandy, what a liability you are." he muttered.

"Don't blame Sandy Tim, she's a good girl with a big heart." George patted Tim on the back. "I for one am pleased to have been part of it all, in spite of the problems it has caused."

"Right, let's get down to business. Can anyone come up with a plausible story?" Jeremy threw them all back into silence again.

They slipped quietly out of Sandy's room and into Hugh's before ordering room service for breakfast and after making his bed look as though it had been slept in Hugh opened the door to the maid.

"Mrs Montgomery will be joining me for breakfast. Leave her tray here please." As they ate they discussed David and his imminent case.

"We can skip whether or not you are a guilty party as I know that you were not. What we have to plan now is how to make sure that the hearing goes as smoothly as possible and that he goes down. I want to draft your statement with you so that you don't have to undergo a long interview with MI6. If my own methods of interrogation are anything to go by, you could be dragged through the mill before they let you go."

"It's not just you who witnessed David's treatment of me though is it? There was Michael and the others who were with you when you found me at the airport. They can all be called, can't they?"

"Yes, they can but I am a little wary of our relationship inadvertently coming out if we involve too many people from Moscow. I could lose credibility if it does, it could be implied that I was involved with the two of you, it wouldn't be the first time a man in my position was guilty of espionage. I wouldn't put it past David's devious mind to try to drag me into it as well. However, the very position I held would have given me access to far more secrets than David could have acquired and there have been no leaks on that front so hopefully no one will take him seriously." Hugh's eyes flashed, "Anyway, he's my catch and I shall break him so badly that he won't know what hit him. Apart from his treason, which is despicable, I will see him incarcerated for what he did to you!"

Together they drafted Sandy's statement and Hugh wrote it in longhand. They both signed it ready for Hugh to get it typed when they would both sign it again.

"That's perfect. The only thing which we can't explain is why you married him so quickly and why you appear to have betrayed him if you didn't know what he was up to."

"I will swear that I fell for him before I really knew him and we got married quickly because he was due to be posted and we didn't want to wait until he came home. A bit like sweethearts marrying before the men went off to fight in the war. I didn't know what he was up to at any time. It was only when he disappeared and you told me about him that I knew."

"We should make sure that is explained in the statement." Hugh re-wrote the statement which said that Sandy had fallen for this Don Juan character before she really knew him. They married in haste as lovers often do and it wasn't until they arrived in Moscow that his attitude towards her changed and he showed his true self. She was unhappy and wished to come home but he prevented it by taking her passport. David took her to a meeting with Hugh so that he could keep an eye on her. This was a mistake on his part as Hugh was able to sense immediately that she was unhappy and that she regretted marrying him. During the interview, Sandy had told of David's lack of candour in Mauritius. Hugh personally witnessed David's treatment of his wife after they had left the meeting. He was abusive towards her and threatened her. Hugh sent him to Warsaw to get him out of the way whilst he arranged to seal his fate as he suspected he would be meeting a contact there. However, David slipped through the net and came home earlier than expected. He then abducted his wife and attempted to send her to Warsaw with papers which he had secreted in her case where he planned she would meet his contact. Hugh believed that he had intended to use her in this way on more than this one occasion but events overtook him and he had to act quickly. He retained her passport so that she would be stranded in Warsaw whilst he made his escape. However, she foiled his plan by hiding until she was found in a state of shock by Hugh and other members of the embassy. David was hunted but he had vanished into some safe house and Hugh personally saw to Sandy's safety and brought her home.

"That's good. You can relax my love, no one is going to try you for treason." He kissed her on the top of her head as he got up to pour more tea for them both and ran his hands through her hair.

"I have him. I will deal with him, he will not get off this one. But the only thing which worries me slightly is will he spill the beans about you and your friends as a last bit of spite?"

"Oh shit, that's just what he will do, like a trapped rat. Oh, Hugh how can we stop him?"

"I have no jurisdiction over that sort of thing. I'm Foreign Office, not local bobby but I think I know how to stop his mouth and it won't be with a kiss."

"This is hardly 'Much Ado About Nothing'!" Sandy laughed.

"Right, first things first." Hugh looked very official as he locked the draft statement in his briefcase and Sandy remarked to herself how different his many parts were. When he smiled, or laughed his eyes softened and he became cuddly and teddy bear like. In his inquisitorial persona, his eyes penetrated your soul and you felt exposed and defenceless. He was acute and clever and unrelenting in his delving for the truth. She didn't envy David his interview with Hugh. She got up to go to her room and get dressed, assuming that they were now going to the station to make her statement.

"I said first things first my girl!" Hugh grabbed her around the waist and picking her up as though she weighed no more than a child he deposited her on the bed. Later in the morning Hugh sighed and levered himself out of the bed.

"Let's get this over with, shall we?" Sandy nodded and stretched before getting up.

"I suppose we better had."

They drove to the station and Hugh left her in the waiting room whilst he took her statement to the office to get it typed. On his return, they sat down with a man Sandy had not seen before but who clearly knew Hugh.

"Sandra this is Robert Green, a colleague. Robert shook her hand and then they got directly down to the matter in hand. Hugh handed him Sandy's statement which he read carefully before putting it beside him on the table.

"If you would sign it please Sandra, and Hugh and I will witness it." That done Robert capped his fountain pen and carefully put it in his top pocket, checked it was straight and facing the way he wished it to.

"This looks pretty straightforward Hugh, just as well for Sandra here that you were witness to most of Montgomery's behaviour."

"Yes, by sheer chance he provided me with the link he had in Mauritius. Once we had that we tried to move pretty swiftly but he must have had a tip off." Sandy looked at Hugh with horror.

"You're not saying that I was his link in Mauritius?" Had he been playing with her all this time believing her to be David's accomplice after all? Hugh looked at her awestruck face in puzzlement.

"Sorry?" he replied.

"What do you mean by I was a link?"

"Oh! I see!" He burst out laughing. "I'm sorry I didn't express myself very well. What I meant was that you gave me the clue when you told me about the drowned Russian sailor. Do you remember that you said they put into shore north of Grand Baie and were out of sight of your party?"

"Yes, Josie and I were going to have a snoop when they all suddenly rushed into the sea to try and save him."

"Well David's *campement* was at Pereybere, just around the corner as it were."

"So, their swimming was just a cover up?"

"I believe so, but I will get the truth out of him later have no fear. No, my dear Sandra I have never suspected you of being anything but a pawn in his nefarious activities. The drowning incident must have put the wind up him when hordes of people suddenly appeared on the scene followed shortly after by one of our diplomats." He patted her hand reassuringly. "David must have scarpered pretty quickly and made sure his presence was noted at the High Commission. According to the security personnel he made a big fuss about having left something behind before the weekend and not having his pass key."

"He was sailing a bit close to the wind, wasn't he?" Robert commented.

"Yes, he was becoming very complacent and we gave him just enough rope. The posting to Moscow was just what he'd been hankering after though he was unaware that I knew this. I wanted him where I could watch him and he played along very nicely." Hugh glanced at Sandy

"I'm just sorry that you became caught up in it all."

"Very well then, we have Sandra's statement and of course you will be writing a report." Robert picked up the papers and stacked them neatly, tapping them on the table to line up all the edges. Sandy fidgeted as he took his time and checked they were completely in synchronisation with each other. She would have scrabbled them up in a heap and stuffed them in the folder in a few seconds. Watching this rather fastidious thin-faced man with the long white fingers of an office-bound man, gave her the jitters. She found she was jiggling her legs in her impatience, Hugh discreetly put his hand on her thigh and pressed it until she was still.

"I think Sandra has had enough of we two fogies Robert, I suggest we part for lunch and we'll meet up again when you've had my report."

"Good idea Hugh. Very nice to meet you Sandra and thank you for agreeing to take the stand at Montgomery's trial. You will not be required to say or do very much as your contribution is merely background information about the man himself and what he attempted to force you to do. The serious charges against him are nothing to do with you and you will probably be allowed to return home once you have played your part."

"Before we go, I was wondering how long I have to wait before I can get a divorce from him. Can I get the marriage annulled if he's sent to prison, do I have to go through another legal hearing or can I start the process straight away?" Robert glanced at her unadorned hands on the table and unconsciously twiddled his own wedding ring as he noticed that Sandy was no longer wearing a wedding band having flung it into the Russian waterfall.

"I suggest you speak to your solicitor about that side of things. All his assets of course will be seized, should he be found guilty, did you wish to claim anything?"

"God no, I'd like to shove..." Hugh coughed quietly and Sandy stopped before launching into a colourful description of where she would like to put his assets.

"You are free to go home now." Hugh said as they walked to the car. "Shall I take you or do you want to ring your father?"

"Do you want me to go?"

"Of course not, but I have to return to London soon to prepare for David's return and my interview with him. It's important that I get my facts straight as I don't want to give him even a slim chance of wriggling his way out of it."

"I see. Just one more night and then I'll go home?"

"I should be able to manage that. I'm easily swayed!"

"Am I definitely off the hook now?" Hugh nodded.

"Completely."

"But what about David's hold over me, how are you going to deal with that?"

"Well, as yet I'm not altogether sure but I'll think of something. Threat or coercion? That's what I have to decide and I can't do that until I've spoken to him."

"Hugh, does he have to come to England. Can't MI6 sort of accidentally bump him off in Moscow? That sort of thing goes on all the time, doesn't it?" She hesitated as Hugh shot her a look of astonishment. "Well the Russians do it when one of them tries to defect."

"Sandra! What a shocking thing to say. We don't do that sort of thing here, we're a democracy not a police state." He glanced sideways at her from the driving seat to see her blush with acute embarrassment at his reprimand. He smiled and patted her knee. "Don't think I haven't considered it. In fact, after we rescued you from the airport and I sat guard over you in the apartment I had a loaded pistol at the ready and I would have happily shot him had he tried to harm you."

"I wish he had. No, I don't really mean that, I couldn't ever bring myself to kill anyone and I'd have hated it if you had been forced to kill him for me." She sat in thought as they drove through the town. As they pulled up in front of the hotel she ventured "Have you ever killed anyone Hugh?" He turned the engine off and swivelled in his seat to face her.

"Let's go inside and I'll tell you a bit about myself."

"Can we have lunch in the room rather than the restaurant?"

"My thoughts exactly."

Over lunch Hugh told her about his time in the Royal Navy during the Second World War.

"Just to emphasise the differences in our ages, you were not even born when I was a young officer serving in the war. I chose to leave university to 'do my bit' and was commissioned initially as an acting Sub Lieutenant which rose to Lieutenant Commander by the time the war was over and I returned to my studies."

"What did you study?"

"Languages. I had been accepted at university to take maths but when I left the navy I was head hunted by MI6 to work for them and languages was a more appropriate degree to have. Up until now I have been pretty much an undercover agent, one doesn't broadcast it far and wide, in fact not even our families are allowed to know, but your involvement with David has meant that I have been obliged to tell you, so I hope I can rely on your discretion?"

"Sure. I won't blab it about that I slept with a real James Bond!" Hugh cuffed her gently.

"Seriously though I'd prefer it if you didn't." He continued. "I studied Russian primarily along with German, French and Polish.

Russia, as I told you in Moscow, was a lurking threat and still is. Hence my postings to these Eastern Bloc countries. I spent a year in Warsaw where every single room was bugged so that we often communicated by writing things down and burning them afterwards. The whole of my career has been related to the Russian problem, even when I was in the Seychelles; idyllic though it was, it was still work." Sandy listened avidly to his history and it was true, it did emphasise their age differences. It was a little like her father telling her about his time in the RAF. She felt very young and naïve.

"As for killing anyone," Hugh addressed her initial question. "Probably. But not with my bare hands or even with a hand-held gun where I could see the victim's face. No, I was instrumental in firing many missiles, raking enemy ships with machine gun fire and dropping depth charges on submarines, but all the men I killed were faceless. Not that that helped me sleep at night, I often imagined what it must have been like to be in a submarine when we dropped the charges and how dreadful it was to be trapped like that under the water just waiting to drown. I think I'd rather be blown to bits than that." He shuddered involuntarily and took Sandy's hands in his. "You are lucky to be born a female and even luckier to be born when you were. During both wars, it was assumed that all men were tough and natural fighters full of testosterone and that any unwillingness to kill was a form of cowardice or a hint that they were homosexual or inadequate in some way. As you know, men were shot in the First World War for breaking under the strain. It was termed as 'lacking moral fibre' and they were executed for cowardice. They didn't shoot men for that in my war but the term 'lacking moral fibre' was still used derisively for the gentler peace loving men. No doubt had I been in the thick of things in the army for example, I'd have had to kill the man in front of me, or be killed. I suppose I would have been able to do it though it isn't something that comes naturally to me. Some men are hardened and brutal naturally, like that man Jimmy you told me about or they are brutalized by the war and find killing easy but I can't see me ever becoming like that."

He got up from the chair and led Sandy to sit beside him on their bed. Still holding her tightly by the hand he continued.

"I hated the killing but I was never a coward and I did what I had to do ruthlessly and without allowing my conscience to interfere with my duty to the Crown. My duty to Britain is my foremost concern and if I had to, I would kill to protect it. That is why I chose to join MI6 when I was approached."

"You must despise people like David. He was born after the war, wasn't he? I think he's about my age and never had it so good. He has no loyalty other than to the god Mammon."

"How well you put it. I thought you were a bohemian artist not a literature scholar! Your reference to Shakespeare earlier and now Greek mythology, what other gems of wisdom are you hiding under that hedgehog hair style?" The tension of the rather emotional recounting of Hugh's wartime experiences broke as they laughed.

"I took English Literature, and History at A level as well as Art, I chose art college because I loved painting but I read all the time, if I haven't got a book I get withdrawal symptoms!"

When they had finished lunch, Hugh resisted the urge to take Sandy to bed and suggested they go out instead.

"Let's go for a walk along the river or shall we take a drive down to the sea?" Hugh suggested.

"Let's go to Exmouth, we used to go there on holiday, the beaches are lovely. Shame we haven't got Lilly with us she'd love it." She looked shyly at him and added "But first, Hugh, can I buy some new underwear? I'm not in the habit of wearing the same knickers for more than one day."

"You've been out of them more than in!" Hugh hugged her to him with a laugh.

"Right Marks and Spencer here we come. Then off to the beach and fish and chips out of the newspaper for supper."

The meeting at the farm was not progressing very well. Whichever way they looked at it they could find no way of denying their involvement with Paul especially as Sandy and Oliver had organised his burial. One word with the vicar would confirm this.

"It looks as though we are going to have to confess everything and hope the courts are lenient." Jeremy sighed. "You, as ordinary citizens who acted out of human kindness, may all get off with a suspended sentence and a fine, but as for myself I will most definitely be struck off and may even face prison. As a member of the legal profession I will be the most culpable as I was completely aware of what I was doing. You too Mike, you're retired so it won't affect your practice but you will be judged likewise."

"I can't have you two taking the worst punishment for something which you were coerced into doing." George said adamantly. "Jeremy, you were tricked by us and Mike you were following the Hippocratic Oath. I shall stand up in court and tell them all that we lied to you and that you, Mike, had no idea that it was a fugitive you were treating and I shall swear that Jeremy never met Paul and believed him dead when he was asked to act for him. They have no way of disproving this if we all stick to the story."

"But what about Montgomery? He knows everything." Tim asked.

"He may not get a chance to even broach the subject. His own trial will take precedence." Jeremy replied. "We need to concern ourselves with what has actually happened here and leave him to Hugh what's his name."

"Talking of him, how long is he going to keep Sandy in Exeter? You'd have thought he would have the decency to ring us and let us know what's happening!" Oliver couldn't explain why he had instinctively taken a dislike to the man even though he had never

met him. "And I still don't understand why he took such an interest in Sandy when she was supposed to be on her honeymoon
with another man!"

"Oli, he was doing his job. We should all be grateful to him for
looking after her." Alice laid her hand on his arm and noticed it
was trembling. "Sandy's going to be involved with him for quite
a while until the trial is over. Try to be patient love."

"All I want is to be able to speak to her damn it!" Oliver had
tried so hard to keep his frustration in check, Sandy had been
home now for well over a month and not once had she rung him
or his family. He had considered contacting Susie and trying to
rekindle what they once had but it was no use. Sandy was the girl
he loved and he wouldn't be able to disguise it from Susie. He
couldn't pretend to her that he loved her as he once did. He was
an honourable man and nothing, not even Sandy' behaviour, was
going to change that. Oliver's face was a cloud of misery and June
and Tim exchanged looks: poor Oliver, the only person who had
the right to tell him about Sandy's relationship with Hugh was
Sandy herself. Tim felt anger burning in him, he was very fond of
Oliver and his heart ached for him. He wanted to tell him and put
the poor chap out of his misery but knew he must not. He swore
to himself that when he had Sandy to himself he would insist that
she told Oliver the truth, surely, she cared enough about him to
do that! Sandy was becoming more and more of a stranger to him,
he thought he knew her so well but it seems that he knew her not
at all.

"I agree with George." Tim took June's hand in his, "We both
do, don't we?" June nodded.

"Yes, I do, Jeremy has the most to lose and we must protect
him. After all he was tricked, initially wasn't he?" Jeremy wasn't
happy with their plan but had to agree that so far it was the best
one they had come up with. His livelihood and his freedom were
seriously in jeopardy, more so than the rest of them. He seemed

to shrink in his chair and with downcast eyes he muttered

"It's against all my instincts and honour but for the time being, unless we can think of another way round it, I will agree. In the meantime, I must find a colleague whom I trust completely and who will be prepared to act for us all should it come to the crunch." They spent the remainder of the evening rehearsing their story and trying to make sure all the facts and dates tallied.

Finally, Jeremy rose wearily from his seat saying "Come on Hilda let's get you home."

"Please stay here tonight everyone. We're all tired and unhappy and a long drive at this time of the evening isn't a good idea." Alice held out her arms as if to encompass the gathering. "I have some cold meats and bread we can eat and room enough for you all."

"Thank you, Alice. Hilda is that alright with you?" At her acquiescence, he sank back into his chair with an expression of extreme exhaustion on his face.

"Thank you from us as well, but June and I will go back to my cottage, it'll lessen the load for you but I wouldn't say no to a bit of bread and cheese before we go." Tim looked affectionately at June, "Is that okay with you?"

"Yes Tim, that's absolutely fine by me."

Hugh and Sandy strolled along the water's edge of the deserted sandy beach their fingers lightly interlaced so that at a glance they appeared not to be touching. Hugh often cast his eyes around them, his instincts telling him that they may be watched. He was aware that he should not be seen to be involved with the witness other than in his official capacity and this made him slightly edgy. They caught sight of some small dunes at the top of the beach and left the waterside to go to them. With one last look around them Hugh pulled Sandy down beside him in the shelter of the mounds and she gratefully snuggled down beside him.

"It's quite warm out of the wind especially with your hot little body next to me." Hugh pulled her to him and they kissed. "I'd like to make love to you here and now but I don't think it's a good idea: apart from the sand getting where it shouldn't, which is very uncomfortable, I have a feeling that I'm being watched. It's probably just the paranoia which goes with the job but I'd rather not take the chance." They hugged and kissed for a few minutes more before pulling apart and sitting innocently looking out to sea. Which was just as well because suddenly a wet dog chased by a young couple flung itself between them and shook all over them.

"Sorry, sorry, Monty come here!" the man called as he grabbed the dog by its collar, "I'm so sorry he's a puppy and wild!"

"Don't worry, I love dogs." Sandy smiled up at him as she brushed the sand out of her hair. The young man smiled back and then a look of recognition spread over his face.

"Sandy?"

"Martin! What are you doing here, I thought you lived in Nottingham?"

"Mum and Dad still do but I've got a teaching job here. I must say it's a breeze after the city, weather's better too." Just then the young woman came panting up the beach, she too stopped short as she reached the dune.

"My God Josie it's you!"

"Sandy, great to see you, who's this?" She flashed a seductive smile at Hugh.

"I'm a friend of the family." Hugh said bluntly and didn't enlarge any further. Sandy took Josie's attention away from Hugh by asking what she was doing now and how come she was with Martin again.

"I thought you two split up after college."

"Yea, well after I got back from Mauritius I was so pissed off and miserable after that shit lost me my job that I gave him a call and he was free so we sort of got back together again." Martin attempted to engage Hugh in conversation whilst Josie and Sandy were chatting but Hugh was not going to be drawn into questions and answers. After a few minutes, he pointedly looked at his watch saying

"We must get back now Sandy." Josie hugged Sandy and scribbled her address and 'phone number on a scrap of paper and they parted company.

"Ring any time, we can catch up." she called to Sandy over her shoulder as they ran after the dog.

"No way!" Sandy muttered as they walked away.

"That was close! Just as well we were behaving ourselves." Hugh remarked when they were out of earshot.

"We could always have made a sign saying 'Coitus do not interruptus!' and stuck it on a post."

"I think that would have the opposite affect!" They sauntered back towards the seafront where the smell of fish and chips drew them to a little restaurant boasting fresh caught fish. Opting for a take-away rather than eating inside they found a bench facing the sea where they sat and ate.

"So, that's Josie, is it? She's very, forward isn't she?"

"Yes, she is always like that, I used to be fond of her but she gets on my nerves. I'd forgotten what she was like before I agreed to join her in Mauritius." Sandy threw a chip angrily at a persistent pigeon. "I'm furious with her actually. If it hadn't been for her grovelling after David and blabbing something told in confidence he'd never have had that hold over me." Sandy stopped eating and turned angrily to Hugh. "I'm surprised I could even be civil with her, she's fucked up everyone's lives just to get into bed with him. And he didn't even want her anyway." A sudden image of her dear Oliver and his stricken face as he had left her in the park flashed into her mind. That was the last time she had seen him or spoken to him. She felt her eyes prick and a tear rolled from under her lashes. "Oh Hugh, what am I going to do?" Hugh put his food on the bench beside him and took her hand in his.

"My dear little girl, you don't deserve to suffer like this. Your friend Josie has just nonchalantly got on with her life leaving a trail of destruction behind her, oblivious to the hurt and complications she has put you through. I would like to pull her up and tell her what I think of her but I cannot." He reached in his pocket and handed Sandy his handkerchief, spotless and ironed just like the first one he had given her. She took it and cried with earnest into it.

"But if she hadn't told David I would never have met you." she sobbed.

"It would have been better if you had not, better for you and for Oliver."

"What about you? Would it have been better for you?"

"You know the answer to that. I struggle daily not to beg you to stay with me. I love you deeply and will never love like this again. But I will say goodbye in the end and one day when you are with Oliver again you will realise that was the right thing to do."

"Oliver. My dear friend Oliver. We were going to get married you know. I was so happy on the farm, we knew each other so well. I've betrayed him and hurt him so much I can't ever go back to him Hugh. When all this is over and you have disappeared from my life what have I got left? Just memories and heartache."

"I know it's sounds trite my love but time does heal, or rather it has a way of shuffling the filing system in your head and your heart. You never forget but the intensity lessens with time, the edges blur and new feelings superimpose themselves over the old ones."

"I don't want any more of these chips. Let's go back now." Sandy screwed the newspaper in a ball and looked around for a waste bin.

"Me neither. Come on then little one."

They drove back to the hotel each lost in their own thoughts. Hugh felt like crying himself, his marriage was a sham and Sandy's relationship with Oliver was potentially wrecked. He didn't really care about his marriage; they had had some good times but Angela had never really tried to understand his commitment to his work and his country. She wanted fun and parties and complained bitterly when he was unable to accompany her to them. She must have started having affairs a long time ago, he suddenly wondered if his children were really his. But it was this little person sitting sadly beside him whom he worried about, not himself. He had compounded her problems by falling in love with her and she with him. Had she been a Josie-like character she would have had fun with him and then callously returned to faithful, long suffering Oliver. He berated himself for allowing his feelings to manifest themselves. He had fully intended to only make contact once a year to see if she was well and had prayed that Oliver would love her enough to take her back. Then she was arrested. And here they were: lovers again with an intensity far greater than before.

Back in the hotel room Hugh ran a bath for them to wash off the sand and sticky saltiness. Whilst it was running he asked Sandy for the piece of paper Josie had given her. "You haven't thrown it away I hope."

"No, here it is." Sandy drew the crumpled scrap from her pocket and handed it to him. "I don't want it. I shall not be getting in touch with her again."

"No, but I might." Hugh made a copy of it in his diary and put the paper in his wallet. "She may be useful."

Hugh had insisted that Sandy ring her mother to say she was coming home until the trial but there was no answer. She rang Tim who was a little abrupt with her which hurt and she had little to say to him in return. She was surprised when she heard June insisting on speaking to her and wondered what she was doing there but didn't ask.

June was quick to pick up the sadness in Sandy's voice. "I am so sorry darling, I can imagine how you're feeling, I just wish I could say something that would make you feel better." Sandy cried a little at the kindness but staunched the tears before Hugh saw them. She heard Tim's voice in the background saying

"Ask her what she's going to do about Oliver!"

"Tell him to shut up Mum. I've just about had enough, I'm shattered and thoroughly miserable about Oliver but I can't help what's happened!"

They slept very little on their last night. After making love they talked and dozed. Then they woke as if synchronised and made love again. They talked over and over about their dilemmas and Sandy begged him to leave his wife and marry her. Hugh refused to make such a promise insisting that she go back to Oliver. Finally, as dawn crept upon them and the dark red curtains turned to pink in the rising sun Sandy fell into a deep sleep. Hugh got out of bed and sat in the armchair. He had made a decision. He would give Sandy time to re-establish her love for Oliver, say six months? During which time, he would ask Angela if she wished to leave him. If after this six months or perhaps he should give them a year, Sandy and Oliver showed no sign of making up he would ask her to marry him. He would not tell Sandy of this plan, she had to believe it was the end for them or she would never make the break. Part of him hoped that Oliver would take her back and that she would learn to love him again and the other part wished fervently that he wouldn't.

Hugh drove slowly on their way to June's, his thoughts in turmoil. It was true that he would be seeing Sandy again for the hearing but there would be no more nights together, no more love-making. He ached desperately for her but dared not allow it to overwhelm him. Sandy sat quietly beside him with her hand warm and comforting on his thigh. They had said all that needed to be said during the night and although Sandy had agreed to part she had cried bitterly and her eyes were still red from the tears. As he glanced at her he thought his heart would break and he very nearly turned the car around to take her back to the hotel.

They finally drew up outside the house and Sandy, oblivious to any who may be watching, threw herself into his arms and kissed him passionately until he gently pulled away.

"Goodbye my darling Hugh." She gulped back her tears and got out of the car. He watched her walk up the path to the front door where she turned and waved sadly before entering the house and closing the door behind her.

Both June and Tim were waiting inside, June rushed to her and hugged her tightly but Tim's face was dark. He took her by the arm and led her into the sitting room.

"We need to talk."

"Not now Dad."

"Yes. Now!" He sat her on the settee and stood in front of her.

"Much as I am pleased to see you have been released Sandy, I can't say as much for your display out there. Kissing a married man for all to see without a care for Oliver who, in my opinion should wipe you out of his life!"

"Tim, leave her alone!" June stepped between them. "Give her a chance to breath, can't you see how upset she is?"

"It's of her own making, she has no one to blame but herself." He pushed June firmly aside. "What did you think you were doing getting involved with him knowing he was married and old enough to be your father?" Sandy got up angrily and faced her father with sparks in her eyes.

"You may be my father but you can't tell me who to fall in love with. I would have preferred it if you and Mum had sat down with me and allowed me to speak first before pitching in with the Victorian father bit!" She glared at him and turned to her mother. "Mum, can you tell Dad that it is over between Hugh and me.

And," she addressed Tim, "Hugh is a decent man, he rescued me from possibly being murdered and he will stop at nothing to put David behind bars. Furthermore, he cares about Oliver even though he has never met him. He loves me but he has forced himself to give me up because he says he is too old for me and I should marry Oliver."

The words came tumbling out followed by a heart wrenching sob and Sandy flew from the room. As she climbed the stairs she shouted back to them "I'm sure Oliver would love to marry a slut!"

"Oh well done," June glowered at Tim, "that was really helpful. She had hardly walked in before you started on at her. Surely you could have at least given her an hour or two to settle. She's been under arrest and she has been frightened. I know you care about Oliver but frankly it's none of your business. What we needed to talk about was Paul's exhumation and not her personal life."

"Damn it June, I'm sorry, but you haven't seen how the poor boy has suffered, he's as thin as a rake and withdrawn and angry at the same time. All he wants to do is talk to her, you heard him at the meeting, if only she would just tell him one way or the other!"

"She will, in time. But you seem to have forgotten what she has been through and what she has made herself endure with no other thought in her mind than to protect everyone else, Oliver included. It is no small wonder that she fell for an older man who offered her protection and affection when she was completely alone in that horrible country with a wicked and cruel husband." She allowed this to sink in before adding "Who do you care more about, your own daughter or Oliver?"

"Alright, alright, you've made your point. I suppose I was a bit heavy handed. I'll apologise if you think she'll listen."

"And stay off the subject of Oliver, she doesn't need you to tell her what she already knows."

Tim tapped lightly on Sandy's door. "Sandy love, I'm sorry, can I come in?" Sandy opened the door to him and he held out his arms for her. She approached him warily then she raised her eyes to his and saw the love in her chubby father's face and fell into his embrace. "I'm so sorry my love, everything has just got on top of me."

"It's okay Dad, I understand but you have to let me sort my own affairs out, no one else can do it for me."

Later that evening as they sat down for dinner Sandy asked her father when he was going back to the cottage. June and Tim exchanged smiles and Sandy exclaimed

"Are you back together? Oh, that's wonderful!"

"It's a trial run darling, just to see if we can stand each other for longer than a day." June laughed and cleared the plates away.

"I hope you can, it would be so good to have the family back the way it was. I'm so sorry Mum, Dad, it was all my fault wasn't it and it hasn't ended yet. I wish we could put the clock back."

"We all do love." Tim agreed.

When they had retired to the sitting room and were relaxing over coffee, Tim interrupted June's chatter "Sandy," He took a deep breath, "there has been a development, Paul has been exhumed."

"What? Why?" Sandy interrupted.

"It's probably thanks to his neighbour who was so vile to Hilda. It appears that she managed to convince the authorities that the grave was empty and that Paul is and has always been somehow 'at large'. Hilda said that they seemed surprised when they found a body in the coffin and of course they have taken it away for identification."

"Oh Christ. What are we going to do?" Sandy cried. "David said he was going to swear I was party to his plans in Moscow but Hugh says he won't be believed; I thought I was safe at last, now we're all back to square one and if David decides to have a last bit of revenge and repeats what he knows…"

"Yes, my love, we're in deep trouble." Tim explained what their only option was at the present. "There seems to be no way out other than admitting culpability but we have to protect Jeremy and Mike." Sandy agree with him about the two professionals but she did not agree that they should just give up and hand themselves in.

"I'm going to talk to Hugh. He may be able to help."

"You had better do it soon then, I half expect the police to come knocking any minute." Tim said. "But heaven knows how he can help, the law is the law my love and even your 'Man from the Ministry' isn't above that."

Sandy was nervous about asking Hugh for help as he had already implied that it was out of his jurisdiction. Also, he was going to be very busy compiling the case against David which of course was the priority. She didn't ring him as he had promised to call her when he had news regarding David's trial and her possible appearance as a witness. They just had to wait and hope that when Paul was identified it would be assumed that he had been recovered by friends at a later date and buried. They prayed that it wouldn't be deemed necessary to ascertain when or how he died as it appeared from what Hilda told them that the reason for his exhumation had been merely to see if he was buried there.

CHAPTER 21

HUGH ENTERED THE ROOM where David sat arrogantly smiling, leaning back in his chair which he had pushed away from the table, his legs were stretched out in front of him, ankles crossed in a nonchalant and insubordinate manner. He looked pale and thin and in spite of his posturing little beads of sweat had appeared on his upper lip and his hands shook ever so slightly. Hugh seated himself opposite him and looked steadily at him. David held his gaze for some time before dropping the front legs of the chair to the floor and sitting up in his chair.

"Now we can begin." Hugh placed the statement on the table in front of David. "I require the truth from you and not these fanciful lies you have written here. Would you care to start again?" Hugh spoke softly his voice betraying no aggression. "I know that there's a great deal you can tell me which would be of use to me and which of course could benefit you. I'm sure you understand what I am saying?" David placed his hands in his lap to hide the shake and replied

"I have told the truth in my statement. I have nothing more to add. My wife and I acted together as a team but she lost her nerve. That's all I have to say."

"Very well. The information you passed on was of little consequence, so I don't need to question you any longer. But as a traitor you may no longer live as a free man in this country and so I shall send you back to Moscow so that you can continue living the lifestyle of a favoured defector. No doubt your contacts will be pleased to see you again and will set you up in a fine mansion in the country." David started. Go back to Moscow to live on the street? No, he had been let down by the Russian bastards who had employed him and abandoned him to die destitute, homeless and penniless. That was why he had handed himself in to the embassy. It had been that or starve. He wasn't expecting this. Thinking he had the upper hand with his implication of Sandy he assumed that Hugh would attempt to bargain with him; he had already planned his moves which involved swearing that Sandy was his accomplice and he also had a card up his sleeve with his knowledge of her involvement in hiding Paul. Hoping to wrong foot Hugh he had intended to use this information to get a much-reduced sentence or failing that he would have the satisfaction of knowing he had revenged himself on that cow Sandy.

"No, you can't do that. I don't believe you. I handed myself in. I admitted being an agent and I was promised a fair trial. I have a right to have my say!"

"You have no rights whatsoever." Hugh replied. "You have one choice and one only. I think you know what that is." David slumped momentarily. He hadn't expected to be beaten so easily or so quickly. Attempting to hide his panic he leaned forward across the table so close that Hugh could smell his sour breath and as he drew his lips back in a sneer Hugh noticed that one of his front teeth was missing. Life in Moscow had been hard for David. Hugh didn't attempt to hide his smile at the thought. David hissed his words and Hugh felt the spray of saliva on his face. He removed his handkerchief from his pocket and wiped the spittle from his cheek. David's breath was foul but Hugh remained where he was: inches from David's face.

"You can send me back if you want but there is a postal service in Moscow *and* a 'phone. I can inform on your precious lover by post. I won't be the only one to lose."

"I'm sure that you will do your utmost to ruin some more lives

Montgomery, but don't be so confident that you will succeed."

"Don't bet on it you pathetic little has been. I'll see you ruined as well if I get the chance." Hugh stood up and called the warder to let him out of the cell.

"I'll leave you to consider the offer: your freedom in Moscow or imprisonment for very many years in England. I may add that capital punishment is also an option, not that it has been implemented since William Joyce in 1946 but I'm sure we could make an exception for you."

Hugh returned to his office feeling very pleased with himself. David's cockiness and confidence had been easier to undermine than he had expected. Either way David chose to go, he was a loser. Hugh opened the statement David had made on his first interview. There they were: all the names, all his contacts in Warsaw and Moscow. By giving Hugh this information David had hoped to reduce his sentence. Not only had he betrayed his country but he had then betrayed British informants who had immediately been rounded up. Amusing in a wry sort of way was the fact that David had passed on inaccurate information to the Russians which had been deliberately leaked to him – no wonder he didn't receive the rewards he had expected. But the very best of all was the list of his communist agents and their contacts in England – how the Russians would love to hear about that betrayal! Hugh went to bed that night a happy man. But a lonely one. He whispered goodnight to the phantom Sandy beside him and fell deeply asleep.

Hugh left David to stew for the next full week. The only visit he was allowed was a brief supervised meeting with one of the British diplomats he had exposed who called him every conceivable name before being escorted back to his cell. All privileges were denied him, and when he asked for a solicitor he was told that one would be provided in due course should he decide to stand trial.

David was brought into the interview room where Hugh and

Robert Green were waiting.

"Your decision please." Hugh prompted him as he sat belligerently silent. "Freedom or life imprisonment?"

"I wish to re-write my statement. I recant everything I've said except for my wife's involvement."

"If you wish, I have no objection to your re-writing it but if it contains lies it will not be treated as a valid statement."

"I still want to re-write it and then I choose freedom in Russia." David had pondered long on his options, life imprisonment was something he knew he couldn't handle; whatever his circumstances, were he to be returned to Russia, they would be better than being incarcerated in a cell for the remainder of his life. But one thing he was determined to try to achieve was to bring Sandy down with him. He hated her with all his being. She had got away from him and was now a witness to everything, she had to be punished. If he couldn't get her for treason, he would get her for harbouring a murderer. On his return to Russia he would immediately write to the chief constable and she would be arrested. It was a poor revenge as she wouldn't get much of a punishment but it was better than nothing. He asked for pen and paper and sat and wrote a new statement:

I admit that my initial statement was not the truth, I have now confessed truthfully and given you all the information you asked for.

He handed the papers back to Hugh who, with Robert, witnessed and signed it. David held his hand out for his first statement saying "You won't want that now."

Hugh ignored him and he and Robert left the room with both epistles.

"Got him!" Hugh remarked as they returned to their office.

The letter was dictated and typed. Addressed care of the British Embassy to be hand delivered to their Russian counterparts.

A flight was booked for David with two escorts to ensure he arrived in Moscow as planned. In the letter, Hugh had named all the Russian contacts David had exposed along with details of assignations and points of contact. He informed them of the flight David would be arriving on and wished them well.

"At least it saves the country of the cost of a trial!" Robert remarked. "It's most irregular Hugh, what you have done, how did you get away with it?"

"Basically Robert, he's small fry and not worth the effort of a trial. He's given us a lead to a bigger catch although he's not aware of it. We don't need him anymore. Let the Ruskies have him, they're welcome to do what they will with him. I've heard that the prisons in Russia are unbelievably dreadful. Of course, he may not even make it to prison."

"That sounds personal Hugh, is it?"

"Yes Robert, very personal."

A handcuffed David boarded the plane bound for Domodedovo Airport along with his two discreetly armed escorts. It roared down the runway, the nose lifted and the plane rose into the air, banked, turned and then headed east. Hugh watched until it became nothing but a trail of vapour in the sky. His task over, he returned home. A satisfactory result though it was, it had two drawbacks; Hugh wouldn't have the pleasure of *witnessing* him being brought to trial and subsequently imprisoned, but the one which was nearer to his heart was the negating of any reason to see Sandy again.

He picked up the 'phone and dialled her number. As it rang the door opened and Angela walked in, bronzed and glowing with health. She was very beautiful, even at fifty and the holiday with her companion seemed to have suited her. She had the contented look about her which indicated that her affair was far from over.

Hugh scowled at her. She was blatantly carrying on with one of his colleagues whilst his relationship with Sandy was about to end for ever as soon as the 'phone was answered. He slammed it back down and turning his back on his wife he walked out of the house.

Sandy lifted the receiver just as it stopped ringing. She supposed that were it important the caller would try again. Lilly hopped about excitedly with her lead in her mouth as they had been about to go for a walk but Sandy hung around for a while longer in case it had been Hugh. He could be contacting her because he had news about the trial. He had indicated that it may be a while before she would hear from him as he would be very busy, but she longed to hear his voice and waited by the 'phone in the hall until June called out.

"For goodness sake stop tormenting the dog, I can't hear myself think with her yapping!"

"Okay Lil' let's go, whoever it was must have dialled the wrong number." *I'm explaining myself to the dog! I must be losing it!*

On her return to the house she asked if anyone had 'phoned but no one had and she put it from her mind.

Hugh drove angrily out of the garage, not bothering to close the doors behind him and turned the car south. It was a long drive to Devon from Sussex and on his arrival the lights were out in the house and all was quiet. He sat for a while outside debating whether to knock or to turn around and drive home again. Impetuosity didn't come naturally to a man of his nature; he always thought before acting or speaking and never let anger control his actions but rather let it hone them. He asked himself what the hell he was doing. This was irrational and would achieve nothing but more torture for them both. But Angela's smug face as she walked into *his* home paid for by *his* hard work and long, sometimes dangerous and unpleasant, postings had been more than he could tolerate. He would divorce her even if Sandy married Oliver and he had no one. It would be better than being constantly cuckolded. He couldn't face the idea of driving back home, in fact he couldn't face the idea of home at all whilst his wife was there. He decided to try and find a hotel for the night. He turned the ignition key and pulled away from the kerb allowing himself one last look at the darkened windows, trying to imagine which room was hers. A light went on in an upstairs room, he must have woken someone with his engine. A face peered out from between the curtains and immediately disappeared again. Hugh turned off the engine and waited for her.

Sandy quietly closed the front door behind her and finished pulling a sweater over her head. She ran barefoot up to the car and flinging her shoes in to the foot-well she climbed in. Dishevelled, sleepy and half-dressed she held more attraction for him than the cosseted and perfectly manicured Angela.

"Hugh!" she gasped as she closed the door behind her. "Whatever are you doing here?"

"I'll explain when we're away from here."

"Did you ring earlier?"

"Yes, I did. But my wife came home and I didn't want to talk in front of her. So here I am."

They drove out into the countryside and Hugh pulled into a lay-by. Taking her in his arms he kissed her softly. "I will tell you everything that has happened but firstly we are going to take a little walk in this hay field. It hasn't rained for a while and the night is warm, need I say more?"

Hugh grabbed the travel rug from the back seat and taking her by the hand he led her to the rick and grabbed some soft dry grasses to make a bed. With the moon as their only witness they made love in the sweetly scented hay until they both fell asleep under the night sky with Sandy tightly embraced in Hugh's arms.

Hugh woke first just before dawn as the blackbirds began their song. The sun signalled its arrival by washing the sky with an orange glow turning the trees and hedges into burning torches.

He looked at Sandy's sleeping form with bits of hay stuck in her hair and one shoe off and one on and mentally photographed it for his memory album. *She's too young for you. Look at her, she's just a child. No, she isn't a child, she's a woman!* He imagined that Sandy would look pretty much the same when she reached fifty, she would never lose her youthful bohemian ways and never be a brittle coiffured beauty, thank goodness. Oliver was going to be a very lucky man if he had the sense to take her back. This thought roused him to wake her; he had to talk to her and tell her what the situation was and he should have done that last night.

"So, my love this is finally the end." Hugh said sadly as he held her tightly to him. "David will not trouble you again and you are now free to resume your life." Sandy remained silent. The time had come which she had dreaded, the goodbye, no more Hugh. She didn't cry or protest; it would do no good.

"Thank you for everything my darling Hugh. I shall never forget you as long as I live." She began pulling the remainder of her clothes on and brushed the hay from her hair. "Once a year you promised, just once a year until I tell you to stop."

"I promise." he whispered in her ear as he held her.

"Hugh?"

"Yes, my love?"

"I have to tell you something but I doubt if you'll be able to help."

"If it's in my power I'll do anything. What's the problem?" He sat up abruptly, "Are you pregnant? It's not David's is it?" A look of horror passed over his face. However would she cope with giving birth to David's child?

"God no! I went on the pill when I was a student and I made bloody sure I didn't miss any when I was being shagged by that shit!" Hugh breathed a sigh of relief followed by laughter.

"You'll always be my little urchin with your imaginative language and gutsy attitude, God how I shall miss you!" He took both her hands in his. "I'm almost sorry that you're not expecting my child. What a little hooligan he'd turn out to be," he added "or if it was a girl then God help me; two urchins to cope with!"

"If I *were* expecting, Hugh, would you marry me?"

"Yes, I would. But luckily for you and for Oliver you are not going to have a baby yet. Oliver will be the father of your children, he is young and fit and he loves you."

"I wish I'd come off the pill then!"

Hugh kissed her gently.

"No, these things should not be accidents, they should be planned. Although I certainly would have married you were it my child, you would never know for certain that I wasn't pressured into it thereby sowing a seed of doubt in your mind that I truly loved you."

"But you do love me I know." Sandy replied. "Anyway, I'm not pregnant so this is all hypothetical. What I needed to tell you is that they've dug Paul's body up!"

"Good Lord! But David's been under lock and key from the minute he handed himself in, there's no way he could have told anyone and anyway I'm sure he was keeping it as a bargaining tool."

"No it's not him. It was probably the woman I told you about, the neighbour, I've no idea what her name is. The others reckon that she thought that the grave was empty and that we had been, and still are, hiding him. She's partly right, we had hidden him, but now they've got his body it's proved her wrong that he's still alive but there's still the question of how and when he died. Also, where had he been when they were looking for him and who buried him? If they examine him they can tell he wasn't drowned in a bog, can't they? And they can work out approximately when he died as well. What the hell do we do?"

"Calm down, calm down my love. Let's take this slowly." Hugh shushed her as her face became flushed with anxiety. "Go through

"He'll be okay when he gets back." Sandy remarked to Hugh as they entered the house. "He's just over protective that's all."

"Mum, this is Hugh." June jumped with surprise as they entered the kitchen.

"Oh!" was all she managed to say.

"I could do with a coffee; would you like one Hugh?" Sandy put the kettle to boil and June, having found her voice offered to cook breakfast.

"No thank you, coffee will be just fine." Hugh smiled. "When your husband returns, I would like you to put aside what you know about Sandy and my relationship and try to address the imminent problem of Paul's exhumation." June nodded.

"Yes, yes of course. It's Tim who is the most upset about you both, he's formed a deep attachment to Oliver you see and... well, I won't go on about that." She caught Sandy's eye. "I am very pleased to meet you and I can't thank you enough for looking after Sandy. I can't bear to think what might have happened to her if you hadn't been there." She shooed them into the sitting room and fussed over where Hugh was going to sit.

"Mum, he isn't royalty! He can sit on the floor if you like." June tittered a laugh and Hugh grinned. It was a very strange feeling for June; this man was nearly the same age as herself yet Sandy was in love with him. They had been intimate, and, she suspected they still were. Hugh wasn't particularly dashing, he wasn't suave like David. In fact, he looked more like a farmer or a builder with his stocky frame, however there was something about him, he had a charisma all of his own, was it his eyes? Or was it his air of unselfconscious authority? June found to her horror that she too was attracted to him. She became flustered and didn't quite know how to treat him. Sandy's humour eased her mother's awkwardness and Hugh, making no pretence of his feelings for Sandy sat down next to her on the settee.

"I would have done it for anyone in her position Mrs Williams."

"Yes of course you would. That man was dreadful, is he going to trial soon?"

"If you don't mind I can't tell you anything. Not at the moment."

After half an hour or so Tim came back and Sandy had been correct, he was in a better frame of mind.

"I must apologise for my rudeness earlier, Sandy tells me she is an adult and I should stop being Victorian." He laughed a little lamely.

"I quite understand Mr Williams, no doubt I'd be the same if I had a daughter." He felt Sandy twitch beside him and remembered their earlier conversation. "Sandy has told me everything about this unfortunate man Paul and I would, if I can, like to help or offer some advice, do you mind?"

"Mind? We'd be eternally grateful for your help."

"Tim darling, what about Mike and the others, shouldn't we wait until they can have their say? We can't just go ahead and make decisions on our own."

"I agree, but this is just a preliminary discussion Mrs Williams, to ascertain whether indeed there is anything I can do. There's no point in involving everyone else if I am not able to help."

"Oh of course not. Please go on, have you any suggestions at all how we should handle this?" Tim asked. "Do you actually know everything we have done?"

"Yes, I told him, I couldn't help it, he questioned me and he didn't miss a thing. I was so alone and angry and unhappy, and I was under suspicion as well, so in the end I had to confess that David had blackmailed me."

Hugh's expression darkened as he recalled the terrified Sandy they had found hiding in the airport when she had narrowly escaped being abandoned in Warsaw and hatred for David burned inside him. He tightened his grip on Sandy's hand.

"I know everything, I extracted the information during my

interrogation of Sandy shortly after I first met her and realised that for newly-weds they were behaving very strangely. I needed to find out what was going on between them and at the same time I had to satisfy myself that Sandy was not involved in his activities. There was something between them and she refused initially to tell me what it was. I am rather good at reading people having had a lot of experience and the poor girl didn't stand a chance. I regret how I tied her in knots but I had to be sure she was an innocent. But I can tell you this, she was prepared to do anything to save everyone from David's exposure."

"But by telling you she was also chancing that you wouldn't report us. Why didn't you?" Tim asked and then realisation dawned on his face. "That must have been when you seduced her. Am I right?"

"Yes, I did fall for her but I resent your use of the word seduce!" His eyes flashed angrily and he paused to take a deep breath. "But as I said outside, our relationship is not what we are here to discuss."

"I don't see how you can help us to be quite honest. If the police decide to pursue it, we haven't a leg to stand on." Tim said glumly.

"Don't be defeatist Dad. Go on Hugh."

"It's not something I would normally get involved with as I am not a member of the legal profession or the police but from what I've gathered you all acted out of kindness and without any thought of gain of any kind. This does not, in the eyes of the law, make you innocent of breaking it. However, I do think that as an acknowledgement of Sandy's role in trapping David who was a traitor to the crown and her willingness to testify against him, I may be able to put a little pressure in the right places."

"That's brilliant as far as Sandy is concerned but it doesn't help the rest of us." Tim was being deliberately obtuse; he instinctively disliked this man irrespective of his rescue of Sandy and the offer he had just made. He had no right to seduce a girl young enough to be his daughter and thereby destroy the love she had for Oliver. He also noticed the way June looked at Hugh and a spark of jealousy stirred in him. "Considering that Sandy was the person who brought Paul into everyone's lives it seems a bit ironic that all her friends and family will carry the can!"

"Tim! I don't believe what I'm hearing." June was shocked. She looked at Sandy's flushed face and turned angrily to her husband, "What sort of father are you? I'd happily go to prison for the rest of my life to spare my only child."

"Hold on all of you." Hugh held up his hand and June fell silent. "Mr Williams, I am not unaware of what you think of me and I am sorry you feel that way but please try to contain your anger. I wish to help all of you and not just because of my love for Sandy. As you said, she was the lynch pin in the whole exercise, remove the pin and the remainder falls apart. By closing the case for Sandy, we close it for everyone."

Tim had deeply regretted his last comment as soon as it had left his mouth. He adored Sandy, she had always been a bit of a liability with her impetuous nature and had needed help getting out of the many scrapes she had manufactured for herself, but for him this was the part of her character he loved the most. Sandy wouldn't meet his eyes, she sat with her head bowed and gripped Hugh's hand. "I'm sorry, I spoke without thinking. I'm just worried about the others." He looked at June who still glared in his direction. "I too would take any punishment to protect my daughter." Hugh waited for the simmering atmosphere to mellow a little. Tim moved to sit beside June and she made room for him on the two-seater settee giving him a small strained smile. Hugh then continued.

"I cannot promise anything at this juncture but I will do my best. I will have to meet with the Tregowans, Professor Small and Dr Squires. Can this be arranged?" Sandy blanched.

"Do you really have to? Can't Dad tell them?"

"Sorry my dear, it is important that I have assurances that none of you will ever speak of this to anyone and I have to hear this with my own ears. I shall have to act very carefully; the department does not approve of string pulling outside their own domain. Of course, it might not even be necessary for me to do anything at all. His body may be re-interred once they have answered the only question they were asked – whether he was in the grave or not, and nothing more may come of it. But it's just as well to be prepared should the need arise."

Hugh stood up and made to leave. "I shall be in touch." Sandy saw him to the door and June laid a hand on Tim's arm to prevent him following. He shrugged it off and turned back into the room with a sigh.

"I suppose I should be grateful but I just feel angry." he muttered as he threw himself into an armchair.

Hugh returned to London and took a room in an hotel, he didn't want to confront Angela just yet. He had made up his mind and that was all that mattered on that front for the time being. After bathing and eating a late lunch he shopped for a change of clothing having left home with nothing. Dressed in clean attire he sought out the one person he knew he could trust completely.

Tim rang everyone concerned and briefly updated them on Hugh's visit. He emphasised the promise he had made to Hugh to remain *schtum* and pencilled in a selection of dates when they could all meet with Hugh depending on his progress and availability.

A week passed and there were no authoritative knocks on the door from the police and no word from Hugh. Sandy was dreading the day when she and Oliver would meet again especially when Hugh would be present. She prayed that Oliver wouldn't guess that she loved Hugh and made her parents swear to keep it to themselves. The time would come very soon when Hugh would be out of her life and then she would tell Oliver everything before she said goodbye to him for ever as well.

Hugh didn't make contact until he had done his research with the help of his friend in the police force. Henry Stiles and he were long standing friends, having been at university together and joining up in the Navy at the same time. They had both been strong patriots and had served for a while on the same ships during the war. Henry had joined the police force on his graduation after returning to university after the war and served his country thus, whilst Hugh had joined the Foreign Office. The case on Paul was a minor affair and was being handled locally, it appeared that there wasn't any urgency attached to it and the Detective Inspector was surprised when Henry made contact.

"It's just routine. We don't need Scotland Yard!" This made Henry worry that his enquiries might prompt them to look deeper into the case and he had to think quickly.

"It's just a pot luck case drawn out of the hat so to speak. We occasionally stick our noses in when we've nothing better to do. Anyway, Charles, how are you? Care to meet for a drink later?"

"Yes, why not, it's been a while since you've been in our neck of the woods. How about seven this evening at the Coach and Horses?"

Over a pint or two they chatted amicably about their lives, wives and children. Henry carefully stayed off the subject of Paul until he was able to nonchalantly slip it into the conversation.

"It's a bit of a waste of police funds to dig him up, isn't it? It's not as though there's a suspicion of foul play."

"I agree, some woman pestered and pestered saying that the grave was empty and the bloke was still alive somewhere. She reckoned that he murdered his mother and then a group of people hid him. I couldn't see what the fuss was about. His name was cleared and he was innocent; an accident apparently. The problem was that even if he was proved innocent in the end, he was under suspicion when he disappeared. We had to follow it up."

"Of course you did. Now you may as well bury the poor bugger again. More expense!"

"Exactly what I intend to do. Interesting little case though. At least it will keep that damned woman out of the station!" They laughed and ordered two more pints.

After Hugh's call to tell them that he thought he had it sorted they arranged to meet at the farm.

"I'm not coming, I don't need to." Sandy refused to discuss it any further. She longed to see Hugh but not in the company of Oliver and his family.

"Okay, I understand my love. It will be best if you stay away. I'll probably go back to the cottage with Tim afterwards, to save the long drive each way, will you be alright on your own?" Sandy rolled her eyes in answer and June smiled and hugged her. "Sorry darling, silly me."

"I don't know why we all have to meet if he's sorted it. Does he want us to put out the banners and grovel our thanks?!" Tim complained as he got the car from the garage.

"Don't be so damned ungrateful Tim. Just drive will you." June slammed the car door and waved goodbye to Sandy as they drove away. Sandy called Lilly and fastened her lead. "Come on Lil' duck chasing time." She walked to the seat she had taken Oliver to on their last final meeting and let Lilly off the lead to do her own thing. She was numb; there was a total emptiness where she should be feeling relief. David was gone and no longer a threat, Hugh had managed to halt any further investigation and Paul's remains had been carefully replaced in his plot. Everything was perfect. Perfect but empty. Nearly four years had passed since she had made that fateful journey across the moor; a series of highs and lows, of terror and bliss. Now there was nothing, absolutely nothing left. She had no tears to shed, what was the point of tears? Oliver's love was destroyed and Hugh was gone. She imagined the relief they would all be feeling at the farm after Hugh's visit, she visualised him getting into his car and driving back to his wife. She imagined Oliver sitting in his room wondering whether she would contact him and debating whether to contact her. Sandy knew that she owed it to Oliver to explain what had happened to her and her only concern was how to tell it without giving him too much pain. As for herself, she didn't give a damn. The future was as bleak as it ever could be – how was she going to carry on living in an emotional vacuum? The only consolation was the thought that Hugh might take advantage of her being alone and spend one last night with her. It was like the last meal before the execution. An exquisite torture.

Oliver and his family thanked Hugh profusely and shook his hand as he prepared to depart. "You are a hero. Thank you." George slapped him on the back, "Mum's the word, that's a promise."

Hugh took Oliver to one side and asked him if he would mind showing him around the farm explaining that he had never been on a working farm and was intrigued by how they survived the hard, endless slog.

"I love it." Oliver said as they walked through the fields and he pointed out the cows grazing in the meadow. "These are milkers, Friesians, they give the best yield. Some of them are ten years old, which is really too long to keep them as they usually go for slaughter at about five or six when their milk dries up. But they are favourites and have given us calves every year, sentimental though it is Mum can't bear to part with them. It's the same with the goats." He remembered Paul and his devotion to Daisy and his speech faltered for a moment, the memories of Paul's happiness at the farm and the sadness of his death suddenly became very real and the joy of Hugh's news was tainted with grief. They had done the best they could for him and through him Sandy and Oliver had come together. Oliver turned away from Hugh to hide his emotion. Hugh gave him a little time then said

"Oliver, I know you love Sandy, she has told me all about you. I'm glad to have met you, you are all that she said you were." It was Hugh's turn to hide his emotions as a desire to hold her once more flooded his senses. "I wish you both happiness." He managed to say before his voice failed him.

"Thank you Hugh, I appreciate it but she doesn't want me anymore, she's made that quite clear. I haven't spoken to her since she got home. She didn't even come here today as I hoped she would. I want so much to talk to her to tell her I love her and that I understand that everything she did was for all of us and that I don't blame her." Hugh struggled to contain his guilt in front of this man. How could he ever forgive himself for what he had allowed himself to do?

"Give her time, let her know you love her but give her time. That's the only advice I can offer." Pulling himself together he said "Now I really must get going. Goodbye and good luck." He shook Oliver by the hand and they walked back to the farmhouse, each deep in his own thoughts.

When he realised that Sandy wasn't going to be at the meeting Hugh had felt a surge of excitement; he would be able to spend another night with her. But after his talk with Oliver he left with a dreadful feeling of guilt. He had never felt so strongly about anyone before his meeting with Sandy, it tore at him like a knife in the chest. He wanted her for himself but the sight of that curly haired young man's pain as he talked of Sandy made him feel like a traitor. He hoped that when Sandy finally told Oliver about him that the blame would lie at his feet and not hers. Maybe she wouldn't tell him. But no, she had to if they were ever going to spend their lives together, they needed to get it all out into the open and then wipe it clean and start again. He drove back to London to his hotel room and wept.

Sandy waited late into the night hoping that Hugh would come to see her.

∩ ◡ ∩

The plane touched down in Domodedovo airport and David's escort, removed the cuffs from his wrists but followed closely behind him as he entered the arrivals. He handed his passport to the officials at the desk and passed through.

"So long, give my love to Hugh." he called over his shoulder as he walked to the exit to begin his life as a defector. Two men fell in beside him as he reached the door. A look of horror replaced his smug grin as they pulled his arms behind his back and fastened them with cuffs. He struggled and looked back pleadingly at his English escort.

"No!" he cried, "I am a British citizen, you can't do this!" His cries went unheeded as he began his journey to the prison cells of Moscow.

∩ ◡ ∩

Paul's final chapter was now closed. George opened a bottle of champagne and everyone toasted the absent Sandy and Hugh.

"Thank God it's over." Alice said. "And thank God for Hugh. Did anyone find out what his last name was?"

"No, I don't think he ever mentioned it, strange, most people introduce themselves fully." George remarked. "He's a dark horse if ever I saw one."

"I don't like to put a damper on the celebrations but we still don't know whether David will manage to throw shit in the fan at his trial." Alistair muttered.

"Hugh told us he had dealt with him. I don't know what he meant by that but judging by his performance so far, I don't think we need to worry. I'm pretty sure he told Sandy what he had done but she seems sworn to secrecy and refuses to say." Tim was glad to see the back of Hugh, but had to admit that he had been a godsend for all of them; except Oliver.

He had watched them closely when Hugh had asked Oliver for a tour of the farm. He had wondered whether Hugh was taking him aside to warn him off Sandy and to lay his claim to her. But when he saw them shake hands and return in a quiet but friendly manner he was confused. Oliver seemed pensive and after finishing his drink he bade them all goodnight and went to his room. Tim prayed that Oliver would forgive Sandy and take her back, but it was asking a lot of the poor lad. He would have to be a saint to do so when he found out about her love affair with Hugh.

Jeremy had been very quiet during the celebrations, sitting alone in the corner he looked tired and strained. George moved to sit opposite him and filled his empty glass.

"Jeremy old man, you look whacked. You must rue the day you met Alistair, I can't tell you how sorry I am to have dragged you through all this."

"All's well that ends well I suppose." Jeremy replied. "I can't say I'm sorry for helping Paul but I must admit I was beginning to regret becoming involved." The bounce seemed to have gone from him and instead of his booming laughter reverberating around the room he emanated sadness and solitude. Putting his full glass on the table he rose with a grunt and moved around the room saying goodbye to everyone. That done, he took his leave and walked to his car. He didn't look back.

CHAPTER 22

AFTER A FEW DAYS IN THE HOTEL where he had thought deeply about what he was going to do Hugh returned to his home. He was not surprised to see a car in the drive which was not Angela's and assumed it must be her lover's. His hackles rose as he slammed the door shut behind him. There was a flurry of movement from the kitchen and Angela emerged slightly pink in the face followed by her companion, a large ex-rugby-playing fellow whom Hugh recognised immediately as someone he had worked with in the past. So, this was the lover she had travelled the Caribbean with. She certainly knew how to pick them; he was the classic tall dark and handsome type and a good few years younger than her, though not the twenty-five years that separated him and Sandy.

"Oh Hugh, this is Anthony he was just passing..." Hugh laughed derisively.

"Did you have a nice holiday Anthony?" Anthony stuttered before beginning to pretend that he had no idea what Hugh meant. "I will give you five minutes to gather your overnight things and then if you don't mind, I wish to talk to my wife – alone!" Without waiting for a reply Hugh turned his back on him as he sheepishly climbed the stairs to retrieve his bag. Angela began to follow him but Hugh stood in the doorway blocking her exit. "You do not need to say goodbye to him Angela, he can see himself out of my house." At the sound of the car pulling away Angela began to explain that it was a thing of the moment and that she wouldn't see him again. But Hugh held up his hands and she stopped in mid-sentence knowing that it was not going to work this time. Hugh had seemed oblivious to so many of her affairs that she had wondered if he condoned them which had made her complacent and less careful about hiding them from him. Now she realised that something had changed and that Hugh must have been building up a dossier against her. She should have known the sneaky way he went about things; it went with his job, though she still wasn't sure exactly what that was, other than he seemed to be posted to troublesome spots all the time, which she had hated.

"I am going to divorce you Angela. I will sell this house and you can have half the proceeds but from then on you are on your own, though I doubt that will be for long." Angela turned angrily to him.

"What about you and your girlfriend? Oh yes, I have heard about your Good Samaritan works, rescuing a damsel in distress, a girl the same age as your son. Have you slept with her yet or is she saving herself for the marriage bed?" She flew at him as though to strike him but he caught her hand before it made contact and held it tightly. He could hardly bear to look at her, she was immaculate though it was still quite early in the day and her hair was neatly done. He looked at the hand he was holding and noted the long, perfectly enamelled nails and threw it from him in disgust.

"That girl is honest and brave, selfless and caring. She puts you to shame Angela."

"How dare you speak to me like that!" Angela's face was suffused with rage, she was used to admiration and compliments, no one had ever compared her unfavourably with some chit of a girl from out in the sticks, an art student no less, probably covered with paint and plaster of Paris.

"I dare because it's true. I will file for divorce today and it's up to you whether we do this amicably or take it to court where I shall name every single one of your beaux."

"And I shall tell them what a dirty old man you are – a girl half your age! You'll be a laughing stock, everyone will know she only wants your money." Hugh was torn between roaring with laughter at her inaccurate assessment of Sandy and throttling her on the spot. He did neither but remained calm and stony. He never realised how much he disliked his wife but now the very sight of her made him sick.

"You may sleep in your soiled sheets in our bed tonight and I shall have the spare room. In the morning, you can pack and stay with your sister until the house is sold. I will provide any funds you may need." He didn't stay to hear her vitriolic reply but shut himself in his office with the door locked until he heard her car drive away. She had packed a bag and had left. He went to the bedroom and ripped the sheets from the bed and stuffed everything, pillows included, into sacks which he flung outside to await the rubbish collection. His next tasks were to ring a locksmith, put a stop on his bank account before Angela emptied it and put divorce proceedings into effect.

Hugh wandered sadly around his home which he loved, the garden stretched out to the countryside beyond and his nearest neighbours were some miles away. *Sandy would love it here*, he thought, then quickly put it from his mind. Even if they ever did marry he couldn't bring her here, Angela's influence on the *décor* and the furnishings was overpowering; it was not his home any more. He rang the estate agent's and made an appointment for a valuation. Hugh walked the house from top to bottom mentally noting what was his and what he would leave behind, sell or throw away. He picked up the silver-framed photograph of his wedding day and put it in the box of rubbish he was accumulating. He noticed a space on the dresser where a portrait photograph of Angela had stood, she had taken it with her but had left the pictures of the boys behind. He dusted them off and stood them back side by side thinking sadly how apparent it was whom Angela loved the most.

Tim and June drove back home the following day to find Sandy was out. She had taken Lilly and left a note saying to expect her when they saw her. Tim immediately assumed she was with Hugh and he bristled.

"She's with that bloody man, isn't she? He should be ashamed of himself!"

"Just stop it Tim. You can't plan her life for her, if that's what she wants you'll just have to accept it." June replied. "It's none of our business, I don't like it either but I am not going to try to influence her one way or the other and I suggest you keep quiet about it as well. You know Sandy, she is stubborn and if you push her one way she goes the other." Tim had to agree. He promised June that he would not say a word to Sandy about Oliver, hard though that was going to be.

Sandy had waited for Hugh all night, her hopes sinking further and further as she realised than he was not coming. He didn't 'phone either and the emptiness gathered in her stomach like a ball of bile. He was gone. He had kept to his word and she knew that she would not hear from him again other than possibly a call in a year's time to see if she was alright. She wondered if he would keep to this promise or stay away, to force her to get on with her life without him. By the morning, she was tempted to try and ring him at home just to hear his voice and she sat in the hall with the 'phone in her hand arguing with herself, frightened to dial the number in case he was annoyed. No, he wouldn't be annoyed, but she knew that even though he loved her he would tell her it was the end. She had to hear his voice just one last time. She dialled his number. The 'phone was picked up and a woman answered it. Sandy slammed the receiver back on the hook. She had forgotten that his wife was back. It was then that she let the tears come. Hugh had gone back to her. Sandy's stomach churned and fluttered as though a thousand butterflies were trying to get out. She wished she had not heard his wife's voice, it made her real, not just an invisible protagonist in the tragedy her life had now become.

Oliver waited daily for some contact from Sandy but none came. He worked diligently on the farm but stayed away from company as much as he could. There was always something needing doing on the far reaches of the farm which kept him away for the day. He often arrived back at the house after George and Alice had eaten, removing his food from the small oven of the Aga, where it had been keeping warm, to eat in solitude. However, as the summer harvests began and he and George worked side by side in their urgency to get it all in before the weather changed, Oliver broke down. As the last bale was stacked he slumped to the stubble in the freshly cut corn field and sat with his head in his hands. George lowered his long body to sit beside his eldest son who had waited so patiently for the girl he loved to come back to him.

"Dad, I'm so miserable." Oliver picked up a stone and flung it away from him then scrubbed his eyes with his calloused hands to wipe away the tears which were beginning to come. "What should I do?" George didn't answer immediately, now would not be the right time to say the wrong thing. He had hoped that one day Oliver would let down his defences and talk to him and now he was doing just that. George pulled his pipe from his pocket and took his time tamping down the tobacco before lighting it and puffing away to get it going.

"Go and see her my lad. It's time."

"But what if she sends me away?"

"Then you'll know for sure. I'm sorry if that sounds hard but at least you will know where you stand." All through the summer George had wondered about contacting Sandy himself and trying to get to the bottom of what was keeping her away. She knew that they were aware of what she had done with David and she also knew that they didn't blame her, rather, they admired her. So, what was keeping her from Oliver? All he could think was that she realised that she didn't love him but hadn't the courage to tell him. But that wasn't the Sandy George had come to know and love. She was honest and fair, she would tell Oliver, he knew she would, if only to set him free. Therefore, she must still care. Maybe she was too embarrassed to face Oliver? Or maybe she was still traumatised by the whole affair. He talked to Alice who was nearly swayed but in the end told him not to go interfering.

"Should I ring or write to her first Dad?"

"No son, just turn up. The shock of seeing you may bring her to her senses. I can't promise, but it's been months now since every-thing was laid to rest and she may be ready to pick up the pieces, just needs the nudge from you." George tutted as his pipe went out and impatiently struck another match to get it going again. Between puffs he mused that Sandy may be feeling abandoned by Oliver in much the same way he was feeling abandoned by her.

"After all, you haven't contacted her, have you? She probably thinks you don't want her anymore after what she's had to do. You're like two magnets, pushing each other away." Oliver hadn't considered this. His memory was of their last meeting when she had told him she didn't love him and he couldn't shake this from his thoughts. Even though in her letter she had said that she did, that dreadful gut wrenching feeling still remained.

"Thanks Dad. You're right, I have to know one way or the other. I'll go tomorrow."

⌒ ‿ ⌒

June's sister, Gillie and her husband Stewart were celebrating their silver wedding anniversary; all were invited to a party at the town hall near her home. Sandy groaned at the thought of it and wracked her brains for an excuse not to go. In the end, she didn't need to, but the reason for her crying off was not one she would have chosen.

Sandy and Lilly walked the same route every day and they were both becoming bored with it, so in the morning before they were due to drive to Gillie's Sandy decided to take Lilly for a good long run to tire her out before the journey, though the solution to tiring a springer spaniel out has not yet been discovered. They set off into the countryside, a route Sandy had looked up on an ordinance survey map. It showed footpaths across farmland and there was even a small tributary which Lilly could swim in. She packed Lilly's bowl and water for them both in her backpack and set off. It was warm and after they had gone some distance they both needed a drink. She sat under a tree in the shade and rested her head against the rough bark. The sun flickered through the leaves and a jay laughed in its branches. Sandy felt at peace for the first time in months. Lilly deposited a stick in her lap for her to throw but she refused.

"Not now Lil', come and lie down here beside me." Reluctantly her little dog settled in the shade and soon her grunting snores were vibrating against Sandy's leg. Sandy closed her eyes and was suddenly transported to the farm, she imagined she could hear Oliver's tractor chugging away in the distance and she allowed herself to drift. In her mind's eye, she saw him stride up the slope to their favourite bank where they had sat many times amongst the scabious and wild cornflowers. She felt him pull her to him and his soft kiss sent a shiver of joy through her. She was woken from her reverie by Lilly licking the tears from her face. Sandy started and looked around in a dazed state, for a moment wondering where she was. She must have slept and been dreaming, but it all felt so real. Glancing at her watch she panicked, it was late and they had to get back or her mother would be worrying and her father angry.

"Come on Lil' we'll take a short cut." She took the map from her pack and studied it. "Yep, I reckon we can cut across here." She showed the dog the route, a small dotted line indicating a path. What it didn't show, however, was a very brambly copse or the farm house tucked in a dell. After fighting their way through the copse they set off across an open field. Sandy put Lilly on the lead in case there were sheep or cattle grazing and they walked on. They passed the outskirts of the farm and were just coming to the brow of the slope when a furious barking sounded behind them. Sandy turned as two border collies bounded up to them. She said "hello there, boys" and reached out to stoke them as they sniffed Lilly from front to back, or rather, from back to front. Lilly shrank back timidly and Sandy spoke to reassure her, but as she did so they both lunged at Lilly, their teeth bared and snarling. One caught her by the back of the neck and the other went for her stomach. Sandy shouted and kicked out at the dogs. She caught one in the ribs and it yelped as it released Lilly, she then laid into the other one, pulling it off and kicking it. Lilly screamed with pain as the teeth ripped her shoulder. Sandy picked up the stick Lilly had been carrying and thrashed the dogs with it until it broke. They snarled as she did so and she was terrified they were going to attack her as well. She mustered her strength and authority and stamping her feet she shouted at them to leave. They must have recognised the command 'leave' as they turned and ran back down to the farm. Lilly lay bleeding and shaking at Sandy's feet. She knelt to inspect the wounds, they luckily had missed anything vital but her shoulder lay open, a tear six inches across oozing blood.

"Bastard bloody dogs!" Sandy shouted after the retreating collies. "If I'd had a gun I'd have shot you bastards!" Poor little Lilly was whimpering and obviously in shock. Sandy picked her up as carefully as she could and began walking towards home. She heard a shout and a whistle from the direction of the farm and a man carrying a shotgun appeared. *Christ is he going to shoot us as well?* She stood her ground as he got nearer preparing her tirade against his dogs. He called out to her

"Wait please miss, it's okay I've shut them in." Sandy strode up to him and furiously held out her injured dog for him to see. Lilly cried constantly with the pain and Sandy's face was scarlet with rage.

"You should sodding well keep them under control. This is a footpath and she was on the lead!" Sandy swore at him. "We're miles from home and she's still bleeding, I'm frightened she's going to die!" Blood from Lilly's wound had soaked Sandy's shirt and was running down her arms.

"I'm so sorry miss, it's the young 'un, he's unpredictable. Then it sets the other one off." He gently lifted Lilly from Sandy's arms saying "I'll take you to the vet. Come on, the Land Rover is just down the hill."

Sandy arrived home courtesy of the farmer in his Land Rover with a still partially sedated Lilly in her arms. She had 'phoned her parents from the vet's and told them to go on without her.

"Is she going to be alright?" June took the 'phone from Tim as he started going on about farm dogs being aggressive and how she should have stuck to the path.

"Yes Mum, she's all stitched up and the farmer is paying the bill."

She kissed Lilly's hot little head and carefully placed her in her bed. The vet had given her some painkillers for when she woke up as she would be very sore and Sandy placed them on the table in readiness, then she made a cup of tea and settled herself beside the dog bed to watch over her. There was the sound of a car pulling into the drive and Sandy thought her parents must have come back early because of Lilly. *Dafties, I said she was alright.* Then the doorbell rang so it wasn't her parents after all. Sandy swore to herself and opened the front door to see Oliver standing in the porch.

"Christ Sandy what's happened?" Oliver had rehearsed his first words to Sandy over and over on his drive and these were not the ones he had planned to say. "Are you alright? Shall I call an ambulance?" For a moment, Sandy wondered what on earth he was talking about and then she remembered she was still covered in blood and her hand which was still holding the door open was caked in it. She burst out laughing. Oliver took a step back in horror thinking she had gone mad and had been trying to kill herself. "Sandy, it's alright, I'll get you to hospital." He reached for her hand tentatively to take her to the car. "Where are your Mum and Dad?"

"Oh Oli, you are such a dear." Sandy controlled her laughter and stood back to let him in. "It's not *my* blood." Reading the question on his lips before he spoke she added "And no, I haven't murdered the parents with a hatchet! It's Lilly's, she's been attacked by some collies."

"Phew, I thought it was yours. Is she alright?" Sandy assured him that she was and told him about their walk. It wasn't until they had analysed the nature of collies and various other breeds of dogs and their suitability to different environments that they both realised they had slipped back into their normal matey ways. It was then that the awkward silence which Oliver's arrival would have caused had it not been for the blood, descended on them like a black cloud. First one started to speak and then fell silent and then the other did the same. Where to start? That was the question. Sandy suddenly felt awkward, ashamed and bitterly sorry for Oliver. For a long time, she had buried the thought of having to speak to him face to face, she had dreaded it knowing that she must tell him all or nothing. Oliver took the lead and blurted out

"Sandy, why haven't you come home? I read your letter and I love you all the more for what you did even if I do think you are an absolute idiot." She looked away from his gentle green eyes dreading to see the hurt which she was bound to inflict.

"I'm sorry Oli, my letter was the truth. But so much has happened since. I don't know where to begin or even if I can begin to explain." Did this mean that she no longer loved him? Oliver's heart sank, she was going to finally tell him it was goodbye.

"Sandy, if you want me to leave you alone just tell me it's over and I'll go out of your life for ever." He looked deep into her eyes to try to read what was in her mind. "You don't even have to tell me why if it pains you so much." Sandy got up from her chair and began pacing the kitchen until Oliver rose also and taking hold of her arm he turned her gently to him and looking down at her sad, tortured face he begged her

"Please Sandy put me out of my misery." She took one last look at the tenderness in his eyes which would be replaced by hurt and disgust when she told him what she had done and tried to commit that look to her memory.

"Oli, come and sit down and hear me out. You will be the one to say goodbye, not me."

"Never, I love you Sandy."

"Tell me that when I have finished my story." Oliver looked puzzled but resumed his seat and waited.

"I have told you most of the truth leading up to marrying David but I didn't tell you what his final blackmail weapon was. I was too ashamed and violated to tell anyone." Oliver listened to Sandy's account of the deliberate spiking of her drink and the subsequent threat of the obscene photographs. He had never felt anger as strong as this before.

"Why didn't you tell me? I'd have killed the bastard!"

"Yes, and ended up in prison!"

"It would have been worth it!"

"Wait Oli, let me finish. I'm not worth it I promise you." The afternoon wore on and as Sandy told Oliver all that had happened with David in Moscow his anger grew in to a raging fury. Banging his fist on the table he shouted out in pain on her behalf.

"Where is he Sandy? Where is that evil piece of shit? If he's anywhere I can lay my hands on him I swear I will kill him!"

"He's somewhere worse than you can imagine Oli. I am not meant to say where, but I will. He is in a Russian prison which I am assured is hell on earth." She paused and took a very deep breath.

"Now is the part where you get up and leave, hating me for ever."

"What could you possibly do to make me do that?"

"Well, you know that I was rescued by Hugh, and it was Hugh who got David sent back to Russia? And it was Hugh who got us out of the problem with Paul's grave?"

"Yes. But what's that got to do with anything?"

"Everything Oli. During that time, we, we, well, we fell in love." She had said it. Now she waited for Oliver to get up and leave. There was silence. Sandy didn't dare look at Oliver, she continued to wait for the scrape of his chair and the slamming of the front door. Neither came.

"Do you still love him?" Oliver asked quietly.

"Yes Oli, I do."

"I see. What are you going to do? He's married, isn't he?"

"Yes, he is married. But that's not relevant really because we have already parted. He says he is too old for me and that I should marry you."

"Yes, he said the same to me."

"When?"

"At the farm. I could tell he was in love with you Sandy, it was so obvious. Otherwise why would he have done all he did for us? But what I didn't know was whether you felt the same. He took me aside to tell me to give you time and to make sure you knew I loved you. I realise now that he was giving you back to me. I liked him Sandy. I could tell he was hurting but he was trying to put things right. I admire him for that." He looked sadly at Sandy, the anguish he had been through waiting and waiting for her to speak to him had been unbearable and now she had told him she loved someone else. He felt the life go out of him. "When you came home and time went by and you refused to speak to me I couldn't work out why but now it all falls into place." He sighed and got to his feet. "I suppose you want me to go now?"

"I'm so sorry Oli, I knew you wouldn't want me after that. I have always loved you but Hugh sort of swamped my senses, I was passionate about him but it was wrong, we should never have let it go so far. He feels desperately guilty about it because of you. I can't say I didn't love him or that I no longer do, all I can say is I'm sorry."

"Do you want me to go Sandy?"

"I won't try and stop you Oli, I don't blame you if you despise me. But please don't hate me for ever."

"I *should* hate you or at least feel anger but I can't. We have been through so much together and you've become a huge part of my life. I can't just draw a line under it and walk away for ever." He stood looking down into her tearful face and took hold of her hands in his. She stood up ready to say goodbye but he held them to his lips and kissed them.

"Sandy, will you come back to me please? I don't care if you still love Hugh, I can't live without you." He lowered his face to hers and gently kissed her lips.

The bells rang as the couple emerged from the church one bright spring morning. He was tall with ginger curls falling around the collar of his morning suit and as the sun caught them they gleamed like copper coils. A massive grin stretched across his face as he faced the cameras, his bride tucked inside his embrace. She was small and even in her wedding dress she still had the appearance of a little urchin dressed in someone else's clothes. She allowed her gaze to wander around the churchyard as if she were looking for someone, then, with a smile she lifted her hand very slightly. In the shade of the trees at the end of the graveyard a figure raised his hand in a blessing then quietly slipped away.